DESOLATION SOUND

a novel by

Marion C. Jensen

FriesenPress

Suite 300 - 990 Fort St
Victoria, BC, Canada, V8V 3K2
www.friesenpress.com

First Edition — 2016

Acknowledgment is given to Grand Central Publishing for the quotation from The Bridges of Madison County by Robert James Waller.

Cover photo courtesy of Richard Trueman, photographer.

ISBN
978-1-4602-7197-1 (Hardcover)
978-1-4602-7198-8 (Paperback)
978-1-4602-7199-5 (eBook)

1. Fiction

Distributed to the trade by The Ingram Book Company

For Dagmar, Minota, and Libby,
my three Muses

CHAPTER 1: DOWN TIME

July, 1992

A man with beer breath leaned over the reference desk. "I'm going on vacation," he wheezed. " I need a list of the titles in the Poldark series. No sense in borrowing ones I've read."

An easy question. Ann Patterson, the librarian, found the answer in the series book.

The next person needed a quotation. A quick look at *Bartlett's Familiar Quotations* and it was found.

She slid back into her chair and staggered back up. The sun had made its leather upholstery molten. The branch library had been recently renovated. Why had the architect positioned the reference desk under the skylight? Why had he nailed the desk to the floor? To prevent someone stealing it? She gathered her skirt behind her to shield her legs before sitting. A dozen people waited in front of her desk.

Beside it, Becky, the branch library's head clerk, was shelving books. "You sure you can cope, Ann?" she whispered.

"Sure. Libraries existed long before air conditioning." Sun burned through the skylight and branded her shoulders. Rivulets of sweat ran into her eyes and dripped onto her cheeks. She dabbed her face with a tissue. It turned red from blush. Why had she put on blush today? To look like a lobster? Heat sickness had sent her boss home, leaving Ann to do the work of two librarians.

Becky glanced at the Post-it notes on their spike.

On their metal spike, the unanswered questions were multiplying like monster blooms. "I'm behind," Ann said, "but I'll polish off those questions during my break."

The clerk frowned. "You need to eat."

Ann laughed. "I need to diet." Answering all those questions would impress the branch manager who was probably at home now, soaking in a tub and drinking margaritas. Ann checked the time. One thirty! She had been at work half an hour. It felt like four.

"So you don't want me to call the central library for a sub?"

"No. I'll be fine." Ann smiled calmly at the next library patron, a skinny man with glasses. "Can I help you?" she asked in a calm, well-modulated voice.

Focus, on the patrons. Be professional. Don't think about heat, don't think about Richard. Or about Desolation Sound.

Another easy question. If they were all that simple, she might get to the book orders this afternoon. Two more quickies. A request for government job postings and one for election brochures. Only ten patrons waiting now.

At Desolation Sound, the ocean was supposed to be bathtub warm. She would swim while Richard read books about the history of the place. He loved facts. Amanda would read too, something fanciful—old-fashioned fairy tales perhaps—the eleven year old had read all the Narnia series. Everyone would be happy. They would be a family again.

"Excuse me!" A bulky woman loomed over the reference desk. "I came here on the bus, in this heat"— her face flushed an unbecoming watermelon pink—"because this library phoned to say a book I ordered was in. Well it's not. A half hour on the bus, and the clerk couldn't even find it. She said to ask you."

"Be right back," Ann assured the others in line as she ushered the angry woman back to the circulation counter. She checked the books on the hold shelves. Yes! "It was filed by title, instead of by author." She triumphantly handed it over. "Sorry about the confusion."

"No harm done," the woman said. "Easy to make mistakes in this inferno."

The librarian fanned herself with a library pamphlet. "Someone's supposed to fix the air conditioning today."

The circulation clerk signed the woman's book out. "You okay, Ann?"

"Me?" She had slumped against the counter. "Sure." She stood up straight and adjusted the shoulder pads in her silk blouse.

"You're on the hot seat, doing the work of two librarians."

"I can handle it. I used to, remember?"

Ten years ago. She'd been the youngest branch head in the Victoria library system, only twenty-five, and a whiz at reference work. To deflect sympathy, Ann picked up a threadbare book from the counter. "What's this?".

"I found that on the floor by the dictionaries. Should we discard it?"

"Are there other copies in the system?"

"No."

The book had impressive Moroccan binding but its pages were yellow, dangling by threads. The title in gold leaf was barely legible: *The Selected Works of Dr. Johnson*. Ann groaned. "Johnson! I had to read him in university. Borrrrring. Preachy!!!" She hefted the book from one hand to the other. "This might be valuable. But we're a public library, not a university collection…still…"

The clerk waited.

"Samuel Johnson is one of the great classics. But does anyone read him nowadays?"

"Ann…"The circulation clerk gestured at the reference desk.

"Do we have to wait all afternoon for help?" a voice bellowed. A horse-faced woman pretended to speak to a younger woman but glared at Ann. "Why don't they put two librarians on this desk?"

The young mother tried to calm her squirming kids. Behind her, an elderly couple leaned on canes. Behind them, the line stretched to the door. A man was noisily counting the folks in front of him.

As Ann sprinted to her desk she noted something unusual in the reference alcove, but her phone was ringing. She slid into her chair. To answer or not to answer? Customers in the flesh had priority but the clerks were too busy to answer the phone. But… Ann panicked. Why couldn't she make decisions any more? What to eat? What to wear? What books to discard? What library patrons to help?

The phone was still ringing. "Sorry," she breathed to the young mother, and answered it. The caller needed the time of high tides at Gonzales Bay on March 20, 1990. Two years ago. The central library would have tide tables that old. Ann jotted his phone number and the question on another Post-it note and smiled at the young mother.

The woman plugged a soother into her baby's mouth. "Do you have information about the La Leche League?"

"Yes." Ann escorted her to the vertical file in the reference alcove.

What the hell?

A whirlwind had struck the alcove. Reference books cluttered the floor—encyclopedia volumes, maps of British Columbia, a Merck medical manual, a New Oxford dictionary. The table bore more mountains of books. At it, a disheveled old man hunched over a Bible. Around him, books tumbled in landslides, but he read on. The poor fellow was probably homeless. His gray shorts were peculiar and ancient. His hair was equally ancient and would have made Einstein's look tidy.

As a professional librarian, she should ask him politely to put the excess books on a book truck, but customers were waiting. Ann handed over the La Leche articles and scampered back to her post. She arrived out of breath. *Exercise is good for me,* she told herself. Some librarians sat like Buddhas at the reference desk and languidly directed customers to find materials themselves. Not Ann. She knew people often needed a personal guide to the information, a *pleasant* guide, not the grouchy librarian of comic strips.

Next in line was the loud, horse-faced woman. Ann smiled at her patiently. Being a children's librarian she had learned to be patient.

The woman leaned across the desk oozing perspiration. "I need the names of Douglas Fairbanks' movies."

Ann ducked the smell and pretended to look at her computer screen. *A librarian shouldn't judge the patron or the question. Each patron has a right to information. All patrons are equal, all questions are equal, and each deserves respect.*

This week she'd answered many odd questions: the colour of King Henry VIII's hair, the number of teeth in an alligator, the date of the last eclipse, the hemisphere in which water drains clockwise, the coat of arms of a remarkably unremarkable family.

She typed "Douglas Fairbanks" into the subject heading space. No more card catalogues! The newly automated catalogue was a miracle. It would list biographies of Fairbanks and show which branch owned them. The screen darkened from its normal green, to black.

Uhh oh!

Last week, the new Novac catalogue had crashed twice, and each time the screen had faded just like this. "Don't you *dare* quit on me!" she whispered to the screen.

Another blast of B.O. "I need the information for the Times' crossword puzzle."

Ann never lost her temper, at least, not at work. "Reference librarians aren't supposed to answer questions from game shows and contests," she said coolly. "I'll make an exception for you, but only because of the heat."

The screen brightened. Two biographies of the once famous actor were here in this branch. She guided the woman to the shelf. The woman thanked her but Ann didn't reply. The sweaty cow had wasted precious minutes and should have apologized to the others in line.

Ann sat down on her chair and leaped up. She gathered her skirt behind her again to shield her legs before sitting. The desk surface was like a hot stove. Was that a wisp of smoke emanating from the Post-its? She moved their spike into the shade and ticked the statistics sheet. Twenty tick marks. In an hour, she had answered twenty questions. Not bad. Damn good for any librarian, let alone a temporary one.

Eight ticks and ten minutes later, she was buzzing with adrenalin. Seven hours on the reference desk was like seven hours on a quiz show. If you answered each question in three minutes or less, you won a clean desk. If you didn't, your prize was a collection of yellow Post-its, to be answered at leisure. The spike was full, a legacy from the sunstruck branch head.

The clock above the library entrance said two thirty. Impossible! Had the clock melted in the heat? No, her watch said the same. Six and a half hours to go, including her dinner break. Sweat seeped through her silk, 'dry-clean only' blouse—Dry-cleanable at six dollars a shot! She should have worn cotton today.

Think cool. Think Desolation Sound! Think of swimming there three weeks from now! Smile!

"Can I help you?" she asked a man in overalls.

"I hope so. I need information about an English gardener."

Honest looking eyes. Scent of earth. Nails straight-cut and grubby. Tanned. Outdoorsy.

"Her name was Gertrude Jekyll," he added. "Specifically I need her design for her garden at Munstead Wood. J-E-K-Y-L-L," he spelled out the name.

"Thanks," Ann's fingers were already flying across the keyboard. "I know Jekyll."

"So where do you keep her?" he asked with a hint of a smile.

The computer screen was black. It was supposed to be green. Was Novac slow or dying? Ann waited.

A child wailed. Had Ann imagined it? No, it was the La Leche woman's child. Heatsick probably. The kid's face was white and glistening.

Focus!

The tanned man crossed his arms.

Don't panic. "Sorry, the computer is slow," she said as she stared at the screen.

The boat trip would be unaffordable on a librarian's pay, but two families would share the expenses. It would be a family vacation. The kids would play. So would their parents. Making bonfires on beaches. Swimming off the boat…in tiny coves in lukewarm water…

"Well?" the gardener prompted.

The screen was still black, as uncommunicative as her husband. In its shadowy depths, her frowning reflection loomed. She pounded on the keys. JEKYLL…JEKYLL…JEKYLL. So what if the keys broke, came unglued, or popped off their pegs like Chiclets? Anything would be better than silence.

A buzzing like a swarm of angry bees…Customers complaining. Not people in line but those at the computer stands. Clerks rustling sheets of foolscap at the circulation counter. Clerks hurrying to the computer stands. Fastening foolscap signs to the computers….

Damn! She should hurl the computer monitor across the room. She should phone the techie who'd recommended the Novac system and hold the phone up so he could hear the buzzing of unhappy customers.

The gardener looked anxious.

"Sorry, sir." she adjusted her shoulder pads and smiled fiercely. "The computers are down. It's a new system. But we have a backup system." She swivelled her chair to the "backup system"—the microfiche catalogue. She thumbed through its ancient hinged sheets, found the "J"s, plucked out the fiche, and fitted it into a dusty microfiche reader.

How long had the man waited in the heat for this display of inefficiency? Blushing, she peered at the dimly lit fiche, wrote a promising call number on a post-it note, and handed it over. "Jekyll will be here, if she's home," she said brightly.

"Here?" He frowned at the numbers on the note.

"On the shelf. Under that call number. Books about her gardens."

"Shelf?" He looked towards the children's section.

"Back in a flash," she told the teenager next in line.

The girl raised clumsily outlined eyes to the ceiling. "I pay taxes for this?"

Ann smiled and strode towards the gardening section with the man in overalls following.

Toppled books in Jekyll's spot! More toppled books further along the shelf! And further still, the culprit. The destroyer of the reference alcove was picking books off the shelf and bending close to read their titles, his nose pressed into their spines. The poor guy was almost blind!

Ann straightened the gardening books and pinched them into place with a gunmetal grey bookend. "Sorry about the mess," she said to the gardener. "People like him have nowhere else to go."

"Like who?" The man looked puzzled.

"Him." She indicated the street person.

"Who?"

"That man."

The derelict was gone. Had he overheard her disparaging comment? She hoped not. "He's gone now—we don't often get street people here in the suburbs. Sorry also about the books on

Jekyll. They must be out on loan, but there are plenty of others here. You might find something in a history of gardening."

The man stared at the spine of a book on embroidery.

"Mis-shelved." She tossed the interloper like a soiled handkerchief onto a nearby book truck. "Sorry."

How embarrassing! She helped him search. Nothing. She crouched to look on the bottom shelf. Nothing. With every move, heat closed in like a warm blanket, suffocating.

Run for it! Break free! Kick off your sensible shoes and find fresh air! Slap a white sign on the door: "Computers temporarily down".

No—make that "Librarian temporarily down".

She turned to the gardener. "Unfortunately, not much is in right now. It's summer, it's Victoria, and it's gardening season." She added a sigh for comic emphasis. This dramatic manner usually went over well with customers whenever the branch's collection was found wanting.

His blue eyes remained cool. He was not the usual patron. Dark, lean, no soft corners to him. What excuse would he buy?

Sorry, sir. The brain of the library has ceased to function. Its neurons are no longer accepting the requests of neurotransmitters. Its memory is inaccessible, and none of its human appendages has any idea when it will be resuscitated.

She smiled like a robot. "The system will soon be up again. When it is, I'll search the collections of the other branch libraries, find Jekyll's design for Munstead and have it held for you."

"But what if nothing's in at those libraries either?"

"You might have to wait a week or so," she said in a tone that mocked this comically inefficient library world.

"That long?" He stared, amazed.

"That's the best we can do." She blushed.

He said nothing.

She should return to her desk. The teenager with the heavy makeup was sitting on it, drumming her heels against it. "Excuse me," Ann said to the gardener, and ran. She gave the girl a withering look. The teenager hopped off the desk and Ann said, "Can I help— "

"Excuse ME," the gardener interrupted. "I'm on a job. I need to order plants. I need Jekyll's plan today."

So gardening wasn't his hobby. That explained the muscular arms and dusty high-topped boots.

"I'll check the other libraries," Ann repeated. The library wasn't a fast food outlet for information. She took her time writing his request on a yellow Post-it. "You'll have to be patient."

"But I'm going on holiday, tomorrow!"

So?

"It's a special project. We're copying the Munstead Wood garden."

"Really!" Ann set down her pen. Munstead Wood had surrounded Gertrude Jekyll's home in Surrey, England. It was the garden dearest to her heart, her first baby, the prototype for all the glorious gardens she later designed. "Copying it here, in Victoria? Is that possible? Our climate is drier than England's. And the original plants may be hard to find."

He shrugged. "If they are no longer in cultivation, I'll find substitutes."

"You'll need a huge site too."

"I have one."

"And time. Time to plant the garden and time to maintain it by deadheading and dividing. And time to order plants. Yet you're leaving tomorrow…"

He laughed. "We started six months ago. Now we're creating the Spring Garden. I just need Jekyll's plant list. I found one in this library last year. It was in a blue book."

"A blue book?".

He looked at his watch. "Sorry, I have to go." He handed her a business card. "Here's my number. I'll return for the plan around five." He turned on his heels.

"Wait!" she said firmly. "If I locate the book at another branch, you'll either have to drive there or wait for it to be transferred here. That's library policy."

"I'll say," the teenaged girl commented to her friend, "Wait, wait, wait!".

"Where are these branches?" he asked.

Ann handed him a bookmark listing library addresses. His shoulders slumped.

Once upon a time, she would have gone out of her way to help people who asked interesting questions. Should she bend the rules for him?

The skylight shone a cone of heat around her. She wiped a tissue across her forehead. It came away soaked with ivory bisque foundation. The shoulder pads in her green blouse had fallen out of position, the pads her husband said drew attention away from her waist. She fiddled with them, conscious of the eyes of the gardener upon her, hopeful.

To hell with library policy! She wasn't a computer! She couldn't be programmed!

"Okay," she said. "For you, I'll make an exception. If I find the plan, I'll tell the interlibrary truck to bring it here by five. We're open until nine. But please phone before you come. I may not be lucky."

"Thanks." He flashed a grin that would have charmed her if she'd had time.

The library's sliding doors opened as he loped through them. Cooler air rushed in, a welcome draft from the outside world. For a moment the inferno was bearable. He must have sensed her staring because he turned and waved. She didn't acknowledge the gesture. She dropped his business card on her cluttered desk. She had bent the rules too often today.

The impatient teenager bent over the desk. "I need stuff for my summer reading course."

No "please." Ann was dripping with sweat, and hungry. *Let the kid wait!*

Ann pretended to have a coughing fit. Blindly, she reached into the top drawer of the reference desk. The KitKat candy bar was still there, still cool, thanks to its foil, but in this heat, not for long. She blew her nose and, sheltered behind the tissue, she sampled the smooth chocolate outer layer, nibbled at the inner crisp wafer-like filling. Her well-deserved prize. Just a mouthful. Enough to satisfy, but not leave tell-tale crumbs.

Three hours down, six more to go! Three of the chocolate bar's four sections had disappeared. She coughed again.

Someone was watching. She could feel eyes upon her.

Not the girl. The teenager was fishing a list of course materials from her purse. Someone else.

In the reference alcove, the street person was staring.

The nerve of him! The old man wasn't exactly skinny, himself!

An hour later, a lull. No one in line. Time to breathe. Time to think. Not about her husband or daughter or the trip, but about book orders.

Ann finished the candy bar, licked her fingers and started reading reviews in the *Library Journal,* four pages, but found the branch head had ticked her choices already. All Ann had to do was fill out order forms. Simple! She'd do that before tackling the unanswered reference questions.

Sweat trickled between her shoulder blades. This was a newly renovated building. Why wasn't the air conditioning working? Something to do with airflow, according to an expert. It would work fine with fewer obstructions, he said. Just eliminate bookshelves. He and the Novac salesman were probably laughing on a boat somewhere, knocking back beers.

An unkempt woman in an ancient housedress approached the desk. The woman held the hand of a young girl, and reeked of gin. Covering her mouth, she muttered a question.

Ann asked her to repeat it.

Red rimmed eyes anxiously veered to the child, and back to Ann. "Do you have anything for kids on death?"

Lord help us all. "Of course I do."

Fairies spiralled upward over the Serpentine Pond in a peaceful English twilight. This fairy tale world was pastel and timeless, a world without death.

The phone rang, shattering that world. How long had she been staring at pictures in a children's book?

"I haven't heard from you and it's after five," a man's voice said. "I wondered if you found the Munstead Wood book…"

How could she have forgotten his question? His business card peeked from under the yellow slips. David MacIntosh. Tangled Garden Landscaping. The words appeared under a reproduction of a famous painting of a chaotic garden. Rendered more chaotic by a muddy fingerprint.

"I'm sorry," she said weakly, "it's been frantic here. The computers are still down. Can I call you back in half an hour?"

"No, I'm on the road. I'll call you. I need that list today."

"I'll do what I can," she cut him off. Demanding type like her husband, but how could she have forgotten his request? Why was she so absentminded? Was it the heat? Or that question about death, the one for which she had sacrificed her dinner break? In an hour, she had collected only three books. There were plenty on the subject for adults. A new one looked particularly good: *How to Go on Living when Someone You Love Dies.* Ann had leafed through it. Excellent. No nonsense about finding "closure," no impossible expectations.

Four years ago Ann had compiled a bibliography for children on the topic of death. She used it to search since the woman obviously couldn't. But only three books on the list were in. The best were out on loan.

Her stomach growled. The mob of patrons had disappeared, probably to fix elaborate meals.

Explaining death to kids deserved sensitive treatment but many books were quick fixes, as soulless as their computer-generated illustrations. One book stood out, a story about a boy and his grandfather waiting for the whales to return. The grandfather's death was depicted as part of nature. The illustrations, in ochre and sepia tones, were quiet and tasteful. But death was not always quiet and tasteful. Three books were not enough, so Ann made out ten reserve forms. The official limit was six forms. Unfortunately, it might be weeks before the child received the books.

And while Ann searched, she found a lovely book of English fairytales, the kind her daughter would enjoy. The illustrations of fairies were soothing. Amanda would copy them.

Get a move on, Ann! Hand in the reserve forms. Deal with the gardening question. Finish the Library Journal orders. Don't think about Edward. Not on the job. Death is impossible to understand. The dead are dead.

She wiped away angry tears and handed the reserve forms in at the circulation desk. "Make these RUSH," she breathlessly told the head of circulation.

"Okay," Becky nodded, when she saw the titles.

A man nudged in beside Ann. The unkempt old man had followed her to the circulation desk. He didn't have books to check out.

Spare me! An admirer! His shorts were once dress pants, made into cut offs. He stood uncomfortably close.

"Hold all incoming calls," Ann told the head clerk "Unless they're from David MacIntosh."

"You haven't had your dinner," a circulation clerk said.

"I know but…" Did a surgeon halt an operation for coffee? Did an opera diva interrupt an aria for lunch? "The chase is on," she explained. "Too many questions, too few answers."

The old man was hovering. She escaped to her desk.

The gardening question first. She phoned the Oak Bay branch library. The municipality was a haven for expatriate Brits. A place where gardening wasn't a pastime, it was an obsession. But the Oak Bay branch had nothing. Neither did any of the other branches. Only the Central Library was left. Ann dialled the reference desk and asked for Colleen.

Colleen found a copy of Jekyll's *Colour Schemes for the Flower Garden.* It included the garden plan for the Spring Garden. But there was a problem. It was on the hold shelf, waiting for a library patron.

"Colleen, be a doll! Please, please, photocopy the plan along with the description of the garden, and fax them?"

"Fax?" Her friend's voice rose an octave. "Faxes are for important communiqués."

"I know, but make an exception! If the gardener doesn't get the plan today, our professional reputation is mud."

"So? What's new?" Colleen laughed. "See you at the book club," she said in parting.

"Book club?"

"At Tara's. Next week."

"Oh yes, *The Bridges of Madison County.* I haven't read it." The button for line three had been lit up for several minutes. "See you there," Ann said. She pressed the button, knowing who was calling.

"I'll go bananas if I hear another chime," a male voice said.

After a few minutes of Big Ben's chimes, most callers hung up. "Sorry," Ann said. "I've been busy."

"David MacIntosh here."

The fax machine at the circulation desk was coughing out paper. Ann motioned frantically to Becky. The clerk handed the fax to her. Ann smiled her thanks. "A fax has just arrived," she said proudly, "with the plan for the Spring Garden."

"Wonderful!"

"You can pick it up at the circulation counter."

"I'll be there in half an hour. And thanks."

Ann allowed herself a moment of triumph. Despite the heat, despite the computer crash, she had answered questions and helped people in need of information. Her eyeballs felt baked. The sugar rush from the chocolate was bottoming out. Only five minutes left of her dinner hour but she would eat later, at home. It had been a busy but productive day and she was happy.

Almost no patrons remained in the library. No wonder, on a beautiful July evening like this. The sun was still high and the light was soft and romantic. She opened the *Library Journal* and filled in more order slips.

At the bottom of one page was an announcement. The provincial library association was meeting in November in Victoria. An opportunity to scout out a permanent job! She noted the dates of the conference in her appointment book.

At a quarter to nine, the usual recording announced that the library would close in fifteen minutes and the closing theme music began. Ann had managed to finish the book orders and most of the Post-it questions.

"Don't you hate that music?" a clerk shelving books remarked.

"Actually," Ann giggled, "I like it." She hummed along and swayed to the beat.

The clerk looked disgusted.

The staff often complained about the corny music. "The Syncopated Clock" had amused people in a simpler era when clocks actually ticked. The tune was mechanical, perfect for a quiz show. Ann waited for the best part, the part where the music paused—the part where you were sure the clock had broken down, where the music stopped and the beat took over, like a metronome beating time.

Tick...tock...tick...tock...tick...tock...

The suspense...would the clock break down or not? If not, would the tune end in a flourish?

The music resumed—but it was the same old tune, only slower, winding down. That's what made the ending so funny—the lack of change.

The lights flickered to signal five minutes before closing. Ten patrons appeared out of nowhere. The clerks hustled to sign their books out by hand. The clerks needed help. Ann grabbed the fairy tale book and ran to their aid. Last in line was the derelict fellow who'd messed up the reference alcove.

"He's been here all day," Ann whispered to Becky. "Poor guy probably has nowhere else to go."

"Who are you talking about?"

"That street person."

The clerk gave her a peculiar look and went to lock the doors. Becky was usually friendly. Maybe she was in a rush to get home.

The derelict placed two books on the counter, a biography of Jonathan Swift and the Bible.

Ann raised her eyebrows at Elsa, the circulation clerk, to indicate amazement. The clerk looked blank. as if she couldn't see the fellow.

Ann blinked. No. He was there, substantial, very substantial, and very untidy. His socks rolled about his ankles. His shorts of some ancient, peculiar fabric, stopped at a strange length just below the knee. The fellow was so fat, he wheezed. His breath was cool and musty but bore no trace of alcohol. He was surprisingly well-read, judging by his book choices. That was strange but not uncommon. Many of life's casualties were well educated.

"My favourite books," the man said, his head swaying back and forth, like an imbecile's. His voice was musical, but hesitant, as though he was unused to speaking. He leaned across the counter and whispered, "Marriage has many pains, but celibacy has no pleasures."

He had quoted *Rasselas*, the only novel Samuel Johnson wrote! The quote was as shocking as lightning from a blue sky.

What about marriage <u>and</u> *celibacy*? Ann wanted to ask, but didn't. She was about to sign the man's books out when she noticed the fax. The fax of the plan for the Spring Garden was still on the counter where she had placed it.

The gardener hadn't come.

Her cheeks grew hot. After all the trouble she'd gone to—phoning the branches, bending the rules! She should have known: the more demanding and charming the library user, the more irresponsible he was likely to be. What a bloody waste of time! She crumpled the fax into a ball and threw it into the wastebasket.

The old derelict stared disapprovingly. Uncomfortable under his gaze, she retrieved the fax from the garbage, walked sedately to her desk, and dropped it into the top right hand drawer. She would keep it there a few days in case the gardener appeared. Then destroy it.

Think positive! You survived another day. You did your best. You deserve a reward.

What better reward than supper—minestrone soup and a boiled egg, along with macaroni and cheese? Mac and cheese wasn't on the diet, but she had cooked some this morning, and there'd be leftovers—her husband limited his intake of pasta. In his eating habits, as in most things, Richard was strict.

But in three weeks, he would loosen up. Life would change. In three weeks, he would be with her and Amanda at Desolation Sound. They would be a family on holiday, together.

CHAPTER 2: TO DANCE AGAIN

On some workdays, she only saw Amanda at breakfast. Tonight, however, the long daylight hours and the heat made sleeping difficult. The eleven-year-old lay awake, her long black hair splayed out on the pillow like a princess. She propped herself up as Ann entered and navigated through the piles of books on the floor to sit on the bed. Amanda loved to hear about her workday so Ann described the day's interesting questions—the one about Douglas Fairbanks, and the one about Gertrude Jekyll. She also described the customers—the strange old man and the bratty teenager, but she didn't describe the sad little girl with the bedraggled mother. Death was a subject to be avoided. She gave Amanda the books of fairy tales.

Amanda pored over the illustrations. "I love the soft colours in this one." She set it on the night table for later. "Want to play the fairy game?"

"The fairy game" was what Amanda called their custom of reading fairy tales together. At eleven, she was too old to believe in fairy tales, but not too old to appreciate their drama.

"It's a bit late. Pick a short one."

Her daughter selected *The Well at the World's End.*

Ann was to be the narrator, so she read,

> *"Once upon a time, and a very good time it was, though it wasn't in my time, nor in your time, nor anyone else's time, there was a girl whose mother had died, and her father married again. And her stepmother hated her because she was more beautiful than herself, and she was very cruel to her. She used to make her do all the servant's work, and never let her have any peace. At last, one day, the stepmother thought to get rid of her altogether; so she handed her a sieve and said to her—"*

Here, Ann passed the book to her daughter.

"Go," Amanda used her best nasty stepmother voice. *"Fill it at the Well of the World's End and bring it home to me full, or woe betide you."* She handed the book back to Ann.

Ann narrated the connecting bit and the next scene. The girl worries that she'll never find the well, and that she won't be able to carry water in a sieve. The girl does find the well, though. She dips the sieve into it, only to have the water run through it. She weeps and a frog appears with goggle eyes.

Amanda took the part of the frog. He strikes a bargain with the girl: if she promises to do whatever he bids her for a whole night, he will fix the sieve. The girl promises. He tells her how to change the sieve.

> *"Stop it with moss and daub it with clay,*
> *And then it will carry the water away."*

Ann read the narrative bit that followed. The girl goes home, and all is fine until one day, the frog knocks on her door.

Amanda read his demands.

> *"Open the door, my hinny, my heart,*
> *Open the door, my own darling;*
> *Mind you the words that you and I spoke,*
> *Down in the meadow, at the World's End Well."*

"Hinny" was such a wonderfully English word! Ann could imagine a grandmother sitting by the fireside telling this tale on a peaceful summer evening like this one. The light filtering through the oak trees was barely enough to read by. The fairy tale made a perfect bedtime story. It came from an old-fashioned, safe world where stories, no matter how gruesome, had happy endings.

"How awful," Amanda said as the story ended. "Having to take a frog to bed, then having to chop off its head, even though it becomes a handsome prince."

"Marriage involves compromises," Ann said with a smile. Not to mention pains, and celibacy. Her daughter was too innocent to appreciate the sexual undertone of the story, or its theme of death in love. That was the great thing about fairy tales: they held different meanings for young and old, and each meaning was complete in itself.

Ann carefully balanced the book on top of a pile of books on the floor. Someday soon, they should buy the child another bookcase.

"That was fun," Amanda said. "The rhymes in the story are like music. Don't you wish people always talked that way?"

"Yes, it would be a better world." Ann kissed her daughter goodnight.

Already the girl had propped another book on her tummy and pulled some tracing paper out of a drawer. Drawing was her tranquillizer, her sedative after a busy school day. She showed Ann the picture—a beautiful enchanted princess stood by a window and called into the night for her maidens. The fairy tale was a Russian version of the one they'd read tonight. She began to trace it.

Ann closed the door and smiled. The fairy game was fun and Ann enjoyed it as much as Amanda. Thanks to it, her daughter had learned to appreciate different ways of telling a tale, and different styles of illustration. As long as the budding artist had a supply of fairy tales, she would be happy.

The leftover macaroni and cheese was excellent. Ann put the pan to soak in the kitchen sink and waited up for Richard. She had seen him only in passing. When she had come home, he'd dashed off to his parents' house to fix their computer. The repair could have waited till Thursday. On Thursdays, he ate with his parents while Ann and Amanda had a "girl's night in."

Richard had no use for the fairy game, and, no time for his daughter either. It was sad. He could have shared so much with her, his hobby of woodworking, his love of forests and wild animals. He could have taken her camping on those weekends when Ann worked. Camping was expensive, he said, and anyway, Amanda wasn't the outdoorsy type. Not a boy, in other words.

But on the boat he would interact with Amanda, teach her about tides and trees, and creatures of the ocean and forests, pal around with her, and explore beaches and trails. Maureen's husband and sons would enjoy that too. Amanda would have the kind of outdoor adventures and the kind of father she'd missed out on till now.

Ann settled down to read the book for the book club. The meeting was next week and she always prepared for it. She opened *The Bridges of Madison County*.

The phone rang.

It was Maureen.

"Ann," she said, "I have bad news. I'm sorry, but we won't be able to go on the boat. Patrick has come down with chickenpox."

*****

The mound of soil in David MacIntosh's driveway was waist high. He had been hauling compost since supper-time, working quietly since the neighbours would be sleeping. He'd rigged a light from the garage so he could see. He had rented this cottage two months ago. The new herb garden would suit its English style. The small house dated from the nineteen thirties. It stood on almost half an acre, with only a few apple trees for landscaping. The original garden had disappeared. That's why he rented the cottage. The garden needed work, and he needed exercise. Especially tonight.

His watch said eleven thirty. He could go for another hour until his muscles could take no more and his body begged for sleep, but he had to save his strength. Tomorrow he would leave on holiday with Gerry. Today at the airport, he hardly recognised his childhood friend. Gerry DeMille was still a giant of a man, but his skin was shockingly white and papery, as if illness had sapped all moisture from it. Sun and fresh air were what Gerry's wife said he needed. She had phoned from England to suggest the holiday. Unfortunately Gerry's father had other ideas. The Lieutenant Governor of British Columbia planned to show off his journalist son to the local bigwigs. David had driven Gerry to Government House, but he would rescue him tomorrow morning.

The boat trip was a perfect way to escape the Lieutenant Governor's itinerary. David and Gerry would mosey up to Sangster Island, gunkhole around Cape Mudge, and re-visit their favourite fishing spots and anchorages. If Gerry was okay.

His voice has sounded so feeble when he phoned from the airport to say his plane had landed early that David had decided not to stop by the library. Instead he drove right to the airport. After the boat trip, he would pick up the Spring Garden plan and explain the delay to the librarian. She was pleasant and attractive, and she'd gone out of her way to get the information. The plant order would wait till after the trip too. He would phone it in to the import dealer. The tree peonies and other plants would take two months to arrive from England and go through quarantine inspection. With any luck, his crew would still be able to use them this fall. But if the plants were delayed, they'd wait till spring. That didn't matter as much as Gerry's health.

It was midnight now. What the heck, he'd work for another hour or so. Humphrey was stretched out in his kennel. Lucky dog! To be able to sleep with no worries.

There'd be plenty of leisure time once they were aboard the *African Queen*. David hoped to God that Gerry would rest.

*****

The conversation with Richard had deteriorated. The grandfather clock in the hallway struck midnight. Ann closed the living room door to let their daughter sleep. Richard had come in at eleven and Ann had blurted out the bad news. But his eyes were bloodshot. She was tired too. The news could have waited till tomorrow.

He sat and glared at the maps and brochures on the coffee table. "I don't care if they're dying," he swept the travel literature onto the floor. "A promise is a promise, and anyway, Amanda's already had chickenpox."

Ann swallowed hard. "But Maureen's two oldest haven't, and the incubation period is fourteen days. They could all catch it. They'd be miserable on a boat."

"And they might be immune, did you ever think of that?" Richard snapped. "Some people always expect the worst. Chickenpox is no reason to back out." His face was red, and his ears too. "Especially with less than a month to go!"

Maureen was the cautious type. "Well, you know Maureen," Ann said. "She doesn't take risks."

"Goddammit. The trip was planned."

He had laboured over the route and planned the anchorages for weeks. Ann took his hand. "I know how much work you've put into planning this, but we can still go."

Richard brushed her hand aside. He rose from the couch and performed a sort of military goose step around the couch. Ann bit her lip to keep from laughing.

He paused at the fireplace, centre stage. "Women!" And the rant began. Women couldn't organize anything. Women were excitable. Ann didn't choose proper women for friends. "Don't you know anyone worthwhile, anyone dependable, anyone who doesn't live life like a soap opera from one disaster to the next? I've had enough of this."

She could feel his frustration, the fear behind his anger, but Maureen was her friend. "Maureen is dependable. She was president of the co-op pre-school, remember? A good one. And she's a good mother too. And her kid is sick."

Richard didn't care about Maureen or her sick child. He was forty-five, ten years older than Ann. His contemporaries no longer had kids to consider. They were free to play tennis, to go on vacations, to live. He had had enough. That's what he always said. And that was as close as he ever came to talking about Edward.

"Ann, if we cancel, we'll have to pay a penalty. And if we go, we'll have to pay double what we expected."

"Never mind," she replied. "We'll go anyway. It'll be worth it, for Amanda's sake. We'll have a good time. As a family." She sounded more confident than she felt. They really couldn't afford the holiday now, and it was *her* fault because *her* friend had let them down.

"I'll solve this." He snapped his fingers. "I'll invite someone else."

"I'll ask around too," she said. Maybe one of the wealthier librarians would go. No, library workers had to give notice months ahead for holidays. But one of the wealthier book club members might be interested. Someone with kids.

* * * * *

Tara Innes clasped *The Bridges of Madison County* to her breast like a missal. "This book was so romantic. I want Ron to read it. If he won't, I'll drag him to the movie."

Everyone smiled, except Ann.

For two years, the eight women had met monthly to discuss books and never, in that whole time, had they devoted more than a few minutes to the book. Tara, the hostess, was her friend, but Tara was intellectually lazy and sentimental. She had chosen the book. Tara herself looked like a romantic heroine in her old-fashioned, white, embroidered dress. Even in this heat wave, the former flower child was as lovely as the Dresden figurine on her mantelpiece.

Ann attacked the delicious layered ribbon sandwiches as the discussion' droned on. Tara described hunting for antiques in Vermont. She and Ron had gone "off the beaten path" and seen the "cute" bridges described in the novel. Cindy Erdmann chimed in that she had seen equally cute bridges in Pennsylvania where she had once attended a nursing convention. She passed around postcards showing some of the cutest. Everyone gushed about them.

Ann contemplated throwing a "cute" fit. Didn't anyone understand that the book wasn't about bridges? Why didn't someone interrupt this nonsense? Were they all too polite? Or too impressed by Cindy and Tara? Both women belonged to the Victoria Establishment, Richard said. Richard cared about such things. Tara had married into an old Victoria family of auctioneers. Cindy's husband was the Deputy Minister of Natural Resources, a ministry that hired Richard sporadically as a forestry consultant.

Ann and Tara had been friends since childhood. They had consulted one another on boyfriends, on parenting and pregnancies, and on gardening. They had joined the same co-op preschool together. Tara flunked courses in high school but she was a talented artist and an asset to the auction house. Ann didn't know Cindy well, but knew she volunteered for worthy causes and she had founded the book club. Cindy was older than the other members, probably about forty-five, but her slim build and positive attitude made her seem the same age. How could an intelligent woman take part in such stupid literary criticism?

Tonight, for once, there would be a proper discussion. This book was dangerous.

A week ago, after Richard's rant about Maureen, Ann hadn't been able to sleep so she read the book instead. She skimmed the pages, becoming madder by the minute. She was still steaming. How could anyone believe such crap?

Cindy put the postcards back in her purse. "The best thing about this book was its lack of violence."

Whoa now! Way off the beaten track. "Lack of violence?" Ann said. "What about the violence to the husband? From his point of view, the story would be unromantic, and upsetting, and tragic."

Tara looked the way she used to during examinations at school, as if she was straining to see something out of sight. She flipped blindly through the pages, as if seeking an answer.

"Who cares about the husband's point of view?" Cindy commented. "He didn't have much of a relationship with Francesca."

"A better relationship than she had with the photographer." Ann reached for another sandwich. Everyone stared, but she ate slowly, savouring the pink and white filling of salmon and cream cheese. Savouring the suspense. The crumbs caught in the low-cut neck of her sundress. She brushed them away. "Francesca and the photographer never knew one another. All they talked about and all they thought about was one thing—themselves. At least Richard was concerned with business."

Tara's looked puzzled. "Richard?"

"Francesca's husband, the farmer."

Tara laughed. "Sounds like *your* Richard."

The others giggled.

Her Richard's rants about forestry were infamous. Ann smiled at the joke. "The book's Richard thought about his sow—"

"Steer," Colleen interjected.

Everyone laughed. Ann's co-worker, a typical librarian, always insisted on facts.

"He thought about his kids too," Ann said. "He took them to the fair."

Cindy groaned. "He *didn't* think about his wife. Francesca and the photographer had just met so they needed to tell each other who they were. Anyway, it's human to be self-centred."

"Even when you're in love?" Ann asked.

"Who ever really knows anyone anyway?" Colleen popped a devilled egg into her mouth.

"So, Colleen, if you're in love, anything goes?" Ann asked.

"This is a fairy tale romance, not reality," her friend replied. "In real life, if I lived on a farm in the middle of nowhere, I wouldn't open my door to a stranger. For all Francesca knew, Robert Kincaid could have been the Boston Strangler."

"Exactly." Ann said. At last the discussion was on track.

"But this isn't a fairy tale," Tara wailed, "Robert Kincaid the photographer was famous."

"So was Ted Bundy," Colleen said.

Tara appeared dismayed. "If Francesca had known more, it wouldn't have been romantic."

"Surely you don't believe that," Ann said. "What about AIDS?"

"Geez, Ann, lighten up! AIDS wasn't around in 1965. All you ever do is trash books." Tara leafed through the pages, muttering. "I'm sure they used protection..."

Ann smiled. Tara was so funny when she became agitated.

Cindy giggled. "It's only a novel."

"I'm positive they did..." Tara said.

"It didn't come up," Cindy said with a straight face.

Everyone laughed.

Tara gave up and closed the book. "Okay, so they took a chance."

"That's not right," a young mother said. "The author should have made that clear. Kids might get the wrong idea."

"*Women* might get the wrong idea," Ann said. "Kids don't read junk like this. This book is dangerous." She threw the novel onto the coffee table. "It's especially dangerous to women."

The romance was too easy and insidious, the heroine too passive. The heroine had no idea what she was entering into. After the hero left, what did she do? She moped. She didn't even have the brains to find out his phone number though he worked for a national magazine. Ann had clipped literary reviews of the book. All the feminist reviewers agreed with her analysis. "The book is dangerous, not just because of the unprotected sex. Think about what it implies for women. Would you live your lives the way Francesca does hers?"

Silence.

Tara looked around as though seeking allies.

Ann enjoyed a foretaste of victory.

A breeze ruffled the sheer curtains in the antiques-filled room. The broiling sun had set. Suddenly life was bearable.

Tonight, *her* Richard was babysitting. How was he doing? Unlikely he'd have the patience to play games with Amanda, but they might watch a science program on TV together. Like the Richard in the novel, he had a lot to deal with, a lot on his mind, his career, and of course, Edward.

He had changed after Edward died, taken up jogging, spent less time at home, less time with them. Had he invited anyone to come on the boat? He hadn't said much since the problem arose. Next weekend he would volunteer at a tennis tournament. Maybe he'd find someone there with plenty of money and plenty of leisure, able to go boating in two weeks.

Tara touched Ann's arm. "I can't believe you didn't love this novel. Didn't it make you cry?"

"At the end, when Richard died, I did. I was upset for him. He was a victim. Not of love, but of his wife's wish fulfilment." She reached for her fifth sandwich.

"Francesca was a neglected wife," Cindy said.

"Yes," Tara said, "so she needed to dance again. Haven't you ever been swept off your feet, Ann?"

Ann kept her face neutral. She had to turn their flank, and march them away from her toward the real enemy, the book. "I'm not the only one who disliked this novel." She reached into her purse for ammunition. "Read these reviews."

Two women read them. The others continued debating whether books should depict unprotected sex. Tara went to the kitchen and came back armed with a cherry cheesecake.

Ann returned the reviews to her purse. The battle was over. The novels lay belly up on coffee tables, under handbags, behind embroidered cushions, like war casualties. Books, even this one, deserved more consideration, damn it. Ann would bide her time and attack again, like Napoleon returning from Elba. She ate two helpings of cherry cheesecake. It was soft, velvety, and romantic. Everyone begged for the recipe.

Cindy talked about her husband's Natural Resources Commission. Ann had heard it all—forest policy was all Richard ever talked about at dinner. She sucked on the last cherry, swallowed it, and fired an opening salvo. "So you don't feel sorry for Richard at all?"

Cindy looked baffled. "He might be appointed to the Commission. It's under discussion…."

"Sorry," Ann's mind whirled. "Again, I meant Francesca's Richard."

Richard's appointment was under discussion! This was wonderful news! If he were appointed, their finances would improve.

"I shouldn't have said that," Cindy said. "It's all hush hush. Richard the farmer was a lousy lover, probably having it off with the steer."

Everyone laughed.

"Okay," Ann said. "Forget ethics, what about aesthetics? What about the book's bridge imagery?"

They stared as if she was crazy. Obviously they thought they had dealt with the topic of bridges.

Ann began the lecture. "If we stick to what we know, we miss what's going on in the world. If we only discuss the familiar aspects of a book, things like contraception and covered bridges, we miss the bigger picture, the purpose of the book, its moral relevance, and the imagery conveying the message. What is the purpose of this novel? Is it just a gentle tale about an affair? Or something more sinister? What images does Robert use to describe himself? Listen to this."

She'd marked the page. She read with exaggerated emphasis Robert's description of himself as an obsolete kind of male animal and as a shaman. She put the book down. "Robert doesn't just give Francesca orgasms; he gives her orgasms of the mind. He practically says he's Jesus come to save her."

Everyone gasped.

"But he's mysterious!" Tara's eyes brimmed with tears. She was a hopeless romantic like Francesca.

"This book isn't about reality, Tara. In the real world, Francesca could have phoned or faxed Robert, or hired a private detective to find him. Francesca was a fool who wanted to live in misery."

Tara wiped her eyes. "You're too harsh, Ann. You're the kind of reader the author describes, the kind who scoffs at great passion. Their love would have lasted."

The others chorused agreement.

The kind who scoffs at passion? Ann gripped her porcelain teacup and spilled tea. Should she concede victory now? Or fight to the finish?

"When I was a nurse, "Cindy said, "I saw suffering every day. This book shows a reality beyond that. I know time passes and people fall sick and die, but I don't want to read about that. I want details of how people lived and loved, of how they triumphed over death. This book delivers."

"I may not know as much as you do, Ann, about literary criticism," Tara sounded hurt, "but I thought the imagery was beautiful, especially when they danced. Listen to this!" She opened the novel and read,

"He was falling into her now. And she into him. She moved her cheek away from his, looked up at him with dark eyes, and he kissed her and she kissed back, longtime soft kissing, a river of it. They gave up the pretense of dancing, and her arms went around his neck. His left hand was on her waist behind her back, the other brushing across her neck and her cheek and her hair. Thomas Wolfe talked about the "ghost of the old eagerness." The ghost had stirred in Francesca Johnson. In both of them."

Tara's musical voice transformed the words into poetry. Into a song about unregulated, un-academic, unabashed joy. Unreal and dangerous joy.

Ann cleared her throat. She had to stop this onslaught. "Why did the author quote Wolfe? Only because he needed a crutch to give this B grade romance some class."

"Ann, you're hopeless," Tara wailed.

The other women looked hostile. Time to declare a truce. Or quit the book club, and nothing was worth that. "Okay, I'll concede this much. If the lovers had met again, which of course they didn't, because the-author-wouldn't-allow-them-to, they *might* have lived and loved happily ever after."

Everyone relaxed. Suddenly another cup of tea was a necessity. The conversation switched to safer topics like kids and food. The battle was over. Ann drank tea and smiled as though losing didn't matter but it did, and she felt anything but peaceful.

CHAPTER 3: BRAMBLES

The next day, the library was a furnace. People dropped in only long enough to sign out holiday reading. Only a few die-hards stayed--a teenaged nerd reading his way through the engineering section, some Japanese students stoically doing summer school homework, and the shabby street person. He stared furtively from the shadows of the reference alcove. Ann stared back. As if the heat wasn't enough, she had to endure this clown watching her. His lips were fleshy, and full. He had the mouth of a sensualist, the mouth of a dirty old man. His brown shorts were disgracefully tight and long, his white shirt was some dreadful kind of hippie thing, voluminous and filthy. He was holding a book up to one eye, and seesawing his head along the print, all the time muttering to himself.

He really was repulsive. Repulsive and sad.

Think of something else, she told herself. She took out a publisher's catalogue and marked reviews of promising new books but the heat made it difficult to concentrate. She drank lukewarm water from a glass on her desk.

The boat trip was fast approaching. They could afford it if Richard was appointed to the Commission, but that was a big 'if'. Money was a problem. A year ago, she had wanted to drive to Disneyland. Richard said they couldn't afford the trip. So they visited Ann's parents instead in Vancouver. Then they drove to Sechelt where the station wagon broke down. A miserable holiday.

Last night at the book club, she'd forgotten to ask if anyone wanted to share the boat. Just as well. Who would want to holiday with the Scourge of the Book Club?

She giggled. Last night's battle had been fun. Waiting for the right moment to attack the members, listening to their half-baked ideas, making them put down their teacups, taking command and flattening their cardboard hero and heroine—the photographer whose greatest passion was himself and the male-fantasy vestal virgin who was as stupid as her pink dress.

She needed to dance again. Haven't you ever been swept off your feet, Ann?

Silly Tara. Upset, because Ann called Francesca a fool. The women at the book club didn't know the basic rules of debate—so they resorted to personal attacks, arguments ad hominem.

Ann, you're the kind of reader who scoffs at great passion

Another ad hominem! Ridiculous!

At least she had goaded them into proper criticism of the book. Even Tara. Tara couldn't analyse but she had read an excerpt, her face tearstained. *She moved her cheek away from his, looked up at him with dark eyes, and he kissed her and she kissed back, longtime soft kissing, a river of it.*

You're hopeless. Tara said that of Ann. Her face was the face of an angel, the face of a troubled friend.

Funny how personally the women took literary criticism. The members usually cut Ann some slack, knowing about Edward, but if Ann had fought on, they would have rallied to the angel's side. Friendships would have fallen. All over a stupid book, a fairy tale for adults.

Ann shifted the publisher's catalogue and went back to reading book reviews, making out book orders. After three orders, she put down her pen.

All she could see was Tara's tearstained face. Ann had upset her friend. Tara didn't understand debate wasn't personal. Maybe Ann should have stopped it earlier. The book club members weren't used to academic debate, except for Colleen who had a degree in English Lit.

Colleen was organizing the programs for the upcoming library conference. Ann should phone her at the Central Library and laugh about last night's debate.

On Ann's desk were some books Amanda had asked her to return to the library. Charming fairy tales. Beautifully illustrated by Dulac and Greenaway and others. Would the librarians at the conference like to learn more about these illustrators? Conference presentations usually centred on boring topics such as "The Internet as Applied to Reference Work," or "Automated Indexes in Reference". The world of fairies would be much livelier.

Ann dialled the central library. "So Colleen, what did you think of last night's meeting?" she asked with a giggle.

"Interesting, and the cherry cheesecake was amazing."

"Unfortunately I had two pieces. I can't seem to stick to my diet!"

"Ann, I must have told you a thousand times that you're not fat. You just have a warped body image."

"Then why is Richard always on at me to exercise?"

"He's a fitness freak."

"About last night," Ann resumed, "wasn't it a hoot the way everyone defended that silly romance?"

A pause. "Actually, I rather liked the book."

"You did?" *No point in trying to disillusion her…Keep on track.* "Anyway, Colleen, I called because I had an idea…"

Ann pitched her idea. The library owned a huge treasury of fairy tales. Many were magnificently illustrated, but most were hidden away in Special Collections. These books were once childhood favourites, and their pictures were fascinating mementoes of simpler times. "I'd like to re-open that world by talking about these fairy tales and their illustrators."

"Sounds too airy fairy to me," Colleen said. "You'd be better to talk about library budgets, or about the Internet,"

Typical librarian. No imagination. The speech would be fun to research, it would impress those in power, and open the door to a permanent job.

Ann elaborated. She rhymed off the names of the famous illustrators, Greenaway, Dulac, Beatrix Potter. Okay, Beatrix didn't illustrate fairy tales but Ann could broaden the topic to children's books in general. And she would illustrate her talk with slides. Edmund Dulac's jewel toned paintings would translate into spectacular slides of exotic subjects like oriental princesses, peacocks, griffins and turbulent seas. A visual feast. And a nice change from computer topics.

It was a hard sell but eventually Colleen caved in. Ann's subject was offbeat she said, but it was probably good to offer a variety of topics to the conference goers.

Ann was sweating as she hung up the phone. A pain low in her stomach signalled hunger. Surreptitiously, she reached in her drawer for a KitKat and tore off its wrapping. The afternoon heat was worse than the morning's. No one remained in the library, except the staff of course, and the old derelict. Now and then, he'd emerge from his barricade of books to select more weighty dictionaries and encyclopaedias. The lucky clerks would have to re-shelve them! The man seemed happy in his bookish environment, and cool despite the stifling heat.

No library users meant no reference questions so Ann happily began researching her speech. First she collected Amanda's favourite books—fairy tales illustrated by Arthur Rackham, nursery rhymes with pictures by Caldecott, Beatrix Potter's stories. She decided to begin with Rackham's *Peter Pan.* She opened the book, expecting to see ethereal fairies. Instead hobgoblins played hide and seek among gnarled and writhing trees. Rackham must have had fun drawing them. But she could contrast his rustic style nicely with that of his suave contemporary, Edmund Dulac.

She would take notes on their art, their choice of subject, and their lives. After reading biographies of Rackham, she looked at Rackham's goblins. They were unruly, obnoxious, cheeky creatures. They spilled out of the pages and thumbed their noses at her and her so-serious topic. She shut the book.

It was too hot to think. She folded the KitKat's foil wrapping into a minuscule fan and looked at the calendar. The conference was on November sixth, three months from now. She should choose half a dozen illustrators, spend a week on each, researching and writing, and allow two weeks for preparing slides. She would finish by October. No, she'd forgotten the boat trip. Add two more weeks. Okay, by mid-October, with time left over for glitches.

The boat trip was only eight days away. Why had she forgotten to ask at the book club if anyone wanted to share the holiday? If Richard didn't find someone, their bank account would suffer. That wouldn't be the end of the world. In fact it might be the beginning. She and Richard and Amanda would be alone together at last, forced into having a wonderful family holiday.

He couldn't stay angry forever, could he? It seemed forever since they had last played tennis or swum together or made love. After their son's death, nothing had pleased him. Not woodworking, not Amanda, not Ann. Only external things, like politics and tennis. Ann had married for love but she was uneasy: Richard had divorced his first wife. Statistics said second marriages often fail. They all needed a holiday, but would a holiday be enough?

Ann sighed and turned again to Rackham's dwarfs. Their ugly, wrinkled faces and limbs were as skinny and gnarled as the artist's skeletal trees. His Peter Pan was a wild, elemental being, unsanitary and devilish, unlike the sanitized Disney version. Yes!! That contrast was interesting. It would give her speech a modern edge. She would contrast Rackham's style to Disney's, and to Dulac's as well. These hobgoblins were important. She should mark this page. She opened her desk drawer to get a sticky note.

The Post-its lay underneath a dirty, leather-bound book. *The Complete Works of Samuel Johnson.* How had it come to be there? Oh yes, she was supposed to decide whether or not to discard it. The book split open as she picked it up. Its binding was failing, dust and loose threads everywhere. On the stained page, the phrase: *It leaves us as soon as it arrives.*

What was Johnson pontificating about?

She skimmed the paragraph.

Time. The fact that the present is impossible to know.

The present ceases to be present before its presence is well perceived, and is only known to have existed at all by the effects which it leaves behind.

The pun was terrible and the phrasing was wordy, but Johnson's insight was modern and acute. No wonder, he had held people spellbound at parties. He had been like a guru in the eighteenth century. People jostled one another to hear his latest pronouncements.

A brown stain obscured the rest of the paragraph. Ann tilted the page towards the skylight to make out the words.

Few people want to examine the present even if it were possible. The greatest part of our ideas arise, therefore, from the view before us or behind us.

Johnson was right. You usually saw the present from the perspective of the past or of the future.

She had hoped for a flourishing career, a loving marriage, and children. But death had intervened. And now her marriage was in jeopardy, her career stagnant, and Edward was gone. But things would improve. Wouldn't they?

Richard had dreams too. He hadn't wanted a daughter. He had wanted a son to accompany him on camping trips, a son to whom he could teach carpentry, and a slim, desirable wife to support him in a powerful government job. Those dreams never materialized.

What did he dream of now? She did not know. She only knew that he had become desperate.

The present was uncertain and queasy. As impossible to contemplate as the concept of infinity. Impossible to endure without hope.

Johnson might be wordy, but he was deep— a nice antidote to the mental indigestion brought on by *The Bridges of Madison County*. She would take him on the boat. She went to the circulation desk, to sign him out.

"Excuse me, Miss."

She inserted a date due slip in the book and looked up. A tall man in overalls, blue-eyed. The Jekyll man. More than a week late for his urgent fax.

"I believe you found that plan for me," he said. "The one for Jekyll's Spring Garden."

"We *had* the plan. It was discarded when you didn't show up. You said you needed it that day. We went to a lot of trouble to photocopy it and fax it here."

He turned red. "Sorry, I couldn't get here."

She shrugged. "You should have phoned. The original might be still at the central library."

"But the project's starting. I'm in a rush-"

"-A week ago, you were in a rush to leave on holiday."

"There was last minute-business, something came up. Illness."

Sure. He looked the picture of health. He was about her age— thirty-five. His forehead shone with perspiration, but it wasn't the perspiration of fever. His eyes were clear, and blue, and steady. He was thin but his chest was broad, his arms strong, and his skin tanned.

Why was she noticing all this? She wasn't a romantic heroine. And he wasn't a hero. He was demanding and inconsiderate.

"Could you get them to re-send the fax?" he asked.

"Sorry," she said with an icy, professional smile. "Faxes are only for urgent library business. They made an exception once. They won't make one again." It sounded unconvincing. Too bad.

He looked startled, as if a snake had bit him.

A thrill of triumph rippled through her.

"Well, thanks for your trouble." He turned to go.

His polite manner cut through her victory like a knife. As she watched him leave, she remembered Tara's tear-filled eyes, Colleen's coolness, and the disgusted look the derelict gave her as she crumpled the fax.

She hadn't always been this prickly. What was she becoming?

* * * * *

Ann flipped open the omelette pan to reveal the golden highlight of her week, perfectly cooked, fluffy, with just the right amount of butter and cheese. Saturday was omelette morning, the start to the weekend, in this case, the August holiday weekend. Today, Richard was occupied with the tennis match and she had to work, but afterwards, the weekend was full of promise. Ann gave her daughter the first omelette so she could return to a television cartoon.

"What time is the first match?" she asked Richard as she refilled the pan.

"Ten fifteen, registration's at nine," he replied with campaign precision. It was only a tennis tournament, but everything he did was important. He smelled wonderfully of aftershave. She loved the way his shoulders met his neck, how his posture was always so militarily correct, how his clothing always fit perfectly. His white tennis shirt, undone at the collar, revealed an intriguing glimpse of chest hair. Long ago, she would have caressed his shoulder, as a signal to return to bed.

He buttoned the shirt, and then fiddled with his empty coffee cup. He limited himself to two cups of coffee. Part of his fitness diet. The first cup he timed to last till his breakfast was ready, but Amanda had taken the first omelette.

Ann closed the omelette pan. "I see the Sooke Art show is this weekend." She set the timer. "We could take Amanda tomorrow, have a picnic in East Sooke Park."

"Oh?" Richard turned his attention to the business section of the newspaper. "Mother wants us at her place at twelve, after church."

Church was essential for business contacts.

"Maybe after lunch?" Ann tried to sound casual. "Or on Monday?"

"Maybe," he said irritably.

Maybe meant *no*. It would rain, or he'd have to mow his parents' lawn. There was never any time now for leisure, only for fitness, or duty. She opened the pan and dropped the omelette onto his plate.

He folded the paper and set it aside. "The Erdmanns want to come to Desolation Sound with us," he said as he began to eat.

"The Erdmanns? On the boat?"

"No, on an ice floe." He laughed in disgust.

Amanda looked up. Ann modulated her voice. "But we don't know them. I mean, Cindy's in the book club and Tom you know through business, but they're hardly our friends, and besides, they don't have young kids."

He forked a piece of bacon into his mouth, chewed it and swallowed. "Mother will take Amanda."

"You mean Amanda won't come with us?" Ann couldn't believe it. "But she wants to come. Don't you dear?"

The girl, her mouth full, nodded.

Richard sprinkled salt and pepper on his omelette, and then wiped the necks of the shakers. "She'd be bored with no one to play with."

"She wouldn't! She's been looking forward to it, haven't you Amanda? Besides, there's no one for her to play with at your mother's. And anyway, I hardly know the Erdmanns. Why would you ask them?"

Then she remembered. Tom was on the Natural Resources Commission, the Commission that Richard was trying to impress. She wiped her hands on the pink apron encasing her like a sausage skin. What other objection could she raise?

"We can't afford to go alone," Richard said, looking up from his plate. "I've already arranged it."

"That's nice." Ann glared at him. "Consulting everyone except me!" How dare he eat with his usual enjoyment? He was complacent, impossible. Consulting his mother and his business acquaintances before consulting her. If you could call this announcement "consulting."

Amanda left the table. Her footsteps rocketed downstairs to the television in the basement.

"It would be nice to go as a family somewhere, sometime," Ann said. She whipped up eggs for her own omelette and poured them into the pan. Richard went on eating, self-possessed as usual. She hated the way his shoulders met his neck, how his posture was always so militarily correct, how his clothing always fit perfectly.

He had done nothing overtly wrong. Maureen's kids being sick had breached Ann's holiday plans. The chickenpox provided a watertight excuse for him to charge in and seize command. The Erdmanns were important; Amanda wasn't.

*****

Brambles twined among wild roses and clambered down moss-covered rocks in search of water. The drought had encouraged them. Ann's hand ached from gripping the secateurs. For two hours, she'd been eliminating brambles from the hill behind her house. The heat was terrible, and though the sky had been cloudy all weekend, it hadn't rained. It was already Monday. The garden clean-up was boring but anything was better than sitting inside, stewing.

The boat trip had become a power trip.

She shouldn't have let Richard choose their companions. She should have tried to find someone herself, at the book club, or at the library. Why hadn't she?

Amanda was disappointed. Richard was angry that Ann hadn't appreciated his solution so he volunteered to stay on at the tennis tournament all weekend. Amanda had a sleepover at her friend Jen's, thank goodness, a distraction from her parents' arguing.

Richard probably hadn't meant to announce it so boorishly. It was just his way. He probably thought he was helping, arranging everything without telling her. But he knew Ann had talked to Amanda about the trip. They would board the thirty-eight foot Bayliner in Richmond, travel up the Sunshine Coast to Gibson's, and up to Princess Louisa Inlet and Desolation Sound, circle Quadra Island and the Gulf Islands and head back to Richmond. A two-week holiday, full of fascinating scenery and fun. No wonder Amanda had run from the table. The poor kid.

He knew Ann wanted a family holiday. Did he really believe their daughter would be unhappy with adults? Or had he just considered the business advantages of a holiday with the Deputy Minister?

His reasons were as tangled as these brambles and roses. In three years, Ann had only managed to clear a small patch on the hill in the backyard. A prickly strand arched downward catching her shirt. A thin stalk with thorns. A junior bramble or a senior rose? The native Nootka roses had straight stalks. This one curved. Ann raised her secateurs to pry the bramble off her shirt. A thorn pierced her glove.

Damn! She pulled off her glove and sucked the wound. She cut the offender down. Then she continued her campaign. Using secateurs instead of fingers, she carefully separated the invaders from the roses. As if cataloguing a book, she noted the differences.

Wild roses had thin, straight stalks, small leaves, and dainty hair-like thorns. Brambles had lightweight, thick stalks, larger leaves and thorns like fangs. The rambunctious brambles were still putting out blossoms. Didn't they realize winter was coming, that their blossoms wouldn't bear fruit?

She grunted as she knelt to hack a thick stalk off at its base. If she cut the bramble down, it would weaken but its roots would bide their time, inches below the ground, ready to erupt. Digging the roots out would be a back-breaking job.

Richard admired their blossoms. And they were pretty—an innocent shade of pinkish white. "Rather like you," he said once in their romantic period. He loved the fruit of the brambles too. There berries were ripening. Ann popped one of the blackest into her mouth and spit it out. It was hard as a stone. The berries needed a few more weeks of sun. They would be perfect after the boat trip.

The boat trip was only a week away. It might not be perfect after all. Bile rose in her throat. She swallowed it. Too much coffee, not enough breakfast, and too much worrying.

Raindrops spattered the warm earth. This holiday weekend had been far from perfect too. Richard was supposed to play tennis only on Saturday, but on Sunday a referee had been sick and Richard had volunteered, and that destroyed the weekend plans. No church, no dinner with his parents. There was a tennis banquet tonight, but he hadn't invited Ann. She wouldn't like it, he said. She wouldn't know anyone there.

Tonight Amanda would return from the sleepover. Ann would cook shepherd's pie, her favourite.

On the boat, what kind of food would the Erdmanns expect? Cindy was nice, but elegant. Would Tom be elegant too? And expect elegant meals? Ann had hoped for a vacation where everyone wore jeans and T-shirts and ate fish. Instead, Richard would be trying to impress the Deputy Minister.

At least on the boat, he couldn't play tennis.

Brambles were becoming an issue. Neighbours had recently complained about brambles invading their yards. Richard scoffed at their complaints. Ann suggested hiring a gardener, but he said they couldn't afford one, and besides, Amanda should help weed. She could use the exercise. The kid didn't need exercise, she needed attention. And Richard himself spent far too much time exercising. He should help weed too.

Ann levered herself upright, and rubbed her aching neck. The rain was wetting her old shirt, her nose was dripping and her hair was filthy. Luckily no one could see. One day she would have a garden under control, one in which she merely had to hoe between orderly plants and stay clean. In Edwardian days, ladies in immaculate, pastel dresses toured their gardens with a trug on one arm, snipping a flower here and there for the parlour. Edwardian ladies never got down on hands and knees. Gertrude Jekyll had been the exception. No pastel dresses for her! The dumpy little woman wore mole-like glasses and heavy boots but she was wild at heart. She had loved dividing perennials and getting muddy. Her gardening boots had been immortalized in a famous painting.

Had that gardener at the library ever found Jekyll's plan? Why hadn't he come to the library when he said? Even if he had been ill, he should have phoned. Maybe he had an excuse. Ann hadn't given him the benefit of the doubt. She shouldn't have lost her temper. He had replied so politely to her rudeness. His blue eyes had been so honest. And he was very good looking.

Maybe if she hired a studly gardener like him, Richard would be jealous. Maybe Richard would pay her more attention.

Not likely. Richard wouldn't believe she could attract a man.

Rain sprinkled her shirt, the first rain in months. It was warm, and welcome. The ground gave off a woody fragrance. Her shirt was soaked but cooling. The blue-striped shirt was an old one of Richard's. Once she had thought it romantic to wear his things, now it was just cheap. She knelt on the damp earth to cut down another bramble. Weeding was mindless entertainment. Maybe one day a robot would scoot over these rocks. Its tiny brain would choose in an uncomplicated binary process, saying 'yes' to roses, 'no' to brambles.

Gardening was relaxing but she should be shopping for clothes for the trip. Amanda might like to come along.

Brambles were important to Richard. She had asked him once to help get rid of them. They'd been walking up the hill, and he paused on a terrace. "You mean clear-cut them?"

She laughed. "Brambles aren't trees."

"What about the animals that live in them, the birds, the squirrels and the quail?"

"Don't be ridiculous, Richard. What about the predators that hide in them? The cats that eat the darling birds? The dear little rats? Anyway, quail and squirrels aren't native to Victoria. And neither are brambles. Not this kind. The native brambles don't arch all over the place."

"I like these." He plucked a blossom and put it in her hair.

"They're choking the native roses."

"Have it your way. You always do."

It was a circle, like most of their conversations. After it, she decided to eradicate the brambles.

In truth, she rather liked brambles, but you had to take a stand, make a choice, and impose order, didn't you? That's what garden design was all about.

*****

David peered through the rain as he steered *The African Queen* away from Fisherman's Wharf. "The fish are waiting," he said to Gerry.

Gerry, wrapped in an expensive rain jacket, gave him the thumbs up. Humphrey barked with excitement. The trip was starting at last two weeks later than planned. David could hardly believe they were going. It felt as though they were running from the law.

Only this morning, the holiday Monday, he had picked up Gerry from the hospital. Gerry had been waiting in the mandatory wheelchair, his smile even broader than his famous television grin. Never had David seen anyone so eager to escape. Two weeks in hospital, with several health setbacks, and rules against cognac and cigars had challenged the television journalist's usual urbanity.

Michael DeMille wanted his son to rest. The heart attack had been a warning, he said. Gerry said he hadn't come all the way from England to lounge in bed. Gerry loved to be active. As a kid at Telegraph Cove, he would play hooky to explore the forest, or the ocean beyond the cove.

David steered past the breakwater. The shore was veiled in misty rain but he could see the Lieutenant Governor's mansion standing high on its hill. Gerry's father was probably at the ballroom window, watching them depart.

David hoped all would go well on the trip. To re-schedule it had been difficult but he had juggled the holiday times of his landscaping crew, rearranged garden inspections, rebooked consultations, and put off a truck-buying trip to Vancouver. He'd even delayed the ordering for Michael's pet project, the Spring Garden. Between hospital visits and running his business, David hadn't had time to go to the library. When he finally got there, the librarian had discarded the plan.

She had seemed strangely hurt and angry. Odd. She had been helpful before, but women could be that way. Unpredictable. Like Jenny, his ex-girlfriend, who wanted time for herself, then resented it when he went fishing. Jenny, who wanted the simple life but also wanted money for expensive clothes. Marriage hadn't even been discussed with the striking Eurasian beauty. Six years of her resentment and remorse were hardly a basis for friendship, much less marriage. He hoped to find something better.

David remembered an interview a friend of Gerry's had done. The British journalist had asked the Prince of Wales and his fiancée if they were in love. The hapless prince replied, somewhat disparagingly, "Whatever 'in love' means." The prince's honesty had cost him the sympathy of the world. But the prince was right. "Love" was a catchall word. Romance was cheap. Friendship, kindness and respect were rare. Sex…well, there were a hell of a lot of women who said they wanted sex, but in reality rated a man only by his pocketbook. Celibacy wasn't as bad as some marriages.

The cabin was quiet. Gerry had fallen asleep on the forward bunk. He was breathing steadily, and his colour was less hectic. David pulled a sleeping bag over his friend and then returned to the wheel.

David's parents were content with one another, best friends even now, forty years after their marriage. Maybe he was wishing for the moon, longing to know the kind of love they shared. Maybe he should consider himself lucky. At thirty-five, he had his rented house, his garden and his independence. He had his health too.

The heart attack had weakened Gerry's fragile heart and the doctors wouldn't consider doing angioplasty or inserting a stent. The journalist was to take it easy, not smoke and rest He would not be allowed to fly home until he was better. David persuaded the doctor Gerry could rest just as well at sea as on land. Gerry was afraid he'd be a burden, but David assured him the *African Queen* was small enough for one person to handle. He'd grown up with boats much larger than the twenty- foot trawler. The patient could relax and pretend the boat trip was a pleasure cruise.

David breathed in the tangy salt air and thought of the two weeks ahead. They would have no agenda. They'd mooch around Cape Mudge, cruise up some inlets on the mainland, go where they pleased, and where the fish were biting.

*****

The rain pelting against the window in Amanda's bedroom marked the end of the holiday weekend. No birds sang in this soggy twilight. Luckily for Richard, the deluge had held off till the tournament ended. He'd be at the banquet now.

Amanda had school tomorrow. After watching several television shows, Ann suggested bed.

Amanda made a counter-offer: bed *and* the fairy game. She pulled a copy of Grimm's fairy tales from a pile of books. "Your choice, this time, Mom."

Which to choose? *Snow White*? No, they'd played that recently. *Rumpelstiltskin*. She showed her daughter Rackham's wonderful portraits of the goblin. The dwarf embodied the spirit of mischief as he danced around the bonfire in front of his cottage. He looked especially nasty as he demanded payment from the miller's daughter.

Amanda laughed at his grimace. "He looks like Daddy when he's mad."

Ann smiled. Luckily Richard couldn't hear this remark.

Amanda was in good spirits. At dinner, she devoured three helpings of shepherd's pie as she chatted about the sleepover. Jen's parents had taken the girls to the beach. They'd paddled a canoe, enjoyed a picnic and a marshmallow roast. It all sounded so normal, so easy, and the kind of weekend Amanda needed.

Ann, as narrator, read about the miller's daughter and how her talent for spinning straw into gold brought her to the notice of the king.

Amanda took the part of the king. In a haughty regal voice, she delivered his ultimatum. The talented woman would die unless by dawn she had spun the straw filling a chamber into gold.

As the goblin, Amanda in a menacing, whining voice, delivered another ultimatum—if the miller's daughter gave the goblin her necklace, he would spin the straw into gold.

The miller's daughter agreed. Ann narrated the result: the king was pleased with the gold, but avaricious.

"What's 'avaricious?'" Amanda interjected.

"Greedy."

The plot repeated itself, a structure common in fairy tales. The King fills a larger chamber with straw, and the young woman gives the goblin her ring. A third chamber is even larger, and if the she can fill it, the King will make her his Queen. Ann, as the woman, made her voice tremble "I have nothing more I can give."

Amanda spoke in a goblin whine. "Well promise me your first child." Her voice wavered.

Ann hesitated. Should they stop the story? No. The tale had a happy ending. Ann resumed the narration. *The Queen gave birth to a beautiful child and forgot her promise. Then the goblin suddenly entered her chamber and—*

-"Mom, I don't like this ..."Amanda snatched the book.

"It's only a fairy tale. Besides, there's a funny bit in just a few more pages."

"I don't care. I don't like it."

And so the game ended. Ann was worried. Amanda seemed to take the fairy tale far too seriously.

To distract her, she said, "Would you like new jeans? I have Friday off. Want to go shopping? I need some clothes for the trip."

*****

Before work the following morning, Ann inspected her wardrobe and began to pack. Years ago, on a camping trip to the Interior, she'd forgotten her nightie. Poor Richard had hunted for a replacement in every overpriced clothing store in the Cariboo. Since then, she always packed carefully.

A patchwork skirt hung at the back of the closet. She smoothed its soft cotton. Its colours hadn't faded with age. She had worn it to a folk festival in Vancouver. She and Richard had snuggled under a sleeping bag, gazed at the stars and listened to a Jamaican band. Men had stared at her then with admiration. Now they didn't. Her waist had disappeared after Edward was born, and she had gained ten pounds, too much for her 5' 5" height. And since she never exercised, it had stayed with her.

The patchwork skirt had proved dangerously easy to undo. Was that only eight years ago? Yes, Amanda was three, and Richard's mother babysat. That was the last folk festival Richard ever attended. Ann wanted to go this year but he was too busy. His taste in music had become more sophisticated. Patchwork skirts were not sophisticated. Pants were what proper boaters wore.

In her bureau was a pair of fairly decent jeans. Beside them was a plastic bag with something pale inside. Tennis shorts! Six years ago, she and Richard had played doubles. Her bare legs had been slim and tanned. She had returned all his shots but not as quickly as she had before children. The shorts were white and pristine. Richard never played doubles now. Doubles slowed him down too much, he said, implying what?

The shorts needed pressing, but white was nautical. She pulled them on, and tugged them past her hips. The waistband that once emphasised a slender waist now gaped a good six inches. She gripped both sides of the opening, and pulled the zipper's teeth together.

No luck. The zipper refused to budge and bridge the gap. In the mirror, her image turned sideways. Her stomach ballooned over the waistband. She looked eight months pregnant. She pinched the protruding flab. Years ago in a fitness test, someone had measured her with callipers and found only a half-inch of fat everywhere. Now there were two inches everywhere, three in spots. She manipulated the bulge and frowned. It was watermelon sized. Was it a tumour? If so, she was sprouting tumours on her thighs and under her chin too. Thyroid? She pulled at her eyelids. Yes, her eyes bulged. She would ask her doctor. No she wouldn't. Bulging eyes meant *hyper*thyroidism and weight *loss*.

The shorts looked crisp and attractive and showed off her tan. She just needed to hide the gaping zipper. In another drawer, she found a beach cover-up, a green cotton one with a jungle print, something Richard's mother had bought in California. Ann pulled it over her head and looked in the mirror. The cotton top flared to her hips, a trifle long, but not bad.

She turned sideways and looked again.

A green pumpkin. Damn. She'd been slim once upon a time.

The face in the mirror flickered, dissolved, changed. Became like hers, but not like hers. Protruding eyes emerged above a fleshy mouth and jowls. The eyes solemnly stared from a dark, turbulent background. Her shape became a male figure, dressed in a ridiculous shirt, and rumpled uncouth shorts. The image of the street person in the library.

Ann shut her eyes. *This can't be happening.*

She opened them. The mouth and jowls became unanchored, detached, and floated upward. The cotton-covered stomach rose like a blimp. It expanded and filled the mirror. It pulsed like a fish's gills, and dwarfed everything except the solemn eyes, which leered at her with loathsome familiarity.

Be gone!

The apparition quivered with emotion, then shrank earthward and settled obediently into a large, solid shape, a woman's shape, a librarian's—hers.

Ann breathed deeply. No need to panic. Her imagination was playing tricks on her. She would never let herself become as shapeless as the old man in the library.

I'll go to a gym on my evenings off. On my mornings off too. I'll exercise like Maureen who's lost so much weight she can wear camisoles. Exercise, even if it means less time with Richard and Amanda, even if it means I have no time to sleep in on days when I work late. Richard would like that. He believes in exercise. But what if I meet someone—library staff or parents of Amanda's friends—at the exercise class? How embarrassing that would be, having them seeing my fat.

Why was she wasting time like this, debating about exercise, and about clothes, worrying about nothing, an apparition? The trip was five days away. She was supposed to be packing. Not dithering. The phone rang and ended the debate.

Richard's mother was calling to ask about Amanda's food likes and dislikes. She would be babysitting Amanda during the boat trip. Ann rattled off a list.

"You shouldn't feed that child so much," Olive said, dogmatic as usual.

"Of course that's not just in one day." Actually, it was.

"The child has a weight problem."

Ann gripped the phone. "She's just growing. Children don't overeat."

"Families do. It's a bad habit." *Yours for example*, implied.

"Feed her what you like." One more word, and Olive could forget about babysitting.

"What about desserts?" her mother-in-law asked.

"We don't eat dessert," Ann said complacently as the white shorts slipped downward. She caught them before they reached her knees. *Damn. That could have happened on the boat. Wouldn't that have impressed the Erdmanns?*

"You don't eat dessert?"

"No," Ann said stiffly. "I have to go. I have to get ready for work. I'll call you tonight." She held the shorts by their waist-band. Crazy to think of wearing them. Soon she'd become like the women who came into the library talking to themselves, wearing mismatched garments smelling of soup and Lord knew what else.

But shorts would be suitable on a yacht. White shorts were elegant, and sexy. Were, and still could be.

* * * * *

On Friday at the mall, Ann was determined to make the most of their shopping trip. The next day, she and Richard would leave. Amanda needed some companionship to make up for that. They found a store where teenage girls shopped. While Amanda pawed through seconds of name brand jeans, Ann took the salesperson aside.

"You sure you want white shorts?" The woman's pencilled eyebrows rose. "We only have black and navy in your size."

"I need white," Ann insisted loudly.

Amanda stared.

Cindy Erdmann probably had ten pairs of white shorts. She'd be decked out in nautical, not librarianish, fashion.

The petite saleswoman didn't examine the racks. "I'm sorry," she said, "Try Chartreuse on the other side of the mall."

"Why?"

"They carry sizes for larger women! This is a store for teenagers."

Ann glared at the petite redhead. The woman hadn't had kids. She didn't have a tummy. She looked like Cindy Erdmann. "Amanda!" she called, and signalled they should leave.

"But they've got Levis…" the girl moaned.

Ann grabbed her daughter and headed out to the mall. There, breathing hard, she felt in her purse for the coupon. It was still there, the last one. Amanda could use a summer treat. They'd make a quick stop at Chartreuse's, then spend some quality mother-daughter time together.

The chocolate coating adhered to the metal spoon like wax. Ann flicked at it with her tongue, nudged the chocolate away until it grew large enough to taste. The coating was okay, but it didn't give a proper buzz. It probably *was* wax--pure chocolate gave a bigger bang, coupled with coffee. A bang. She needed one.

Amanda had finished eating and was drawing princesses on her paper napkin. You could tell they were princesses by their dangling earrings.

I shouldn't be looking at clothes. Ann thought. *I should be buying groceries for the boat tomorrow. But what the hell.* "How about another sundae?" she asked. "One to share."

"Oh yes" The girl's round face flushed with pleasure.

Nice to see her happy. The kid needed some perks before grandmother set her on the straight and narrow.

Amanda frowned. "But, Mom, we don't have another two-for-one coupon."

"It doesn't matter. My treat." Ann fished in her bag for a five dollar bill. "Could you go to the counter, dear? I'm a bit tired after all that shopping."

Amanda went. Ann couldn't face the woman at the counter. The sundaes were mountains of whipped cream and cherries and chocolate sprinkles, enough to satisfy any normal appetite. Generally, Ann wouldn't have ordered seconds. Or, to avoid comment, she'd have driven to a different ice cream parlour— the one down by the library—for seconds.

Families were eating at the picnic benches outside. Nice that the restaurant had put money into landscaping. In the shade of mugho pines and ivy-covered trellises, an older couple ate tiny ice cream cones. The man laughed at something the woman said and she tenderly wiped a speck of ice cream from the corner of his mouth. Ann stared. Would she and Richard laugh like that one day?

Ann remembered he had laughed when she'd asked to play doubles a year ago. *You couldn't keep up* he had said. He had jeered when she wanted to go to the folk festival. *Folk fest was for the young.*

She was only thirty-five. He was ten years older but didn't look it. *You couldn't keep up.* What had he meant? That he didn't want to play doubles, or that he didn't want her?

If she dieted, she could put him to the test.

Amanda arrived with the sundae on a cardboard tray. Ann zeroed in on the soft white mound like a wolf stalking a tender lamb. Dieting could wait until after the boat trip. So could the test of Richard's affection. She needed this, now.

CHAPTER 4: HAPPY LANDINGS

The *Maybelle* shuddered as it pulled silently away from the pier in Richmond. Cindy hauled up the bumper things on the sides of the boat, and Ann hustled to do likewise, but by the time she reached one, Cindy had them all in their brackets and was relaxing on the bow. Sun blasted from the white deck. Cindy rubbed sunscreen on perfectly modelled arms and then lounged back, her bathing suit revealing only slim beauty. Even the round "First Mate" cap she wore could not detract from her looks. Cindy had bought the hats as a joke. Ann's hat was the same as hers. Richard's said "Captain" and Tom's said "Galley Slave".

"I refuse to wear that one," Cindy said as she gave it to him. "Maybe it will inspire you to cook." She kissed him.

Ann sat down carefully on the bow and arranged her T-shirt to hide her stomach. Her new white shorts already bore black streaks, probably from carrying the fishing gear. She'd fuss about cleaning them later. Now she would relax. "Care for a midmorning beer?" she asked as the Fraser River sped by. "Might as well get into the holiday spirit."

Cindy laughed. "Why not? The boys would probably like one too."

Ann passed the men en route to the fridge. They were conferring over charts, Tom in the captain's chair and Richard at the table. Down in the galley, she opened paté she'd bought in an expensive deli. Calorie-laden, but she was on holiday. The pounds would add up anyway since power boating called for very little exertion. Underneath the bar, she discovered drinking glasses, blue ones with gold trim, surprisingly classy. Wine goblets, old fashioneds, and tall glasses perfect for beer.

"Care for a brew, boys?" she called up to them, imitating Cindy's breezy manner.

"Sure," Tom replied with a smile.

Richard nodded, his eyes on the chart. They had reached the mouth of the Fraser and soon would be in open waters. In his captain's hat he looked like a movie star. He was tanned, greying at the temples. She wished he would glance at her. After all, the weather was perfect, the trip was exactly as he had planned, and his wife was fitting into it seamlessly.

She arranged the glasses on a wooden tray, along with a plate of paté, grapes, and crackers. The snack looked as appetizing as anything in *Gourmet Magazine*. She lifted the heavy tray and negotiated the steps to the salon. "You must try this paté, boys," she said as she surfaced in the salon. "It's local, made from juniper berries and venison and—"

The floor rocked. She grabbed for the handrail, then the glasses. Two wobbled, and fell, spraying beer on the charts and on the floor.

"You okay?" Tom asked.

"Sure. A bruised elbow, that's all."

Glass, beer and soggy crackers littered the stairs. She picked up the shards of glass first, and then blotted the beer with kitchen towels. Tom mopped the charts. Luckily they were plastic coated.

Richard looked up from the charts. "Cleaning rags are under the galley floor," he said.

She felt his eyes upon her as she put the tray on the galley counter and lifted the heavy cover of the cubbyhole. Inside were rags and garbage bags, cleaning solutions of all kinds, but no carpet cleaner. "Gibson's will have carpet cleaner," she said. Gibson's Landing was less than an hour away.

"Use something on that stain now," Richard said. "If it dries it'll stink."

"Yes, Sir," she said lightly.

He was charting the course or he would have helped. He didn't mean to be so bossy.

She did her best on the stain, and then reassembled the snack. She washed the grapes and plate, and replaced the broken glasses with smaller plastic ones. Cindy wouldn't mind drinking from plastic. Balancing the tray on one hip like a barmaid, Ann mounted to the cabin. Without disturbing the charting operation, she put the men's glasses into the holders cleverly slung from the corners of the table. Ships' furniture needed that kind of detail. The ocean could upset everything.

She offered crackers and paté. Tom thanked her. Richard waved the snack aside and crossed to the controls. He'd forgotten his beer, so she took it from its holder and passed it to him.

"Cheers," he hoisted it, smiling at Tom. Not at her.

The bow wasn't comfortable at full speed, so the women moved to the top deck. Ann clung to the vinyl seat. Whitecaps played on the water near Wreck Beach. "It's a bit rough, isn't it?" she said to Cindy.

"It often is at the entrance to the Fraser." Cindy took a cluster of grapes. "These grapes are yummy."

Ann would have eaten the grapes but she suddenly wasn't hungry. The water was a peculiar green and alarmingly strewn with debris. Thank goodness the men had both been through the Power Squadron course. They'd be careful. Richard liked to take risks, but Tom was cautious, and Richard wouldn't cross him. His career depended on Tom's good will.

"I feel we're in safe hands," Ann said. "Even though it's Richard's maiden voyage, you and Tom have several trips under your belts."

"Short trips. This one is a treat. Tom's always wanted to see Desolation Sound. Thanks for inviting us along." Cindy passed the tray to her. "Thanks for the snack too. I'm stuffed."

Cindy had eaten a couple of crackers, but somehow the whole round of paté had vanished. The diet would begin the minute Ann was back in Victoria.

"Richard's very fit," Cindy commented.

"Yes." Ann was used to hearing that. And the unspoken comparison to herself. Richard was more than fit. He was bright and aggressive and had the energy of a much younger man. "He jogs around Elk Lake every weekend. He's been doing that for five years *and* he plays tennis. I should too. Look at me."

"You look fine. Gardening must keep you in shape. Keeping fit is important. Tom and I hike. It gives us a chance to talk. We go for long walks several times a week."

"You do?" Ann tried to keep envy from her voice.

"Three or four miles. Around a nearby golf course, or on the Lochside trail."

"I'd like that." But Richard wouldn't. Walking was too slow for him. "But," Ann added, "I'm too busy. Till Christmas, I'm working full-time."

"That must be hard with a child at home."

"I'm used to it. I went back to work when Edward died."

"Of course." The woman's voice quavered. She cleared her throat. "I guess it takes your mind off that."

Don't begin the trip on a lugubrious note. The water was becoming choppy, the shore more distant. Ann pointed to a strip of sparkling white sand. "Isn't that a beautiful beach?"

"Yes, we should buy some recreational property here. Tom wants to buy a boat, but boats aren't suitable for young grandchildren."

The swells were building, lifting the bow up and down. Ann swallowed. "It's a perfect day," she said to convince herself.

The men came up on deck. "Are you girls gossiping again?" Richard asked.

"Telling wicked stories," Cindy grinned, "About you."

Ann held out her beer glass. "Want the rest of this, Richard?" Her stomach was rolling like the waves. Gravol time. She should have taken some before they set out.

Richard brushed the rim of the glass with his hand, and then took a swig. "Not a bad day! At this rate we should get up to Egmont by supper time."

The horizon was bobbing ferociously behind him.

"You don't look well, Ann," Cindy said. "You okay?"

"Just getting my sea legs."

"Cindy's a good sailor," Tom said, patting his wife's bronzed knees. "She grew up around boats."

"I'll just go down to the cabin for a minute," Ann said.

Richard looked disgusted.

"To unpack," she said to prove she *wasn't* deserting the ship or being unfriendly, but still he looked angry.

In the tiny stateroom, the scent of diesel oil and bilge merged and smelled like vomit. She tried to slide the tiny window open. It wouldn't budge. So she tried not to breathe. With every swell, the suitcases on the bed slipped sideways. She leaned over to unzip Richard's bag. A wave struck, and she fell onto the bed. The stripes on the suitcase's plaid cover waved green and beige and brown. She took out her husband's good white pants, and staggered with them to the tiny wardrobe. She hung the rest of his jackets in it.

Richard had brought his grey linen dinner jacket! Did he plan to treat the Erdmanns to dinner at an island resort? That would sink the budget, but it might help his cause. If so, he should have told her; she would have brought a dress. The wardrobe was full now. She might be able to squeeze in raingear and deck shoes but her clothes and his socks and underwear would have to go in the cubbyholes.

A swell hit the boat. The wardrobe doors banged shut. The wall thrust up and down. She balanced against it like a blind person, and returned to Richard's bag. She pulled out socks and crawled under the low ceiling to stow them in the cubbyhole at the foot of the bed.

From above, came the sound of laughter. Everyone was laughing, even Richard—Richard who never laughed any more. The sound penetrated through the ceiling porthole, open in the adjoining bathroom. The "head," she must remember to call it—a tiny utilitarian space. Ann entered the head and screwed the porthole shut. She reached for the Gravol. In the wardrobe mirror, her face was as sweaty and pale as a sea creature's.

Her stomach heaved.

"Anyone for coffee?" she inquired breathlessly an hour later. She stood on the side deck of the *Maybelle,* arms poised to seize a sturdy window frame, if a wave struck. The delicate white railing wouldn't support a woman her size.

Cindy smiled down from the top deck. "Later, Ann. We're just coming into Gibson's Landing. We'll have lunch there."

Tom beckoned. "Come up top and learn about docking."

"Okay." Ann squinted dubiously up at Richard. He was intent on the charts, his head haloed by the sun.

Along the shore, dark evergreens staggered up rocky promontories. The ocean was blue grey except for a wide band of muddy, pale green water, like the wake from a giant boat. In this muddy ribbon, branches bobbed, along with grasses and shrubs. Roots grasped skywards like the fingers of drowning men. No wonder they were called deadheads. She shouted up to the trio.

"Watch out for deadheads. I don't like the murky water either. Anything could lie underneath"

Tom yelled back. "It's just the runoff from the Fraser. The river's unusually high this year so there's plenty of that. We need to be careful here. But once we're away from Gibson's, it should be smooth sailing."

Thank God. Ann climbed the ladder and said to Cindy, "Want to go shopping in Gibson's? I need a few things."

The hardware store was a cornucopia of small town delights. After buying carpet cleaner, Ann examined its treasures. Amid the flotsam and jetsam of tackle and tools were two sets of drinking glasses with plastic trays to match! Swizzle sticks in carnival pinks and greens looped merrily over the side of each glass. One set was striped blue, black, and gold. The other had neon pink sea stars with the word "Gibson's" diagonally across them.

Cindy looked at them. "Not much selection, I vote for the striped."

Both sets had merit. If Richard were here, he could decide, but he and Tom were at another store checking out fishnets. They'd meet later for lunch. Which set would look better in the *Maybelle*?

"The cabin's upholstery is beige," Ann said. "So pink would brighten it up, but blue stripes would go better with the blue glasses already in the bar."

She took a glass of each type, tested the weight, assessed fragility, and scraped her fingernail across the designs to check their permanence. She held each up to the light.

"Liquor looks nicest in pale or clear glass, but mixers and pop look nice against any colour. Those blue-striped glasses are heavier and better quality. The pink ones are like the cheap glasses given away by gas stations. Their decorations may wear off."

Which would Richard prefer? He liked dark colours and often wore navy blue or black. His favourite sweat top was dark blue. But that was clothing. Did the rules apply to furniture? Would glasses classify as furniture? Were the striped ones dull? The pink ones were livelier, and they were proper souvenirs of Gibsons....

Cindy was staring at her.

"We should ask the boys," Ann concluded.

"Why?" Cindy's ponytail swayed as she laughed. "Tom would drink out of an old boot."

Ann frowned. "We have to live with our choices," she said, but Cindy was already asking the salesgirl the prices.

Cindy returned and whispered. "Five bucks for the striped, four for the pink."

"Five dollars. Five EACH?"

Cindy made a face. "'fraid so."

"Damn," Ann broke out into a sweat. "I should have thought of bringing extras from home. We've never chartered a boat before. I didn't know what to expect!"

Fists curled, she stared at the glasses. A pink set would cost forty dollars, far too much. And she'd have to buy all ten. If she didn't, they'd clash horribly with the glasses already in the bar....

Cindy put a hand on her arm. "Are you okay, Ann?"

Ann spoke from her trance, "Sure, why?"

"It really doesn't matter, you know."

"What doesn't?"

"What we choose." The woman's blue eyes were worried. "Let's buy those instead." She pointed to stacks of cheap disposable glasses sitting on top of a Styrofoam cooler.

"Plastic glasses for wine?" Richard's face flashed, sneering. "Let's try another store."

"We've been to three already," Cindy said, "Gibson's isn't Victoria."

That was true. Three stores. No point in delaying the decision. With an imperious air, Ann marched to the counter and announced to the teenager there, "I'll take four of the Gibson's glasses. And four swizzle sticks too. They look jolly."

At the outdoor café, crumbs in wicker baskets was all that remained of the fried chicken, but the jug of beer was still half-full. Ann heaved her parcels onto the table. Shopping had worked up a thirst. The glasses would come in handy.

"You're late." Richard tapped his watch.

"Did you get crabmeat?" Tom asked with a smile.

Earlier that morning, everyone had discussed menus and Richard had drawn up a schedule. Crab dip was the appetizer for tomorrow's dinner.

"No crab dip," Cindy said. "We haven't been grocery shopping yet." She spoke slowly. "We've. Been. Shopping. For. Glasses."

Ann unwrapped her treasures. "Here they are! With their very own swizzle sticks too!" She hooked a swizzle stick over a glass and held it up in triumph.

"Hideous," Richard said.

"The best that Gibson's had to offer," she said lightly.

"A waste of money, and time."

Damn him. Impossible to please. "MY money, MY time. This was my treat, a holiday treat." She seized the jug and poured beer into the glass. Sea stars floated in an orange sea, and then were marooned in air as she gulped. *To hell with him. She was on holiday.*

No one spoke. The sky was blue. The beer was excellent. She refilled the glass. Over its neon pink rim, beer erupted like a snowy volcano. She calmed it with a swizzle stick. Richard mopped the tablecloth. She looked around the café and raised the foaming glass in a toast. "Happy landings," she said to the man at the next table who seemed familiar.

The man twisted toward her in a kind of leer. He was heavy, uncouth, and ancient. His white shirt was loose and his brown shorts looked rusty, but he appreciated her. His eyes said that.

"Nice pub," she said to him.

The heavyset man twirled his fingers at her. "There is nothing," he said, "which has yet been contrived by man, by which so much happiness is produced as by a good tavern or inn."

She giggled. He must be a Shakespearean actor, he was so longwinded.

The man expelled his breath like a whale. He turned to the fried chicken on his plate and ate as though riveted to it. Never before had she seen anyone eat with such gusto. His forehead broke out in a sweat and the veins swelled. Between bites, he wiped his greasy fingers on his shorts. His manners were terrible, but he was happy. Ann stifled a laugh. She glanced at Richard expecting him to sneer at his neighbour's manners, but Richard was too angry to notice anyone but her. She didn't mind. The beer compensated for the seasickness, and the broken glasses, and Richard's affronted tastes. She ordered chicken to go along with it.

In a blissful daze, Ann shopped for groceries. They were on holiday. Time didn't matter. Tom looked a little strange when he mentioned it was too late to continue up the coast as planned. Instead, they would anchor at a nearby island for the night. Ann had another beer after they anchored. The men fished.

Ann would have talked to Cindy but the woman was engrossed in a glossy magazine. Ann staggered to the stateroom in search of something to read. She rejected books on Victorian illustrators and Samuel Johnson's works. Books like those deserved more sober contemplation. She chose a travel book instead. On the way to the main cabin, she stopped by the galley, checked that Cindy couldn't see her, and reached into the cubbyhole in the floor.

"Fish on!" Richard called.

Ann dropped the chocolate bar into the cubbyhole and ran with the others to the back deck.

Richard landed a fifteen pound salmon. "Dinner," he said.

No one was hungry after the chicken at the café.

"For tomorrow night," Cindy said.

"We'll barbecue it at Princess Louisa Inlet." Richard held it up. His mood had improved. He posed for a photo.

*****

Ann was just finishing her midmorning beer when Egmont came into sight. The village was tiny. A restaurant overlooked the dock. The umbrellas and tables on its patio looked inviting but the *Maybelle* would stop only long enough to refuel before beginning the long haul up Jervis Inlet. Richard was on the top deck at the controls as they approached their berth on the outermost finger of the dock. Ann stood at the stern, prepared to tie the bumper-pads—called-fenders—just as efficiently as Cindy on the bow. Tom was at Ann's elbow, ready to assist.

They were inches from the dock when the boat instead of coming gently into the finger, rocked violently along it, and swayed sideways towards it.

Ann looked questioningly at Tom.

He leaped onto the dock, and leaned his full weight against the stern. "The current's got us!"

An invisible sea monster was churning the water and pushing them toward the corner of the finger.

"Take her out and try again," Tom shouted. "Damn!" The boat bucked toward him.

The corner of the dock was splintery and sharp and surprisingly low in the water. If their stern hit it, the fender was hanging too high to blunt the impact. Ann staggered to untie the fender. The knot was difficult. *Don't let us hit*, she prayed. *At least not till I lower this fender.*

The engines stopped. They were drifting! The hull was almost on top of Tom. He pushed frantically against it. Ann wrestled with the knot.

Why had Richard insisted on taking the controls? Why had Tom let him? Tom was way more experienced but he was too easy-going. Richard wasn't familiar with dual engine powerboats, and he'd been drinking. Actually everyone had been, just a few beers. And anyway, no one had known about the current.

The knot came loose. Ann freed the fender, and positioned it lower.

"Atta girl!" Cindy shouted from the front where she too was adjusting fenders. "We'd better—"

The boat shot forward. Ann jerked backward, grabbed frantically for the railing and missed, hit the metal barbecue, and fell heavily onto the tackle box.

She caught her breath. Her right arm had been scraped by the barbecue. But she was still holding the fender's rope. Losing the fender would have been dreadful. She straightened her first mate's cap.

Tom and the dock were receding at the speed of light. Richard must be following Tom's advice, taking the *Maybelle* out to try again. But at top speed? Two men docking a small fishing boat gunned their engine to get out of the way. One made a rude gesture. The owner of a giant yacht yelled as the *Maybelle* missed it by inches.

Ann secured the fender.

A rope lay coiled by the cabin door. Tom could use it to tie the stern to the dock. She stumbled forward, gripped a handhold by the cabin door, picked up the coil and waited to throw it to Tom.

The engines stopped again. They were far away from shore. For a moment all was silent.

Then from the top deck, curses. "Ann, where the hell are you? Get up here and spot for me. NOW."

She dropped the rope coil and started up the ladder. The boat was rocking and she was dizzy from the beer so she placed each foot securely on each rung and made it to the top. "Fifty yards from the dock," she shouted.

Richard hunched over the controls, his captain's hat on his head. Had he heard her? She put one foot on the upper deck. "Fifty—"

The boat hurtled backward. She reached for the railing and grabbed air.

She landed in a puddle on the deck. Her thigh was scratched, her shorts torn, but she was alive, and wet. The boat's wake was pouring over the stern like a waterfall. She eased herself up onto the cooler, and retrieved her hat from the puddle. Richard must have decided to back into the berth.

A pole rested beside the ladder. She could use it as a barge pole to fend the dock off. The dock, and Tom were fast approaching. To be precise, the corner of the dock was. Tom was running for his life. On the cooler, Ann braced for impact.

There was a sound of splintering wood as the boat impaled itself, then a loud splash, and a crunching.

"Ann!" Richard scurried down the ladder. "Why are you sitting on your fat ass? You're crew!" He rushed past her to examine the gouge in the hull.

Two fishermen ran to their rescue. One hauled on the bowline to stop the impaled boat from swinging. The other helped Tom ward off the stern.

Fat ass?

Cindy grimaced sympathetically at Ann,

Nothing excused rudeness. "I wasn't sitting!" Ann roared. "I was spotting. For you…and I…fell…." She gasped for breath, "It wasn't my idea," she screamed,"…to charter a thirty-eight footer. You should have chartered a boat more your size."

Tom could hear. So could the people on the dock, even the two fishermen who'd come to help. The whole world could hear. So what?

"Hand me the boat hook!" a fisherman yelled as the boat slowly dislodged itself.

"Ann!" Richard relayed the message.

"Boat hook?" She looked around for a hook.

Richard turned, mimed disgust, and seized the pole by the ladder.

"Oh," she said loftily to no one in particular. "The *barge* pole."

The fisherman used the pole to steady the stern next to the dock. A peaked cap hid his face. The cap said 'Rent-a-Wreck', the kind of cap Richard wouldn't have been caught dead in. The man's shoulders were shaking. With silent laughter.

From above came less restrained mirth. On the restaurant patio, under gaily fluttering umbrellas, eyes peeped and fingers pointed at the entertainment—landlubbers in white shorts and ridiculous captain's hats, pivoting in a powerboat around a dock, going nowhere.

"Lend a hand," Richard snarled at Ann. "See that," he pointed to the coil of rope on the back deck. "That's a rope. R-o-p-e. Give it to Tom to tie the stern."

Ann tossed her first mate's cap overboard. "Up yours, Captain."

Cindy looked at her.

Ann's chin rose. Richard could fetch the rope himself.

Cindy conveyed the coil to the fisherman in the peaked cap. He thanked her absently, his attention on the water roiling behind the boat. He pointed there. Beside him, Tom stared. So did Cindy.

What were they staring at? Was the boat leaking fuel? Ann had heard of boats blowing up. But that was propane, not diesel. Or was it? She sniffed. There was no smell, none she could detect. Anyway if there'd been danger, Tom would have had them off the boat at once. He was the responsible type. She looked again at the man in the peaked cap. Lean, muscular. She'd seen him somewhere before, or someone who looked like him.

Richard bent over the side of the boat measuring the damage with the palm of his hand. "Not too bad," he said in a more civil tone, but he was talking to Tom now, not Ann. "The damage is above the waterline. We can patch it and still reach Princess Louisa Inlet tonight as planned."

Tom grinned. "Say Captain," he said. "Did your plans for tonight include barbecued salmon?"

"Yes, why?"

"Wasn't there a barbecue on the back deck?" Tom's eyes twinkled.

"Yes..." Richard turned. "What the hell..." He stared at the back railing, and then gazed at the frothing water.

The barbecue had been a nice one with cedar handles and side trays. Expensive, too. He thrust open the gate to the swim deck and knelt there, bending to the water, his Captain's hat lopsided on his head. He looked as though he was praying for the god of the sea to regurgitate the barbecue.

Ann giggled. "So much for dinner." She patted the cooler on which she sat. In it was the fifteen pound salmon, Richard's.

He glared. "If you'd helped, this wouldn't have happened."

She grinned.

"It's not funny," he said. "Grow up."

"I brought chili, sir," she said with cold fury. "We can eat that."

"Chili's not salmon." His bottom lip protruded like a pouting baby's.

On the dock, Tom and Cindy clutched one another in paroxysms of mirth.

The fisherman in the awful peaked cap winked at Ann. "I can recommend the restaurant's fish and chips," he said helpfully.

She had entirely lost her appetite. She remembered him now. The fellow in the library she'd been so rude to. The gardener.

CHAPTER 5: KILLER INSTINCT

In mid-afternoon, the engines' thrust buzzed through the bed, angled the floor upward, and sent the door of the wardrobe swinging crazily. From the bed, Ann kicked it. A moment later, it resumed its wild dance. She kicked again. She was drunk. And ready to kill Richard. He'd been awful during the docking, and worse afterwards.

After the docking, they'd needed to unwind so they ordered lunch on the restaurant patio. The fish and chips were excellent, Cindy said, but Ann was too angry to eat or to speak so she stuck to beer. Cindy tried a few cheery topics then lapsed into silence. The men ate doggedly, unwilling to discuss the missing barbecue and the hole in the boat while most of Egmont's population sat around listening, ready to laugh. The patio was as quiet as a funeral parlour. Only the two fishermen at their table in the corner were talking.

Every word of their conversation was audible. The gardener discussed the merits of various fishing lures, dodgers and flashers while the heavier man gloated over the rock cod he'd caught that morning. He spoke in a well-modulated voice with a trace of an English accent. The gardener lounged on the corner bench, one foot on it, the other on a yellow dog, probably a lab. The Englishman's cheeks were grizzled with the beginnings of a beard.

If the two men noticed the silence around them, they didn't show it. They seemed to be making an effort to behave normally.

The sky looked like rain, and Richard looked like thunder.

Below, at the dock, their boat was being patched. Ann thought of the long afternoon ahead, the trek up Jervis Inlet to Princess Louisa Inlet. To break the silence, she asked Tom about fishing in Jervis Inlet.

"The water's too deep for salmon, but we might catch red snapper or lingcod."

Richard looked up from his chips. "We won't have time to fish," he hissed at Ann. "We need to reach the rapids at the entrance to Princess Louisa Inlet at slack tide. Thanks to your dawdling at Gibson's yesterday, we'll have to race to get there."

"*Have* to?" she countered. "This is a holiday and we're supposed to be relaxing."

His mouth thinned. "*You* could stay here."

The modest log cabins on the nearby hillside would be quiet and the food at the restaurant was edible. "I just might, Captain Bligh."

Titters around them. The locals were nudging one another.

Cindy looked at her husband. "Anyone for dessert?" she asked cheerily.

Tom scanned the menu. "Mud pie! And homemade blackberry pie too!"

"Yes!" Ann banged her empty beer stein on the table.

"No!" Richard reached for the bill. "Let's get going." He strode off, leaving Cindy and Tom and the good people of Egmont staring.

Ann and the Erdmanns caught up to him on the wharf. They walked to the boat together. Or rather, Cindy and Tom walked hand in hand beside Richard. The dock wasn't wide enough for four so Ann dropped behind. She could imagine what it looked like from the restaurant above. *The wife as a dog.*

The door of the wardrobe banged again. The books on top shifted but stayed put, thanks to a low railing. Richard was going full throttle up Jervis Inlet. The reverberations were numbing. The room was spinning. Ann crawled up to straighten the books and then knelt to examine the wardrobe lock. The clasp on one door was broken. She could tie the knobs together, but why bother? Why bother fixing anything?

After lunch, to be a good sport for a whole hour, she had sat on the top deck in drizzle, as her husband cut a frothy scar through the smooth black skin of the inlet. Deserted coves flew past, gulls and sailboats too. Hikers appeared on a hill, probably hunting for petroglyphs but vanished before she could comment. Life became one long drone of diesel engines. Conversation was impossible. Being a wife was impossible.

"I have a headache," she said, and went below.

Among the books on the wardrobe were two book club selections. She weighed them, one in each hand, like a goddess of justice. She would lend whichever was lighter to Cindy. She could transform the holiday into a reading holiday. No, Cindy wouldn't abandon her man for fiction. She'd stand by him, on the rainy deck, wrapped in a weather-proof jacket. Her ass was the proper size.

Nine more days of this. Two to reach Desolation Sound, three there, four coming back through the Gulf Islands, nine wet days, floating in this dingy chicken coop, and why? To visit the Mecca of west coast boaters. Travel magazines always showed Desolation Sound under blue skies. Travel magazines dealt in illusions and hope.

Today she'd rather be anywhere else. At home, watching television with Amanda. At Richard's parents' house, talking to Olive. At the library, discussing rainforests with kids in the summer reading program. At the book club, arguing with Tara.

Outside the cabin's tiny window, raindrops had begun to prick the water's surface, but other than that, the surface was smooth.

For some reason, the boat had slowed. Above, on deck, something heavy was being pulled and pushed. Her shipmates were probably raising the bimini, hoping the awning would keep them dry. But nothing on board was dry. The bedding smelled like a mouldy dishrag, the smell so sour, even the diesel fumes could not mask it.

Air! I need air! If I don't have air, I'll be sick again. With clammy hands, she pried at the window catch. It didn't budge. She rested a minute and tried again. No luck. *If I have to break the glass, I will!* Gasping, she summoned all her strength and swung her fist back.

A man's hand undid the catch and slid the window open.

"Thank you," she said and turned, expecting to see Tom.

Her saviour emerged from the shadows, an elderly man in an old-fashioned shirt and stockings. "Being in a ship," he said, "is like being in a jail, with the chance of being drowned."

"Yes." Where had she heard that comparison before?

He gestured toward the window. "I too have had trouble like this with windows in Scotland."

"It was horribly stiff," she said. "Richard must have shut it. This cabin is bad enough without being airless."

The man grimaced. "In Scotland, even in the well built houses, the windows are shut, the result being foul air."

Was she dreaming? She rubbed her eyes, but he was still there, his loose white shirt billowing in the breeze. His face was fleshy, ruddy and raw-boned, his lips thick and sensual for a man so old. He appeared to be about seventy.

He smiled. "I am truly sorry to make such trivial criticism. Scotland is generally a wonderful place."

He was fat, almost repulsive, but something about his formal manner set her at ease. "Who are you?"

"Someone who has been watching you."

A stalker. She sat on the bed. The face, the brown shorts, the large shirt. Yes, she'd seen him at the library on that hellish hot day when time seemed to stand still. Just before the library closed for the night, he had waited in the checkout line, reading the Bible and Jonathan Swift. He had talked to her, and quoted Samuel Johnson.

The stranger nodded his shaggy head, as though he followed her thoughts.

He'd been in her bedroom too. When she tried on clothes for the trip, he'd been there in her mirror like an apparition of her worst self. And in the café at Gibson's, he'd sat at the next table. He'd wolfed down his food and leered at her.

Strangely, she was more curious than afraid.

He moved to the dresser. "That is my book, you have been reading, or rather, not reading." He twirled his fingers at the battered leather book. He picked it up and held it open at its frontispiece, a portrait of a fat old man wearing a wig, a white wig like his, but tidy, not perched like a hat over wild grey hair. The man in the picture wore a decent black suit. Were these rusty brown rags the remnants of that suit?

"You're Samuel Johnson?"

"You may address me as Sam."

Samuel Johnson. A person so charismatic that partygoers in the eighteenth century stood in rows around him to hear his words of wisdom. An extrovert who thought deeply about the human condition. A scholar who devoted years of his life to compiling an English dictionary "The Great Lexicographer," she said slowly.

"Yes," he said.

"But you're so…" She almost said 'fat'. "Large…I mean larger than life."

"As God made me, I am."

There was something soothing about his words, something that went beyond. An answer maybe to the unspoken question, a core of understanding, but there were other questions to be answered now. "Why are you watching me?"

He made a bow. "I am here to accompany you."

"A guide, a guardian angel?" She laughed.

He remained serious.

"Why you?"

"It was considered appropriate."

"Because I'm a librarian? Because I love books, and you did too?"

"Partly that...but mainly…because I lived and I was married." He looked at the rain-dimpled water, and his expression brightened. "I too have travelled. I once went as far as the Hebrides islands. They were reputed to be a lonely and unpolished part of the world." His protruding eyes flashed with passion. "I found them otherwise. That journey was the highlight of my life."

His gaze bored into her. She took a steadying breath. The cabin was vibrating with light as if someone were holding a mirror and bouncing sunbeams off the dark panelling. The journey to Desolation Sound took on the allure of an adventure. "I'm glad you're here on this voyage, Sam."

His face gleamed and blended with the general brightness. The light wavered. Like a candle, it sputtered and died, and the stateroom was as dark as before.

She was standing in the draft from the open window. Rain spattered the books on the wardrobe and splashed her cheeks. She shook herself and said aloud, "If I'd eaten lunch and not drunk it, I wouldn't be seeing things. Hallucinating because of low blood sugar."

Hollow laughter resounded through the empty room. She ignored it and searched under the rain gear in the wardrobe for emergency rations. Mars Bars.

Someone knocked on the door. She froze.

It opened. Richard entered.

"I thought you were driving the boat," she said, too startled to be angry. Holding the candy bar behind her she backed into the bathroom where she pretended to get a roll of toilet paper from the vanity. She hid the chocolate bar under a towel.

He sat on the bed. "Tom's taken over the wheel, we've got time," he said. "You know…" he patted the rumpled bed.

It had been months since the last invitation. Did he mean it? Her cheeks grew warm. "The others are on deck, just above us."

"We'll shut the portholes. The engines' racket will give us privacy."

"Okay," she said, her fingers already undoing the button on her shorts.

*****

It was quick, thoughtless. He went to sleep afterwards, his mouth a satisfied O, his toned body at ease. Ann lay on the edge of the bed, as far from him as possible. To touch him was inconceivable. His body was his, not hers.

Had it been prompted by the beer, or by the bruising his ego had suffered at Egmont? Or did he enjoy the danger of being intimate only inches away from the others?

Quietly she rose, went into the bathroom, retrieved the Mars Bar, and ate it sitting on the toilet.

En route to the upper deck, she paused in the galley to get a drink of water.

The toilet flushed. Richard was up. He entered the galley and passed, without speaking, without looking, on his way to join the others.

Carrying a book, she followed him to the rainswept top deck. Why had she given in to him?

Three hours later, she was still wondering that. On the draughty deck, she pretended to read a travel guide while he talked to the others about forestry, or more accurately, shouted, competing with the drone of the engines. She shouldn't have given in, not after the way he treated her at Egmont. She should have resisted, but the need had been too great. He always got what he wanted. He knew her weakness.

Cindy nudged her. "That's Camp Malibu."

The children's camp overlooked the rapids. Ann checked her watch. Five thirty precisely. Slack tide. Perfect. Richard had achieved his goal.

"Some camp." Richard sounded envious. He watched the kids slipping like otters down an elaborate slide into a pool. Shrieks and splashes enlivened the grey evening.

"It used to be a fancy hotel." Ann read the information from the guidebook.

"Not a bad location," Cindy said. "The view's spectacular. I bet some developer has his eye on that property."

"Sure," Ann said with sarcasm. There'd been many sad sights along the coast—abandoned salmon canneries, abandoned Indian villages. "At sea, nothing lasts," she said.

Not even love. The way he spelled out 'rope' to her, the way he scorned her attempts to spot for him and the way he blamed her for the loss of the barbecue. Their love had crumbled like those abandoned buildings. Since Edward died, the family had become unglued. She had hoped this holiday would patch what was lost.

Edward would have been like those kids sliding into the pool, an eight year old laughing, not thinking or worrying about the future. He and Amanda swam in life jackets at her parents' cabin in the Interior. At three, he was a terror. He loved pushing people into the pool and would scream with joy. At preschool that fall, he learned to be considerate and became a credit to his mum.

The children's laughter faded as the boat traversed the rapids and entered Princess Louisa Inlet. Cliffs towered above. Down their black surfaces swept hundreds of miniature waterfalls. The falls were probably enchanting in sunlight but in rain, they were monochromatic and dismal.

The largest waterfall dominated the head of the inlet, the famous Chatterbox Falls. Like an actress much photographed, Chatterbox Falls didn't live up to its reputation. Tom tried to take the *Maybelle* in for a closer look, but too many boats jostled for front row seats. Mooring nearby was impossible. Mooring at the small wharf was also impossible. Powerboats took up every inch. Others anchored offshore and swung in dangerously wide arcs while their owners lounged on deck in plastic chairs, playing cards, and drinking. They listened to Muzak for which they kept their generators buzzing.

Ann shuddered. So much for Princess Louisa Inlet. Would Desolation Sound be equally disappointing?

Tom stopped at a safe distance from the swinging powerboats. The last thing the *Maybelle* needed was to smash into one of them. Richard lowered the anchor but the floor of the inlet sloped too steeply. The anchor didn't catch so he and Tom rowed to the rocky shore and attached two lines to saplings.

When they returned, Richard stood on the back deck and dabbled a hand in the water. "The temperature's not bad. Time for a swim."

The water was milky, and pockmarked by rain. None of the other boaters was swimming, not even the kids. Richard began to strip, revealing toned muscles, unusual in a forty-five year old. "You need exercise," he said to Ann. "Come on in."

One push, that's all it would take. First, she'd warn him about the jellyfish. He'd scoff as usual. Then she'd put her hand on his back. A moment later, he'd be floundering among the creatures, caressed by their red and white slime. He'd struggle onto the swim deck, an ugly look on his face and an even uglier red rash on his legs. He'd think a man-of-war had stung him, but she'd correct him. "Lion's mane jellyfish," she'd announce with librarianish glee, knowing the rash would torment him throughout the night, maybe even kill him.

But did pointing out a fat ass justify murder?

"Richard, you shouldn't swim here," she said. "The guidebook says even the white jellyfish here can sting, and the red lion's mane jellyfish are worse." She embroidered the facts with a literary reference. "In a Sherlock Holmes' tale, several lion's mane jellyfish sting a man and he dies an agonising death."

There. Her librarian's conscience was clear. If he perished, it would be not from lack of information. .

He stared indecisively at the turgid water, and then at a lively group hiking up the hillside from the wharf. "How about a hike beside Chatterbox Falls instead? We can take pictures."

He took command. Like an eighteenth century explorer, he rowed everyone to the foot of the waterfall. A sign at the base said the rocks were dangerous, but he stood on them anyway. He took photos. He perched on one rock and hopped to another, surveying the falls with military precision from every angle, up and down and sideways. He wanted to capture the force of the water, its power. He set off upwards on the trail beside the falls to photograph it from above. A seagull screamed a warning.

"Richard," Ann ran and tapped him on the shoulder. "Up there, don't climb across that mossy rock face."

"Why not? From the far side, I'll get a better picture."

"It's unsafe. I've read about it. A woman writer climbed across it with her kids. Moments afterwards, the moss gave way and hurled downward. She realised she and her kids had been close to death, and also close to something inexplicable, something she called the *curve of time.* Richard, *she had recognized that rock face. She'd dreamt about it.*"

He sneered. "If it's not jellyfish, it's moss. For you, the sky is always falling, isn't it?"

"Nothing impresses you, does it?"

"Not sensationalism. She was a woman and a writer, what do you expect?" His words were scornful but he turned back. He set off on a lower trail looking haunted, captured, like a bear in a cage, "Ann's scared," he said to the Erdmanns, "so we'll hike to the cabin instead."

"I'm *not* scared," Ann said fiercely. "And the writer was a naturalist *and* a scientist *and* a mother. She travelled up and down the coast. She often had unexplained, unscientific experiences. Not everything is as straightforward as you'd like it to be."

"C'mon you two," Tom said, smiling. "It's not worth quarrelling about. It's getting too dark for photos anyway. Let's go back to the boat and have a drink."

"When we've seen the cabin," Richard decreed.

Ann trooped after the others. She could have said a friend of the writer had built the cabin. Or said why bother seeing the cabin if the writer was so stupid?

As Richard walked along the boardwalk, he enthused about the lush rainforest, the moss, the trees. He was probably trying to impress Tom. The trees were ancient and anorexic. Moss clothed them, moss of a particularly evil green colour. Moss cushioned the boardwalk too and made it slippery. The lush green masked the ugly reality.

Richard plunged on through giant dripping ferns and Douglas firs. Rain drummed on the wooden boardwalk, urging human sacrifice. *Tie him to one of his precious trees. Make him confess his true feelings.*

A shadow appeared beside her. Thinking it was Tom, she turned around. The shade was taller and fatter than Tom. It came into focus.

Sam!

Marching along, Sam matched his stride to her shorter one. Leaning on a thick walking stick, he blew a tune under his breath, a merry Scottish reel.

"Why are you happy?" she asked. "You like crummy vacations?"

Sam gave her a sidelong glance. "Too many travellers affect to be disgusted by all they survey."

"But this is truly ugly, this moss, these trees…"

"The joy of travelling is in the journey, the anticipation."

She barked a laugh. "Anticipation of what? A mouldy cabin?"

He sighed. "Pleasure is very seldom found where it is sought." He touched the moss with the tip of his walking stick as if admiring it.

"Not here at Princess Louisa Inlet for sure." She kicked a boulder out of the way. If I'd stayed home, I would have missed crashing into the dock, this downpour, and Richard's temper."

He smiled. "Our brightest blazes of gladness are commonly kindled by unexpected sparks."

"I guess it was rather funny, losing that barbecue, seeing the locals watching us, meeting up with that gardener."

Sam stared at her. "The jest which is expected is already destroyed."

"Richard never laughs at things I think funny."

He paused next to a fir tree. "Endeavour to be pleased." He beamed as though he'd just divulged the secret of the universe.

Easy advice, but who could be pleased with such an expedition…with such a husband… with such a rainy rainforest? This hike was miserable. She would return to the wharf and wait there. She turned to leave. The spindly branch of a fir tree brushed her cheek. She would have pushed it aside but its moss was amazingly soft and alive. Seen up close, it was a beautiful, sunny shade of green. In fact, up close, out of the mist, everything, the leaves, the bark, the wooden walkway, were intensely alive.

Richard was marching ahead like some kind of general. She smiled. He was ridiculous, his anger was irrational but they both had much to overcome. The journey to happiness might take years. Sam understood that. He was the first person she'd met who understood that. And his advice was simple; *try to be pleased.*

Sam strode on, whistling.

She hurried to catch up. "Okay Sam. I'll make you a promise. Today, and for the rest of this vacation, I'll change my tune. I won't promise to be *pleased*, but I'll endeavour not to pout."

*****

Gulls swarmed over the water off Cape Mudge. "A good sign," David said to Gerry. "Might be a herring ball there. Salmon love herring."

He attached a new leader and lure to his friend's fishing line, and moved *The African Queen* closer to the feeding birds. The Fishfinder showed the ocean floor sheared downwards. A giant group of black dots floated across the screen.

"Herring ball!" He put the engine into neutral and grabbed his rod. "No barbecued Spam for us tonight," he said and cast his line.

Twenty minutes later, he had netted two coho, one a seventeen pounder. "What a beauty!" He admired it despite the gusting rain. "Good for the heart too!"

Gerry nodded. "Mine maybe. It would take more than salmon to heal a hard heart like yours."

"Not that hard. I still get weak at the sight of curves like these." David ran his hand lovingly over the fish. The tail was wide and silver, the gums clean and white, and the shape chunky, yet symmetrical. He took up the filleting knife. In a few minutes, the fish was ready for the barbecue. He picked up the other coho.

Gerry put his hand on David's arm. "Let me try filleting. It's time I stopped being so lazy." He took the knife from David.

David was pleased. The journalist had bobbed in the boat all afternoon in the rain without complaining. He seemed to have acquired a more robust attitude since his heart attack, and took pleasure in everything. He loved life.

Unlike some people. Like the fellow in the captain's hat leading the group down the wharf at Egmont. A controlling type, out of control. What made people that way? Fear? And his wife too. At the library, she had seemed strong, eager to please and mortified when the system failed, but not fearful. At the bungled docking, her temper had blazed. But afterwards, she turned into a doormat. Another casualty in the relationship wars.

Such a waste. She was attractive, but strangely unaware of her voluptuous appeal. Why didn't her husband take pleasure in her? The strong yet sexy legs, the easy athletic way she walked.

He opened his tackle box and found a pale blue lure. No point thinking about her. Might as well fish as think about another man's wife.

Hectic colour brightened Gerry's cheeks as he finished cleaning the fish. Had the job been too much for him?

His friend grinned his famous television host grin. "This is as close to paradise as I'm ever going to get," Gerry brushed fish scales from his expensive yellow rain jacket. "It reminds me of the old days, fishing at Telegraph Cove."

The trip was working out well. They'd been right to go ahead with it, but Gerry was still recovering. "Let's call it quits for today," David said. He put the lure back in the tackle box. "I'm starving."

CHAPTER 6: DESOLATION SOUND

They left Princess Louisa Inlet early the next morning. On the trip back down Jervis Inlet, a south-easterly rocked the *Maybelle* so badly that Ann lost her breakfast. She went to bed, closed her eyes and slept.

Two hours later, she woke. The rocking had stopped, and so had her seasickness. Sunlight floated in the room, mirroring ripples onto the ceiling. The boat was no longer moving. She ventured out onto the back deck. Tom was assembling fishing rods. All around, fishing boats bobbed like toys in a bathtub. Wind had swept the rain clouds away to a pink line on the horizon. This sunlit world was as bright as a child's painting.

"Richard's on the upper deck," Tom said, "using my official cell phone for a business call. Cindy's up there too, fishing. Want to try your luck?" He held up a rod.

His manner was casual, unlike Richard's. Tom probably never lost his temper. Unlike Richard. Unlike herself. No wonder Tom had risen so high in the Natural Resources Commission.

"Why not?" She would endeavour to be pleased. "What's a cell phone?"

Tom explained the new phone technology as he attached a lure to the line. He tested the lure's action on the water, and handed her the rod. Its reel buzzed as she followed his instructions and pulled the line thirty times, measuring out enough line for the depth of water. She set the brake.

Tom taught her to raise the rod and then suddenly drop the tip. This jigging action apparently made the lure swim like a small wounded fish and attracted larger, would-be predators like salmon.

"Easy," she said after a few tries.

"Jigging takes patience," he said. "Women have more sensitive hands. Maybe that's why native Indians believed women were better than men at fishing." He took a bottle from the cooler. "Want a beer?"

She shook her head. She wanted to concentrate on this new skill.

He fished, sitting on the railing, and said Richard was phoning to set up another hearing for the Commission. Though Richard wasn't a member of the Commission, he had attended most of the hearings, travelling as far as Princeton, Vernon and Prince George. Tom was impressed.

Ann wasn't. Each trip meant absence from his family. If she complained Richard would get on his high horse. If the province was to have a policy on natural resources, *everyone,* environmentalists, politicians, biologists, and ordinary folk should attend the hearings. Everyone, a representative mixture, not just foresters like him. People should care about forest policy and forest tenure.

As if everyone had time for that! Richard took the Commission so seriously, she hardly dared ask about it. Tom talked about the Commission in a way she could understand. He answered her questions. He wasn't stuffy, she bet, even when he was at work. On holidays, he considered fishing as important as politics. A person could relax around a man like that.

Those two fishermen at Egmont had been like that, laid back and pleasant, enjoying their vacation though they didn't have a powerboat or fancy clothes. A guy who wore a Rent-a-Wreck cap didn't take himself too seriously. You could probably talk to him about anything, about fishing or gardening or politics.

Why couldn't Richard be like that? The minute he put the phone down, she bet he'd stop the fishing and they'd be full speed ahead. He'd never change. Never relax. Not even on holidays. He'd been that way ever since Edward died. In a rush. Running from death.

He had been different when she met him. Newly divorced, he'd been visiting SaltSpring Island with friends. She and Tara were swimming at St. Mary Lake's Tarzan swing. From the water, she'd watched him climb the dead tree to the rope. He had swung far out over the lake, before letting go. He brought the rope to her in the water. Everyone cheered as she gripped the tree and stood and launched herself outwards, enjoying the rebound of the tree, and the wonder of letting go and dropping into the water.

At the Vesuvius pub afterwards, they basked in the light from the setting sun and talked about their ambitions. He wanted to go into politics. She wanted to oversee the children's departments at the public library. They both wanted a family. He took her hand, and she felt the sinewy purposeful strength of him, so unlike that of unfocussed younger men. The desire for children cemented the relationship. After just a couple of days, he asked her to marry him. She'd been flattered. For a month, he wooed her, saying he would commit himself to making her happy. Unlike his ex-wife, she would be an educated and intelligent mate and a wonderful mother for their children. She was proud to introduce him to her parents in Vancouver. He presented himself well, and showed no sign of temper, and neither had she.

She'd seen him as an older, wiser partner and lover, her equal. But after Edward's death, Richard became overbearing and ambitious, even on the tennis court. At work, she was still competent, but at home she lost her way, lost her voice in the relationship—plodding away, hoping to reawaken love.

Hopeless. Ann moved to the shadowed side of the boat. Fish were fond of shadows, she'd heard. And shadows suited her mood. She couldn't "endeavour to be pleased" with Richard.

"Yet it is necessary to hope," Sam said at her elbow. "Though hope should always be deluded."

"How did you know what I was thinking?"

"Every man may, by examining his own mind, guess what passes in the minds of others. Besides, I never speak unless I am spoken to."

A ghost with good manners!

"Why should I hope?" she asked, glad to say what was in her heart.

Sam swung a portly leg up over the boat's railing and perched in sunshine, smiling at the sunlit boats and water. "Hope itself is happiness, and its frustrations, however frequent, are yet less dreadful than its extinction."

As he spoke, he touched every one of the struts on the ceiling of the back deck as if he was counting them. Then he ran his hand along the wet railing, lifted his fingers to his lips and tasted the salt. He seemed determined to acquaint all his senses with the essence of his surroundings.

"Sam, you say happiness is hope. But in your novel *Rasselas,* the hero and his friends search for happiness. They don't find it. It's impossible to find, you wrote. You don't mention hope. Another time, you said human life is everywhere a state in which much is to be endured and little to be enjoyed. Again no mention of hope."

He propped his chin on one finger. "I try on different views. Context is important."

"And the way you speak is so convoluted with all those 'buts' and 'yets'. It's confusing even for a librarian, and it's contradictory."

"I scrutinise life in its complexity. New things are made familiar, and familiar things are made new."

"It's annoying," she cast her line out into the dark water. "Anyway, you can be hopeful about me. I've decided to take your advice. I'm endeavouring to enjoy myself, despite Richard. And I'm hopeful of catching a fish. So by your definition, I'm happy."

Richard climbed down the ladder from the top his telephone in hand. Tom offered him a rod. To Ann's amazement, he took it. He began fishing in the sunshine, as far away as possible from her. Sam curled up between them and slept in a crumpled mass on the cooler. Tom vanished upstairs to fish. And maybe to give them privacy.

They fished side by side. The sun's rays became blinding. The reflections of sunlight on the water probably looked like a flashing mirror to the fish below and the fish went into hiding. The fishing boats vanished too. Only two remained of the dozens there an hour ago.

Hidden behind his sunglasses, Richard could have been thinking anything, impossible to guess. He never stood still this long.

Ann's arms felt like dead weights, and her legs were buckling. She sat down beside Sam on the cooler and propped her rod against the railing, keeping a hand on it to feel any nibbles. This morning she had learned to move the rod to compensate for each wave's upsurge and down-swell. She was almost too tired to do that now, yet she was strangely calm and strangely certain a fish would bite.

Tom moved the boat closer towards the point in order to fish in the back eddy of the current. Ann reeled in and the boat surged on the crest of the waves toward land. Cindy was rattling dishes in the galley. It was lunchtime. Funny, Ann wasn't hungry.

"I'm taking orders for drinks," Richard said to her. "Want anything?"

Sam stirred, opened one eye, and then shut it again like a watchdog.

"No thanks," she said, surprised. This was the considerate husband she remembered the Richard who had wooed her and taken her to Mexico.

*****

Marigolds in clay pots had ringed the hotel terrace where the Mariachi band played. She savoured her margarita's bold flavour and the raucous music and looking forward to her birthday dinner. Richard had made a reservation. Evening breezes ruffled the surface of the water. Waves of sun mirrored themselves on Richard's face as he dried his hair. They both wore swimsuits. He photographed her as she sipped her margarita. He was into photography then, and also woodworking. He had wanted to photograph a female Mexican farmworker that morning but Ann wouldn't let him.

He fished in his gym bag and slid a square package across the table. "For you."

She rummaged in the white tissue paper and felt something smooth and cold, an ornament. She pulled it out, two glass dolphins leaping from a smoked glass sea. No, not glass, abalone, purple and luminous. Delicate gold edged the dolphins' tails and fins. "It's wonderful, Richard. I love dolphins." Their backs were rounded and smooth and their clear glass reflected the sun.

"I bought it at the dolphin show this morning. I thought you could put it on your night table where you could see it first thing in the day and last thing at night."

She kissed him. "You're such a romantic."

They toasted one another and listened to the band.

*****

They had once been a couple, they had once been romantic. Now they stood on separate sides of the boat, fishing. In mid-afternoon, Cindy relieved Tom at the controls, to allow him to fish too. Every now and then Cindy had to start the engine to keep from drifting ashore. Richard groaned every time. He worried the noise would scare his fish off. *His* fish. It was funny how badly he and she both wanted a fish. Funny, to agree on something. His skin was turning an alarming red so Ann went to the top deck for sunscreen.

Tom was fishing off the bow and Cindy was at the controls, a *Good Housekeeping* magazine propped on the dashboard.

"Should we start dinner?" Ann asked wearily.

Her friend looked up from her magazine. "The generator would scare the fish."

"Isn't it time to find an anchorage?"

"Yes." The older woman rolled her eyes. "Tom would fish all night."

"I'm beginning to think Richard would too. Let's give them half an hour more. Then we'll take charge and eat, right?"

"Right." Cindy gave her the thumbs up.

On the back deck, Ann slathered sunscreen on Richard's shoulders. He smiled, and for a moment looked happy. Ann took up her rod and cast.

Whitecaps formed on the black water. The wind was rising. Tom was smart not to push on to Desolation Sound today. The weather was uncertain, and they needed to relax. But they also needed to find shelter, or the boat would rock all night.

Her rod twitched. A wave, or a spasm of her arm muscles? The tip of the rod dipped. Once, twice, clean and rough.

"Fish!" she yelled, lunging to let out line. "Bite!"

Tom and Cindy came running. Richard reeled in. Ann's reel sang as the line went out.

"It's not a coho," Tom said beside her, "the way it took the hook."

The line went slack. In the whitecaps, her quarry had disappeared.

Something splashed forty feet off the starboard bow.

"A chinook," Tom yelled. "A big one." He grabbed the net. "Let him play himself out," he said to Ann. "It might take a while. If you get tired, I can take over."

"Sure," she grunted, bracing her legs against the railing and trying to control the rod. Its handle dug into her thigh. She considered herself strong, but the force on her arms and thighs was unbelievable. No wonder rod holders were invented.

Sam awoke and cheered her on.

Richard came and put his arms around her to steady the rod. His breathing on her skin was as excited as a lover's.

She shook herself free. This was her fish, not his. Her opponent hidden beneath its watery shield was an unknown, magnificent force. A prize she in the world above could only sense, and lust for, and covet.

Twenty minutes later, her line went slack.

"Lost him." It was as though a dear friend had vanished. "He's broken the line."

"Don't be too sure," Tom said.

As if in answer, an enormous weight bent the rod. The line shot through the water and sped alongside the hull. Ann hung over the railing to see. The water was black and opaque. Near the front of the boat, a flash of white. "Is that him?" she shrieked.

"Yes," Tom said. "Crossing our bow." He held out the net and captured a handsome, thirty-pound chinook. The fish shimmered unearthly and silver, the hook embedded in its narrow jaw.

Cindy photographed Ann holding it. Ann laughed as she posed. "It will just be another boring photo of a fish." She was trembling with excitement.

"Amanda will like it," Richard said.

Sam threw his wig in the air. "Madam, that fish is a miracle."

And it was.

After that, Richard wanted to catch a fish himself.

"It's already five o'clock," Ann said. "What about anchoring?"

"There are plenty of coves nearby," he answered.

Ann thought of dinner. She glanced at Cindy, but Cindy shook her head. Dinner would wait.

Ann fished beside Richard. He stood as still as a sentinel as the sun dropped. The wind rose and waves splashed over the bow. Ann began to feel queasy. From far away, she heard Tom shout it was time to look for a place to moor. Reluctantly, Richard reeled in.

The first cove they found was only large enough for the sailboat already there. The next held six boats already, but it was spacious, and its rocky promontory would provide shelter from the wind.

After the excitement of fishing, Ann only had enough energy to prepare a simple meal—salad, and salmon steak, with hummus and pita bread for an appetizer. Cindy made the salad. Ann drank a few beers and put the fish under the broiler. The salmon would take twenty minutes so she suggested moving to the back deck for appies and beer. The last rays of sun turned the sky into a blaze of coral and red. Onshore, an abandoned cabin turned to gold. The scene was idyllic, or would have been, but for the heavy beat of their generator, necessary to run the stove.

"You, there, you in the powerboat," a fellow in a striped shirt waved from the deck of a nearby sailboat.

"Hi." Ann waved her glass in reply.

"How long are you going to keep that thing going?" The voice was angry.

"Not long. Only a few more minutes."

"Some people are so rude," Ann commented to Cindy. "He could have asked politely. He could have invited us over for a drink or something."

Tom smiled. "Sailboats despise us powerboats."

Richard's cheeks reddened. "Arrogant twit," he yelled. "You don't own this cove."

The sailor shrugged and continued furling his sails.

"Just for you, jerkface," Richard yelled, "we'll keep our generator going for an hour."

Ann laughed. "Atta boy, Richard!"

"Actually Richard…" Cindy said quietly. "Look at the pennant on his mast. He's a member of the Royal Vancouver Yacht Club."

"So?"

"They have a right to anchor in this cove," Tom said.

Cindy put her hand on Richard's arm. "Listen," she said soothingly, "it's not worth getting upset. The salmon steaks are broiling. They'll be done in a few minutes. Besides, generators *are* noisy."

"Too noisy." Richard glared at Ann. "We don't have an alternative, thanks to Ann."

Ann put down her beer. It had been a wonderful day. She had caught a fish and she had sensed Richard's love. And now, he was blaming her for losing the damned barbecue! *And* blaming her for taking his side. She reached for another beer. Richard hated her drinking but to hell with him!

The salad was a gourmet mix of edible native greens. The bread had been baked fresh the day before. The salmon was delicious, everyone agreed as they discussed tomorrow's trip into Desolation Sound. Ann kept glancing at the nearby yacht. The owner was taking down sails, getting ready for the night. He had spoiled their day. And their dinner, the dinner to celebrate her catching her first fish. She took a few bites of salmon and set down her fork.

"I'm going over there," she said. "I'll take the dinghy. I'll tell that jerk he ruined our day, and I hope he's happy." She went out on the back deck. "You there," she shouted.

Richard's fingers bit into her shoulders. He pulled her back inside the cabin and sat her down at the table. His lips were white with rage. "What do you think you look like, drunk and fat, ready to pick a fight? He's a member of the yacht club. Don't you have any manners?"

Ann's face burned and her lips trembled. She couldn't let this go. "What did you call me?"

"Drunk."

"*And*?" She dared him to repeat it.

He moved to the other side of the table.

"Ann…" Cindy reached out a comforting hand.

Ann stood, eye to eye with Richard. "Maybe I'm not perfect," she spluttered, "unlike you, but I'm your *wife. You* yelled at that sailor. Why can't *I*? He spoiled *my* day. And you just made it worse. Don't talk to me about manners. Manners begin at home."

In the stateroom, she shook with rage. *Fat and drunk.*

Drunk. Maybe, but everyone had been drinking.

Fat. After years of veiled hints, at last he'd said it. Said it in front of the Erdmanns for whom *she* was supposed to be on her best behaviour. Of course, *he* could impale a boat on a dock and act as if it was her fault. He could sound off about government policies, even to the Deputy Minister. *He* could criticize her for the lost barbecue though it had fallen after *he* rammed the dock. *He* could yell at strangers and blame her when she'd tried to support him. Up till now on this holiday, she had tried to be civil. To be a proper wife. To be perfect. Why would he insult her in front of everyone?

Why would he care what the sailor thought?

Tom had laughed about the ongoing war between powerboats and sailboats. It was funny. But all Richard cared about was social status. Richard used to have a sense of humour. He used to love her. This afternoon while fishing, it seemed he still did.

Tears splashed on the bed. She impatiently swiped at her cheeks.

Why did he make such a big deal about her flaws? Why did he always consider other people ahead of her?

Fat. He'd actually said it. In front of everyone. The truth.

Why? *Because he can.*

"I've been far too lenient, Sam." She hiccupped. "He deserves to be punished. I've had enough." She hiccupped again.

Sam sat next to her on the bed. "He that too much refines his delicacy will always endanger his quiet."

"I'm not being delicate, damn it." She burped. "Richard insulted me."

The ghost clasped his hands behind him and paced the cabin like an ugly but authoritative college lecturer. "There are many reasons for insults." He paused a moment, his finger coiled in the air as though to capture a thought. "Of those with whom nature and virtue oblige us to converse, some are ignorant of the art of pleasing, and offend when they design to caress." He held up a second finger. "Some are negligent, and gratify themselves without regard for the quiet of another."

A third finger rose. "Some, perhaps, are malicious, and feel no greater satisfaction in prosperity than that of raising envy and trampling inferiority."

Which was Richard? "Number three," Ann sniffed. "Malicious. His favourite sport is trampling inferiority and insulting anyone less perfect."

"Whatever be the motive of insult," Sam said gently, "it is always best to overlook it."

"Overlook rudeness?" She blew her nose. "Why?"

Sam's eyes held hers. "Folly scarcely can deserve resentment, and malice is punished by neglect."

There was something comforting about old-fashioned words. "You sound rational, Sam, but you're dead wrong." She realized what she had said. She hiccupped. "Sorry, don't 'endanger your quiet', Sam; 'dead' was an unfortunate word choice. I meant to say you don't know Richard."

Sam stared as if he was willing her to understand something.

She realised that if Sam had been following her, shadowing her on this holiday, he might know Richard very well, intimately, in fact.

"I can't overlook this. I'll…" she searched for inspiration, and then laughed. "I know, *I'll* embarrass *him* in front of his friends…" Her voice became fierce and she felt something almost like joy. "I'll tumble him out of his goddamn complacency. I'll mutiny. Abandon ship. Go home. Hire a boat or a plane to take me there. Wouldn't that be funny? Imagine his embarrassed explanations, imagine his loss of face, and imagine his horrible reaction when he realizes he isn't in control."

Sam patted her hand. His hand was massive, a jet ring on the little finger, yet it passed through hers, and she felt nothing. "Do not endanger your quiet," he wheezed.

His voice was soothing. Suddenly, she was sleepy. It had been a long day—beginning with seasickness, and ending with rage. She settled on the bed and pulled the damp blanket over her. A woolly peace descended, a peace rarely known since Edward died.

Sam was right. If Richard was malicious, that was Richard's problem. Richard had been embarrassed when she imitated his behaviour, and he'd acted out like a child—just as he had acted out at Egmont. He was probably too drunk to know what he said.

Endeavour to be pleased, was Sam's advice, and there was plenty to be happy about. Look at the facts. They'd made love at Princess Louisa Inlet hadn't they? Today, he had come to help her fish and had hugged her to steady the fishing rod. He wouldn't have done that if he didn't desire her. If he didn't care.

And he cared for Amanda too. He often seemed cold to the child but today he had insisted on taking a photo of the fish *for Amanda.*

* * * * *

Sunlight shimmered on the curtains of the cabin. Through the porthole to the top deck, came the sound of quiet conversation. The others must be up there, letting her sleep below. The clock on the wardrobe said a quarter to one. Fourteen hours she had slept! A sound sleep, the kind she hadn't had for years.

She felt peaceful, renewed. Last night, she had been angry with the sailor, and with Richard. Both of them had had too much to drink. Today, last night's quarrel seemed petty and slightly humorous. Richard was such a snob he had capitulated to the rude sailor. She had taken Richard's side only to have him insult her. She had been furious, but Sam had wisely calmed her anger. "Sam," she said, "You should bottle your wisdom, and sell it."

Sam sat at the foot of her bed, absorbed in a guidebook.

All was quiet. No motor sounds, no generator pounding. The boat had stopped. That could mean only one thing: they had reached Desolation Sound.

She drew back the window curtains. The ocean was calm. In its pearly mirror, monstrous green islands stood half submerged admiring their reflections. Some of their humped backs bore scars from ancient storms, bare spots where trees had fallen. Others wore untouched, virgin forest. Behind the islands, in the blue distance, mountains marched inland to the sky.

She slid back the window and breathed deeply. No whiff of diesel or creosote or propane tanks. No jetties or roads or shabby general stores. The air was pure. The sunlight was like a blessing, giving her permission to relax.

"So this is Desolation Sound, Sam. It's wonderful."

He looked up from the guidebook. "Depends on your point of view. Captain Vancouver saw these same pines and arbutus and maples and islands," Sam read. "But he said this place had 'as gloomy and dismal an aspect as nature could well be supposed to exhibit.' He named it Desolation Sound and summed up saying, 'Our residence here was truly forlorn."

She smiled. "As I remember, the captain was only here for three weeks and it rained the whole time." She stretched in the sunlight. "Do you think the water is warm enough for a swim?"

Sam turned a page. "The ship's botanist agreed with him. Mr. Archibald Menzies remarked that 'the smaller islands were naked and rocky; and the larger ones were wooded with pines of a stinted appearance. This added to the broken, rugged and gloomy prospect. The captain used almost the same words, writing 'an awful silence pervaded the gloomy forests.'"

"It's not gloomy. It's peaceful. Captain Vancouver hated Desolation Sound. He cursed it for its inconsistent tides and its lack of edible berries. He cursed its mountains for blocking the view. His mood improved when he encountered two friendly Spanish ships here." She laughed. "If he'd lived in our world of crowded freeways, he would have appreciated this peacefulness. He was lonely and frustrated. He couldn't find a route to the east. Men always want what they can't have and ignore the beauty around them."

She pulled her hair into a ponytail. "Sam, as you said last night, there's no point in being angry at insults. Today, I won't drink."

Her white shorts were smeared with oil and dirt from fishing but she pulled them on anyway. She no longer cared what she looked like. A new world waited outside, a world of innocence, ready to be explored.

She went up on the top deck and lazed with Cindy in the sunshine. She was telling Cindy about her plan to speak at the librarians' convention when Tom yelled from inside. "I've been listening to the weather forecast. A gale is coming. We must find shelter now." They should leave the open water immediately.

That's the way it was on boats, Ann thought. You lived minute to minute and took nothing for granted. Already a southeast wind was causing choppy waves. Clouds moved in. Desolation Sound would live up to its name. Everyone scanned the shore for shelter.

If they couldn't find safe anchorage they would need to proceed eastward up to the end of Waddington Channel.

Waves slapped the rocks. The water looked cold and uninviting.

She should have swum earlier when it was calm.

A flash of white on shore. A rock? No. Sunlight? No. A gap in the trees, and inside it, framed by greenery, white masts. The bay was as picturesque and tranquil as an old-fashioned daguerreotype. If only there was space for them! She called out to Tom.

The chart showed a dangerous sand bar at the entrance to Roscoe Bay, but the tide was high so Tom turned the wheel. "Good spotting," he said to Ann. He pointed to the chart and grinned. "There's a lake near this bay, Black Lake. It's supposed to be good for swimming."

"Excellent!" Ann said. She and Richard could swim together after all!

As they reached Black Lake the sun emerged and turned it blue, yet another contradiction in this contrary world. On the lakeshore, a large, shelving rock formed a convenient diving platform. Cindy spread a towel next to Ann on it. Tom and Richard dived in. Ann would have too, but didn't want anyone to see her old black swimsuit unraveling at the seams. There were other swimmers in the water too.

It doesn't matter. Tom and Richard are far out in the water and Cindy's not looking, and besides, Cindy's a friend. Ann stripped and dove.

The water was as warm as a swimming pool. She surfaced and called to Cindy, "Coming?"

"Not yet." Cindy shielded her eyes. "After I finish this article on Princess Di." She put on sunglasses and took up her magazine.

Tom and Richard were in the centre of the lake. Ann didn't often have a chance to practice the butterfly stroke, her fastest stroke. Using it, she caught up to them. She turned onto her back to float. Above was sky, below, water. This world was clean, blue, uncomplicated.

Further out in the lake, a dog barked. She turned over to watch a couple of men throw a floating stick for a yellow dog swimming with them. The animal, probably a lab, yelped for joy. It clamped the stick in its jaws and returned it to them. They threw it closer to shore. They seemed to be coaxing the dog toward land.

"This is heaven," she said to Richard, praying he would for once drop the stern mask.

"Yes," he said. With his wet hair hanging in his eyes, he appeared boyish, casual, like the man she'd married. "You're still a good swimmer, Ann"

Was he trying to compensate for last night's criticism?

He splashed Tom. The two rolled and plunged and executed duck dives. Ann joined them, and was dunked by Tom. She dunked him in return. Manners were forgotten. She remembered how to play.

Afterwards, she floated blissfully on her back. Who cared about threadbare swimsuits or a few extra pounds? Her body wasn't perfect, but it was strong.

Cindy was missing all the fun. "Come on in, Cindy," Ann hollered, "It's wonderful!"

"Later," Cindy shouted. "The article is getting interesting."

The dog's owners hurled the stick towards Cindy's rock. The dog grabbed it and emerged on the rock, its blonde coat dripping. Cindy moved her towel just in time. The dog shook itself. The spray of droplets was visible even from the centre of the lake. The owners called out apologies. Cindy made a sign that she was okay. The dog wagged a greeting as its masters neared the rock. Suddenly, Cindy stood up, dropped her magazine, and executed a streamlined racing dive into the water.

Was something wrong?

Cindy joined her husband and treaded water. "The view from shore was intriguing," she shook hair out of her eyes, "Much more interesting than Princess Di. They were definitely centrefold material." She giggled. "And pleasant. They wished me good afternoon as they scrambled into their clothes and vanished into the woods."

Tom grinned. "Poor guys. Probably thought they had the lake to themselves, and didn't expect company."

"Not female company, anyway." Cindy hugged him.

Richard, likewise, swam to Ann. Underwater, his hand circled her waist and brought her close. Feeling the familiar warmth, Ann forgave everything. She laughed. "This is like old times." Long ago, they had swum like this, like dolphins together, skin to skin.

"Like SaltSpring," he breathed.

"Yes."

"Remember the Tarzan swing?" she asked. On Saltspring, the rope dangled from a skeletal tree cantilevered out over the lake. The tree's dead branches formed a primitive ladder up to the rope.

He smiled. "Yes. You swung off it on your first try, I remember. You were frightened, but I'd never seen such determination."

"You were good too, in fact you were gorgeous." Though he was thirty-five, he had run up the trunk like a teenager. He'd swung far out over the water, and then let go. Trying to impress. She was worth impressing then, being young, and attractive, with a well-paid job.

Underwater, his hand worked its way toward her breast. "And," he whispered. "I'd never seen such breasts."

His breath fanned flames. Ann gulped and glanced at the others, and smiled. "Richard and I will swim in now, I'm getting tired."

"Yes," Richard said. "What time is it anyway?"

"Five?" Tom squinted toward the sun. "Six? Does it matter?"

"Ann and I should hurry back, start the bar—...the generator."

"Don't rush," Cindy said. "There's plenty of time." She lay back in Tom's arms, "I'm happy here. We may never find another place like this."

On the rock, Ann and Richard towelled one another off carefully, a prelude to future explorations. Ann's skin tingled. *Yes.* This was how it was to desire and be desired. This meltingly aware and incomplete state. This was how it had been on SaltSpring. She might be heavier now and less independent financially, but not too fat or too dependent. Richard hadn't changed. He could still play Tarzan.

Richard put on his runners. Breathlessly, she wrapped the towel like a sarong to hide her less than desirable legs. Her shoes lay on a nearby ledge warm from the sun. She reached for them and then saw next to the runners, a black stain. A stain that might have been a crevice or a shadow, but its glistening skin was slowly stretching and contracting.

She shrieked. She had to warn the others. She stood, cupped her hands and shouted to Tom and Cindy, "There's a leech here!" Her voice echoed off the rocky shore.

Cindy waved to show she had heard.

A cloud passed overhead. The lake turned black. Ann grabbed her runners. Shivering, she said to Richard, "If I'd seen that leech, I'd never have gone swimming. There are probably hundreds of them…hiding there…on the rocks…on submerged logs…on the bottom-- Whole families…lurking anywhere your feet or your fingers might touch.."

Richard walked silently to the trail, and then stopped. He looked at her. "Do you have to make such a big deal out of everything?"

"Sorry." She took his hand.

He held it until they were out of sight of the others. Then he shook it off with disdain.

"Better hurry," he said. "We're the cooks tonight. And Cindy and Tom will be hungry."

CHAPTER 7: PARADISE

Ann moved from stove to sink, testing pasta, and stirring sauce.

Once upon a time, he would have laughed at her reaction to the leech, and would found it cute. Once upon a time, she would have used the leech as an excuse to seek safety in his arms. Not raised the alarm to everyone on the lake. He hated her nervousness. She hated his anger. Fear and anger were different sides of the same coin. Ever since Edward died, any small event could trigger them.

"That sauce smells fabulous," Cindy said. She and Tom were in the salon now drying off after the swim. Richard had started the generator and vanished to the upper deck to phone a client.

Ann added wine to the sauce. She would make up for her faux pas by cooking a fantastic dinner and top it off with a fantastic dessert. That should soothe Richard.

"The increased fees should go for forest renewal," Richard said, between mouthfuls of pasta. "The government should spend it on replanting, and on retraining loggers for other jobs."

Ann drank the excellent Pinot Noir and tuned out. Late afternoon sun glinted on the metal masts of sailboats seeking shelter from the whitecaps beyond the cove's narrow entrance. Here, the water was calm and probably warm enough to swim in. Richard was riding his usual hobbyhorse—the need to increase provincial stumpage fees. He had hardly noticed the appetizer of sundried tomatoes in warm brie spread on crackers. He hadn't commented on the Caesar salad dressing pungent with anchovies and garlic or on the clam sauce. He also didn't notice the fact that Tom was silent.

To interrupt the lecture, Ann passed him the bottle.

Tom seized the opportunity to get a word in. "What you're saying, Richard, jibes with our government policy. But, off the record, Richard, I'm worried about that policy. We'll have to be very, very careful how we implement forest renewal and retraining."

Richard opened his mouth to speak but Tom continued, "Loggers might agree to more inspections and to selective logging, but not to an increase in stumpage fees. Raising fees will price lumber out of the foreign market. Mills will close. Logging companies will fail. Jobs will disappear. Retraining loggers won't make a dent in the resulting unemployment—"

"In the short term," Richard interrupted, "we'll suffer. But that's because our provincial economy is in limbo. Why? Because it's based on primary resources. We've squandered those resources, and we'll pay for our sins." He glared with righteous indignation. "Replanting trees plus retraining loggers are our only hope of salvation in the long term. If we don't give the forests a chance to renew we will face reduced forest yields." He poured himself another glass of wine. "More?" he asked Tom.

Tom refused, but Richard poured him some anyway. The Deputy Minister smiled. "You want to save the trees at any cost."

Richard didn't notice the sarcasm. He continued to rant. Maybe he was right about stumpage, but even at home he was always on about it. Why couldn't he talk for once about normal, unimportant, personal things? Ann took the dirty dishes to the sink and served the apple pie she'd made at home and frozen.

"Retraining will save the economy-" Richard shovelled pie into his mouth.

"-Dinner was perfect," Cindy said

"So's this pie,"Tom added. "A real treat here in the wilderness."

Richard frowned. He didn't appreciate the interruption or the pie. She might as well have served leeches. "Retraining is the answer," he waved the bottle.

"That's what my advisers say," Tom said, "but retraining for what?"

"Jobs. Jobs in computers—"

"Get real! Many loggers have a grade eight education."

Richard raised his voice. "Damn it all, look at the big picture, Tom! Loggers can work as cooks or tour operators. They can take service jobs...whatever."

"McJobs," Cindy said.

Tom set down his wine glass and said quietly, "Richard, how many cooks and tour operators does a logging town like Port Alberni actually need?"

"Plenty, damn it."

"Richard," Ann put her hand on his arm. "Tom's *lived* in Port Alberni. He worked as a logger there before he became a forester."

"That was an excellent meal, Ann." Tom finished his pie and dabbed at his mouth with a napkin. "I agree with you, Richard, that raising stumpage rates will help the economy. If we do it slowly. If not, it could cause economic chaos. We can't create service jobs overnight and—"

"-Sure we can," Richard shouted. "It's part of the process."

There was silence.

What was Richard thinking, lecturing to the Deputy Minister of Natural Resources?

"It's simple." Richard stood. "First," he thumped the table, "retrain the loggers in carpentry. Second," he thumped again, "establish secondary industries. Third...keep the wood here and export only the finished product. Tom, don't talk about being careful and going slowly. This is an emergency. We need to act now, not worry about unemployment. The transition period would be short and sweet. I know. I've studied unemployment statistics. In fact," he added with a self-satisfied smile, "I've been working on the problem.

"I've had enough," Ann said. "I'm going outside." She grabbed a book from the stateroom and marched past the now silent dinner table towards the back deck.

Cindy looked concerned. "You okay, Ann?"

"I'm fine," she growled as she shoved open the sliding door. "I just want to read while there's still daylight."

Richard stared. She positioned her chair so she didn't have to look at him, and opened the book. The words on the page blurred, but she pretended to read. A small waterfall gurgled by the boat's mooring lines. Normally she would have found the sound soothing.

The group at the table was silent. Tom and Cindy might think she was angry at them. To reassure them, she casually swivelled her chair and said, "Cindy, I'm catching up on my book club reading. You should read this." She held up the novel *Pillars of the Earth.*

"I have," the older woman answered. "Remember I chose it?"

Of course! Instead of sounding casual, you sounded brain dead.

Conversation resumed. They talked about the itinerary. Tom wanted to explore Desolation Sound, and then, depending on the weather, spend a day fishing off Cape Mudge on Quadra Island. Cindy liked that agenda because she wanted to visit the pub on Quadra Island. The discussion was cordial.

"That's settled then," Richard said. He re-launched his rant on forest policy, pouring forth random thoughts about everything from pulp mills to the cost of newsprint.

No one else spoke. Richard was drunk, too drunk to realize he was boring his guests. Too drunk to praise his dinner, the dinner made especially for him.

"Damn it all." Ann pitched her book toward the water.

Sam caught it. "Madam," he whispered. "Reflect a while. There is nothing worse in life than to be married to a peevish man. Nothing can please."

She hadn't noticed Sam, hunched like a black shadow on the ladder.

"I've been here all afternoon," he said. "Listening to this sublime waterfall."

"What makes you an expert on relationships?"

"I was married, Madam."

Married? Sam was sloppy and definitely had a fat ass. Who would marry him?

"Dear, dear, Tetty." His voice shook and he bowed his head, looking lugubrious. "I pray for her forgiveness. She was not in the best of health, being many years senior to myself, but in the beginning, we were happier than most."

"But?"

"But she relied on the bottle, and withdrew to her bed, and after that was no more company."

By 'company', he must mean lovemaking. A passionate marriage to an older woman until alcohol entered the picture. "Was *she* peevish?"

He sighed. "No. Tetty was like you, too willing to please……" His figure wavered and became a wraith. "Easily swayed by food, by drink, but nevertheless, I should have shown my love more fully."

"Marriage is full of pain," Ann said. "To quote a certain eighteenth century expert'

The ghost coiled in upon himself. "I should have shown my love more fully." His face convulsed in a paroxysm of despair as he shrank and disappeared.

Poor Sam. Richard would never feel that remorse. Sam had persuaded her to ignore Richard's insults. But she would teach Richard a lesson. The water was dark and calm. She still wore her bathing suit. What if she dove in now for a lengthy swim? Richard would regret his behaviour.

A second later she was underwater. The black velvet depths urged her to forget, but anger propelled her through the water in a strong crawl, the stroke that had won provincial championships when she was a teenager. She swam toward the entrance to the cove. Sailboats' lines clanged against masts. On board, dishes clattered, children's voices twittered like birds at twilight.

On board other ships children were laughing. Children were being bundled into sleeping bags, or sitting on deck, playing board games, children like Amanda. Amanda would have loved sleeping on the boat. Instead she was in Victoria, watching TV, eating popcorn if her grandmother permitted it, laughing along with the canned laughter.

This could have been a family vacation. Richard had been angry because he'd wanted Maureen's boys to come. He shouldn't always want what was impossible.

Night was falling. Waves crashed on the sandbar warning her not to go further. She circled back near a small fishing boat, *The African* something. The rest of the name was hidden until the boat swung around on its mooring line. *The African Queen.* The boat was almost as ramshackle as the one in the famous film. An awning sheltered the back deck. Towels hung from it. Someone was smoking a pipe, a pleasant smell. Someone laughed.

"Cape Mudge, tomorrow," a voice said.

"And more salmon. If this wind lets up. Otherwise we'll stay here and play chess."

A dog barked and raced back and forth along the deck. It must have seen her. A yellow dog. The one in the lake. Two heads peered over the side of the boat.

The eavesdropper plastered a smile on her face. "Nice evening for a dip." She waved cheerily at the gardener and his friend, hoping they didn't recognize her, and turned abruptly to swim back to Richard.

"That was a damn fool thing to do," Richard said when she emerged dripping onto the swim platform. "Going off without telling anyone. We thought you'd fallen overboard. We took the dinghy out, looking for you." He handed her a towel.

Tom opened the gate for her.

So Richard had worried. She'd only been gone half an hour but the sky was now as black as the water.

"You were ridiculous," Richard said, "getting angry over nothing."

Nothing! So much for remorse! "Nothing? You call it nothing?"

Tom disappeared discreetly.

She followed her husband inside, banging the sliding door shut behind her. In the salon, he headed straight for the bar. Ice clinked into a glass.

"I wonder," she said, "If you think it's clever to insult me in public."

"Don't be ridiculous," he whispered, "I often praise you, but on this trip you've been moody most of the time."

"Look who's talking! You keep saying you've had enough. If that is true, why don't you leave?"

"Don't start that again," he took out a bottle, "and don't disturb the others." The smell of cognac wafted through the lounge. "Want some?"

"No," she said, shivering. Drinking might warm her, but it wouldn't repair what had come between them. Didn't he see the encroaching shadows? First the small differences—his playing tennis alone, and then the larger ones—his travelling to hearings, and now, the public insults.

"I'll sleep out here, tonight," Richard said.

* * * * *

"You're a good watch dog, Humphrey." David patted the dog warming his feet, and gazed at the lights of the boats in the cove. Which one was hers?

Gerry said, "Remember that boat, the *Maybelle*?"

"Who could forget it?" David stroked his new-grown beard and laughed. "Such a stupid name."

The journalist tamped the tobacco down in his pipe. "A ship of fools."

"A marriage of fools," David replied. "Marriage, someone once said, has many pains."

"Not in my case," his friend answered, "though I'm not sure my wife would always agree."

David laughed. Seeing the married woman so unexpectedly again, had brought back feelings he'd rather ignore. He gestured with his coffee mug towards the direction in which she had swum. "With our luck, the *Maybelle* will be fishing tomorrow at Cape Mudge."

"Probably," his companion said. The pipe glowed as he lit it.

"That was a close call at the lake today," David mused. "Even with this beard, I thought the blonde on shore would remember me from Egmont."

"Luckily you showed her something else to remember." Gerry punched him.

David yelped, and Humphrey growled, ready to protect him. David tickled the dog's ears and Humphrey lay down again.

Gerry lounged in his chair, his feet up on a tackle box, and puffed on his pipe. "Or maybe it was the woman in the water you were trying to impress. You couldn't keep your eyes off her, I noticed. Perhaps you've forgotten the rest of that quotation, "Marriage has many pains but celibacy has no pleasures?"

Damn. You couldn't hide much from Gerry.

"The southeaster's still blowing," Gerry said to his now silent companion. "Maybe we should stay here tomorrow."

"No thanks, I've had all the woman trouble I need."

"This is a nice spot, especially the lake. Quite alluring."

In the dark, David smiled, and remembered what the woman's swimsuit had revealed.

"It's been a wonderful vacation," his friend added. "Nothing like it back in England—the fish, the clean water, the uncrowded coves, and every night, a cookout."

It had been fun, David reflected. Almost like being seventeen again, rowing out of Telegraph Cove in search of whales. Joyful, except for the constant concern about his friend's health. But this trip was drawing to a close. Only four days left. Afterwards, Gerry would stay with his parents at Government House until he was well enough to fly home.

David smiled. "I hope your dad doesn't mind me spiriting you away like this. He hinted he'd like to come along."

"I'd rather have you as a nurse. He would have fussed and laid down the law. No drinking and certainly no swimming like our dip this afternoon."

"The doctor said mild exercise, and we didn't overdo it."

"No, and it did me good."

"Anyway, I guess your dad's keeping busy with all those formal receptions he has to host."

"Don't worry about Dad. He's not much of a sailor, anyway. He's happiest in his garden dreaming about Gertrude Jekyll." Gerry puffed on his pipe. Sparks like shooting stars flew off with every puff. Brilliant against the moonless sky.

Had the woman made it safely back to her boat? She was a strong swimmer so there was no reason to worry. Her shoulders cut through the water. Did she swim every night? Maybe he should follow Gerry's suggestion and stay longer in this cove. No! Gerry would guess why, the minute he proposed it.

"What was the name of that girlfriend of yours?" Gerry asked.

"You mean Jenny? She's nothing to me now."

The other man chuckled. "When we get back to Victoria, maybe you should look her up."

*****

Ann woke early and looked for Richard in the main salon. The curtains had been drawn back, the lounge had been folded up, and his pillow and blankets were neatly stacked. She went to the back deck. It was empty. Last night he'd been '"peevish," to quote Sam. He hadn't shown remorse, but anger meant he'd been frightened. That meant he cared. Yes, he had insulted her, but he had been drunk. Why ruin the holiday over it? She would make peace.

She climbed the ladder to the top deck. He was there, talking on his cell phone.

"But don't wait up for me," he said, then seeing Ann, added, "that's all I can arrange right now. See you Thursday." He put the phone into its holster so quickly it fell out. He bent to retrieve it.

"Anything wrong?" she asked.

"No, Peter Bryant wants a meeting, that's all. On Thursday to discuss the Carmanah thing. I told him not to wait for me. To go ahead with it. I can't be expected to attend every meeting." An aggrieved tone now, whereas before on the phone, his voice had been breathy with enthusiasm. He was still cross.

"About last night," she said, "I was stupid to be upset and to worry you. I'm sorry."

No answer. His cheeks were an angry red. At last, he said, not looking, "You should be."

"How about coffee?"

He nodded.

She hastened below. She'd have to turn on the generator to make coffee, and that would wake Cindy and Tom. The neighbours wouldn't appreciate the noise any more than that angry sailor had. It was a shame to disturb such a peaceful morning. She opened the galley window. The air was as sweet and warm as the breath of a lover. It caressed her hair, and sent shivers down her spine. The sun was just peeking over the entrance to the cove. A new day. A new start.

The African Queen was crossing the sandbar, moving silently, departing to fish probably. The awning was down, the fishnets upright on either side of the cabin, the two men standing at the wheel. Their voices came over the water, the words muffled but excited. Passing out of the cove, the boat blazed in the gold of the rising sun, and the men gave a spontaneous cheer.

A golden moment. Her heart recognised it. Her brain catalogued it, and welcomed its joy, the way an elderly person welcomes a child, not envying youth, but recognizing what is lost.

Enough moping. She would enjoy this final day in Desolation Sound, beginning with a proper breakfast. She turned the generator knob and ended the morning calm.

A huge log floated by. *Pay attention, Ann!* Luckily, it missed the boat. They were chugging east up Waddington Channel, and she was on the top deck, leaning on the railing, and supposedly spotting for debris. But after the delectable waffles dripping with syrup, she could barely keep her eyes open.

Concentrate! The sunlit water was green with yellow flecks in its depths, a dreamy green, like a mirror, but deeper, blacker. She needed soothing. Richard's mood changes were strange. Last night, so angry he slept in the salon. This morning, so matter of fact he had brushed off her apology as if last night had never happened. And still no affection.

Focus! Look for debris!

The more she stared, the more the water became transparent as air, became a medium in which she could thrive. Last night she could have swum for hours, listening to happy boaters and their children, feeling free, her anger dissolving, melting into the water.

Deadhead on the right! Wake up! Stop daydreaming!

Behind her, a voice wheezed, "Almost every man has some art by which he steals his thoughts away from his present state."

"I shouldn't daydream. Richard doesn't."

Sam arranged his great bulk on the white vinyl couch and rolled his stockings down as if to suntan. "It is not much of life that is spent in close attention to any important duty. Many hours of every day are suffered to fly away without any traces left upon the intellects."

"Really?" She stretched. "So it's normal to let my mind roam?"

Sam looked ridiculous with his old fat knees exposed but he had such a compelling manner of speaking that you overlooked superficial flaws.

He said solemnly, "We suffer phantoms to rise up before us—"

"Phantoms like you, I suppose."

The ghost went on as if she hadn't spoken. "We amuse ourselves with the dance of airy images, which after a time we dismiss for ever and know not how we have been busied."

"Richard used to relax by reading and doing woodworking but now he hates to waste time."

"Do not deride such happiness." He wagged a stern finger. "Many have no happier moments than those that they pass in solitude. Ah yes, abandoned to their own imagination, which sometimes puts sceptres in their hands or mitres on their heads, shifts the scene of pleasure with endless variety."

She thought of Amanda sketching princesses, herself enjoying Rackham's fairies, and the fairy game. "Things are different nowadays. We don't have servants. We believe work is the key to a successful life. Not imagination."

"But imagination is a source of happiness." Sam's face shone with enthusiasm. His skin became dazzling and he almost tumbled off the couch in his eagerness to lecture. "It is easy in these semi-slumbers to collect all the possibilities of happiness, to alter the course of the sun, to bring back the seasons, and all the blessings of all climates, to receive and bestow felicity, and forget that misery is the lot of man."

Ann grinned. "Of *man?* Try being a woman. But you're right. Other than chocolate, I love curling up in a comfy chair with a novel. Richard says I should read about political and environmental issues instead, and become political."

The ghost gave her a pitying look. "Others are afraid to be alone, and amuse themselves by a perpetual succession of companions."

"He's certainly made a lot of friends at the hearings, nice people, like Tom. Richard's way more sociable than I am. I have friends I see at book club meetings. I should call them more often, I guess. Be more like him."

Sam raised his unruly eyebrows. "The difference is not great; in solitude we have our dreams to ourselves, and in company we agree to dream in concert. The end sought in both is forgetfulness of ourselves."

Forgetfulness of self. Wouldn't that be wonderful?

Sam rolled up the sleeves of his shirt. In the sunlight, his flesh was blinding. It blended with the whiteness of the vinyl seats.

Ann rubbed her eyes. When she looked again, he was gone. She ran her hand along the vinyl seat. It was still warm.

She heard the dinghy motor start up below, and realized the *Maybelle* had stopped. No need to watch for deadheads. Cindy was on the main deck and she pointed to the whitish shore. "Oysters," she said. "The boys want to gather some."

Richard and Tom motored across the channel to an oyster bed. There they pried the chalk white shells off the rocks and tossed them into ice cream buckets. In their swim trunks, they looked like teenagers. Maureen's boys would have loved activities like this. And Amanda would have too. Oyster gathering looked like fun.

Back aboard, Richard laughed as he counted and re-counted the oysters. Dinner would be oysters along with crab. Just to hear him laugh was enticing. Ann felt happier after talking to Sam. He made her feel as if everything she thought and did was normal. He insisted that most of life was spent doing unimportant things. There was nothing wrong or right about escaping into imagination.

Maybe Richard needed companionship, as Sam suggested. He certainly enjoyed being with Tom and Cindy. Maybe he feared being alone. He should talk to her about that, become more human, like Sam. He should talk about Edward.

For dinner Richard broiled the oysters and served them in a pungent curry sauce. He dished up crabs in a lemon-garlic broth. At home, he never cooked. At home he insisted on two vegetables per meal. Here, vegetables weren't even on the menu. And instead of talking about stumpage fees, he talked about prying oysters from rocks. He stretched and said, "I wouldn't mind staying here in Desolation Sound for an extra day. It's so beautiful."

"But we need to fill our water tanks, don't we?" Cindy asked.

"We can fill them here," Richard replied.

"Here? With salt water?"

"We found a waterline in the forest. Don't know who put it there. It was just there."

"Like an answer to our prayers," Tom said. "An invitation to extend our time in paradise."

Richard smiled. "In the channel, the water was warm. How about a swim after supper, Ann, and then a game of cards?

What had got into him?

The swim was magical, and so was the game of cards. The magic lingered into the next morning. Before breakfast, there was not full-fledged lovemaking, but at least a cuddle and a peck on the cheek that left her wanting more. Instead of planning the day's itinerary after breakfast, Richard actually took a paperback mystery up to the top deck. Ann joined him on the vinyl seat.

Sam was right. The enemy was habit. She and Richard needed to escape themselves.

Richard's green T-shirt and khaki shorts skimmed his flat stomach. What would he do if she leaned against him, the way Cindy sometimes leaned against Tom? Ann leaned over and patted his muscular quads. He was in excellent shape, thanks to jogging and tennis. What would happen if she let her hand wander? Cindy wouldn't notice. Shaded by a straw hat, she was re-reading *Pillars.* Richard might become amorous, the way he was in Mexico. In Mexico, the hot sun combined with tequila made them randy as rabbits. Their daily routine: make the vast king-sized bed, and then unmake it.

Ann discreetly loosened the top three buttons of her sleeveless blouse just a tad more than was decent, but not enough to embarrass him. She reached past him to pick up one of Cindy's magazines and brushed his arm.

No reaction. Not surprising. Cindy could proudly haul Tom below saying she needed him to wash her back. Richard wouldn't go for a strategy as obvious as that. Ann crossed her legs, and hoped he'd notice how nicely tanned they were becoming.

He kept on reading. She opened the magazine and immersed herself in the latest Hollywood gossip.

"How about a beer?" Tom appeared at noon with an armful of cottage brewed beers.

"Sure," Ann said, yawning. "It might put me to sleep, though." Reading about movie stars and royal celebrities and their perfect bodies was depressing. Sunlight revealed the spider veins on her legs, and her fat ankles. Twilight was much more romantic,"dusk," they called it in England. At dusk, fairies flew over the Serpentine pond in London.

"How's the book?" Richard asked Cindy.

"Just as good the second time around. I'm glad I chose it for the book club."

"Follett keeps his plots simmering." Richard twisted the caps off two beer bottles for the women.

"Thanks," Cindy said. "This isn't a thriller like Follett's other books. It's historical with great descriptions of monasteries and battles."

"Life was harsh in medieval times. No one went cruising." He drank from his bottle. "How do you choose books at the book club? Do you draw up a yearly list?"

"We used to, but we didn't like to be locked in case something fabulous came along or the chosen book was a stinker."

"Bestsellers can be stinkers. What about mysteries?" He held his book up. "Not for you literary types?"

Cindy laughed.

Ann turned away, disgusted. How often had she told him about book club meetings, only to meet silence? And yet here he was, talking about something other than business, laughing, asking for information, conversing! He could be polite to strangers but not to her. She stormed down to the galley for leftover cream cheese dip and crackers. Plus beer. She deserved one.

That afternoon, boredom set in for Ann. Everything was too perfect, and everyone drank too much. Tom and Cindy lay asleep on the lounges, pillowed by one another. Sam slept on the back deck. Instead of cuddling, Richard read his whodunit. Ann went to the galley.

It was already five o'clock. The sun was still high but they hadn't eaten lunch, other than crackers with the beer. She put together a salad of radicchio and red leafed lettuce, and, for pizzazz, added anchovies and boiled eggs. That, plus steaks and French bread would be dinner.

Waves lapped at pebbles on the too peaceful shore. No one stirred. It would be good to push on to Cape Mudge tomorrow. The two fishermen would be there now, barbecuing salmon Indian style, and laughing about nothing. Here it was too quiet. She turned on the generator to wake the sleepers. If they didn't want dinner, they could at least play Scrabble.

They played three games. Ann won two—voiding her tiles to win the second with the word 'scholar'. Tom won the third game and Ann immediately suggested a rematch, despite groans from the others. Cindy said her brain was tired. She passed on the first round. Fuelled by beer, Ann crowed as she managed to void again, using the word 'epistle'.

"That word's archaic," Richard said, disgusted.

Tom lavished praise on her.

Scrabble was a librarian's game. Luck entered into it too. All the letters had been distributed and she had only three, an 'e', a 'c' and an 'a'. She chuckled as she placed the word 'aces' using the s in 'epistle.' Richard still had a full load of seven letters.

"I surrender!" Tom declared, and refilled everyone's glasses. He had switched from wine to a rich silky port, a proper after-dinner drink.

Not that they'd eaten yet, but who cared when you could beat your mates so thoroughly? Ann and Tom toasted one another's prowess. Richard was silent. "That was fun," Cindy said.

"How about another game?" Richard said suddenly, competitive as always.

Ann was amused. The sun set as she mixed up the tiles for a fifth game.

"Say, Richard," Tom said as he placed his tiles on his rack. "How's your luck running on those Fidelity shares?"

"Not bad. The company was taken over and they jumped from sixty-five cents to eight dollars."

"What shares?" Ann looked at her husband.

He filled his glass with port. "Some stock I bought a while ago," he said offhandedly. "Tom, I hear you lost a bundle on Dynamix. I—"

"When?" Ann interrupted, "When did you buy shares in Fidelity?"

"Years ago." He frowned as he removed a tile from his stand and exchanged it for another. "Peter Bryant put me on to them. All the foresters bought them."

"Years ago….? Six months ago I returned to work fulltime because you said we needed money. And you played the stock market?" She dropped her tiles on the floor. With shaking hands she gathered them up. "How many shares did you buy?"

"A few." His cheeks reddened.

"How many?" In front of the others, he'd have to answer.

"Ten thousand, maybe twenty."

"Twenty thousand! While I skimped on meals...while I told Amanda we couldn't afford Disneyland this summer...we couldn't afford to pay anyone to help in the garden! We couldn't afford a housecleaner... We couldn't afford this vacation!" She dumped her Scrabble tiles on the table and swept them toward Richard. They skidded along the table's surface onto the floor.

Richard ducked to pick them up. "You were never interested in stocks, Ann. It was a good deal."

"Too good to tell me about?" She quivered with rage. "It was *our* money you gambled with. Exactly how much did you make?"

He blushed to the roots of his hair. "A couple of hundred grand."

"No!"

"You should be happy," he said. "It's a nest egg for the future, safely invested. Trust me."

She pushed past him on her way from the table. "I'll never trust you again."

"Don't say that." He reached out an arm. "Come and finish the game."

"To hell with the game."

CHAPTER 8: THE TWO DOLPHINS

The sight of his silk pyjamas folded neatly on the bed in the cabin decided it. Brand name pyjamas, blue and green striped, she'd spent part of her last paycheque on them so he could be suitably attired in case he met the Erdmanns on the way to the toilet at night. The secret investment and profit. While she saved, and worked extra hours, time she could have spent with Amanda, hours they could have spent playing or shopping or just being together. What else was he hiding, a mistress, a second wife? How much had he made, two hundred thousand? Or more? She'd damn well find out.

She picked up the silk pyjamas, opened the cabin door and hurled them into the salon. Let him explain *that* to the Erdmanns .

*****

At Quadra Island the next morning, she followed through on her decision. When they docked at Herriot Bay, she carried her suitcases through the salon. The others were at the table planning a trip to the general store. Ann paused to speak to the Erdmanns. "Thanks for being such good shipmates. I enjoyed meeting you, Tom. Sorry to desert you all."

"You're not leaving!" Tom rose to his feet.

"You know why. It has nothing to do with you or Cindy. I hope you understand."

Cindy's mouth dropped. She looked at Richard.

He followed Ann to the back deck. "Give me those suitcases," he hissed.

"No."

He accompanied her along the wharf and up the ramp to the road. She stopped beside a bramble-covered hedge under a home-made sign that said "Island Cabs."

"You can't do this," he said, his back as straight as a corporal's.

"I can."

"It will be all over Victoria."

"Not unless *you* broadcast it. The Erdmanns won't. They are my friends. Friends don't humiliate friends."

Again he tried to take the suitcases.

"Let go." She swung one at him, ready to fight. Several of the islanders were watching. If he wanted humiliation, he'd have it.

"You're being ridiculous," he said, but he backed off.

A rickety cab pulled in next to the general store. She piled her suitcase and her bag of books into it. At least she had books for comfort. And Sam. .

* * * * *

Five days later, she poured a cup of tea for Sam and one for herself and sat down again at the kitchen table to continue taking notes for her speech. Sam finished his tea, and smacked his lips. The sound was oddly endearing. She poured another cup—his sixth. The spicy fragrance of the English Breakfast tea was reassuringly normal. She poured more for herself too and opened an old edition of *Winnie the Pooh.*

Sam twirled his fingers at the library books. "No place affords a more striking conviction of the vanity of human hopes than a public library."

"Why? What's wrong with libraries?"

He gulped down his tea and belched. His manners were delightfully disgusting. Here was a man who enjoyed his food and drink.

"Who can see the wall crowded on every side by mighty volumes, the works of laborious meditation and accurate inquiry, now scarcely known but by the catalogue, and preserved only to increase the pomp of learning, without considering how many hours have been wasted in vain endeavours?"

"In the public libraries, we discard books that aren't borrowed." She had very nearly discarded Sam's work. "Some worthy books aren't popular."

"And some mediocre ones are." He sighed. "How often imagination has anticipated the praises of futurity, how many statues have risen to the eye of vanity?"

"Right. Some authors only write for fame."

Sam nodded. "How often wit has exulted in the eternal infamy of his antagonists, and dogmatism has delighted in the gradual advances of his authority, the immutability of his decrees, and the perpetuity of his power."

"What a mouthful!" Ann said. "You're too harsh. Not all writers are vain or vindictive or power mad. For example, vanity didn't motivate the men who wrote and illustrated this book, and it's one of the wittiest books I know." She handed him *Winnie the Pooh.*

Sam turned the pages, his lips pursed. He leaned close to inspect an illustration of Eeyore's house and flipped back to the beginning of the chapter in which Eeyore's house disappears when Pooh, a bear of very little brain, mistakes it for a pile of sticks. Pooh rebuilds it without Eeyore realizing what happened. Sam read and looked up from the book, his eyes twinkling. "To be sure there is wisdom here." He continued reading.

"Look at the illustrations," she said as Sam finished the chapter.

"As good as Hogarth's," he agreed.

"Were they drawn out of vanity?" Ann shook her head. "No. Kids love them. The illustrator, Ernest Shepherd, lived through the horrors of the First World War. Perhaps because of that, he delighted in small, human things like Eeyore's tail and Roo's nose."

Sam pointed to a picture of the Hundred Acre Wood. "Here is an ideal world, a peaceable kingdom."

"True. Today, parents wouldn't let a child wander in the woods, but children still enjoy Christopher Robin's rambles."

"Do they? The words are oftentimes difficult."

Ann had wondered about that. Was the book aimed at children? Did people have to experience war and violence to appreciate the bear's gentle bumbling? "Maybe, but my speech is about pictures, not words. Everyone, even young children, can appreciate pictures. Maybe the pictures will inspire them to read the text. As a librarian, my mission is to publicize books. Even yours, you vain, dogmatic, power-mad author."

He laughed.

"It's good to hear someone laugh," she said.

For five days, she'd been alone with Sam. When she arrived home, she explained to the neighbour who looked after the mail and the indoor plants that she got the flu on the boat and had to cut the vacation short. She phoned Olive with the same story, and asked her to babysit so she wouldn't pass her germs on to Amanda. She spoke to Amanda and told her the highlights of the boat trip. Amanda seemed wistful. Ann suggested enrolling her in a summer camp but Amanda refused. "You need to be with other kids," Ann said.

"I like Jen." Her daughter whispered. Jen was Tara's daughter.

Amanda sounded strangely timid. "I'll arrange some playdates and some sleepovers," Ann said. "And when I'm better, we will have some special mother/daughter times together. Go shopping. Have lunch. Talk."

"Okay." Amanda sounded happier.

Ann hung up and went to work with Sam on her speech.

The five days that followed were happy ones. She didn't think about Richard. She didn't think about her weight. She didn't think about his investments. Someone who deliberately withheld information was not worth thinking about.

*****

On the front porch, the August heat was baking the marigolds in their Mexican clay pots. She watered them. The geraniums next to the mailbox were also limp so she gave them a drink too. A neighbour backing his car out of his driveway waved. She waved back. It was Friday morning and he was leaving for work.

"It feels odd, Sam, lazing here. Usually by eight, I'm on my way to the library."

The ghost yawned. "I seldom woke before noon."

She laughed. "Too much partying! I'm amazed you managed to compile a dictionary. Today I need you to use all your literary skills. I have to boil my notes down to create six short, lively biographies. I'm worried. I have two binders full of notes. How will I condense them and give my speech focus?

Sam bent to sniff at a mauve petunia. "You can learn much from the study of people's lives. Each has its share of tragedy."

"I hadn't thought of focussing on tragedy but audiences love disasters."

In the kitchen, she scanned her notes for tragedies. "You're right, Sam. Arthur Rackham had his share of trouble. He made tons of money, but money couldn't help his invalid wife. And success cramped his creativity. He wanted to paint serious portraits, but he felt driven to please the public, even when he was dying. On his deathbed, he completed the drawings for *The Wind in the Willows*. Should I really emphasize all that? Wouldn't it be depressing?"

Sam shook his head. "Show the dark side. If nothing but the bright side of characters should be shown, we should sit down in despondency, and think it utterly impossible to imitate them in *anything.*"

She grinned. "And that would be *really* depressing. But my listeners will want something light too. The slides will provide relief. They'll show these artists' talent. They'll have nostalgic appeal, reminding the librarians of their own childhoods and the books they loved. They'll depict worlds that were pastoral paradises, free of environmental hazards, free of conflict and divorce. Unreal worlds." Tears welled up and she ducked her head so Sam wouldn't see. She'd better avoid thinking about marriage or she'd never finish.

In search of something happier, she flipped through *Winnie the Pooh.* "Ernest Shepherd's drawings bring out Pooh's loveable qualities. Shepherd liked people, and got along well with A.A, Milne, the reclusive author of the book. Amanda loved this book but never copied these drawings. Funny, because as a toddler, she loved to draw animals..."

She skimmed through the book. "I'll emphasize this story's environmental theme. Pooh destroys Eeyore's house by mistake then goes to all kinds of trouble to build him a new one. Such a simple story, but it could be a parable about environmental destruction. The author doesn't harp on it and Shepherd makes it comic, but the story is both comic and tragic, depending on your point of view."

"Like marriage," Sam said.

Her marriage.

Richard would be in the Gulf Islands preparing to return the boat to Richmond. He'd be home in two days, and Ann was still angry. He'd be angry too. What effect would their anger have on Amanda? If the girl's parents could not make peace, her world would be ruined, the house of sticks would be scattered.

Every event had a tragic and comic aspect. When things went wrong on the boat, Cindy and Tom laughed. Richard didn't. He kept playing the perfectionist. In fact, Ann half expected to receive a cell phone call from him and a lecture about deserting the ship.

But he didn't call.

*****

That night, she couldn't sleep. She turned on the bedside lamp. On her night table, the dolphin ornament caught the light. Seven years ago Richard gave her that ornament. She had wrecked that evening.

Instead of accepting the gift gracefully and enjoying the music of the mariachi band, Ann had ranted about the female farm-worker, the one Richard had wanted to photograph. The woman was harvesting grain and looked lovely in a red dress, her baby secured in a sash. After two margaritas, Ann speculated that the woman's husband probably visited a taverna every night while she babysat at home. Ann gestured recklessly with her glass. Tequila bathed the table.

Richard wiped up the spill. He slung the towel over his muscular shoulders and grinned. "Luckily the kids work too," he joked. He leaned back in his wicker chair and squinted at the sky. "Cozumel was a good choice for a holiday. The weather couldn't be better."

He pondered taking a year off work to teach forestry in Mexico. They could play tennis and swim. He leaned toward her with enthusiasm for the future, his arms on the scratched Formica table. The dolphin ornament shook. Its facets sent light shimmering over his face.

She interrupted with two objections. One, he'd be teaching men, not women. Two, he assumed she'd quit her job, the job she had struggled to keep through pregnancy. Men always considered their work more important than women's. "Reproduction is work too," she said.

"Hardly," he leered at her.

He found it easy to leave their daughter and their beautiful baby boy. Ann began to cry. Her tears made the dolphins double and waver. Their delicate dorsal fins and hard round bodies were beautiful. The female farmworker was beautiful too and *she* hadn't abandoned her baby.

Richard gestured to the waiter for the bill.

Ann sniffed. "What do men care about the survival of the species?"

He laughed. "Those margaritas pack a wallop don't they? Our species doesn't depend on domestic work anyone can do."

Anyone can do.

"Don't cry, honey," he said. "We're here for a good time."

He asserted with his usual air of authority, that Mexican women could improve their lot, get better jobs, if they didn't move so slowly, get jobs in factories, producing shoes.

For men like Richard.

Away from their kids.

Become pampered and independent "like our women." He cupped the statue of the two arched forms, the larger dolphin leading the way and protecting the smaller.

Pampered.

Ann had returned to work when Edward was just one month old. Richard said they needed cash. Cash for holidays like this Mexican one. Ann pushed back her chair, ready to leave.

He quickly said he appreciated all she had done for him.

For him. Her superior.

The setting sun ignited the ocean waves. They glowed red and black, like coals, and lapped at the shore, shifting the sand, warming the breeze into a dragon's breath.

She gathered up her swim bag and sunglasses. "I'm leaving."

"Don't."

She sat down.

He looked baffled. "I wasn't talking about you, Ann." He took her hand. "I thought you were more intelligent than this."

His first wife had been unintelligent. Ann was the intelligent version. A trainable dolphin.

"Richard, scientists recently discovered dolphins are only trainable up to a point. After that nature takes over." She trotted out statistics about the value of women's work.

Richard interrupted. "I hope one day you'll learn to value my gifts." He looked at her, his eyes dark with pain. "What are we arguing about?"

The breeze from the water was suddenly cold but she had one more point to score. "About values. Is making war more valuable than taking care of children?"

"Yes. Men fight to preserve their homes, their wives and kids."

"We laugh when we see Hitler in old newsreels, he looks so ridiculous, but what about Churchill and Stalin? Does anyone laugh at them? Does anyone laugh at you?"

She grabbed her beach bag from the table and knocked the ornament. It spun round and round. The dolphins turned, and their gold fins sparkled. With mesmerizing rhythm, the dolphins leaped in their amethyst sea—together, graceful and natural, male and female, eternally together.

Richard moved first. As the ornament neared the edge of the table, he reached and with practised reflexes, caught it…

Later that night, she had blamed her outburst on the margaritas and he had forgiven her.

But the margaritas hadn't been to blame. Now, seven years later, she could see her mistake. Until now she had assumed that Richard had changed after Edward died. She had believed that anger at the loss had warped him, the same anger that she lived with—anger at the injustice of the brevity of their son's life, the loss of his future, of their dreams. And that was true. But long before Edward died, Richard had assumed the role of her teacher and leader. On the day he met her, he had remarked how similar their values were. But their values were different. That was the problem.

Had he rescued the dolphin ornament out of love or anger? Ann closed her eyes. *I hope one day you'll learn to value my gifts.* Those words still stung.

My gifts. Was this one a token of love or of subservience?

The sides of the dolphins were smooth glass, the water a rough-cut amethyst. Rough waters the dolphins had to navigate, the larger one taking the lead.

The ornament was beautiful. Once it had been a reminder of how destructive her temper could be. Now she saw its hidden message.

On Sunday morning, Ann made coffee and heated cinnamon buns, and ate a late breakfast on the front porch. After a turbulent sleep, her thoughts were as cloudy as the sky. What had she dreamt? The nightmares were forgotten, but Richard would be home in less than an hour.

The day was cloudy and cool with an autumn chill, a good day for gardening. She finished her coffee. "Sam, I'm too tired to work on my speech. I want to gather blackberries. Richard loves them."

"Excellent idea." Sam lounged on the porch swing. "It's good weather for vegetables, and for the animals who eat those vegetables, and for the animals who eat those animals." He settled himself down for a nap.

"But first I have to water the marigolds." She filled the watering can. The Inca marigolds were like those in Cozumel. That holiday was a surprise gift from Richard. A token of love? His purchase of Fidelity shares another surprise gift? It seemed out of character. But after Edward's death, both of them had become unpredictable. She put the watering can down, and thought about money. Richard handled their finances. He said they couldn't afford the boat trip, but he had lied. Why? Because she wouldn't know the difference. She never examined bank statements, asked questions, asserted herself. At the library she was efficient but at home she was lost.

Sam was snoring. She woke him.

"Sam," she said as she picked berries, "Richard should have told me about those stocks. He may have thought I was too young to understand such things."

Sam was busy eating. The blackberries were ripening one at a time as though doled out by a parsimonious banker. Some were still hard, green nipples. Others were semi-soft and red and bitter. Only the black ones, swollen with juice, were worth eating.

She sampled a couple. They were brimming with moisture, warmed by the sun, and intoxicating as wine. She licked her fingers. "Sam, I need to show him I'm not a child. I need to learn about our finances but I'll try to approach the subject carefully, without blame or anger. I'll tell him I'm glad his investments have paid off. I'll say I'm relieved I don't need to find a permanent job so urgently. Then I'll ask him to show me exactly where he's invested every penny."

The plan sounded harmless. But Richard would be furious about the holiday. Would he even talk to her? Silence was a great weapon against impertinent questions.

The gravel on the driveway crunched. A car was pulling up.

In panic, she hid with Sam in the brambles.

Richard carried two suitcases into the house. He appeared tanned and rested. Maybe he would be lenient.

"Wish me luck," she said to Sam, and followed her husband into the front hall.

When he saw her, he set his suitcases down. His face reddened. "I hope you realize you made a marvellous impression on the Erdmanns. You ruined the holiday, and a damned expensive one it was too." He stomped past her to bring in boxes of food and bedding.

She could imagine the joy with which he had packed the boxes, the delight with which he'd trundled them in a wheelbarrow along the dock and up the ramp to his car.

He piled a box of bedding in the hallway. "Where's Amanda?"

"At your mother's."

"Still?" His frown deepened.

"I told her I had the flu. I told Olive I needed to recover, and asked her to keep Amanda till you returned. We talked about your mother's birthday—it's next week—that's all. Olive and Amanda don't need to know our problems."

"*Your* problems, you mean."

He huffed out to the car again for three more boxes. He set them with marvellous efficiency on the kitchen table. She watched, fascinated by his fury the way a rabbit is hypnotized by a snake rearing to strike. He scraped a box cutter along the side of one box. Packages of crackers and bottles of condiments spilled onto the table. Among the mess were three KitKats. He shoved them in Ann's direction. She cringed.

He picked up the ketchup. "I guess you're pleased," he said as he put it into the fridge. "The boat's barbecue cost six hundred dollars to replace. Just a little extra, and *you* thought it was hilarious when it fell overboard."

The barbecue didn't just *fall*. *She* had stumbled against it and loosened its fittings, but *he* had dislodged it by smashing into the dock. *Let it pass*, she said to herself. *Keep quiet*.

"And the Erdmanns, what about their holiday?" He slammed the fridge door. "Cindy would have liked to have another woman for company but *you* decided to back out. Not that you were great company—overeating, drinking too much, losing your temper over a game of Scrabble."

A dragon breathed down her neck. *The money issue was important*. "It *wasn't* just a game of Scrabble," she blurted out.

Sam looked worried.

Richard was right though about her excessive eating and drinking. He was right about Cindy. He wouldn't admit it but he'd probably missed Ann too, his mate, the woman with whom he had swum once upon a time. Men always masked hurt with anger. Women too, as Sam had pointed out.

She put her hand on his angular shoulder. "I let my temper rule me. I shouldn't have left the boat. And you're right, I do eat and drink too much. I've let myself go. I wouldn't blame you if you want a divorce."

His lips curled, in a smile of satisfaction or of pain. "I haven't mentioned divorce, have I?"

"No."

"What you need to think about is your behaviour."

"Yes."

"Okay," he said.

It was over. So easily. He had forgiven her! She moved to hug him. He moved away. But he had accepted her apology.

There was something else, something else she needed to discuss, but what? Something about his mother? "By the way," Ann said, breathing deeply to restore her composure. "About your mum's birthday. It would be nice to have some of her old friends to tea. After all she'll be seventy-five."

He assessed the proposition. "Yes. Mother would like that."

Sam gave her a thumbs-up signal.

"Afterwards, we could celebrate with a family dinner."

"Fine. Meanwhile, be sure to apologise to Cindy for ruining her holiday." He went to check the telephone answering machine for messages.

She was dismissed.

Oh yes, she remembered now—*it wasn't his mother's birthday—the subject she meant to discuss*, but she was too exhausted to discuss money now.

*****

Richard was called out to Vernon, the next morning and was gone for two weeks. Ann had plenty of time to locate bank statements, and read about budgeting. As she unpacked his suitcase, she said gently, "Your mother loved her birthday present."

A blank look.

"The turquoise jacket," she prompted.

"Oh?" He headed for the shower.

"And her party." She went to the bureau to get photos of the gathering. "Look at these."

He dropped his underwear into the laundry basket.

"Amanda took them," she said to interest him. It was a lie.

"I'll look at them later." He smiled. "Glad the party was a success. Mother deserves it." He shut the glass door to the shower and turned on the water.

End of conversation. He'd missed the party. As far as he was concerned, Ann's contribution had been minimal. He didn't even ask for details. She had planned the party and made it happen but he wasn't interested, and didn't care. Ann marched to the shower stall

Sam stood guard there. "Gratitude is a fruit of great cultivation. You do not find it among gross people."

Gross? Ann smiled. Did he consider Richard gross? No, Sam must be talking about humanity in general. Sam had been at the birthday party. He helped her remember the birthday guests' names, and he breathed patience into her when Richard's mother complained about her son's absence.

"My book club is meeting next Tuesday, Richard" she shouted over the roar of the water. "Cindy will be there, I'll tell her then that I'm sorry about the holiday."

"It's about time," he said from the shower.

She stored his suitcase on the closet shelf. She set out clean underwear and socks for him. She considered what to say about his investments.

He emerged, and quickly grabbed his robe. "By the way," he said, drying his hair, "there's a reception next Saturday night. A launch for the Natural Resources Commission. Wine and cheese at Government House. The appointees to the Commission will be announced. Everyone will be there."

"Wives too?"

"Yes, including Cindy."

"I'll talk to her then," she said.

He examined his wardrobe. While he was away, she had arranged his suit jackets next to shirts in appropriate colours. Would he notice?

"I may buy a new suit," he said. "Something conservative, well cut. Suitable for an appointee."

"I guess we can afford it now," she said with a smile. She pointed to the stockbroker's reports on her night table.

"About those stocks, Ann. I bought them on the advice of our stockbroker. It was no big deal. I thought you checked the monthly statements."

"I do. I didn't see those."

She waited for him to explain, but he said nothing.

She couldn't believe he had hidden them but what else was she to think? Especially when she found records showing that he had withdrawn fifty thousand dollars from his stockbroker account a couple of years ago. Seed money for the stock venture? She could have cross-examined him, but she didn't want another quarrel or another apology. She wanted information. "From now on, I'd like to see the monthly statements. Just in case you kick off, and I'm left a helpless widow."

He smiled. "Hardly likely."

"You never know," she said, only half in jest. He would tell her everything. Or else.

CHAPTER 9: PILLARS OF THE EARTH

Ann had never been inside Government House. She marvelled at the height of the ceiling in the ballroom, and the tall windows. She thrilled to the sound of the bagpipes announcing the arrival of the Premier. Beside the Premier was Lieutenant Governor DeMille. The portly man beamed at his guests. Ann waited with Richard in the receiving line, enjoying the breeze from the windows.

On this September evening, the breeze carried the scent of the roses planted around the vice-regal swimming pool. The view of the ocean was intoxicating too. The Olympic Mountains reared high in the sky, dwarfing everything, the ocean, sailboats, trees and houses. Their snowy peaks had never seemed so clearly etched, their bases so hazy and transparent. A magician might have hung them up in the sky as a mirror to catch the last rays of sun.

Magic permeated the evening. She could sense Richard's excitement. Tonight, he would receive his appointment. He had received the call a few days ago and was ecstatic. His new pin-striped suit showed off his military bearing. As usual, several of the women were eyeing him. Ann didn't look too shabby herself though her outfit was far from military. Her simple, but sensuous, sarong skirt touched the floor. The skirt's orchid batik matched perfectly the blue of her sleeveless blouse. She had owned both for years. Until she lost weight, she wouldn't buy anything new. But she had splurged some of Richard's ill-gotten gains on a new hairdo. Her hair was upswept, with tiny ringlets in front of her ears. A romantic style, the hairdresser said, to go with the skirt. Amanda called the hairdo 'awesome'. Richard hadn't commented. Ann fiddled with the ringlets and wondered if they were too youthful.

A waiter brought champagne in glasses engraved with the provincial crest. The drink was delightfully chilled, perfect. Men in dark suits and women in expensive-looking dresses circulated on the balconies and main floor of the ballroom. Chandeliers lit the gilded ceiling, though their light was un-needed. The glow of the setting sun made everyone look glamorous. An aide announced Ann's name and took her glass from her so she could shake hands with the Premier and the Lieutenant Governor. The aide handed her glass back. Richard ushered her toward a group of politicians talking about forest policy. Ann excused herself, saying she'd be in the pool garden. He gave her an absentminded nod.

She could have gone up to Cindy and Tom. She had seen them in the crowd and waved, but she would need a few glasses of champagne to get up the courage to apologize.

Most of the guests in the pool garden were admiring the view of mountains and ocean, but the flowers in the garden were just as spectacular. Santolina, sun roses and rock roses overhung the low rock wall behind the beds. Shrub roses reached high then tumbled in a mass of blooms. The colours were soft pastels and greys but some lemon yellow dahlias provided a warm accent. Who had planned this romantic Mediterranean garden? Strolling beside the pool, loving the sultry heat, she could have been in Torremolinos or Amalfi. She half expected to hear a mandolin playing.

"Champagne?" a waiter at her elbow suavely replaced her empty glass with a full one.

This was the way life should be. Champagne flowing, civilized men and women and an equally civilized garden with just enough colour to jazz it up. Like her outfit. Its bright blue contrasted with the safe, sober neutrals on the other women. The colour suited her dark hair, but was it too bright? Was her hairstyle too wild? She tugged at a ringlet. Should she have asked the hairdresser to cut her hair into a more disciplined shape?

"Hello. Are you on the Commission?" a burly man in a tuxedo asked. He was bearded, blonde, and his voice was well-modulated with a trace of an English accent.

"No," she replied, "my husband is, or soon will be. He's being appointed tonight." She should make small talk. "Aren't the hors d'oeuvres marvellous?" A tray went by. "Look at those! Cheese straws, olive stuffed sandwiches, even devils on horseback, don't you love that name? Such a yummy combination, bacon and scallops..."

The man smiled. He raided the tray and laid a goodly selection on two paper plates. He wore a wedding ring, she noticed.

She demolished several devils on horseback and licked her fingers. "Victoria is at its finest on occasions like this."

"I'm more impressed by the flowers," he said. "This pool garden's recently been redone. Normally it's off limits to the public, unlike the other gardens here at Government House."

"I didn't know any of these gardens were open."

"They are, from sunup to sunset, every day of the year."

He must be an aide to the Lieutenant Governor.

"I've been admiring the design," she said. "I should come here for ideas for my own garden. I see they don't have brambles like I have."

He laughed. "They have lots," he waved toward the woodland area below the terraces, "down there. Volunteers are clearing them out."

"People volunteer to do that?" Ann laughed.

"If they appreciate Garry Oak meadows." He talked about eco-systems and camas and other native plants. He seemed very knowledgeable.

"You work here?" she asked.

He looked evasive. "No I'm visiting, on holiday from England, but I walk in the gardens."

She snagged a smoked salmon cheese puff off his plate. "Actually, I have Garry Oaks too, not in a meadow though. People think they're ugly trees, but I like their shapes. Rackham would have too."

"Rackham?"

She washed the cheese puff down with champagne, another excellent combination, and waved her empty glass at the woodland. "An artist who drew gnarly trees and gnomes."

"Oh, you mean Arthur Rackham."

She giggled. "He was gnarly himself, a skinny Cockney."

The man glanced at her, and then picked up his empty plate. "That woman on the steps is Joan Greenwood, the president of the garden volunteers. You should ask her about brambles. I'll be back in a moment. With more sandwiches."

She giggled and took another glass of champagne. "I'm sticking to the good stuff."

The Englishman frowned.

"I know you," she said slowly. "You were at Egmont, weren't you? I didn't recognise you all cleaned up."

"Yes, we'll talk about that when I return." He dashed off in the direction of the ballroom.

Where was Richard? She squinted up at the ballroom windows. He was still there, talking to his important friends.

The sun set, and the sky turned a moody blue-green colour, darker at the edges like the inside of an abalone shell. A breeze played with her skirt. A warm breeze. The pool might be warm too. She contemplated the water, tested it with a tentative finger. The water was heated, almost too hot. It was a perfect night for a swim. She slipped off a sandal and dipped her foot in the water.

She should be inside, mingling with the pillars of society. Richard wanted her to. He was probably wondering where she was. And Cindy and Tom were probably with him, waiting for apologies. Ann sighed. She rose, put on her sandal and slogged around the pool and up the steps to the ballroom. A group of people stood at the top of the stairs. Among them were the burly Brit and the demure looking president of the volunteers. Ann waved at her to be friendly, but somehow couldn't phrase a proper question about brambles.

A man stepped from the crowd and blocked her way. "Ann, isn't it?"

"Yes." He was tall, lean, with blue eyes, outstandingly handsome in his tuxedo, a regular Prince Charming, but he had the wrong Cinderella.

Then she recognised him. "The other man from Egmont! What are you doing here?"

"A friend invited me. Anyway, I had to come. All the Government House staff members are here, and I'm the contractor for these gardens. It's an official function. What about you?"

"Same. I didn't know you were officious?" She frowned. That hadn't come out right.

He grinned. "Sometimes. But not when I can help it. Is your husband here?"

"Yes, why?"

"I thought you might be looking for him."

"Why?" Suddenly rebellious, she repeated, "Why?"

"I wouldn't know," he said, his eyebrows raised.

"I'd rather talk to you. You were at Desolation Sound. I went swimming there…It's too bad it all had to end." Her eyes filled with tears.

"End?"

"I had to leave paradise, come back," she waved her glass dramatically, "to this." Champagne sprayed everywhere. She gulped the rest to keep it from spilling.

"I'm taking you to your husband." The blue-eyed Prince Charming put a firm hand on her elbow. "Is he inside the ballroom?"

She shrugged him off. "Did you see Princess Louisa Inlet with all the dripping trees? It's a goddamn tourist trap." She hiccupped.

He smiled. "Wait outside by the pool while I get your husband." He steered her back toward the pool. "Yes, I've seen Princess Louisa Inlet. It's beautiful, rain or shine."

"It's a goddamn tourist trap." She had to convince him. "Fish hate it. The water doesn't flush out. It's only fit for…jellyfish." She hiccupped again. "And for Richard…I should have pushed him in." She giggled. "I should have."

"You need coffee."

"I need…champagne." She beckoned to a waiter.

"No you don't." Prince Charming took the glass from her and waved the waiter off.

"I hate this," she said hiccupping.

"Oh oh!" she said and was sick into a santolina bush. Her senses reeled with the scent of its grey leaves, the slightly musty smell of newly watered earth.

She raised her head. Prince Charming was still there. She hadn't imagined him.

"I don't feel well," she sniffed.

"Stay here," he said. "I'll bring coffee."

"Yes." She subsided on to the rock wall, and then turned abruptly to be sick again. She was disgusting. What noble volunteers would clean up the mess? Perhaps it would fade overnight, blend into the earth. With clammy hands she pulled at the soil, piling it over the evidence.

The smell of coffee on the night air was overpowering. He'd brought some for himself as well.

"Thanks," she said. She took the cup in her dirty hands and stared at it, unsure of her stomach. Her skirt was dripping wet, her sandals too. "I'm awful, aren't I?"

"You drank too much champagne, that's all. Anyone could." His eyes searched the crowd.

"The party was beautiful and I had to spoil it." She hiccupped. "Like Desolation Sound. That beautiful watery world. " Her romantic skirt was soaked with champagne.

"I'll fetch your husband," he said.

"No! Please don't… he'll kill me…"

The man's mouth twisted. "What's his name?"

"Richard, Richard Patterson. Everyone knows Richard. He's tall, important, distinguished. In a cream coloured suit."

"I'll search the ballroom. Don't move."

"I won't. I would rather die than go in there."

He vanished.

She was disappointed in herself. She eyed the shimmering pool. It would make a beautiful final resting-place. She wobbled toward it.

On the other hand, the lawn chairs looked awfully comfortable.

They were. She lay back in one. Above her, stars emerged.

"Secular quests always end in comic disappointment. Haven't you read my *Rasselas*?" Sam heaved his bulk down into the lounge chair beside hers and smiled companionably.

At least *Sam* still liked her. "I'm in rough shape, Sam, like your Prince Rasselas. He should never have left his Happy Valley to seek happiness. I should never have gone to Desolation Sound, or to this reception."

"Happiness is not to be found on earth."

A tear made its way along the bridge of her nose. The pool would be a fitting end for her. Drowned like Ophelia, dying for love.

"On second thought, come with me." Blue eyes had returned. He looked worried. Had he seen her contemplating the pool? Or talking to an invisible Sam?

"Not to the ballroom," she said. "No way."

"Just as far as the steps."

He escorted her as far as the steps to the ballroom, and made her sit on the bottom one. He beckoned to the Brit, whispered something, and the Brit disappeared into the ballroom while he mounted guard over her.

Sam was there too but she couldn't speak to him now, with an onlooker. Anyway, talking was too much trouble. She closed her eyes. Would this dark night ever end?

More whispering. The Englishman had returned.

"Richard will meet us at the car," the handsome gardener said. "Come with me." He helped her to her feet. His hand was firm on her waist as he led her past the pool to a wrought iron gate. He unlatched it and helped her down a short flight of concrete steps, then along a path by a cedar hedge.

"Where did you park?" he asked when they emerged in front of Government House.

The circular driveway was crowded with limousines, and sedans. None looked familiar. Besides, sleep was more important.

"What kind of car?" he asked.

"A Nissan, a station wagon, top of the line."

"What colour?"

She dozed off. He shook her gently. "What colour?"

"Blue."

"Is that it?" He pointed to a vehicle parked under the *porte cochere*.

She pried her eyes open. "Yes. And Richard." Her heart sank.

The light from the lamp in the *porte cochere* glared on Richard's white shirt. He greeted them brusquely. "Thanks for your help. I'm Richard Patterson."

"David MacIntosh. We met at Egmont. I was fishing—"

"-Oh yes," Richard quickly interrupted. "It was kind of you to see my wife to the car."

"Not at all. Wouldn't want her to go missing."

"Not like the barbecue," Ann chortled.

"She ate something that didn't agree with her," David said.

"Sure she did." Richard made no effort to assist her as she teetered toward the car. "They're announcing the appointees to the Commission now. The most important moment of my life, and she decides to be 'ill.'"

David's eyes narrowed. "If you like, I can drive her home so you're not away from your official duties."

Richard considered a moment. "Actually, that would be very convenient. It's not easy to handle her when she's like this."

Ann rallied. "Richard, I didn't mean-"

"Thanks" he said to the gardener. "You've come to our rescue again. If I can ever be of help to you, here's my card."

The gardener looked puzzled. Then he pulled one of his own cards from his pocket. "Here's mine."

Richard was being formal, the way he was when he was angry, but the champagne was at fault.

"Richard," she tried again. "I-"

"Don't. No explanations. You damned near disgraced me in public."

Her mind coiled around apologies and belligerent excuses then relaxed into inarticulate fuzz.

She was in a truck on Foul Bay Road, heading north. She couldn't remember getting into it. Or driving from Government House onto Rockland Avenue, and the other streets.

"I'm sorry," she looked at David. "You probably wanted to stay at the reception too."

"I'd rather drive you home. Are you okay?"

"I should never have drunk that champagne. And my hair." She reached a tentative hand up to push a ringlet from her eyes. The effort made her head swim.

"It looks fine." He turned onto Beach Drive. Richard must have given him directions. "Sometimes, it's better to cut loose. You seemed to be trying too hard to be correct."

"Yes," she closed her eyes. "Ever since Desolation Sound." The terrible disgrace of being drunk there too, of leaving the boat. Of leaving Cindy and Tom too.

"What happened there?"

"Nothing was right. Except the fishing, and the swimming. We lost the barbecue. Then Richard told me he'd been investing our money, and I lost my temper. I left."

"Left? You mean you abandoned ship?"

"Yes. On Quadra Island. Took a cab, then a ferry, then a bus—home."

` He chuckled. "And Richard has been angry ever since?"

"Since? He's never *not* angry."

The gardener was silent, concentrating on the road. "Marriage has many pains, but celibacy has no pleasures."

Sam's words! "A friend of mine said that." She looked around. Her famous friend lay scrunched up in the space behind the seat, sleeping. "What about marriage *and* celibacy?" she asked in a belligerent tone. "There's not much to recommend that."

He sighed. "Why is Richard so angry?"

"If I knew, I'd be a happy woman."

The streets began to be familiar. She pointed out her house. He parked, and offered to escort her inside.

"I can manage," she said. She opened the car door. She felt foolish enough already. If he gave her a friendly hand, she knew she would melt, and he'd despise her for that, and for being drunk. Regretfully she summoned up shreds of dignity. "Thanks for the offer, though," she said with a smile. "It was kind."

*****

"We all make mistakes," Cindy said when Ann phoned the next day.

Ann propped her throbbing head on her arm. "But that was a pretty big mistake, spoiling your holiday."

"Don't worry about it. So long as the fish were biting, Tom was happy. And I had a whole week of relaxing and reading and sunning. The weather was glorious."

Feeling relieved, Ann picked up the List and ticked off the first item: *Apologize to the Erdmanns.*

"Anyway, Ann, I'm more concerned about you, and Richard."

Cindy was sympathetic but her husband headed the Commission. How much should Ann tell her? On the other hand, Cindy was becoming a friend and she had been on the boat and seen plenty. She deserved an explanation. "Cindy, I was angry. That business about the stocks…Richard should have told me. He risked our money on them. He probably would have told me eventually as a surprise. But everything's okay."

Cindy would know this was a lie. Ann decided to confess. "Actually, it's not okay. Cindy, I can't go on like this. I'm not supposed to question him. He treats me like a child." She began to cry. Like a cry baby but she couldn't help it. "That's okay, I mean, I can live with that, but I can't stand his lying."

The phone line was quiet.

Cindy must be appalled. She admired Richard. Everyone did. And pitied him for having a bad-tempered wife, a wife so disloyal and stupid that she criticized him. Calling him a liar was stupid. Who would give a liar a position on a government commission? Ann had just killed Richard's career. "I shouldn't have said that," she added quickly. "Please, Cindy, don't repeat it to Tom."

"I won't of course."

The older woman sounded tired. Political wives never revealed their hurts.

"Ann, I can understand why you're angry but what do you intend to do about it?"

"Do?" Should she tell Cindy about the List? Ann cleared her throat. "I'll do what I should have done: I'll read bank statements, stockbroker's reports, find out where our money is going."

"Right. Tell Richard that."

"He says he meant to tell me."

"Maybe. Everyone has secrets."

Secrets.

Did Ann have secrets? None really, except one. Just to think of it made her blush. Seven years ago, she'd danced with a man at a preschool fundraiser—just danced, nothing more—a wonderful man—she was pregnant with Edward. The man had a girlfriend, the supervisor of the preschool. Out of jealousy, Ann had made the woman's life hell. Ann never told Richard—it was too awful.

"Honesty is good for relationships," Cindy said.

At the library, Ann believed in free access to information. But at home? *Why was home different? Because of Edward?* She gripped the phone.

"Ann, honesty can be difficult. Tom once told me there was no hope for us. All our friends were having families but I couldn't get pregnant. I felt I'd stolen from him the one thing he wanted. I couldn't talk about it. He was leaving me. We were growing apart. I realised I had to be honest with him. I told him how I felt and we decided to adopt."

"Maybe Richard wants to talk about Edward," Ann said, "and I haven't given him the opportunity." She said that to be agreeable but didn't really believe it. After her performance at Government House last night, she couldn't imagine Richard wanting to talk about anything except her behaviour.

She looked again at the List. He had left it on the kitchen table, before going to a restaurant for breakfast.

*****

The beat changed and Ann managed to shift her steps to the new pattern, or rather, to an improvised version of it. From far away at the front of the gym, the orders came, mercilessly loud and stern. "Four, three, two, one," the instructor's hand was up, her fingers collapsing as she counted. At 'one' she chopped both hands downwards and the variation she had warned them about began. That is, began if her audience heard the warning. The instructor's headpiece wore a microphone so that her commands could compete with the blaring rock music. At times, they couldn't.

"Fantastic," the leader shouted. "You're doing fine." She smiled at something, maybe at her own prowess, not at the exercisers. Few of them were obeying orders. Three were already at the drinking fountain, not even keeping their feet moving as dropouts were supposed to do.

"Ten minutes left." The instructor's outfit clung to toned buttocks and minimal waist.

Show-off. Who wore spandex these days?

"Grapevine!" Miss Spandex's right hand shot up, her fingers dictating. She swayed her non-existent hips lithely in the dance movement.

Step right, step left, right foot behind, step left. Ann grunted, her feet hidden somewhere below her bust. The others in her row were puffing too. Even Sam. All were older than Ann but no one was as clumsy.

"You're doing great! I wish all my classes were this good."

Sure you do.

Praise inspired the front row keeners to nod at the instructor and form a warm bond. A grey-haired grandma added a few extra twists of her own and a bare-waisted bimbo wove in some bumps and grinds.

Damn it, where was Emily, the usual teacher? This was a substitute and she had it all wrong. Ann would quit if this woman taught another class. Ann didn't need this phoney cheer. Miss Spandex wasn't perfect—she had a measly belly and skinny arms. Didn't she realize that?

"Strong arms!" The instructor's arms pumped imaginary iron, her fists pulled tightly into her chest while her face contorted in a smile.

Among the slackers in the back row, Sam merely stepped side-to-side following the example of two blue haired matrons. Next to him, an expressionless, angular blonde did the minimum. A grim-looking woman checked her watch.

"Smile!" the order came. They smiled.

Thank God there aren't any mirrors, Ann thought. *We'd die laughing.*

She puffed through another twenty lunges. The dreadful circle time came next. Everyone formed a circle and kicked, everyone but Ann. She tapped her feet, pretending she was doing low impact. Half-heartedly, she raised her right leg. It dropped to the ground. She hoisted it again. *Don't quit.*

Sam had given up and was sitting in the bleachers, nodding his head to the music. She thought of joining him, but then remembered Richard's List.

- Aplogize to the Erdmanns
- No more scotch, wine, champagne or beer.
- No more chocolate.
- No more tantrums.
- No more chitchat about books or children at political gatherings.
- No more frumpy clothes like the outfit you wore to Government House.
- No more ice cream.
- No more untidy hair.
- No more bitching about housework.
- No more complaints about your mother-in-law.
- No more book club meetings.

Two weeks ago, he had given the list. Feeling weak, on the morning after the reception, she had agreed to every item, except the last one. "I can't quit the book club…I love it."

"Reading is sedentary," he said. "You need exercise."

"Reading exercises the mind."

"Discipline." He glared like a sergeant.

"Right." She was too hung over to argue.

What had he said to David last night? What had David thought? Luckily she didn't remember. David had been kind to her the same way she was kind to library patrons who came in stinking of booze. Richard was right. And so was Sam. She had to get a grip on her emotions.

Richard stared coldly.

He must care or he wouldn't have made the List. "I can't quit the book club. I've read the September book and besides, I'm hosting the October meeting. Maybe after that I will. You're right. It *is* a waste of time. The book discussions are lame. My friends would rather talk about anything other than books. They're nice people though, Maureen and Tara and Colleen…and Cindy."

"<u>If</u> you make improvements in these other areas, I might concede on this. Have you apologized to Cindy yet?"

"I phoned her this morning."

"So you're ready to sign?"

"Sign?" She was confused.

"At the bottom of the list. I want commitment."

'Kick!" the instructor ordered. Ann raised her leg a couple of inches. She puffed through the kicking routine. The last two weeks had been torture. Every night an exercise class or a walk. In a way it was a relief to have someone else take over her life, try to make her into a respectable member of society—someone bossier, stronger, more energetic, more disciplined.

She attempted another kick. Maureen had lost weight by doing aerobics. It could be done. Richard's List was ridiculous, like a peace treaty with clauses, a guide to perfection. In the old days, he'd never have given her such a list without joking or laughing and hugging her. There'd been no humour or love in his eyes as he handed her the pen. He was ridiculous but if she met the List's conditions, perhaps he'd change too.

Wait till you see *my* list, she almost said, but she took the pen and signed. Nothing on *her* list seemed that important.

Ann's ankles throbbed. The clock on the gym wall moved imperceptibly toward the half-hour. She needed a drink, something strong like whiskey.

Sam joined the circle. His brown shorts were modestly loose-fitting and he kicked with gusto. "I couldn't drink so I drank nothing at all," he whispered.

"But I thought taverns were your favourite hangout. I thought you loved wine."

"I did, for eight years after Tetty died. Then I found I couldn't take a little wine, so I abstained. Abstinence was as easy to me as temperance would have been difficult. Tea became my drink."

She stepped side to side between attempted kicks. "I've noticed."

"I drank thirteen, twenty cups at a time."

She giggled. "You would do well at the book club meetings."

He twirled his fingers in exaggerated imitation of the instructor's counting.

A ringlet fell into her eyes. She stopped moving, pushed it back and secured it with an elastic. Richard said no ringlets. She should wear her hair in a bun or have it cut into a professional looking style.

"Can I interest you in a wig, Madam?" Sam asked as he kicked. He pulled a white woolly mass from a pocket, perched it like a cap on his brown hair, and pirouetted.

She laughed. "That thing looks like a sheepskin."

"Fashion makes sheep of us all. If you like ringlets, wear them. Forget the list."

"I can't forget it. Richard is right. I'm a mess. I saw the photos from the boat trip. I was wearing my new shorts. Ugh. The shorts were too tight, and they were stained. And my face was as podgy as a pudding. No, I need exercise. By Christmas, I'll lose thirty pounds."

Sam cast an appreciative look at her. "No more than ten. Women should be plump. My Tetty was short, but her bosom awakened my amorous propensities."

"Amorous propensities!" she laughed.

The class was doing the Charleston now. A man arched his back dangerously as he stepped and kicked. The instructor should stop him. She should coach everyone individually. But she wouldn't do that. If she paused the routine, even for one second, the fitness illusion would shatter.

"Remember the slogan, 'No Pain, No Gain'?" the instructor shrieked. "We don't believe it anymore. If you feel pain, you should stop, do something else."

Hah. The whole class felt pain. This was a dance of death.

Ann cursed through the weights exercises, and complained through the abdominal exercises. She would have liked to curse the instructor, but she wouldn't. *No more tantrums*, she warned herself as she lay on the floor stretching. She would become a pillar of society.

When she stood up, the room swayed and she almost toppled.

Some pillar.

She righted herself. The class was over. Following Sam's example, she made an elaborate bow to Miss Spandex.

Afterwards, her leg muscles were so sore she used her grocery cart at the supermarket as a walker. When she arrived home, she asked where Amanda was.

"In bed," Richard didn't look up from his newspaper, "asleep."

She had hurried home, but had arrived too late. Recently she had been too busy in the evenings to talk to Amanda. The kid was spending too much time on her own. Ann dumped the groceries on the kitchen table where Richard was reading. "How was dinner?" she asked.

"Great. Chicken and dumplings," he said with a yawn. "Be nice if you'd cook homey meals like that. Maybe you should take a cooking class."

"I'd like to," she said, determined to have a positive attitude, "but I'm out five nights a week now, with exercising and working. Maybe in the spring when the aerobics class ends."

"Do what you like." He returned to his paper.

He seemed annoyed. He'd never complained about her cooking before. As usual, he must be comparing her to Olive. She said lightly, "You and Amanda will become spoiled by eating at your mother's. We can't have that."

"Mother likes to have us."

She had meant it as a joke.

"Ann, don't feel you have to punch a clock here. You don't have to cook every night. Amanda and I can look after ourselves just fine."

She changed the subject. "It's foggy out, isn't it?"

No answer.

She stood on tiptoe to put some Halloween candy on the shelf over the stove. They'd be safe from her there. On impulse she opened the package and withdrew two small chocolate bars. "Want to hear about my exercise class?"

He shrugged. "What's to hear?"

"Not much. There was a new instructor though, not as good as the regular one, and the music was way too loud. I'm getting used to it." She said it all in a rush, knowing he wouldn't respond.

He didn't.

She should eat. It was almost ten o'clock. She took a package of instant noodles and added some chopped chicken to it. Experts said you shouldn't sleep on a full stomach. Hers ached from doing sit ups. The thought of food made her queasy but the new exercise regime was only temporary. By the time of the library conference, she would have lost enough weight to ease up on it.

The List didn't mean he didn't love her. It meant he didn't love her the way she was. She told herself that as she went up to their bedroom and put on her nightgown. It became her slogan. She repeated it that night, and every night, as she lay beside him, sleepless, while he slept.

CHAPTER 10: LOST IN THE FOG

Fog softened the stucco cottage and the oak trees, and gave the scene the pastel fragility of an impressionist painting. The leaves were already falling. David raked them into the pile. He'd been cutting back perennials that had finished blooming, cleaning up the beds. He set a match to the pile and stood back, content to move slowly, glad the fog hid him from his neighbours. Too much had happened recently. To absorb it all, he needed time, and privacy.

The telephone call from England two days ago had changed everything. Gerry's wife had been too upset to say much. A heart attack. Another. It had been expected, but it was still a shock and unbelievable. Two weeks ago Gerry had been at the reception at Government House, laughing and poking fun at the bigwigs, and helping David rescue Ann. Now Gerry was gone, his presence as insubstantial as the sparks flying up from the bonfire.

Despite the damp air, the fire burned. The fog sealed off everything, eliminated all distractions. He might have been on an island, alone with his dog. As kids at Telegraph Cove, he and Gerry used to take the canoe out in fog like this, against parental orders. Damn foolish. He and Gerry knew it, and would hug the shore to get home safely. They always had survived to tell the tale. They had always taken chances. Till now.

Gerry wasn't the cautious type. He had lived bravely. Despite his weak heart, he wanted a last holiday. Thank God, he'd had one.

David's eyes stung, but not from smoke. He wiped them on his sleeve.

Gerry said that when he moved from Canada to England, the thing he missed most was gunkholing. With all Gerry's wealth, that's what meant the most—puttering around in the tiny fishing boat, anchoring wherever he pleased, taking risks. He said he could never have that kind of holiday in civilised Europe, could never have had that freedom. At Desolation Sound, they'd been like kids again, fishing and camping, and talking. There, time had stopped. If there was a deity, He'd smiled on them. That was the way life should be. No clocks, no watches, just nature keeping time.

After the phone call, it would have been nice to talk to someone about his loss, someone not a member of his family. A woman, preferably. But he hadn't called Jenny for months, hadn't wanted to, and there was no one else. So he phoned his landscaping crew and told them, and said he wouldn't be at work for a while.

He considered flying to England for the funeral, but decided against it. He'd already said goodbye to Gerry. Nothing would be more perfect than the memory of the bright October day when he'd driven his friend to the airport. Gerry had looked one last time at him, and given him the high sign. A performer to the end, leaving on an upbeat note.

David sat on the front steps, called his dog, and buried his face in Humphrey's fur.

* * * * *

While Richard patrolled the kitchen, checking food sales slips, inspecting cupboards, Ann cut chicken into bite-sized pieces and tried not to inhale. The chicken flesh was sickly white. Three weeks had passed since The List, three weeks without a candy bar, a drink, or a trip to the ice cream parlour, and now, after a bout of the flu, she didn't crave any of that. She'd lost three pounds, half of what she should have. Richard hadn't noticed. Because she'd been sick, she'd missed two exercise classes. There was a class tonight. She had to go. At the rate she was losing weight, it'd be a year before she could play tennis.

On the other hand, maybe she should skip the aerobics class. The clerks at the library were saying she should let up on the exercise.

Her stomach clenched. She swallowed bile as she piled the chicken pieces onto a plate.

"I can't do it, Richard ... three aerobics classes a week. I'm getting too far behind. The garden's a mess. I haven't finished my speech for the conference. I haven't even read the book for the book club. I want to cut back to two classes a week."

He paused in his investigation of a cupboard. "They say if you don't have time for exercise, you're too busy. Why not drop the book club? Learn some social graces instead."

She gritted her teeth. "I socialise at work *and* at the book club."

He straightened the cereal boxes. "With people who count? "

"Cindy's in the book club."

"*And* Cindy's hosting the next social for the Commission."

Ann could see where this was going. "I might help her," she said loftily, "when I'm feeling better."

"*I* never get sick. You wouldn't either, if you got more fresh air. The garden needs weeding."

She sighed. "I know. Maybe I should hire someone."

Someone like David MacIntosh. She remembered him in his tuxedo at the reception...lean without a pound of excess flesh on him...kind enough to bring her coffee and drive her home....kind enough to take pity on a fat drunk. No, he was the last person she would hire.

Richard was saying something.

"Sorry, I missed that," she said.

He scowled. "I said gardening's good exercise."

"But not intense enough, and I want to lose weight quickly, be trim like you. Maybe I should start jogging with you at lunch time."

He paused in the middle of arranging soup cans and smiled. "Downtown? You'd come all the way downtown on your lunch hour? You couldn't get back in time. Jog around the library parking lot instead."

The library parking lot? Was he kidding? Tears sprang up and she swallowed them. He had all the answers. Like his mother, he always knew best. Was it a genetic trait?

She stirred the albino chicken into the noodles. The steam smelled like plastic. The recipe was a no-fat, no-flavour one from a health food store.

A spasm racked her. She clutched her stomach. A little thing like flu wouldn't stop people like Richard and Olive. They kept their resolutions. They were superhuman.

Sam leaned over the pot of boiling noodles. "Resolutions," he said, grinning. "I have all my life long, been laying abed till noon. Yet I tell all young men, and tell them with great sincerity, that nobody who does not rise early will ever do any good."

She felt better. Sam was fun.

Richard smiled. "It would be nice if you'd offer to help Cindy."

"Help her?"

"With the social."

That wasn't on The List but she considered it. She'd see Cindy at the book club meeting if she wanted to volunteer.

"I'm too busy," she said, and Sam smiled.

*****

Ann stared around Cindy's comfortable and elegant living-room in search of a target. Dieting didn't help her temper, and neither did Richard's suggestion she help Cindy with the Commission's social. Retired people like her hostess had time to volunteer. Ann didn't. So far she had only written up four illustrators—Rackham, Dulac, Shepherd, and Kay Nielsen. Two more to go plus slides to organize, and the speech to compose. The library took up her days and aerobics took up her evenings. She couldn't remember when she and Amanda had last played the fairy game, much less had a girl's night in.

"Ann," Cindy, as hostess, started the discussion, "you've read *Pillars of the Earth*. What did you think of it?"

The other women waited.

Ann picked up the book. On the boat, to be friendly, she'd told Cindy she loved the book. "On one level, I enjoyed it, but it's not the epic it pretends to be. It's a sexist male fantasy."

The book club members looked at one another, and dug frantically into the smoked salmon dip and the cheesecake. *All the lovely forbidden foods.*

Cindy cleared her throat. "I liked the adventure. Follett's books have plots, unlike some we've read."

Ann smiled. "The hero's wife dies in childbirth in the forest, then along comes a convenient nymphet whom he rapes. That's a plot?"

"That's just the opening…to grab your attention. What about the part about the religious orders and the burning of the monastery, and all the details about the monastic rule?"

"Yes," the members chorused.

"What about the insecurity of medieval life, the diseases?" Another woman entered the debate.

Cindy nodded. "And the wonderful description of how the cathedral was built?"

Colleen joined in. "Built step by step over four decades, despite world events like the crusades and famine, Follett did massive research into things like the laws governing licenses to hold markets. Some facts were new to me, like the fact that markets were not considered to be in competition if they were two-thirds of a day's journey apart."

"Forget the facts," Ann said. "This is fiction. What about the dialogue?"

Silence.

Ann continued. "I just about fell off my chair laughing when the heroine was afraid of her brother losing his 'career' as a knight."

"Ann," Colleen's expression was grim, "you never like the books we discuss. Maybe you shouldn't be in this club."

The others looked at Ann.

Her stomach ached as though someone had punched her. She struggled to breathe. These were her friends—Cindy and Tara and Maureen and Colleen. Were they kicking her out?

"Just kidding," Colleen said.

Should she apologise for stating her opinion?

"The next meeting is at your place, Ann," Cindy said smoothly, "so it will be your turn to choose the book—presumably one you like."

What book? What titles had she seen on the library's new fiction shelf? "How about *Possession*?"

Colleen groaned. "That book, I can hardly lift it. Library patrons complain to me all the time about it, how wordy it is, all the Victorian poetry in it..."

"I liked it," Ann said. "If you skip the poetry, it won't be much longer than this." She threw *Pillars of the Earth* onto the coffee table.

"I hate long books," Maureen said. "Librarians like them 'cause you can read on the job."

Ann had known Maureen for years. And her friend still didn't know what librarians did? "We don't read on the job. We read on our own time. It's not part of the job, but we read so we can advise patrons which books are worthwhile."

"Yeah," Colleen said. "Literary books with descriptions about spoons sitting on blue checked tablecloths."

The others laughed. Colleen referred to a dreary novel everyone, except Ann, hated.

"Novels about dysfunctional families," another woman chimed in. "Novels about incest and alcoholism."

"*Possession* isn't about families," Ann said, "it's about love."

More laughter.

She realised what she had said, and blushed.

Colleen made a face. "I'm sick of flavour-of-the-month best-sellers. Just for once I'd like to read a classic. I might not make it to the October meeting."

"Me too," Cindy said. "I'll be busy around that time."

Was Cindy deserting her too?

Cindy shot Ann a pitying look. "I'm organizing the Commission social."

"Richard told me," Ann said. "Do you need help?"

"Sure." Cindy sounded surprised.

Ann was equally dumbfounded. She took a moment to recover, and then offered to lend members her personal copy of *Possession.*

The former scourge of the book club would become its saviour. The former social embarrassment would prop up her husband's career in her spare time, as he requested.

Had she lost her mind? What spare time? Why would she want to become a political wife? She hated political functions. But she had offered. She would have to follow through.

*****

The Commission met over lunch in the dining-room of the Harbour Towers Hotel. Lunch went better than anticipated. Ann had behaved impeccably, and hadn't even spilled the shrimp bisque soup onto the white tablecloth. That would impress the Commissioners. On her right was Brian Hughes, a government fundraiser, on her left, the head of the United Way campaign, across the table, Peter Bryant, chairman of Olson Logging. *Pillars of the earth.*

Peter made the lunchtime conversation pleasant. He had met Ann when he was involved with Amanda's co-op preschool, but he was too much of a gentleman to refer to Ann's behaviour there.

She played with her napkin as the business meeting commenced. Richard chaired it and called for reports. Cindy, as head of the social committee introduced Ann, her latest volunteer, and described arrangements for the Commission social. Ann would look after the liquor, hire a bartender and rent glasses. After a brief discussion of costs, the meeting moved on to other matters and Ann breathed easier. The costs had seemed exorbitant to her.

The view of the harbour was enchanting. Nautical flags flew from the boats. It was a fine October day, the kind where, if you owned a boat, you might think of taking it for a cruise.

During coffee, Brian Hughes, whom she knew slightly, leaned towards her and said, "Say, how's Richard doing with the Maynards?"

"The Maynards?" Ann hadn't heard the name.

"Tribal Logging. You know, the company opposing clear-cut logging. He made a brilliant speech when they staged the rally on the grounds of the Legislature."

"He did?"

Brian chuckled. "That joke about the bicycle was priceless,"

She laughed obediently. "When was that?"

"Two weeks ago."

The chairman of the United Way campaign overheard. "That Richard. You should have heard him last week on the phone to the Premier. He's got guts. Threatened to resign unless the Commission got more funding. He'll go far."

"Oh?"

The men exchanged glances.

"Sorry," she said. "Of course I remember now. Typical Richard, wasn't it?" But her response was feeble. She was obviously out of the loop. And she was furious. Richard did communicate sometimes, but always with enough lack of detail to discourage discussion. With her, he controlled the flow of information. With these people and with his mother, he turned on the tap.

That afternoon, she angrily shovelled weeds from between chrysanthemums in the backyard. "Idiot!" she said to herself. She had taken time off work to attend the meeting. She would take more time off to help with the social. Yet she was a fool who didn't know what her husband was doing on the Commission because he hadn't told her. That rally, that phone call to the Premier, he hadn't mentioned any of it.

"From now on, he'll tell me about his business, as well as about our finances. Or else…"

Sam faded into the oak trees as if terrified.

She carried the shovel and a bucket full of weeds toward the compost heap.

Richard drove up. He stepped from his car but she said nothing.

He gave the bucket a cursory glance and laughed. "A bumper crop of chickweed. When the rainy season starts, it will flourish. You should weed once a week." He turned to inspect the shelves of carefully labelled boxes of fertilizer and seeds in the garage.

Ann stared at his neat, complacent head. "*You* should!" she said, her voice low. "You've got time…." she gasped for breath. "Time to play tennis, to mow your parents' lawn, repair their computer." Her fists curled.

He looked at her as though she'd lost her mind.

Her fists uncurled. *No tantrums.* It was on the List. "Sorry," she moaned. She had to find a more mature response than fury.

"You know I'm travelling to Vernon tomorrow, to Kelowna the next day," he said. "I don't have time for pastoral pleasures."

Pastoral pleasures? Was he kidding? "Okay," she said. "Amanda will help me weed."

"That's better. You'll soon be a gardener like Mother. She hoed potatoes the day she gave birth to me."

"Was she hitched to a plough?"

"Olive was a prairie woman," he said icily. "She knew how to make a home. Still does. And how to keep herself in shape."

His mother never read a book. "And what about these prairie women's minds?"

He raised his eyebrows.

"When they're pulling ploughs and applying fingernail polish, do they read anything, even a newspaper? Do their husbands talk to them about their jobs? About rallies, about phone calls to Premiers?"

His cheeks grew red. "You're being ridiculous."

"*You* are."

He knew what she meant, but pretended he didn't. He was so smug, so imperturbable.

"Oh, I could…" She had to make him pay attention. She raised the shovel. It sailed across the garage, missing his head by inches.

He ducked in time. His lips turned white with rage. "See a counsellor," he said. "You need help."

*****

Fog surrounded the house like white wool. Amanda was in school, and Richard was in Kelowna. Ann sat in the living room. She had helped him pack and had tried to explain her rage. She apologized. She hadn't meant to throw the shovel. It just happened.

Don't bother making excuses, he said.

She had to keep busy. She couldn't sit here all morning, and then sit in the library all afternoon and evening. She would prune Richard's brambles.

Where was Sam? She needed someone to talk to, to tell her she wasn't all bad. How could she have thrown that shovel, she, a librarian, a civilised being? It was a miracle he hadn't been injured. The shovel had struck the potting bench, quivering like a dart in a dartboard. It could so easily have struck his head. *He could have died.*

In the garden, she sniffed back tears as she cut back the branches whose fruit had wizened.

Where was Sam? He must be hiding in the fog. White wisps swirled around the garden, carrying with them the fall scent of smoke. People were burning leaves, cleaning up. It was time she cleaned up her behaviour. If she saw a counsellor, the counsellor would want to know the history of their marriage, would ask when things began to go bad.

Why had she thrown the shovel? Richard had said something. Something about ploughs. No, *she'd* said that, about his mother being hitched to one. He'd said something about women keeping themselves tidy.

It was all such a stupid tangle. Had been like that for years, a sad mess.

She hacked at the brambles. Her hair came unpinned. Black curls hung in her eyes. She pinned them back. Romantic tendrils were dangerous. She'd get her hair cut tomorrow into a crisp, no-nonsense helmet style like Colleen's hair, like the hair of most librarians.

The oaks' soft presences loomed overhead like ghosts. In the distance, the low chords of a foghorn sounded, announcing, along with the fog's cool breath that summer was over.

She had thrown the shovel. Strange she couldn't pinpoint why. In the library, if someone asked for a half-remembered title, she could fill in the blanks with a few keystrokes. But yesterday afternoon was a blank, except the result. Richard's lips white with fury, Richard shaking with rage…

No one to talk to. Even Sam was repulsed by her behaviour.

The native wild roses next to the brambles bore tiny rosehips, fruit too insignificant to justify their existence. Maybe she should get rid of the wild roses as Richard suggested. They were neither useful nor productive. A hundred years ago, settlers had seen them sprawling across green meadows and were reminded of home. But now those settlers slept in the crowded cemetery at St. George's

Church and condos sprawled across the meadows. Cultivated roses had replaced the wild ones.

She put her secateurs into her bucket. She would let the roses live. She would do no more damage. She would make an appointment with a counsellor. She needed protection, against herself.

A bulky figure loomed out of the mist. "Sam!"

He looked sad. "It is better not to quarrel," he said. "Who knows where it will lead?"

"I'm scared," she said.

*****

At aerobics the following night, she pondered the history of the quarrels. When had they begun? When Edward died? No. In Mexico? No. Earlier, when she was pregnant with Edward. Yes. Richard hadn't wanted another child because he wanted freedom. Freedom to play tennis? Freedom to make love to her? Or freedom to leave her? That mess at the co-op pre-school when she'd antagonized everyone, maybe that made him realise he had not married perfection. She'd made up for that by becoming one of the most efficient presidents the co-op ever had. Edward had loved being in the three-year-olds' class there.

The aerobics class ended with stretching and relaxation. Sam lay down on a mat beside hers. Ann stared at the lights on the gym's ceiling.

Everyone always commented on the Amanda's quietness, but also on her stubbornness. The girl was at an awkward age, too young to date, too old for toys. She was docile now, but soon the temper inherited from her mother would emerge, and guarantee an unquiet life.

Tears welled up and rolled down to the mat. She had failed as a wife and as a mother.

The aerobics instructor came up after class and told Ann she was doing better, and not to expect too much from herself. She must have noticed something was wrong. Ann hastily assured her that she enjoyed the classes.

Driving home, Ann lectured herself. *Get a grip on your emotions or you'll end up muttering to yourself like the crazies in the library.*

Sam smiled in sympathy.

Amanda was like Richard. Disciplined, careful, focussed. It was strange—what Ann disliked in Richard, she loved in her child—the discipline in doing homework, the careful setting of the table, the way she could lose herself in homework. But Amanda needed attention.

Did Richard?

And suddenly Ann knew the origin of his coldness, the reason for the quarrels—*the other woman.* Not a real woman, of course, but an *ideal,* a slim, ministering angel of the hearth, someone to cook homey meals, someone to press cooling cloths on Richard's fevered brow, someone who made life easy for everyone. As a child, he'd known cheerful, uncomplicated women like Olive. Small town women like Cindy who'd given up nursing to work part-time for her husband. That's why he loved being in the Interior of British Columbia, the relaxing countrified atmosphere the simple life. Sometimes when he returned from his trips, it was as if he were still gone, as if he wanted to bury himself in the past.

He needed a woman like Cindy who never lost her temper. Cindy had volunteered to host the social even though her split-level house was too small to hold eighty people, let alone dance in. Ann's living-room with its polished oak floor would be perfect for dancing. And Richard would love her to host.

When she arrived home from aerobics, she phoned him. He wasn't in his hotel room, but he returned her call the next morning.

"Richard, I have an idea," she said.

He pointed out that Cindy was good at arranging parties. Ann countered with the fact she'd arranged plenty of parties herself, socials for the co-op pre-school, functions for the library, his mum's birthday celebration. He said this was different, the members of the Commission were used to the best. She promised gourmet quality hors d'oeuvres, said she'd make them ahead of time with Cindy as planned. Amanda would help and serve them at the party.

"You do realise the Minister of Natural Resources will be there," he said. "We have to keep this classy. Some of the forestry reps are loggers. They may not fit in. We'll have to monitor the liquor."

He wasn't really anxious about the loggers' drinking. They'd be on their best behaviour. He was anxious about *her,* after the fiasco at Government House.

"Don't worry," she said. "I won't drink."

She chewed her nails and waited.

"Okay," he said, at last, his voice measured, unenthusiastic. "Will you arrange for music? There'll be dancing."

"I'll discuss it with Cindy."

"Remember to invite the representatives from all the districts and their spouses."

"Cindy has a list."

"Don't expect help from me. I'll be tied up all that day with meetings."

"I won't."

"Well, I'd better get back to work," he said.

Before he could hang up, she asked, "Did you get my message?"

"The hotel said you'd called. My meeting went late last night."

She laughed shakily. "I mean the message I left among your suits." She'd packed for him, matched socks to pants and ties to jackets, enough for three days, and then, before she closed the suitcase, scribbled a message on a piece of paper.

Silence.

"I didn't want you to leave thinking I hated you. I don't. I love you Richard. I know my temper is the problem. I didn't intend to throw that shovel."

More silence.

"Do you love me?" she asked.

"Of course. Did you see the counsellor? Are you working on your anger?"

"Yes. I'm meeting him again today, and on Friday. He thinks you should come too. I'm trying, Richard." Tears threatened. She blinked them back. "I need time. We both need time. Time together." She had an inspiration. "I know! I could take Friday off. Fly to Kelowna for the weekend."

"I'll be in Vernon then, not Kelowna."

"The calendar says you're in Kelowna on Saturday."

"The meeting's been moved. I'll be busy all day. It wouldn't be worth your while."

She couldn't fight it. He obviously didn't want to see her. "Richard, maybe, when this is all over…"

"When what is all over?"

"Oh, you know, the social, the Commission…everything. Maybe then, we should take a few days, go somewhere, Seattle, Oregon…?"

"Maybe."

She said goodbye.

He couldn't have sounded less enthusiastic. He was a spoiled child nursing a grudge. The more she tried to please, the more he sulked. His excuse about moving the meeting was fishy. As if he were hiding something. Another woman? Never. Richard was too proper. Not like her, a woman who with any encouragement would lust after men like Peter Bryant, or David MacIntosh. No, Richard was making excuses because he was angry. And who could blame him? Would anyone want to spend a weekend with a murderess?

He couldn't see that they needed time together. When was the last time they'd been happy? At Desolation Sound, sunning together on the top deck, swimming together at that lake. She smiled as she thought of Richard reaching for her under the cover of the water. Cindy and Tom had been amorous too, Cindy inspired by the two naked men probably. Something in the air at Desolation Sound had encouraged romance. But it was temporary, fleeting.

It was lunchtime, time to leave for work—but she would phone Cindy first, tell her the change in plans, and arrange cooking sessions twice a week. The social was on October 28. The hors d'oeuvres would be amazing. She would whip the house and garden into shape. Impress the Commission, and, two weeks later, the book club. Impress everyone. And Richard?

CHAPTER 11:
A TANGLED GARDEN

Cindy saw the recipe cards in Ann's kitchen, and laughed. "What's this, Ann? A reference library of quiche recipes?"

"They all looked yummy."

"Don't worry. The politicians will be happy with basics like this bacon and onion quiche." She held up a card.

Richard used to appreciate her cooking. Would basics be enough? "I couldn't decide."

Cindy stared, the way she had in Gibson's when Ann pondered which glasses to buy.

"Cindy, I've postponed the quiche decision till our next session. Tonight, we're making crab puffs and Hawaiian chicken roll ups. The first batch of crab puffs is in the oven"

"So that's the delicious smell." Her friend examined the recipe for Hawaiian rollups. "Quite a list of ingredients—cooked chicken too."

Ann pulled Tupperware containers from the fridge. "I shopped last night after work, and prepared the chicken. The crab puffs smell done." She took them from the oven. They were steaming and beautiful. She could have sampled one but didn't. She left them to cool on the counter.

Cindy chopped onions. "You're one busy lady, Ann, volunteering for this and for the librarians' conference too. How's your speech coming? I've forgotten the topic."

"Illustrators of Children's Books at the Turn of the Century." It was a mouthful. "That's the working title. I'll choose something snappier later. The subject is illustrators of famous kids' books, books like *Winnie the Pooh* and *Peter Pan*. Classics never go out of fashion."

Cindy looked up from stirring the filling. "If you say so. My kids liked more modern books, the vocabulary was easier."

"I may give a second talk on modern illustrators." Ann tried to sound confident. "But kids still love the classics. They can guess the words' meanings. At least Amanda can."

What if the conference librarians shared Cindy's opinion? No, they loved nostalgia. They'd beg for a sequel to the speech. Ann could volunteer to deliver a sequel at the national conference in June. Back by popular demand. An expert. Employable even in a job market that favoured computer expertise.

No. Employment didn't matter. Thanks to Richard's profitable investments, she didn't need to work.

"Yes you do." Sam sat on the counter eating a crab puff. "You are an instrument honed to seek out information. What would you do at home?"

Ferret out exotic recipes? Give impressive cocktail parties? Clean immaculate toilets? Ann shuddered. Sam was right.

Cindy flattened bread to encase the rollups. "Have you made this recipe before?"

"No. It looked tasty and it can be frozen. That's the criterion. I bought plastic containers for each hors d'oeuvre." She opened the cupboard to show off the containers, all labelled.

"Wow! What a librarian!"

"I want to do my bit for the Commission."

"Richard must be impressed. What does he think about having the party here?"

"He's happy. And it's fun to do something together."

That wasn't far from the truth. She'd phoned him several times in the Interior. The party was like a magnet between them. Whenever he seemed distant, she only had to mention it and he became attentive. The worst was over. So now it was safe to confide in Cindy. "Richard and I haven't got along well lately. I guess it was obvious on the boat."

"Yes," her friend said warily.

"I'm going to counselling. Richard suggested it."

"Is he going too?"

"No, it's mainly my problem. Things are looking up."

"They are?" Cindy frowned. "Listen, Ann, I never know how much to say…how much advice to give…when it's a friend…I wouldn't want you to get hurt."

"Hurt?" She laughed. "Me?" Richard was the one in danger. Should she tell Cindy about the shovel incident? Joke about it? No, the story wasn't funny yet. It would be, later, once she'd figured how to tell it.

"If you ever need to talk, Ann, I'm here." Cindy squeezed her hand.

Odd. Cindy wasn't the sentimental type. Time to lighten up. Ann giggled. "Stress is good for me. Have you noticed I've lost weight? I'm almost into a size twelve." With hands on hips, she paraded like a model.

Cindy didn't smile. "I never thought you were fat, Ann."

"Of course I'm fat."

Her friend gave her a long look. "You're top heavy, Ann. Most of your weight is in your bust."

"And at my waist." Ann looked down at her apron. "My hips aren't bad. I've been going to aerobics for a month now, Richard's idea, and I've started weight training too, just one circuit, after the aerobics. To get these arms under control."

"Richard's too skinny. Your arms look fine to me. So do your legs."

"They need definition. All that swimming when I was a kid put on blubber." Ann preened, running her hand over her new severe hairdo. "I got my hair cut too."

Cindy was quiet. After some consideration she said, "Ann, I've told you before, you're not fat. It's your clothes."

"My clothes?"

"They're so…librarianish."

"What do you mean, 'librarianish'?" Ann glared.

Her friend laughed. "Sorry. I know how you hate stereotypes. I meant "matronly." All your bulky dresses and blouses, your shoulder pads, your oversized T-shirts and jeans…they make you look like a tank. What you need is a new wardrobe. Want to go shopping? I can help you choose things that fit, things that skim your waist, and show off your legs."

Why not? She could afford it now. No frumpy clothes, Richard's List had decreed.

"Okay. I need something new for the social. Richard expects me to look decent."

Her friend frowned. "Do it for yourself, not him."

"Okay, okay." Cindy was into personal best motivation. Like the trainer at the rec centre who'd cautioned Ann not to overdo exercise. "For myself. But I want to please Richard too. He's travelling so much. He's stressed."

Cindy's eyes were troubled. "You are too."

The plastic containers were beautiful. In one evening, they'd made rollups, crab puffs *and* spanakopita—three hors d'oeuvres! So they were ahead of schedule. Tomorrow they'd make more. The crab puffs were works of art. She would have loved to show them to Richard and Amanda, but Richard was away and Amanda was asleep. Ann ate a stray crumb of puff pastry. Excellent.

Now that Cindy had gone home, the house seemed empty. Sam was dozing beside the television. Ann turned it on and flipped through sitcoms to a political debate on economic cutbacks and the federal deficit. Boring. She needed a diversion from those crab puffs. The grandfather clock in the hall struck ten. She turned off the television and worked on her speech.

At the dining-room table, she read her notes on Beatrix Potter. The nineteenth century artist had lived in a world without computers or economic cutbacks, a world bounded by her garden fence. Lucky lady! Nowadays Beatrix would have had to compete with computer graphics. She would have had to justify to publishers the relevance and marketability of her tale about a harmless rabbit. Her 'job' as an illustrator and writer would have become a hobby, nothing more.

Like my job. What will I do after this job ends? What if I can't find another position? Sam was right: I need to work, but my profession is dying. How useful is it now to know the peculiarities of indexes, and the intricacies of cataloguing and classification? In 1992, people don't care about quality of information, just speed. Soon, the Internet will handle most information needs.

She was staring at her notes on Beatrix Potter instead of distilling them down. *Wake up!* She needed a cup of tea.

In the kitchen, the appetizers were still on the counter. She should put them into the freezer, but they smelled so darn good, especially the rollups and crab puffs. She was starving. She had only had a salad for dinner. She deserved a reward after all her cooking efforts tonight. Besides, she had already lost some weight—enough to get though aerobic classes without pausing. *And no one would see.*

An hour later, the crab puffs were gone. There were a few chicken rollups still left but only because the curry powder was spicy. She needed something to offset the taste of curry, something like dessert. In the freezer was a blackberry pie Richard's mother's favourite. Ann could buy another. And pie deserved a proper accompaniment. A bottle of port was in the liquor cabinet.

The clock struck twelve as she finished the pie. She wiped her fingers on a tea towel, and returned to the fridge. It was overflowing. The food in it needed to be organized.

The clock struck one as she went to bed. She lay there, unable to sleep. Her stomach groaned. Pain radiated in her chest. Her body couldn't take the overload of food.

She rose and went to the washroom, and made herself vomit. It felt wonderful. Then she opened the medicine cabinet and looked for a laxative.

An hour later, she was back in the kitchen, cooking hors d'oeuvres to replace the ones she had eaten.

*****

Autumn rain splattered on the skylight above her desk as the library opened for the day. She tried to project a confident image. She'd weighed herself before work. She hadn't gained an ounce. She had replaced the appetizers. Except for the bags under her eyes, no one would know, not even Richard, about last night's sins. No one would know, but she knew she was slipping, sliding downward. Where would it end?

Sam passed by with an armload of books. "Madam," he said. "Be of good cheer."

"How can I be cheerful when I'm a fallen woman? I can't live up to Richard's expectations or to yours. And this morning I'm in no mood to listen to your noble principles."

"Principles, alas, are not practice." He wagged a finger. "I had a friend, a poet, who was a man of compassion and elegant maxims, but ignoble. We are but human."

"I didn't gain any weight last night but today I feel weak. Will I ever get back to playing tennis? I couldn't even hold a racquet today. I need to change."

"Be as you are." His chin stuck out belligerently.

Ann liked that idea. Twice recently, she had been told she was okay. By him, and yesterday by Cindy who said she was not fat.

"Excuse me," a faded woman approached the reference desk. "Could I see the consumer reports on dishwashers?"

A flurry of library patrons followed. A retired mechanic wanted information on 1982 Oldsmobile hubcaps. A pre-school boy needed his reading logbook stamped. He'd read five whole books in one month and he proudly chose the stamp, an ostrich with its head in a book. An old lady requested information on melanoma. Ann photocopied an article in a medical encyclopaedia. Sam followed her to the photocopier where none of the staff could see them.

Ann smiled. "I feel happier keeping busy, Sam, and feeling useful. In a larger library, I would ask a clerk to do this but I like the routine of photocopying. I hope that old lady is okay. I worry when I see people consulting medical reference books. Self-diagnosis can be dangerous. Even so, information should be available to everyone, including people who don't have computers. That's what libraries are about: access to information." She handed the article to the old woman and her gratitude was reassuring.

Ann settled at her desk with another biography of Beatrix Potter. "I love being a librarian, Sam, though most people would find it boring."

"Like compiling a dictionary," Sam said. "That is generally considered as drudgery, a task that requires neither the light of learning nor the activity of genius. Something to be successfully performed without any higher quality than that of bearing burdens with dull patience, and beating the track of the alphabet with sluggish resolution."

Ann laughed. "Don't pretend you didn't love your work too. You, famous as The Great Lexicographer and as Dictionary Johnson."

He waved aside her praise. "A 'lexicographer' I defined as 'a writer of dictionaries, a harmless drudge.'"

She took notes on Beatrix Potter's ill-fated romance.

He stared at her. "It is wise to be humble, madam. Fame is as fleeting as shadows."

"Maybe, but if this speech makes me famous, I might wind up with a permanent job."

"Excuse me, Ma'am." A workman came up to the desk. "I'm here to fix the air conditioning."

She laughed. It was October. Fixing the air conditioning now was like trying to patch a marriage when the marriage was over.

Not that hers was. And Richard would be home tomorrow night.

*****

He would arrive at ten. He would see the hors d'oeuvres as a sign of her repentance. She would tell him about the counsellor and her plan to become more even tempered. Ann was excited but also nervous and glad to keep busy. Tonight's project was baby quiches and mini pizzas. Cindy sliced onions and mushrooms. Amanda rolled out the dough. Ann fried bacon and tried to think of something other than Richard. "What theme should we have for the decorations at the social?"

"Theme?" Cindy looked blank.

"How about trees?" Amanda said. "A forest. I could make some giant cut-outs."

"And we could decorate the cake with small trees." Ann was excited. The decor would be amazing. She blotted the bacon and began whipping eggs for the quiches.

The phone rang. Amanda answered. She talked for a few minutes, and called her mother. "It's Dad. He won't be home this weekend." She handed over the phone and disappeared into the dining room, obviously disappointed.

Richard had to extend his stay in Vernon. He had to check some research for a gathering the Commission was sponsoring, a mini conference on mountain pine beetles.

He'd been gone four days. Today was Friday and her parents were coming to dinner on Sunday but Ann didn't argue. She talked gaily about appetizers and about her research for her speech. He expressed no interest but she babbled on, pretending, for Cindy's benefit. He said he'd be back on Monday and to say hi to her parents.

Afterwards, she finished beating the eggs, and asked Cindy to chop the bacon.

"Where's the bacon?" Cindy looked in the fridge.

Missing. She'd left the cooked bacon on the counter but it was gone. So was Amanda.

Ann found her daughter in the dining room, drawing a princess and a magic carpet. "What happened to the bacon, Amanda?"

"I wanted some." She looked guilty.

"Half a package?" Ann quivered with rage. "It was for the quiches! You knew that. If you keep on eating this way, you'll be enormous."

Tears fell on the princess.

"I'm telling you this for your own good. You don't want to end up like me."

The girl rose clumsily from the dining table and ran to her room. The door slammed.

Ann returned to the kitchen. Ham could replace the bacon. Why hadn't she thought of that? She wrenched open the fridge door, aware of Cindy's curious eye.

She would have to tell Cindy something, but not everything. "Richard and I quarrelled before he left for Vernon, and now he's decided to stay there a few more days, that's all. Amanda's disappointed. She's not old enough to understand. The counsellor said it's quite natural for spouses to quarrel."

Cindy spread tomato sauce on the pizza dough. "Tom and I quarrelled a lot when we were first married over his fishing. I left him for a month and moved in with my parents. Tom was always planning weekly fishing trips with his buddies. He had to learn that marriage was give and take. Now he takes two fishing trips, one in the fall and one in the spring, and I go on a trip somewhere too."

"You and Tom seem so happy. Richard and I, since we had kids, spend very little time together. Except one trip to Mexico. He's often away on Commission business. But he's never extended his stay. I should be more nurturing."

"You're not his mother."

Ann laughed. "Thank God. She's a saint. But you and Tom present a solid front to the world. We don't."

Cindy's expression was guarded. "With losing your son, you've both been through a lot."

"Yes, that was hard, but I'm over it and so is Richard, and anyway that was five years ago. I can talk about it now. But Richard won't. Any problem seems to set us adrift. His only interest seems to be his work."

Her friend spread sauce on a mini pizza. "Richard's always been ambitious. What's more important to him, his career or you?"

That was hard to answer. The List showed he cared, but now his main concern seemed to be the upcoming social.

"Have you thought of separating?"

"No. We have a religious and social commitment. That's why I'm seeing the counsellor. Richard's changed." *For the worse.* "This morning, the counsellor asked me to think about when we were first married and I remembered the sweater Richard gave me the first Christmas. It was a fisherman knit, an unusual style, like a jacket. Dark green, his favourite colour. He said that wearing it, I looked like an Irish goddess."

"Young love." Cindy's cheeks dimpled.

"I wore that sweater everywhere. Then I became pregnant and forgetful. One day it was gone. I searched the library's Lost and Found. I hunted in every corner of our house, even the crawlspace. I searched his mother's house too. Finally I had to tell him."

"But you'd had the sweater for a few years?"

"Three." Ann sighed. "I'll never forget Richard's face when I told him. It was as if I'd deliberately discarded his offering, and him." Her voice quavered. "Even now, every time I pass a store that sells fisherman knits, I look for one like it."

Cindy put the can of tomato sauce down. "Why? Because you want a similar sweater or because you want to fix your marriage?"

For love, of course. If you define love as obsession, determination, pain.

Ann changed the subject.

*****

On Monday morning, Richard set his suitcase down in the hallway. "I don't want to hear more apologies or any more talk about feelings. I want to see results."

He had cut short her speech about how she felt awful about throwing the shovel, about how she really loved him.

"I'm still going to aerobics," she said. "And I've had my hair cut." She patted her helmet. " And you should see the freezer."

She led him to it. The bulging packages there ignited enthusiasm. Within a couple of hours, he phoned an order in to a butcher for meat for the barbecue, bought a new propane tank, and scrubbed the floor of the back porch, though the party was two and a half weeks away. She was relieved to see his energy directed in a positive way. Perhaps he wasn't holding a grudge. But was Cindy right? Was he more interested in his career than in her?

When he finished the porch, he emptied the pail over the railing, and looked at the garden "I thought you and Amanda were going to tackle this. This is what people will see. Nothing is in bloom except those brown things. And weeds along the driveway. These shrubs!" He pointed to a wilted rhododendron. "Horrible. People won't arrive till six but there'll be enough daylight to see this mess."

Luckily Amanda was at school. She had weeded the driveway, or tried. "I'm sorry." Ann picked up the bucket and the brush. "What with counselling sessions and work and cooking and aerobics, I haven't had time for gardening, or even for Amanda. And it's been raining. Maybe I should hire someone."

"You'd better," Richard said, to her surprise. He opened his wallet and fished through cards. "What about that fellow we met at Egmont? I have his card."

"No! Not him!"

"Why not?"

She grasped for straws. "His firm looks after the grounds at Government House. He probably doesn't do small jobs."

"This is hardly a small job. 'Tangled Gardens Landscaping'," he read from the card and laughed. "That's what you have, a tangled garden. Phone now."

With lead in her heart she said, "Okay."

It was almost noon. The gardener was probably working. She could leave a message and have time to think what to say before when he called back.

David answered after two rings.

"Hello," she said. "This is Ann Patterson."

"Oh yes Ann, how are you?"

He remembered her of course. Who could forget the drunk beside the Lieutenant Governor's swimming pool?

"I wondered," she said, "if your company does residential work."

There was a pause. Had she insulted him by asking?

"Occasionally," he said. "Between larger projects."

She hesitated. Richard motioned for her to hand over the phone. He was used to getting faster results. She hung on to it. "Are you between projects now?"

"In a way. I've been taking some time off."

"But you are working?"

"Depends."

She took a deep breath. "We have a gardening emergency."

"Emergency?"

"We need an instant garden."

He laughed. "It's October. Most gardens are slowing down by now."

"Ours has to be presentable in two and a half weeks. We're having a barbecue and dance. There'll be lots of politicians and bigwigs here." Apropos of nothing she added, "I hope it doesn't rain."

"Stuffed shirts come unglued in rain," he said.

She stifled a laugh. "Do you have time for this? It's not exactly a small job."

"I'll be there tomorrow at four."

*****

Ann hoped Richard would confer with David. Unfortunately, the gardener arrived early.

"Richard's jogging," she said as she ushered David onto the back porch to view the soggy garden. The rain was pounding off the porch railing, but he was dressed for the weather in rubber boots, and a sturdy waterproof vest and jeans. He surveyed the backyard. The hill didn't look as awful in the rain, but wait till he saw it up close. He walked with her up the makeshift path. Sam accompanied them, swinging his walking stick with an energy she'd never seen before.

"Watch your step," she said, following David with an umbrella. "These stones are treacherous. The rain may have undermined them."

He paused by the burgeoning brambles whose wizened fruit even the birds despised. He examined the so-called 'vegetable garden', a forest of stakes bearing minuscule tomatoes and gigantic dead leaves.

"I've tried," she said lamely. "But everything kind of got out of hand."

He knelt by the faded dahlias to examine the soil washing down the terraced ground.

He toured the complete garden in silence. For some reason, she appreciated his silence. She didn't have to apologise any more, just let him appraise things as they were.

Afterward, they returned to the shelter of the porch.

"What kind of garden do you want?" he asked.

"I don't know." She wiped a damp strand of hair from her forehead. "Up till now, I just wanted to keep ahead of the weeds. Something natural, I guess." She thought of Richard. "And showy."

"If you want a show, put in more chrysanthemums. Those bronze ones over there echo the colour of your house."

"Yes…" Ann wasn't convinced. Richard had criticized the mums for being brown.

"But?"

"I like chrysanthemums, but I want more, a design, something visible, and"— she searched for the word—"permanent."

"Perennials and shrubs?"

"Yes, a proper garden."

"For that, you'd have to do major preparations." David pointed up the slope where the rain was forming a waterfall of mud. "The soil's washing out. You need a couple of retaining walls."

"Richard said I could spend what is necessary. He wants the garden made decent."

"Decent?" David's teeth gleamed.

"'It's an embarrassment." After all her labours, it hurt to admit the truth.

"Hardly. You've made a good start. The site's unique with the rock and all. This garden could be spectacular."

Tomato plants straggling, wild grass erupting, brambles reaching upward. What was he thinking? Was he envisioning the Hanging Gardens of Babylon and counting on a wage only King Nebuchadnezzar could afford? After all, he was used to being paid by Government House.

"I want to keep it simple," she said. "Maybe you should just plant some heather on the bank to stop the erosion." It sounded dull to settle for that.

"Like the ones over there?" He pointed to dreary mounds along a neighbour's driveway.

She shuddered. "No. Not in patches, more massed and…wild the way they grow in Scotland." Behind her, Sam who'd been to Scotland nodded agreement. "I want a natural garden. Don't make it too tidy. Leave the wild roses, and some brambles. Under control of course."

He laughed. "Nature's not easy to control."

It had been a long time since she'd made a man laugh. The sound was welcome.

"My husband likes brambles even though they're wild and prickly. Their berries are so juicy. He'll talk to you when he returns. In the meantime, would you like some coffee?"

"Sure. I'll have another look around, then come down for it." He sprinted up the hill. The rain was descending in torrents now, but it didn't seem to bother him.

Had she expressed Richard's wishes? Richard might like globs of heather. She filled the coffee-pot, put out donuts bought especially for the consultation, and thought about the gardens of her neighbours. Many of them had ponds. Would Richard like one? She had always dreamed of the garden as a wild place, a place of flowing water.

She poured coffee for David when he came in and confessed. "What I really want is something different. Some neighbours have ponds."

He studied the view from the dining room window. He paced back and forth then came to a halt. "A waterfall?" he asked, his eyes merry.

"Yes!" Her dream garden had one. "A small one, of course, like the one at Roscoe Bay. I love the sound of water trickling over rocks. So full of life."

"Like the one at Roscoe Bay?" He looked speculatively at her. "Where you swam that night."

And she had hoped to remain businesslike. He was so close, so vibrant and healthy, sitting now across from her. She cleared her throat. "Could the garden be completed in two and a half weeks?"

He thought a moment. "Normally I wouldn't have men to spare, but it's the end of the season. " He squinted as he counted on his fingers. "Three days to clean up the rock, sort out the plantings, get the brambles under control, and see what we have to work with. Three more days and three men to truck in and distribute topsoil. A week to build retaining walls…"

"Retaining walls?" That would be expensive.

"You need one there," he pointed to the ground by the dahlias where erosion was worst, and there." He pointed to the vegetable garden. "Planting will be the easy part. It could be done in a day or two, depending on what you and your husband select. Yes, I can do it, or most of it, in two weeks, but we have to start now. Do you have time this afternoon to visit a nursery?"

She drained her coffee, ignored the plate of donuts, and left a note for Richard to meet them at a garden centre.

Standing between displays of red and yellow chrysanthemums, Ann debated the merits of each. "Red's garish," she told David. Richard hated red.

"But it looks fresh against the browns of fall," David said.

"Yellow fades into brown," she said.

"But it's goes with the bronze mums you already have."

She agreed. Yellow was more natural in the fall than purples and pinks.

Richard frowned as he came up to them. "Didn't you hear me calling?"

"No." Ann said. "I was thinking about colours."

He looked from her to David. "So what's the plan?"

"No plan yet," the gardener extended his hand. "I'm just learning your preferences."

Richard appeared mollified. He turned to Ann. "You look as if you're off to the Hebrides. Dressed fashionably as usual."

For the first time that afternoon, Ann thought of her appearance. She hugged her bulky cable patterned sweater. Richard wore white jogging shorts. "The shadows are cold. I dress for the shade."

Richard's lips curled. "She never cares what she wears."

"Sensible woman." David cleared his throat. "As for your plan, I'll draw up a few ideas and bring them around to you tomorrow. For the work to be completed on time, I'll need your confirmation by Wednesday."

"Then you'd better give the drawings to me. Ann will dither. She's been fooling around in that yard for years."

"Fooling around?" Ann was speechless.

"Some people have no sense of design." Richard confided to the gardener. "You should have seen the place last spring. Red rhododendrons next to yellow. I had to laugh they were so hideous, so she dug them up and transplanted them while they were in bloom. They died of course."

Ann tried to smile, but her cheeks burned. Her husband wasn't an expert landscaper either, and even if he were, he didn't have to behave like this in front of a stranger.

"The garden needs a little help," David said. "The chrysanthemums are lovely."

His smile melted her resentment. She had an ally, a friend. "We want to have more," she said, surprised at how easily the word 'we' came. "Do you like the red or the yellow mums, Richard?"

"Neither. I like the colour white, not that you'd ever notice. White's in good taste."

"We could paint the mums white," she said.

The gardener laughed. Perhaps the world was not a deadly serious place after all.

"She's hopeless," Richard said.

She said brightly, "I don't know why he ever married me."

"A mistake," he said as if he were talking about the weather. "I like dahlias," he told David. "Big ones, dinner-plate size. Nothing prissy. Something to make a splash." He strode to a display of monster dahlias.

"How about a waterfall?" David asked with a smile.

Richard spun around, his face transfigured. "Where?"

"On the rocks, above the dining room window. Something to look at while you're eating or holding cocktail parties. It would suit the site."

"Have you done waterfalls?"

"Several, including one at Government House. I could show you a portfolio of my work."

"Don't bother. The gardens at Government House are superb." His voice trembled with excitement. "A waterfall it is. Just keep the price down."

Like a shark, he manoeuvred between Ann and the gardener and asked about rockery plants. He whisked David off to see the Japanese maples. Ann stared at his departing back, and then at the mums. She said to the sales girl. "I'd like forty mums, mixed colours, red and yellow, please."

She could do what she liked. It was fall, damn it. Bright colours were needed. There were shadows enough ahead.

*****

The following night, the gardener spread the plans on the oak table in the dining room and explained the details to Richard. Ann served coffee and was careful to say nothing. The garden paradise must be Richard's idea. The plans showed two retaining walls edging the grassed area. On the hillside, jagged rocks rimmed the waterfall and edged a small stream above it. A brilliant red Japanese maple overhung the stream, while a star magnolia guarded the pond below the waterfall. Green, leafy water plants hid the mechanisms of the pump and the pipes.

The Commission would be impressed. From the back porch they would see flaming masses of red and gold mums and the glowing crimson maple. The garden would be spectacular, but it would be beautiful in other seasons too. In the spring, the mums' new leaves would provide a green foil for yellow daffodils and white magnolia blossoms. In the winter, Oregon grape and viburnums would brighten the path up to the brambles and wild roses, each of which would have their own, well-defined, sunny corner. David had put a lot of thought into the plans and had understood the need for keeping these things separate.

Richard asked questions, had David substitute plum trees for the crab-apple trees along the driveway, and inquired about prices and schedules. The cost was reasonable. The job would take three weeks.

"But the party's in two," Ann said.

"We'll plant everything, except the driveway before the party," David said. "We work rain or shine. In fact, rain's better for tree planting."

"Good." Richard turned to Ann. "Can you be here at the house tomorrow?"

"It's Thursday, I'm working."

"Can't the precious library operate without you for a few hours? Someone has to be here."

"Why not you?"

"The Commission's meeting."

They stared at one another. Whose career was more important?

"Listen," David said. "It's not a problem. We bring our own tools. If you want, you can leave us a key for the house. We're bonded."

Richard frowned. He didn't usually allow workmen such a free hand.

"If Government House trusts you, I guess we will." Ann smiled and took her husband's hand.

He pulled his hand away. "Yes," he said. "Just make sure to lock the place up when you leave. Ann always forgets."

CHAPTER 12: THE SUNDIAL

It was fun to be able to laugh. Not that David criticized Richard but Richard's opinions about the unlocked house, about her work, and about her taste in colours became hilarious when there was someone to laugh with. Laughter had been missing for too long. It opened up the future. So did the plan for the garden. It was wonderful not to be thinking of past sins, not to be apologising, and to have something new, something creative, to look forward to.

Ann left work early on Thursday, as anxious to see the garden as a mother to see her newborn child. The buzz of chainsaws greeted her. Amanda and Sam waved from the brim of the hill. On it, two men were using chainsaws to clear the brambles from the rock.

"It's a big job," David said. "They've been at it since morning." He paused in double-digging the beds next to the stream. Sweat dampened the back of his shirt though the day was cloudy and windy.

"I didn't think bosses would work that hard."

He shrugged. "It keeps my men motivated. Besides I like the exercise."

The chainsaws ceased. The men piled the debris. Sam walked uphill to inspect the job, easing his ascent with his crooked walking stick.

"You want this compost here?" a man came up with a wheelbarrow.

"Yes."

The man dumped the compost and David spread it on the bed. Four large rhododendrons lay on a tarp beside him. They were leggy and their leaves were yellowish. David gestured to them. "They will appreciate their new home. They haven't had much of a life in that bed under an overhanging roof."

"Look at their roots, mum," Amanda said. "They're the size of my baby finger!"

"Rhodos always have tiny roots," David said. "In transplanting, I try not to injure them. " He picked up a plant and settled it in its new location, heaving the large shrub into place as though it weighed nothing. He watered it, topping up the water as it disappeared into the loosened earth.

"They already look happier," Amanda said when he'd planted all four.

The men were filling the truck with an astonishing amount of garden waste.

"Our fourth truckload," David commented.

Sam picked his way back down the bare hillside.

"Amazing," Ann said Without the brambles, the hill looks different. I never would have guessed the rock could be so attractive. It's like an abstract marble sculpture, so clean and pure. I can see hollows where the stream will flow, and the small indentations alpine plants will love. And the oaks add interest too."

David nodded. "Beautiful."

"Like a fairy tale landscape," Ann agreed.

Amanda said, "Like Arthur Rackham's pictures."

"Who's he?" David asked.

"An awesome artist. His trees look like skeletons. Like those." The girl pointed to the scraggly oak trees.

"Garry Oaks." David said. "People either love them or hate them. Once there were forests of Garry Oaks in Victoria. But most have fallen victim to progress."

"I love them," Ann said, "and the wild roses too." It was wonderful he admired undisciplined nature. "What a transformation after just one day. I can't wait till Richard sees it."

David stared at her, and picked up his shovel. "The day's are getting shorter so I'd better get busy." He went to dig a new bed under the dining-room window.

Ann turned to go into the house with Amanda. She asked him if he'd like something to drink, juice or water.

"No thanks. We have water. And we had a break."

Inside, Amanda had juice, and Ann drank coffee as they examined the landscaping plans. Usually they had cookies too, but today the cookies were forgotten.

*****

The following day at a branch librarians' meeting, Ann couldn't stop smiling. Richard had reviewed the transformation as though he was an expert landscaper, but he pronounced himself satisfied. During dinner, he talked with her about the garden. They had a new interest in common. Ann was so optimistic she planned to shop for dresses with Cindy on the weekend.

At the meeting, Colleen brought the librarians up to date on the conference. It would last three days. November 5 to 8, a Thursday, Friday, and Saturday. Ann would miss the Saturday session because she had only three days of holidays left, one of which would be October 28th, the day of the Commission social.

After the meeting, Colleen pulled a paper from her binder. "I found this, Ann, and wondered if you'd be interested."

It was a drawing by Rackham. Ann had seen it before, but she was pleased by the friendly gesture after Colleen's hostility at the book club. She thanked her friend and said, "About my speech—what do you think, should I call it 'Illustrators of Childhood' or 'Pictures from the Past'?"

Colleen frowned. "'Pictures from the Past' sounds more homey." She closed her binder. "Ann, I don't want to pour cold water on your topic but it isn't exactly trendy. Could you make it more relevant? Maybe psychoanalyze some fairy tales?"

Ann's temper flared. "Trendy? These artists didn't care about trends. Their work is timeless. As for psychology, their drawings have depth. Take Kate Greenaway's pictures of children for example. Kate said herself 'There was always something more—behind and beyond everything.' The great Victorian art critic, John Ruskin, found her pictures erotic."

"Fascinating," the other librarian said, "But…academic."

"Academic?" Ann could hardly speak. Ruskin and Greenaway were famous. Her revelations would rock the audience.

"Yes, academic. Maybe your topic would appeal to special libraries. But in public libraries, the emphasis now is on computers."

"I've worked on this topic for months," Ann spluttered. She struggled to control her temper. "I can't change it."

The other librarian sighed. "Don't take it to heart. It's just my opinion. Look, with this speech, and that political cocktail party and redoing your landscaping, you've got a lot on your plate. And you're having the book club meeting at your place too. Can I help by bringing something like veggies and dip?"

Ann was seething as she drove home. "Colleen's lucky to have a fulltime position," she said to Sam. "She meant well, but she isn't an authority on audience tastes. And she has no clue how much this speech means to me, or how much I've put into it. Trends are fine but there should always be room for tradition."

Sam sighed. "You raise your voice when you should reinforce your argument."

Ann barely listened to him. She was still fuming when she arrived home.

David's crew were dumping compost behind the retaining walls. The walls curved along the contours of the hill and so would the new beds. David himself was planting the new red and yellow chrysanthemums next to the bronze mums by the dining-room window. The colours looked wonderful against the dark compost. Not brown and ugly.

"Hi," Ann said. "The mums look fresh. Are you going to plant those too?" She pointed to flats on the back porch.

"Yes."

"Can I help? I need exercise."

"Sure."

She donned her gardening gloves. She and Sam moved the mums in a wheelbarrow. David tipped the plants carefully out of their containers and placed them in a random pattern on the soil. Even if it rained on the night of the party, the mums would be spectacular.

"You're awfully quiet," he remarked. "A hard day at work?"

"Yes. It's good to be outside." She sniffed the mums. "I love their smell, don't you?"

"Like ginger."

"Like Christmas. If I could afford to plant on a grand scale, the way Gertrude Jekyll did, I'd have a whole border of mums."

"Except in her day, mums were kept in pots, and not used in borders. But I agree. It's fun to think big." He grinned. "You remind me a bit of Jekyll."

"Is that a compliment? She was a frumpy spinster."

"And a rebel. She liked natural gardens. Her contemporaries liked bedding out plants in geometrical designs like circles, ribbons and squares."

"Richard's type of garden."

He laughed.

She blushed. "David, about Gertrude Jekyll, I'm sorry I lost my temper that day at the library."

He looked up from digging, his eyes unperturbed. "I appreciated the effort you made to find that plan."

He had every right to be angry but he wasn't! She should copy that kind of attitude.

He smiled. "I'm finished here so let's have a look at the retaining walls."

She followed Sam up the steps to the lower rock wall. Sam sat under the oak tree next to it while David tested the mortar mixture in the builder's wheelbarrow. Apparently the mixture was okay, because he helped the builder heave a boulder into place so its jagged surface faced upwards.

"Only one more row to go," the builder said.

The seams between the rocks fit so well, they needed very little mortar. "It's like doing a jigsaw puzzle," Ann said, in wonder.

"You get a feel for it," the workman said. "Some people make a hobby of building walls."

The wall further up by the vegetable garden was finished. Its mortar had dried to a putty colour that blended pleasingly with the greys and oranges of the rock. David inspected the side of the wall that would bear the weight of the earth.

"Did you ever get the information on Jekyll?" Ann asked.

"Yes. A couple of weeks later, from the central library."

It was strange he had delayed getting the plan when he had needed it right away.

David examined the structure in silence. He seemed to have forgotten her. A breeze had come up and she shivered. Twilight blurred the garden. She could hardly see Sam. The men were loading the truck getting ready to leave. She should be inside cooking dinner. Amanda would be hungry and Richard would be home soon.

"I couldn't come to the library that day," David said, "because I had to pick Gerry up at the airport."

"I liked Gerry," she said. "I met him at Government House too." On that awful night when she drank too much.

"Did you recognise him?"

"Of course. You and he helped us dock at Egmont, remember?"

"I meant, did you recognise him from television?"

"From television?" The burly man had seemed familiar. The slight English accent. The kind eyes above the beard. She gasped. "He's Gerry DeMille, isn't he? I read something about him recently. The journalist who reported from the Gulf War."

David's mouth became grim. "He always was an adventurer."

Was? As if he'd…"Oh yes! I remember now. The article wasn't a biography, it was an obituary. It said he'd been on holiday in Canada. But he was always clean shaven on television so I didn't…recognize…I'm so sorry…I didn't realise…" Involuntarily she reached out and hugged David.

"It's okay." The gardener's voice was muffled. He patted her on the back as though *she* were the one needing comfort.

She remembered Gerry's laughter echoing across the water at Roscoe Bay, and his kindness at Government House. Just one month ago. It was unbelievable. The loss must be terrible. This explained why David seemed quieter and why he seemed to prefer to work alone rather than with his men. He was in mourning.

"David, you told me you were taking time off work, when I phoned to ask you to do this job. I didn't realize why. I'm sorry."

He cleared his throat. "You didn't know. Life must go on. " He smiled. "We grew up together at Telegraph Cove. Gerry's dad was poor then, working as a logger. Soon afterwards, he bought his first logging operation, and made his first million. Gerry and I were friends for thirty years. I'm glad we managed to get out on the water one last time."

She swallowed hard. "The Lieutenant Governor, Michael DeMille, is, was, Gerry's father?"

"Yes. That fact wasn't mentioned in the newspaper article. Michael hasn't given interviews to the press. He wants to grieve in private. He's devastated. You don't expect to outlive your child. Michael planned to stay in office for four years. Now he's thinking of retiring to his farm."

"The DeMille Estate! That huge property out on the peninsula."

"Michael loves English gardens particularly Jekyll's designs."

"So he hired you," Ann said.

"Not at first. He had a gardener but the project was more than he could handle. I took over last spring. The first garden I planted was the aster garden. You should see it now."

"I'd love to. But I thought you were working on the Spring Garden."

"It's been planted. Michael wants to duplicate all the Munstead Wood gardens."

How many was that, half a dozen? "You don't sound enthusiastic."

David shrugged. "Turning Canadian farmland into a Jekyll garden is a bit like importing London Bridge to Arizona. I try not to be cynical. The project means a lot to Michael. He wants to make the gardens a memorial to Gerry." David's voice became hoarse. He bent to prod the wall, testing its strength. "Gerry didn't even like perennial borders. He called them a smorgasbord of plants, unappetising, with too many colours and too many plants."

Ann laughed. "Unless there's an artist in charge, like Gertrude Jekyll."

Some trucks had left now but two remained. Men were dumping an orange tarp full of brambles into one. David watched them, lost in thought.

"So what kind of garden do you like?" she asked.

"One like this," he said, "growing out of its surroundings and merging with them. A garden that's both wild and controlled, a garden with character." He pointed down the hill. "I love this kind of terrain—rock and water. A balance between what is flowing and reflective and what is unmoving and hard."

"Yin and yang," Ann said. "Solid rocks and flowing water."

"Changing with the light. Shadows can make the rock seem to move, and make the water seem motionless."

Nothing was what it seemed. Light and shadows could change death, love, and hate. She thought of Sam, and his advice to endeavour to be pleased. Attitude was everything.

They walked down to his truck. The steps were dim, as if under water. As if she were swimming to a new world.

David looked at the pile of brambles in the other truck and smiled. "In Chinese, the word for landscaping means 'digging ponds and piling mountains.'

"Pretty rough trade, gardening," Ann said, joking.

"Mountains have meaning to the Chinese. They believe that qi, the vital breath in nature rises in the heart of mountains becomes sluggish as it streams to the sea, but once drawn up to heaven, it swirls in clouds, becomes alive again before it falls as rain on the mountains."

She tried to understand. "So the vital breath of nature never dies, it just takes on different forms."

"Yes." She became conscious of him standing next to her, vital and alive. He noticed her staring but said nothing. In confusion, she said, "Your company's so busy, are you sure you have time for this job?"

"We've finished planting the Spring Garden. Our contracts at the Legislature and at Government House at this time of year involve easy work like raking and mulching. So yes, we can afford the time."

He said goodnight to the men. "That's the second truckload of brambles," he commented as they drove off. "Funny, you kept the brambles."

"We couldn't use herbicides because of the birds, and because…well, to tell you the truth, Richard likes brambles." She was surprised how defensive she suddenly became about Richard. "To smother them would have taken acres of plastic so I've been digging them out."

David smiled. "Talk about hard work!"

"Gardening's good exercise." She couldn't believe she said it. One of Richard's favourite maxims. Maybe yin and yang were reversing.

* * * * *

It fit! Ann whirled in front of the mirror, admiring the subtle colour of the crimson dress, and the way its plunging neckline was hidden by the demure bolero jacket. It was only a size twelve. Strange. She must have lost weight. She hadn't been exercising. Lately, she hadn't had time. She'd been too busy preparing for the social.

"See," Cindy said when Ann emerged from the dressing room. "It's perfect. Not full about the hips, a short waistline. Just what you need. Your legs look great."

"They do?" Ann looked at them. In the mirror, Sam smiled approval.

"And," Cindy said, "that awful haircut has begun to soften."

"Awful?" The bobbed hair had grown in, curling at the ends. "It's lost its shape. I was thinking of getting it cut again for the party."

"Don't. It looks natural, not like a helmet."

Maybe only Richard liked helmets.

* * * * *

The next day was Thanksgiving, but the meal at Olive's was hardly a celebration. Richard was late because he was jogging. Then he talked about dryers and Olive talked about her bridge club. Ann asked polite questions. Amanda was silent.

Ann wished Cindy and Tom hadn't been away that weekend. She could have asked them to dinner, or Tara and Ron, or she could have skipped dinner altogether, and contemplated the changes in the garden. The landscaping was on schedule and Richard was happy to keep his very own bramble patch. She told him about David's friend Gerry. Richard hadn't met the journalist, but offered David his condolences.

In mid meal, Amanda asked to be excused from the table. She went to the kitchen with her sketchbook. Recently the girl had only been interested in the garden, and in drawing. She wasn't watching television, and wasn't doing homework. That was unusual, but maybe she was becoming a teenager. Ann would discuss it with Richard.

Richard skipped pumpkin pie to put a new belt on his mother's dryer.

"You work so hard, dear," his mother called to him while Ann did the dishes.

Amanda's marks at school had begun to slip. There'd been a call from her teacher, Ann hadn't told Richard about. When they arrived home, she followed Richard into the den. "Richard, I wondered if we could talk about Amanda. Her teacher says she's having trouble at school."

"Can't it wait?" He picked up the phone. "I have a client to talk to."

"On Thanksgiving Day?"

He closed the door.

A couple of hours later, he joined her in bed. He was soon asleep. Ann lay stiffly beside him. At two, she was still awake. He was leaving for Vernon tomorrow at nine. There was no time to talk. He could fix dryers, he make phone calls, he could save forests, but he had no time for his daughter's problems. She shook him. "Richard, wake up."

"Wha—" He rolled over, and pulled his pillow over his head.

Furious, she threw the pillow across the room. "Don't you care about Amanda?" she screamed. "She's failing at school."

He propped himself up on one arm. "Do you realise it is three o'clock in the morning?"

"You have to listen to me sometime."

"Not now." He grabbed his pillow and a blanket and left the room.

She could have run after him. In the old days, she would have.

On the breakfast table, was a small tape recorder. Ann turned it on. Richard's voice was emotionless, as dispassionate as a doctor listing symptoms. It repeated the list of grievances, the same ones as before, but with one addition, the fact that her unbecoming, irrational behaviour set a poor example, and was at the root of Amanda's learning problems.

How dare he say that? He hadn't even heard the teacher's remarks.

The recording ended with a warning. "I realise you're busy with the party this week, but I won't be patient forever."

She stared at the revolving spools of tape, waiting for something more, some shred of affection, of hope.

A knock sounded on the door. She switched off the machine and went to answer it.

"Do you mind if I use your phone?" David asked. "The shrubs have arrived from the nursery, but I'd like more Oregon grape."

She ushered him into the hallway, and then backed into the kitchen so he wouldn't see her sleepless eyes.

He began to dial, then looked at her and stopped. "Are you okay?"

"Sure. Just a bad night."

She turned toward the window. Two men were hauling a Japanese maple up the bank, the tree Richard had chosen.

"Four days until the party," she said, "and the garden is looking wonderful."

Richard couldn't take Amanda on the boat trip, Richard didn't want to discuss her schooling, and Richard didn't want to talk, period. Except a monologue on the tape recorder.

"That maple's a gorgeous red," she added. Her voice broke and she hoped David wouldn't notice. She bustled over to fill the coffeemaker. "How about coffee?"

"No, thanks."

"I'm in a bit of a rush," she said, putting energy into her movements as she emptied the dishwasher and put the tape recorder away in the pantry. "I have to get to the library. And a housecleaning service is coming here any minute now. I'm so lucky. Richard said I could hire one. He wants the house, as well as the garden, to look their best. Everything's in great shape."

"And the marriage?"

She closed her eyes. "What marriage?"

David moved swiftly. He held her like a brother, an uncle, offering comfort. His arms were strong, his shirt smelled of the earth, he was reassuring and solid. She leaned against him for only one tempting, satisfying moment.

"I shouldn't have said that," she said, drawing back.

"But it's true?" His voice had certainty.

She nodded. "This morning, at least. We quarrelled last night." She tried to smile. "I need coffee badly. You sure you don't want any?"

"Okay. Sounds good. I've changed my mind."

She filled a cup and held it out. "Thanks for all you're doing. The landscaping, I mean. It's wonderful."

His eyes met hers over the proffered cup. "Could I do more?"

Their hands touched briefly. His blue eyes were dark with an urgency she pretended not to understand.

"No," she said. "I can handle it."

*****

Twirling in front of the bedroom mirror on the day of the social, Ann remembered the electric touch of his fingers, the promise of passion in his eyes, and wished she could tell Richard, make him jealous, and make him take notice of her. Richard was too busy struggling with his tie to comment on her new dress. He was cursing because he'd cut himself shaving. He didn't see that the crimson dress made her skin look flawless, and her eyes huge. In the mirror, her face was pretty in a plump sort of way, her breasts full, her waist…well…at least her legs were okay.

If only David could see her.

This morning he had come for coffee again, and she'd invited him to the party. He said he really didn't like that sort of thing. He asked her to bring her coffee outside and watch the waterfall being turned on.

Water gurgled among rocks and ferns and emerged at the brow of the hill. From there it fell in lovely long cascades, past the oaks. The stream coursed through the rocky crevices as though it had always been there and disappeared into a pool at the bottom of a grassy slope. Sam was so delighted that he dipped his feet into the pond. She could have done the same.

Water pulled the whole design together. The pond reflected the grey sky. The other elements of earth and air and water were there. And fire too, in the crimson leaves and flowers. She loved it all, she said. In fact, she would go shopping right away to buy lights. She would string them among the trees so the guests could admire the landscaping after dark. The evening would be perfect, thanks to David.

The gardener seemed to share her joy. He took her hand, and for a moment she'd thought he was about to kiss her, so she pulled away. Richard didn't deserve such treatment.

In the bedroom mirror, she smoothed the crimson material over her hips. It was nice to be wanted.

Sam looked questioningly at her.

For the party, Sam had also taken pains with his appearance. He wore a new wig. He'd brushed his brown coat and for once had tucked in his shirt. He appeared ten years younger. Almost presentable.

The doorbell rang. "Amanda," she called. They would greet the guests as a family. Amanda wore black and looked very grown up as the members of the Commission poured through the door. The members admired Amanda's green and yellow streamers there and the clever tree motif. They headed for the bar in the kitchen. The day of meetings had made them thirsty. Ann made small talk and tried to remember names, with Richard's help. When everyone had arrived, he took command of the barbecue. Delicious odours of roasting lamb and chicken circulated through the house.

Time for hors d'oeuvres. Amanda and her friend, Jen, sallied forth with them and returned minutes later with empty platters.

"One guy ate five stuffed mushrooms," Jen said and giggled. "Then he ate four more."

Amanda helped herself to two mini-quiches. Her black dress looked less sophisticated with crumbs on it. Ann herself refrained from eating since there would be salads later, and dessert, a huge chocolate cake decorated with the motto of the Commission, "Resources for All." Tom Erdmann saw the cake on the sideboard and asked where Ann bought it. She'd baked it that morning.

Cindy tossed a salad. "The sun has set but people can't tear themselves away from the garden. It's gorgeous. How did you get it done?"

"An excellent gardener. Actually, he's not quite finished. Next month he'll plant trees and shrubs along the driveway."

"Those lights are pretty too."

Richard was smiling. All seventy delegates had come, plus their wives. Ann felt a cold sort of pleasure in the thought that she had at last succeeded in making him happy. He stood at the barbecue, in his element, joking with a group from Vernon. Beside him, more lamb and chicken were marinating, ready to be cooked.

Ann carried a tray of appetisers to the living room where the Minister of Natural Resources was talking to Peter Bryant. The Minister took a couple of Hawaiian rollups and complimented her on the party. Ann commented on the good turnout. Then the Minister moved on, leaving her with Peter Bryant.

She blushed with embarrassment. Would she ever be able to be near Peter, and not recall the co-op pre-school fundraiser and the way, dancing with Peter, she had forgotten her husband? "How's Julie?" she asked. Jealousy clogged her throat.

"Busy. Saltspring Island agrees with her. She would have come tonight, but she's expecting again."

"Again? That makes three!" She tried to hide her dismay. No one had three kids nowadays. She herself had settled for two, and been left with one.

Peter's hair was grey at the temples but the grey emphasized his green eyes and tanned skin. He talked proudly about the pre-school his wife had established near their home on SaltSpring.

Envy struck. Life on SaltSpring...with a loving husband. "That's great," she said. She smiled and was about to move on when Peter stopped her.

"Ann, I thought of calling you a couple of weeks ago. After the Commission lunch meeting. Richard phoned me."

"He did?" Richard knew Peter through business—Peter owned a logging company—so a call wasn't unusual.

Peter seemed to search for words. Finally he said, "He wanted to talk about marriage...."

Ann coloured. Why would Richard talk to a business acquaintance about that?

"He wanted someone to sympathise." Peter's lips drew down in an expression of distaste. "Well, I didn't."

"I don't understand. *Sympathise*?"

"Because I went through a divorce. He thought I'd approve."

"Approve? *Of divorce*?" Numbness crept over her. Richard would never say that word to her, yet he would talk to Peter about it?

Peter's eyes were kind. "Ann, I know what it's like to feel locked out of paradise. I hope you will find happiness."

She tried to laugh. "It's probably just Richard's midlife crisis."

Peter shook his head. He gestured with his glass in the direction of the porch.

By the barbecue, the crowd had thinned, enough to show Richard talking to a young woman, his arm around her waist. Even as Ann watched, the woman reached for Richard's hand and squeezed it. She was a delegate from Vernon. When she'd introduced herself at the door, Ann had been vaguely puzzled. Something about the woman was familiar. She'd seen her before, somewhere.

Sam looked at Ann with sorrowful eyes.

Music began to play, a catchy tune. People in the dining-room began to dance, but Ann stared through the porch doors at the couple by the barbecue.

Open windows…a view of a garden…on a September evening.

At the Government House cocktail party, the woman had been standing with the Minister of Natural Resources by the open window. The setting sun had illuminated her white dress. A slim brunette, tall too. Not unlike Ann herself, as she'd once been. Richard's type.

Ann stumbled to the kitchen to find Cindy.

One look at her, and Cindy said, "So you know."

"Yes." Ann's lips were numb.

Cindy sighed. "I can't believe he invited her here, to your home."

Ann's tongue was a lead weight. Her lips were numb and could hardly form the question. "How long has it been going on?"

Images flickered past like sequences from a silent movie. Images of herself trying to fit into the white shorts…spilling the tray of drinks…images of Richard presenting her with the list…close-ups of herself doing aerobics, throwing the shovel, …a still shot of Richard with his arm around a stranger.

CHAPTER 13: RUMPELSTILTSKIN

Around them, people replenished drinks and helped themselves to salad. The kitchen was no place to talk privately.

"Come with me." Cindy led her into the hallway. "I wondered how much to say. It was difficult to give advice."

"You *knew* all the time? Even before the boat trip?"

"Tom told me." Cindy put a hand on Ann's shoulder. "Among the people on the Commission, it was common knowledge."

"No!"

Images of faces at the lunch meeting. Images of herself perfecting her report to the Commission, requesting time off work to attend the lunch meeting. Images of the members of the book club, of Tara and Maureen and the others.

Ann drew a deep breath. "What about the book club? Do they know too?"

"No, though they suspect something is wrong with your marriage."

"Why?"

"From the way you attacked *The Bridges of Madison County*."

The camera zoomed in for a close-up of the wooden bridge on the book's cover, then out for a full-length image of herself, the High Priestess of Culture, condemning the romance. Funny, when she knew so little about romance.

"I gave that book a hard time." She tried to laugh.

"Not as hard a time as you gave yourself." Cindy's voice broke.

Richard had played on her ignorance and her need to believe in his love.

From the dining room came the sound of laughter and a Latin beat. Richard wouldn't be dancing. He'd be outside alone with the mysterious beauty, flaunting their relationship to his colleagues who knew about it, and to his wife who didn't.

Sam nodded gravely.

On the boat, Sam had said some people escaped into fantasy and others sought out company instead. She picked up his reference to Richard, but not his reference to 'company' assuming it just meant companionship. Yet that was the word he used of his wife Tetty. She was no more 'company' after she took to the bottle.

"Cindy, why didn't you tell me?"

Her friend nodded. "I almost did, after the lunch meeting. I guessed from what you said, he hadn't told you a thing about the Commission. That was unkind. And he expected you to volunteer for it, knowing you would come in contact with people who knew about the affair. That was also unkind, and stupid. It was almost as if he wanted to be found out."

Tonight, if she'd gone out to the porch, she would have stumbled on the truth. Peter Bryant had spared her that. He was a true friend.

A drunken logger stumbled past, looking for the washroom. "What's up?" he said as he passed. Cindy directed him. "Great party," he said, eyeing Ann. "Great hostess." She realised her bolero top had come unbuttoned, exposing cleavage. She buttoned it up.

Images flashed of choosing correct clothes for the lunch meeting. Ann snorted back laughter.

Cindy looked alarmed.

"Cindy, he wasn't the only stupid one. I was so nervous about that lunch meeting, I went shopping to impress his friends, to show them what a gorgeous wife he had. I thought a glimpse of lace under my suit might do the trick. I tried on a ridiculous black lace teddy, squeezed myself into it, and bought it. What a hope! Me, the un-sexy wife!"

"They wouldn't think that."

"Okay, undesirable, unwanted. On the shelf." Ann giggled. "A very librarian place to be."

"How can you laugh?"

"Shock, I guess. So many years, thinking he was angry because of Edward's death, trying to regain his love. How wrong I was. It's as if I'd been watching a film all these years, a film about marriage. Feeling guilty because I'd dragged him to such an annoying movie. Blaming myself. Hoping it would improve." She laughed shakily. "I was so absorbed in blaming myself and in hoping for improvement, I never noticed he'd left the theatre."

Had someone turned up the volume of the Latin music? The beat pounded, bringing memories of Mexico and of arguments there, and arguments since. Arguments over petty things, her habits, always hers, never his.

"All these years, Cindy, I never gave up hope." Ann was crying now.

"I know."

"I thought… if I tried…I could revive his love." She smiled and wiped her eyes with her sleeve. "An impossible task." The List, the self-improvement, the attempt to win love by volunteering her cooking and her home for the social...

"We should get back to the party," she said. "No, actually, I don't feel a bit partyish." She stared at Cindy. "So love was never at stake."

"No."

"I fought for it because I thought he was angry and depressed, but he was guilty and self-indulgent, for years."

"Yes."

A cool breeze ruffled her skirt. The hall door was open. What if she left the house and never came back? No, Amanda would suffer. She would have to take her with her, and that was too much to contemplate.

"Love is so fragile. I tried to love him. But he wanted freedom. It's funny, you can't half-love someone. I remember a poem by John Donne from high school. About the shadow on a sundial, and about love:

'Love is a growing, or full constant Light;

And his first minute, after noon, is night.'"

Cindy leaned against the hall table. "I knew things were beyond hope when I asked Richard about planning another cruise. We were on the top deck of the *Maybelle* in Desolation Sound. It was a sunny morning, and things seemed to be going better between you. He was more relaxed than I'd ever seen him. When I asked him about a cruise, he gave me the strangest look, as though I was crazy. He said you two had separate friends, experiences and futures. When you abandoned ship, I was glad. I thought 'okay, that's it, the end.' But afterwards, you kept saying things were fine. I tried to believe they were, but at the lunch meeting, I realised they never would be."

Ann shut her eyes. "I couldn't admit it, Cindy." So many standards to hold up, so many expectations, and now nothing. "Our life together was hopeless. And I will end it now."

She strode to the back porch. Richard was scraping the grill and the brunette was picking up napkins and paper plates.

Ann glared at Richard. "Please don't bother to tidy up. Just leave, and take your girlfriend with you."

His expression wavered between belligerence and guilt. Like Rumpelstiltskin. She almost laughed.

"Have you gone mad?" he asked.

"I've gone sane. Several of your *friends*," she gave the word sarcastic emphasis, "have enlightened me."

A look of disbelief, then a quick smile. Of amusement? Relief? Guilt? His eyes flitted to his girlfriend. The woman looked ashamed, and he put a protective arm around her. "Ridiculous lies and rumours. Only someone neurotic and jealous would believe them. Marina and I work together."

"Jealous?" Ann asked. "No, I'm not. Neurotic? Yes, to stay with you. If you leave now, I'll behave properly. I realise you want to impress these people so I'll make your excuses. I'll tell them you went upstairs because you weren't well. Now leave."

His face turned red. An explosion was imminent. Ann escaped into the house.

She was chatting in the living room with a delegate from the Kootenays when Richard appeared.

"How dare you order me from my own house?" he hissed.

"I beg your pardon?" She cupped her ear as though she hadn't heard.

The delegate could not hide his amusement.

"I'm staying," Richard's face was white with anger. "Damn it all, this is unfair. It's my house and my party."

"And a very nice party it is," said the Minister who'd obviously overheard only the last words. "We need to cut loose once in a while."

"I'm afraid Richard isn't enjoying the party," Ann said. "Something he ate disagreed. Maybe the dressing on the shrimp salad. He's leaving."

"No I'm not." His face turned purple.

"Don't worry about us," the Minister said with concern. "We'll carry on, but you should lie down, Richard. You don't look at all your usual self. What a shame."

"Isn't it?" Ann oozed sympathy.

The delegate from the Kootenays coughed to disguise a chuckle and Ann had no doubt the story would be around the gathering in minutes.

Richard turned on his heels. With a half wave, he vanished in the direction of the back porch. Presumably to find his girlfriend and leave.

The guests told her the party had been marvellous as they scurried out the door. Peter Bryant volunteered to talk to Richard, but she knew it would do no good. She thanked him. Tom would have stayed to help clean up, but Cindy persuaded him that she and Ann could handle the mess. Amanda looked worried. Ann told her Richard had been called unexpectedly to Vernon. Something about a forest fire. Ann thanked Amanda for helping and sent her to bed.

Three hours later, the house looked as though the party had never happened. Ann put down the vacuum cleaner and dragged herself to the kitchen table, a bottle of Mouton Cadet in hand. "Tell me everything," she said to Cindy.

Marina Wilcox was a wildlife biologist from Vernon. Richard met her five years ago when he was there on a contract. The beauty was divorced with no children and lived in a posh lakeside condo. She and Richard were often seen jogging together and playing tennis. He had stayed at her condo. Colleagues in Vernon assumed they were married.

Ann saw, in retrospect, the road signs of adultery—the regular absences, the shunning, the public goading, the curt exchanges that passed for conversation. After two glasses of Mouton Cadet, she saw the true Richard. A man living a hoax, a man relieved to be found out. A stranger. After five glasses, she constructed a realistic model of herself. A stupid woman who'd accepted that hoax.

Day came. Ann phoned the library and called in sick.

After Amanda left for school, Ann went through Richard's closet and bureau. She took his freshly ironed shirts and tumbled them into a garbage bag, his suits too, and all his carefully sorted socks. Everything he owned, in ten garbage bags. She and Cindy deposited them at the end of the driveway. Then Ann left a message on his office answering machine, telling him to collect the bags or the garbage truck would.

They were gone that night.

*****

Two days later she was still asking herself questions. Why had he brought the woman to the party? To show the world his love for Marina? To end his marriage? Why hadn't he simply asked for a divorce? Because he still loved her in some corner of his heart? Or because he was embarrassed after years of expecting perfection? Why had he expected perfection? Why had she mistaken coldness for warmth? He must have met the woman shortly after Edward died. He must have wanted comfort, comfort his distraught wife couldn't give? Why hadn't he comforted his wife, why hadn't he talked about Edward? Out of fear? The questions led nowhere. No one knew the answers, except Richard, perhaps.

On Halloween day, Ann wore green makeup and a long red wig to work. The branch librarian was delighted with her disguise. Ann couldn't have felt more witchlike. She could hide her anger behind the mask, but how would she manage at the library conference next week, and at the book club the following week?

She pinned decorations of black cats and pumpkin around the story time area in preparation for a visit by a class of fifth graders. She picked up a smiling red devil, stuck a pin into his bottom and fixed him to her broomstick.

Richard was a coward. He hadn't fought fairly. For years he had anaesthetized himself from all her interests—the book club, the library, Amanda—he had divorced his first wife and he knew how to operate on an unwanted marriage. He had prepared like a surgeon for the final revelation, the amputation. But he hadn't prepared for her anger.

"Madam," Sam said, "The cup of life is bitter enough, without squeezing in the hateful rind of resentment."

She ignored the remark and painted her fingernails blood red.

Anger added drama to the Halloween stories. The fifth graders squealed at appropriate moments. Anger added terror to the games. So did darkness. She turned out the light and said, "I found a body in the library, and it had been here for some time."

She passed a grape around. "Here is his eye." *His critical eye.*

She passed spaghetti, "His brains," she said with glee. *The clever brains that never made long-term plans.*

"Marriage has many pains--" Sam whispered.

"Yes," she said, and continued the game.

That night, Amanda was going out trick-or-treating. Ann sat on her bed and described the scary game. Some kids had hollered with fright. Amanda laughed. "I played that game at camp."

Ann clutched the childish Holly Hobbie bedspread. What could she say about Richard? Amanda was still a child. She looked sophisticated in a black dress until she spilled crumbs on it. She thought Halloween was funny. But she was almost at puberty.

The pink bedspread was unsuitable for a girl her age. So was the room's pink and white décor. Richard had vetoed redecorating. Just one of many plans he refused to make.

Sam tapped his foot on the floor. "Lasting dislike is often the consequence of occasional disgust."

"Occasional?" Ann whispered.

"Planet Earth to Mom." Amanda nudged her with a book.

She realised Amanda had been talking.

Amanda held a book out. "Would this picture make a good slide for your talk?"

In black and white silhouette, a king held his daughter at arm's length from a suitor, but the two young people lunged together comically, determined to kiss.

"Not bad," Ann said. The picture illustrated the story of the Golden Goose.

"Who drew it?" Ann asked.

"Arthur Rackham."

"Thanks. Rackham didn't often do silhouettes." She marked the page with a paper clip. "Amanda, I've been thinking you need a new bedspread, and new paint in your room. It's a bit childish."

"What about Dad?" the girl said doubtfully.

"He won't mind."

After Amanda went out with Jen, Ann, still in her witch costume, answered the door. In between trick-or-treaters, she sat with Sam in the living room. She told him her plans to redecorate.

Sam snitched a candy from the bowl on the coffee table. "Our own felicity we make or find."

"I want to make her happy. And make myself happy by sending the decorating bill to Richard." She reached for a Halloween chocolate and knocked the book by Rackham off the coffee table. It fell open at a picture of Rumpelstiltskin. The goblin wore shoes too big for him. When his true nature was revealed, he looked ridiculous as well as angry.

Amanda had never liked *Rumpelstiltskin* because of the threat against the baby. How would she like the news that the straw had not been turned to gold and the King did not love the Queen?

*****

Four days later, shopping with Amanda for a bedspread, Ann waited for a good moment to tell her. Amanda chose a blue and white quilt to go with the new decor. They cleared the bedroom of furniture. Ann left her to box up her books and decorations and went downstairs to the kitchen, where Sam waited to help her rehearse her speech.

The painter was coming tomorrow. So was the conference.

Amanda appeared in the doorway with her old Holly Hobbie bedspread. "I'll store this in the attic."

Ann nodded.

"Can I sleep in the den till Dad comes home?"

"Yes, while he's away."

"Is he away for good?"

"Yes, or back only for brief visits." Ann cleared her throat. "He's living somewhere else."

It was awfully blunt but Amanda didn't need fairytales. Some of her friends had divorced parents. She was old enough to understand.

Awareness broke like a wave over the girl. Her features dissolved, became childlike. "Will you still be my mum?" she asked in a strangled tone.

"Always." Ann hugged her daughter. Richard's daughter.

It was almost eleven when she left Amanda. And now there were only twelve short hours before Ann was to deliver the speech. She poured herself a fourth cup of coffee. She hadn't looked at the notes in weeks. How was she going to pull the facts together, make sense of them? She stared at the bulging file of notes.

"Allow me to look at those, Madam," Sam said.

While he read, Ann paced. A lock of hair fell into her eyes. She brushed it back. Tomorrow she would ask Amanda to glue it into place with hairspray..

Truth is better than a lie, she told herself.

Tomorrow, Olive would be here to direct the painter. Decorating would distract the girl, and so would school. Ann would ask Amanda's teacher to keep an eye on her. She'd be okay.

Divorce wasn't the end of the world, was it?

Sam looked up from under bushy eyebrows. "Madam, you must try to be calm."

"Yes." She mustn't think of anything now, except her speech.

He shuffled the papers. "Life isn't restful. Nature will indeed always operate, human desires will be always ranging; but these motions, though very powerful, are not resistless."

"Maybe."

"Nature may be regulated and desires governed."

"You're right," she said. "I have to get a grip."

He put down the file. "To contend with the predominance of successive passions, to be endangered first by one affection, and then by another, is the condition upon which we are to pass our time." He blew his breath out like a whale pleased with himself for having spouted.

Ann sighed. "Emotional upheaval is becoming a habit with me. But tonight I have to think about these illustrators and their tragedies."

He tapped the sheaf of papers on the table. "Show not just the melodrama, but the moral."

"A moral? Would a modern audience like that?"

"Of course. Show, as I did in my essays on the lives of the poets, how pride in art leads to overconfidence and neglect of art." Sam rose from his chair and loomed over her, seeming to fill the room. "Take as your moral the vanity of human wishes. It's a grand theme. Show fame playing with human lives. For myself as an author, every publication was a new period of time from which some increase or declension of fame was to be reckoned. The gradations of a hero's life are from battle to battle, and of an author's from book to book."

"And a librarian's from job to job?" She smiled.

"Don't jest. All is vanity." He sighed mightily, then sat down and assumed the bent posture of an old man. "You can't depend on fame. Mark what I said in the preface to my dictionary!" He wagged a finger and quoted, "'I have protracted my work till most of those whom I wished to please have sunk into the grave, and success and miscarriage are empty sounds: I therefore dismiss it with frigid tranquillity, having little to fear or hope from censure or from praise."

He paused, obviously expecting applause.

"Frigid tranquillity?" She smiled. "In the end, is that the correct moral attitude? What about joy"

He scowled. "At that time, my wife had died recently." He nosed his way through her notes on Edmund Dulac.

His remarks seemed pointed. "I don't want fame," she protested, "and I'm—"

The phone rang. Richard said hello.

"I'm too busy to talk," she said.

"As usual."

Sarcasm. After seven years of trying to please.

"I want to come by," he said.

Want. No 'please', no 'if it's convenient'. "Sorry. The conference is tomorrow. I'm preparing my speech and trying to deal with Amanda, and everything."

"Something has come up. We need to talk."

"Talk to your girlfriend." She hung up.

Minutes later the phone rang again. On the fourth ring, she answered. "I'm going to unplug the phone, Richard."

Silence.

"Should I call back?" David MacIntosh asked.

"Wha...? Sorry." She attempted to put some warmth into her voice.

"I don't want to interrupt. I just wanted to tell you I'm free to come by a week from Thursday to plant trees."

"Exactly what Richard and I were discussing," she lied. "We're not sure we will go ahead with that after all."

"Oh?" he said, his tone pleasant. "Should I cancel the nursery order then?"

"No...yes...I don't know." This was terrible.

Silence.

"I'll phone you," she hoped she didn't sound as ragged as she felt, "later...next week...when we've decided."

He said goodbye, and she shuddered. She hoped she hadn't been rude. She hoped he would understand.

She went back to her notes. The phone rang again. It had to be Richard.

It was.

"You don't care," he said, his voice muffled, almost unrecognisable, as though he'd been drinking, or was ill.

"You made damned sure of that," she snapped. "I told you I have to work tonight."

"We should reconsider things," he said.

We? "Are you tired of her already?"

"Don't hang up, please. Remember how I've supported you all these years since Edward died."

"You mean how you kept to yourself."

"Kept my worries to myself. For your sake."

It sounded as though he wanted to come home. Had he realised he really cared for her. Did she really care for him?

"Richard, I don't have time tonight to hear your version of our marriage. Why exactly did you call?"

"I've had some news," he said slowly.

"What news?"

"You remember those stocks, the ones I told you about at Desolation Sound?"

She laughed. "The ones I found out about, you mean. The ones you bought with *our* money."

"Yes, well..." His voice trailed off. He cleared his throat. "Today there was a correction in the stock market. They took a dive. Lost eighty percent of their value..."

"You mean we're poor?" Ann's heart thumped. There would be bills for the half-finished landscaping, lawyer's bills, bills for redecorating Amanda's room. Richard didn't even know about those yet.

"Will we have to sell our house?" she asked.

"Not exactly. I have my salary from the Commission. And you have yours—"

"Only till Christmas," she interrupted. "It won't be easy to get another job. You should have thought of that before you rented your love nest."

She hung up. No way could he move back in. She'd sell the house first.

She wiped sweaty palms on her jeans and sat down at the kitchen table. She and Sam wrote out prompt cards, and rehearsed. Her speech would have to be perfect. Her future, and Amanda's, depended on it.

CHAPTER 14: IT'S MIDNIGHT, GOOD MORNING

Amanda waited up to hear about the speech. Ann admired the newly painted bedroom, made hot chocolate for both of them, and told Amanda what she wanted to hear.

The conference room at the Empress Hotel had been a lovely apple green shade like the rooms Amanda admired in books about Buckingham Palace. The fireplace's white mantel overflowed with carved roses. Ann felt like a Queen standing there. Her huge audience of librarians sat on marvellous gilt chairs, eager to learn. They were astounded by her revelations of the sad facts of the illustrators' lives.

Fact: Rackham's painstaking drawings for *Alice in Wonderland* found no favour with his contemporaries. Fact: He never had time to paint serious portraits.

Fact: The illustrator of the Oz books quarrelled with their author. Fact: He suffered when more fashionable Dorothys replaced his podgy version. Fact: His contemporary librarians ridiculed his poster style and banned the Oz books from their libraries. Fact: the artist had become an alcoholic and died alone.

The slides had been a hit, especially Amanda's favourite, Kay Nielsen's picture of the daughter of the King of the Ebony

Islands. The painting showed the white maiden in the arms of a fierce cloud/warrior.

Fact: Neilsen's book had never been published: World War I intervened, and after the war, costs soared, and fantasy became unfashionable.

They also loved the slides of Kate Greenaway's fashionable, doll-like children.

Fact: Those same children aroused the prurient interest of John Ruskin. The famous Victorian critic corresponded for decades with Kate, discussing details of the children's clothing. He was more interested in her creations than in the shy, dowdy spinster.

Amanda snuggled into the hide-a-bed in the den. "Did you read the poem Kate wrote?"

"Yes, after they saw slides of her drawings."

'*A lonely soul, I am ever alone.*
If love ever comes it is quickly gone—
Nothing abides and nothing stays.
I think I have found it, but only to know
How very soon it is all to go.
The sunshine is followed by falling snow.'

Fact: The haunting poem was evidence of another unhappy life.

Fact: Beatrix Potter, the creator of Peter Rabbit, lived a repressed existence as an artist before she escaped in middle age to marriage.

Fact: Ernest Shepherd knew the horrors of World War I before he created the portrait of gentle Winnie the Pooh.

Amanda nodded. "Amazing how joy can come from sadness. What about Edmund Dulac, his picture of the Princess and the Pea?"

Amanda had chosen the slide. Its butterfly colours shone like stained glass and showed the artist's genius for colour and the oriental simplicity of his line drawings.

"They were awestruck," Ann said.

Fact: after World War 1, Dulac's books lost popularity. They were too expensive to produce, and he sought other outlets for his genius.

"I ended my speech with my message," Ann said, "the vanity of human wishes. These illustrators wished for happiness. They worked harder than we can conceive in our age of computer graphics. They achieved fame. But fame often brought misery. Even so, their art, like medieval cathedrals, is distinctive and impossible to imitate. It will bring joy to future generations."

"And to the librarians in your audience?"

"I thought they'd never stop clapping. And afterwards, one showed me an edition of Dulac, she'd treasured since childhood. Seeing that book was the icing on the cake for me, the end of a perfect day."

Amanda went to sleep smiling at her mum's success.

Fact: It was all a fairy tale.

The audience was ten ladies, and one gentleman, all over sixty, not one person with influence, not one with jobs to offer. The librarian who introduced Ann, commiserated with her afterwards, and said it was a pity the *Surfing the Net* workshop ran at the same time.

Sure the oldsters had loved the speech, but they weren't critical. Neither was Sam. He sat in the front row, cheering her on and urging her to smile.

So Ann smiled when a retired librarian said that modern children preferred action books to fairy tales. She smiled when another librarian praised her research as if Ann had consulted primary sources, visited the artists' homes, and read their correspondence. She smiled when the gentleman politely suggested she should give a second lecture on modern illustrators. Maybe, at the national librarians' conference, she boasted, a safe boast, since no one there would attend national conferences. Then a woman said she had read *Winnie the Pooh* to her children, years ago. Her three-year-old son had loved the illustrations. Of course, that was before Disney adapted them but they still enchanted him.

Ann nodded. Long ago, her kids had also sat in a big chair with her, listening as she turned the pages. Edward had a stuffed toy he called Mr. Bear. Amanda and he had had tea parties with Mr. Bear.

She said her son had loved Winnie too, and then she escaped. At the conference cocktail party Sam stayed by her side. She drank sherry, and tried not to mind when librarians did not even pretend interest in her speech. The head of BCLA suggested Ann volunteer as a speaker for local clubs 'desperate for entertainment'. With professional dignity, Ann said she might publish the speech in a library periodical.

As Ann drove out of the conference centre's parking lot into the November rain, she was a wreck.

Sam did his best to console her. "Think of the pyramids, Madam, a monument of the insufficiency of human enjoyments. Think of the Egyptian king, amusing the tediousness of declining life by seeing thousands labouring without end, and one stone, for no purpose, laid upon another."

"I didn't labour for no purpose. I wanted to impress the librarians. What a fool I was. Colleen told me no one would be interested."

"Don't blame yourself for the wild vicissitudes of taste."

"My topic was utterly unfashionable. Is everything I touch going to turn to straw?"

"The misery of man proceeds not from any single crush of overwhelming evil but from small vexations continually repeated"

"*Small!* Easy to say. *You* aren't without a permanent job. *You* aren't going to lose your home!" She manoeuvred out of the hotel parking lot. Rain ricocheted off the hood of the car. Wake from passing cars sprayed the windshield.

"Sam, that woman's remark about *Winnie the Pooh*. She didn't know about Edward obviously."

"Obviously."

She pulled over into a parking space. She couldn't drive. On a rainy November night like this, Edward had looked up at her so trustingly as she hustled him into his snowsuit. There was a school concert and they were late. The school auditorium was packed. They sat in the back row. Her son whimpered and said he couldn't see. He wanted to climb onto her lap. She wouldn't let him. The place was so hot she couldn't bear the idea of holding a child.

The concert began with a procession of children to the stage. Amanda led it. The spotlight was on her. Her hair curled around her shoulders and she looked like an angel. Then she sang. The audience was spellbound. Her singing was so beautiful Ann cried. Amanda hadn't told her she had such an important part.

She finally took Edward on her lap so he could see his sister, but he didn't look, he rested quietly against Ann like a hot damp rag. Obviously, he was ill. Ann told Richard, and they left the concert and rushed their son home to bed.

"Sam, I thought it was just the flu. I went to work the next day. Richard's mum babysat. At four, she phoned me. Edward's fever had spiked and he was screaming.

"I phoned Richard at work. He came home. Edward's skin was blotched with purple. I'll never forget the drive to the hospital that dark, wintry afternoon. Richard raced through red lights."

Traffic lights blinked red yellow and green. She was conscious of Sam sitting beside her silent. How much of this sad story did he already know?

In the dark, his bulky form was barely discernible. His breathing was laboured as though he struggled to control his emotions. After a while, he spoke. "Life is uncertain. Most men find that, of the good or ill which he has experienced, a great part came unexpected, without any visible gradations of approach; that every event has been influenced by causes acting without his intervention."

"Sam, am I never going to be happy again? And what about Richard…he's so unhappy and so lost…"

She mourned for all that was gone, and for all that might have been. It felt good to share with Sam what she couldn't share with anyone else. "That was five years ago, Sam. I've read so much about grieving. Anger is one stage, and I'm stuck in it. C.S. Lewis went beyond that stage to the point where he could say all is well. Sam, I thought the trip to Desolation Sound would unite my family. I thought this speech would guarantee employment. I was wrong."

She wiped her eyes. "But Sam, there have been moments of happiness. I have enjoyed talking with you. And Amanda and I were happy, researching that topic, living in a dream world."

"Remember the hero of my novel?" Sam said gently, "He thought he had the world before him, and so he left the Happy Valley. Such are the effects of visionary schemes. When we first form them we know them to be absurd but familiarize them by degrees, and in time lose sight of their folly."

"Poor Amanda. I encouraged her to copy illustrations. A fat lot of good that will do her in this world of computer graphics. She's the misfit creation of a bookish mother."

"All is not lost," Sam said gravely. "You have learned and studied. "We always rejoice when we learn and grieve when we forget."

"Amanda is waiting up for me. What will I tell her about my speech?"

Sam smiled. "Tell her the truth. It was magnificent. As good as I could have given myself. You pursued perfection. To search is not always to find, and to find is not always to be informed. And thus to pursue perfection is to chase the sun."

"Yes, an impossible dream." She started the car and drove a few blocks to the central library. The building hulked black and unlit over the street. Headlights moved through the downpour in an endless chain of false cheer. Like Sam's wisdom.

"You know my marriage is finished, and so is my career. You know the future. Librarians will become obsolete.

"Who will need our help finding information? Only the cripples of the computer age--people who can't surf the tidal wave of information. Right now, some nerd is probably devising software to answer their most common reference questions.

"You know the future, Sam. You should have told me I couldn't please the librarians and I couldn't please Richard."

"We that live to please must please to live."

"Don't spout nonsense, Sam." She turned to him. "Why did you encourage me to give that speech?"

He didn't answer.

In the back seat, the books she'd used for research fell onto the floor. Stupid books! Stupid Sam! "I'm sick of fairy tales…and tradition and…advice…And you. You never had a child. Your child didn't die. You're useless. I wish you'd get lost."

Sam's features wavered. His shoulders shimmered. His profile flattened into transparency, he wavered and vanished.

He was gone. Her friend, her confidante, her counselor. He had helped her survive the trip to Desolation Sound. He had helped her survive today. He would have helped her survive the weeks ahead.

"Sam, I'm sorry. I didn't mean that. I was angry. I should control my…" How long would he be gone? A few minutes, or forever? Did time matter to ghosts? He couldn't leave like that. He liked her, and she liked him.

Rain formed a curtain on the windshield. Her watch said almost ten. Time to go home.

She opened the back door of the car and chucked the tumbled books into a box. She staggered with it up the library steps, and dumped the books in the book chute. They lumped and bumped their way back to well-deserved oblivion. If only she could clear clutter from her mind as easily. She needed to be realistic, consider her circumstances, and work out a plan for the future. A future without Sam.

But first, she had to tell Amanda a fairy tale about the conference.

*****

Candles lent a festive air to Ann's living room. Like cave dwellers, the book club members exchanged news about the previous night's storm and power outage. Tara had eaten cold potatoes for dinner like her Irish ancestors. A branch from a Garry Oak had damaged Colleen's deck. Native Indians would never camp under oaks, she said, yet municipalities built houses under them.

As Ann poured wine, the conversation turned to Christmas. A cookie-baking session was suggested. Holiday plans were discussed. Ann bustled around as hostess, passing hors d'oeuvres, pouring wine. She had decided to not divulge the fact that Richard was gone. No one there except Cindy knew that.

Ann asked Cindy to open the book discussion.

Cindy held up her copy of *Possession.* "I made it to the end!" she said triumphantly.

"I bet you skipped the poetry?" someone said.

Colleen chuckled. "All those verses about ash trees. Ann probably chose the book because her husband's a forester."

Cindy smiled. "I even liked the poetry," she said bravely. "I also liked the description of Victorian society. How trapped the women were then."

"The heroine was pretty modern," Colleen said, "being bisexual."

"What did you think, Ann?" Cindy asked.

Years seemed to have passed since she read the novel. What was it about? A graveyard search on Halloween, letters between two poets? Ann leafed through the book. "I think it would make a great movie," she said in desperation. "Especially the scene in the graveyard when they dig up the evidence."

"Evidence?" Colleen looked puzzled.

What had they unearthed? Hair...a lock of hair...that was supposed to prove...what?

Tara laughed. "I never thought I'd hear a librarian say a book would make a great movie."

"Well it would," Ann said stodgily. This was terrible. She had never forgotten a plot before. *Don't say anything. Don't reveal your ignorance!* Book reviews would have jogged her memory, but after the conference fiasco, she had lacked the energy to locate reviews. The coffee pot was empty. "I'll make more coffee" she said and escaped.

With shaking hands she measured coffee. She was in no shape to discuss books or anything else. The novel was enormous. Blindly she flipped through the pages. Nothing was familiar. And the book was far too long. To skim through it would require superhuman effort. Like Sam's.

Rain spattered against the kitchen window like a child tapping, seeking entrance. Ann opened the window. "Sam?" she called.

The wind in the oak trees sighed a response. A presence seemed to be hidden in their branches, a shadow, proud and aloof. She stared, trying to make out its shape. Then she remembered the coffeemaker. She'd forgotten to turn it on. Everyone would wonder what was keeping her so long.

She turned it on, and returned to the window. "Sam, please, I'm sorry I was angry. It wasn't your fault that no one wanted to hear about Victorian illustrators. I shouldn't have blamed you. I need your help. I've been thinking so much about Richard and my job I've forgotten everything else, especially this book. Have you by any chance read it?"

"No," a voice behind her said. "And it wouldn't help you if I had."

She whirled around.

Sam's white shirt was undone at the collar and he laughed the way a young man would. "I seldom read a book all the way through."

She was disgusted. "And you called yourself a literary critic?"

He twirled his fingers at her. "The reader may be weary though the critic may commend. That book is good in vain which the reader throws away."

"Be serious. Some difficult books are excellent. Like this one." She showed him the novel. "The author is brilliant."

"He only is the master who keeps the mind in pleasing captivity; whose pages are perused with eagerness, and in hope of new pleasure are perused again; and whose conclusion is perceived with an eye of sorrow, such as the traveller casts upon departing day."

"Exactly. I was sorry to reach the end of this book, and I loved its theme. The author showed that we never know the truth about history. History is irrelevant compared to love." Details of the last scene came back. "Thanks Sam, now I remember enough to bluff my way through the meeting. Come with me."

The coffee was ready. She was as jittery as if she'd drunk six cups of it. In the living room she poured coffee. The others stared.

"You'll be relieved to know I didn't bring reviews tonight. As Samuel Johnson said, 'That book is good in vain which the reader throws away'. I want to hear what *you* thought of the book."

Somebody laughed.

"Awful," Colleen said. "Except for the mystery about the secret love affair. Boring. Far too many literary references. Why on earth did you choose it, Ann?"

"It was beautiful, especially the ending."

The others waited, probably expecting her to hammer home her opinion as usual.

What had happened at the end? A lovers' reunion? A separation?

Sam opened the book at the last page. She read it and her eyes filled.

A reunion and *a separation.*

She remembered now. Two modern researchers find evidence in the poems and letters of a famous Victorian poet that he had an affair with a woman poet. From other sources, they find out he had a daughter. They conclude that he never knew about her and lived a sad and limited existence. But when they exhume his body, they are puzzled to find a lock of hair. They can't explain it. The truth had been lost to history, and they can't explain it. But at the end of the book, the author reveals it.

"Listen to this," she said and read aloud from the final page.

The poet meets a fiery young girl in a field of flowers one hot May morning, and, from her free manner, he knows she is his child. Nature has uncovered the truth and justified his life and his love. He gently asks the child to tell her mother two things—one that he has been looking for her—and two that he won't disturb her. He makes the girl a crown of flowers and in exchange asks for a lock of her hair.

Ann read that far, and began to sob.

Cindy took the book from her and read on. The poet kissed the little girl matter-of-factly, so as not to frighten her, and went on his way. The child met her brothers on the way home. In the rough and tumble, her lovely crown of flowers was broken, and she forgot the message, the message that if it had been delivered would have changed history's view of the poet's life and love.

This torrent of tears was embarrassing. Ann tried to smile and failed.

She felt a comforting hand on her shoulder, Colleen's.

Love was gone. Everyone knew. It was a relief not to have to barricade herself against friends, against herself. In life as in literature, Nature had revealed the truth.

*****

In a chastened mood, Ann walked in the garden. A foghorn sounded as she climbed the steps to Richard's bramble patch.

Last night, she had tried to keep the truth from the book club, and failed.

Fact: Love had gone. Richard had planned his escape for years.

Fact: good friends made life bearable.

Lately, she had neglected her friends for other goals, the garden, the social, the List, the conference. She would arrange outings. Sam could join them.

The storm had wrecked Richard's dahlias. The proud white flowers hung on bent stems and begged to be cut down. Cold had blackened the chrysanthemums' leaves. She took out her secateurs and began chopping them, cutting them off at six inches so they would have some protection against frost and snow.

All was quiet. The spectacular waterfall's pump was turned off because frost threatened. The azaleas bore grey-brown leaves. The brambles' polished stalks formed skeletal cages around the oak trees. The blackberries had wizened.

Amanda loved blackberries. As a child she used to lead her brother up here. They would emerge with purple faces and hands. Amanda loved to tell Ann a riddle.

First I am white as snow

Then as green as grass I grow

Next I am as red as blood

Lastly I'm as black as mud.

"What am I?" Amanda would ask.

'I don't know,' Ann would lie.

"Blackberries!' the child would say, popping a berry into her brother's mouth.

When the two of them weren't outside, they loved to paint at their child-sized easel. Once they had painted a bear together, their arms around each other and Ann had taken a photo of them.

The picture faded and another took its place—three-year-old Edward in the hallway, looking up trustingly, his eyes bright with fever, as she bundled him into his coat.

Ann blew on her fingers to warm them. "How can I leave these memories, Sam? I should have taken more photos. Change, like death, allowed no time to prepare."

Sam stared at the burlap bags below on the back porch. The nursery had delivered the saplings in them yesterday—plum and birch and Saskatoon berry. Ann had forgotten to cancel the order.

"I should plant those," Ann said, "before the weather gets too cold. Richard would be annoyed if I don't." She laughed shakily. "Sorry, I keep forgetting I don't have to please him now. It's a bad habit."

"Possibly," Sam said.

Did Sam agree or disagree? His expression was hard to read. She felt the need to defend Richard. "He bought this house because I loved wild roses." *The old Richard*—an ardent newlywed striding into the house to kiss her, a strong swimmer who'd wooed her at Salt Spring Island. *The new Richard* had plotted to leave her. She should face facts and erase that dream.

"Cindy wants to introduce me to her brother," she said.

"Life admits not of delays." Sam's head shook violently as it did when he was emotional. "When pleasure can be had, it is fit to catch it. Every hour takes away part of the things that please us, and perhaps part of our disposition to be pleased."

The loss of pleasure and the loss of the ability to feel it. She could not imagine anything worse.

*****

David eased a plum tree into its hole, pulled soil around it and surreptitiously watched Ann and her daughter. Like most of the neighbours they were raking and burning leaves on this windless November day.

He was surprised when Ann phoned yesterday. A couple of weeks ago, she had told him she might cancel the tree planting. Another odditiy. Today, when he asked about the party, she froze a moment. Then she smiled and said her guests had loved the landscaping. Something strange was going on but it was none of his business. Ann had made that clear enough when he offered to help that day. Probably another quarrel with her husband. Over the cost of landscaping? He hoped not.

He fetched another sapling from the deck. Weeks ago, he had dug the holes along the driveway. Planting was just a matter of watering them in and replacing soil. After the driveway, he started planting in the backyard. The smell of smoke reminded him of cooking fish over a fire on the beach with Gerry last summer. It was a fall smell, signifying the end of the season. And in a few days, David would return to work on the grounds of Government House. He carried a birch to its place near the stream.

"Feels like snow," Ann said as she raked leaves from the rhodos by the dining room window.

"Those clouds aren't heavy enough. Excellent weather for working outdoors." He planted the birch and fetched another from the porch where Amanda was sweeping leaves.

"Good job," he commented, "If those oak leaves stayed on the deck, they would stain it."

Ann was raking brown leaves from under the transplanted rhodos. He stopped to chat. "I see the transplants are putting out buds. They're happy."

"Thanks to your care." Her voice faltered, and she took a deep breath. "I've enjoyed the garden steps and the path up to those oaks. I go up there to think." She smiled, but her eyes were huge as she watched Amanda struggling to carry a garbage pail full of leaves.

"Paths are useful. They restore order to the most chaotic gardens. If you see a design in a garden, you enjoy it more."

On the other hand, Amanda had seemed overly excited to see him. She was going to visit a friend but insisted on working in the garden. He set the birch down and took the garbage pail from her and dumped the leaves on the growing pile.

"Horizons do that in paintings," the girl said, "The princess is in the wind, and snow is falling and she is lost in a strange land. Her feet are pale in satin slippers. She is looking for something but the snow is hiding it. But she can see the horizon line, and she knows it lies beyond that."

The girl was strangely elated. Was she okay? "Exactly," David said. "You need the horizon line to get your bearings."

Amanda sat on the bench by the stream, and watched him plant the birch tree. "The bark of that tree is pale, as pale as the princess' skin."

Definitely the girl was dreamy, talking about a painting, maybe. Ann had said her daughter was artistic.

He raked earth around the root ball, stood back to check that the tree was straight, and staked it. All around leaves were falling like confetti but this young birch would hang onto its gold coins until December.

Ann's hair flew into her face. Vulnerable. She brushed it away as she raked and scooped up leaves. Her face seemed younger, and strangely blank, the face of someone grieving. Her body was strong and voluptuous, a body made for lust and for love. When she phoned, she apologized for her rudeness, and said to finish the planting after all. He hoped that he would get to know this woman but today she was remote and quiet. Even so, he loved being here for this brief time. The musty smell of smoke and earth was one last surge of summer heat. Soon it would be winter and the icy soil would smell metallic.

Ann looked at him. "What if…" she paused for breath..."What if you can't tell earth from sky, or weeds from cultivated plants. What if everything you counted on is tangled and not what it seemed?"

She sounded lost. A couple of weeks ago, she had been delighted with the landscaping and excited about the party. Something must have happened at the party. Her husband was an ambitious so-and-so. David had half a mind to phone him, tell him to care for his wife. That if he didn't, someone else would.

"I'm an expert on tangles," he said, "so I called my company, the Tangled Garden. In gardening if everything is jumbled, you can impose order. You can choose where to make a path and where to draw the line."

"You make the choice sound easy," Ann said. "As easy as a kindergarten workbooks where you choose a dog from a row of cats."

He grinned. "I used to tease the teacher and pick a cat."

Ann looked straight at him, flushed and beautiful. "It would be wonderful if choosing was just a matter of binary thinking."

"Binary thinking?" he asked.

"Thinking the way a computer thinks. It selects a bit or doesn't. A computer has only two choices. Cat or dog. Yes or no."

"Like picking petals from a daisy," he said lightly. "She loves me, she loves me not?"

"Computers don't consider how, or why, or wrong or right."

"Sometimes something larger takes over, plants the daisy, or digs the path or programs the computer. You could call it fate. You go with what you are given."

She smiled. "You *are* talking about gardening, aren't you?"

Her words were humorous, but she trembled, and he knew how difficult this situation was for her. A cloud passed in front of the sun and the world turned black.

"I think there's going to be another storm tonight," he said.

"I love storms. I'd like to build a cabin here in the garden where I could stay and see the lightning flash and the thunder crack"

"Gertrude Jekyll had a wee cabin like that. She called it her Thunder House. A place where she could experience the force of nature and be safe."

"Wild, but controlled," Ann said, shivering, "what a combination."

A car horn sounded. Amanda left with her friend. Ann suggested coffee. She hoped in a way that he would say no, but he didn't. At the sink, they took turns washing their hands, and then he sat at the counter. He had sat there often, but this time she was conscious of his eyes. She felt a heaviness, a heat, a longing to hold and be held. The way Richard used to hold her. She went to the cupboard. "French Roast or Mocha Java?"

"It's not coffee I want." He sounded amused. His hands came around her from behind and clasped her waist. "Tell me to go," he said. "And I'll leave right now."

On the nape of her neck, his breath was unsteady. His hands radiated warmth, but she must separate herself from this life-giving heat, and make a moral choice. Richard had been gone only two weeks.

No, damn it, he'd been gone for years. And even though her body wasn't perfect, this man wanted her. Why worry? The choice was simple.

She leaned back against David and became ravenous, crossing the line from the propriety of friendship into the unknown. Glad that he could not see her face, she savoured the wonder of his closeness. "I want this," she said and moved her hips.

"This?" He laughed.

"This." She swayed shamelessly and reached behind.

He caught her hand and turned her to face him. His skin was ruddy with desire, but his eyes were clear, questioning. "You're sure?"

"Yes."

Already it was too late to turn back. Already her appetite was arcing, the juices flowing hot through her thighs, her throat, and the veins in her arms. With greedy fingers she outlined the curves of his mouth, the forbidden fruit she'd often wished to consume. His lower lip was generous and full unlike Richard's. She took it between her teeth and sampled.

Sweet, yes, even sweeter than anticipated. She closed her eyes to appreciate it more.

In search of new pleasures, she moved lower to the angle of his jaw and feasted on the abrasively masculine texture, the tantalizing salt taste. Yes, this was how love had been once upon a time, on Saltspring Island with Richard.

David pulled back from her.

She opened her eyes and attempted to focus. Had she disgusted him?

"My turn," he said with a smile.

His lips on hers provided and withdrew an intoxicating taste of what was to come. She told herself she had to endure this waiting, remember her manners. She was starving, and he was preparing for a banquet, setting out cutlery and napkins, arranging flowers, and polishing fruit. Groaning, she politely bore the pain, until she could no longer. Mutely, she brought his hands to her breasts. The breasts Richard had once adored.

His touch was gentle, and reverential, unlike Richard's. His hands circled and clasped, again and again until she no longer cared about manners. Good or bad. Right or wrong.

The sheets were tangled in an impossible knot at the bottom of the bed. With her toe, Ann nudged them over the edge, and phoned the library. She said she was ill, only the second time she'd lied that way.

"Now, how about that coffee?" she asked much later.

CHAPTER 15: THE SOLITARY WANDERER

Ann chuckled as David ate another serving of pasta. She loved a man with an appetite, in bed and out. As a lover, he was tireless. Best of all, he hadn't made her feel self-conscious. She couldn't resist brushing his arm with her breasts as she served fruit for dessert, even though Amanda was watching.

Over dinner, they had talked about the weather, the garden, his crew, her book club, an even exchange of topics, but David seemed quiet. Sam rose from the table and began to pace. She wished he would sit down. The grandfather clock in the hallway ticked louder. So loud, she couldn't think of a thing to say.

Dessert was eaten in silence.

Ann became conscious of Amanda looking from one adult to the other. Was she mature enough to sense the change?

The girl wiped her mouth with a napkin. "Is Dad coming to see us soon? I want to show him my new room."

Ann blushed. "He hasn't phoned. I think he's still in Vernon." Did the girl truly miss her father? Or did she perceive David as a threat?

David quickly diverted the conversation to a drawing of a queen displayed on the fridge. He talked easily with Amanda, but as soon as he finished eating, he said he had to leave.

At the front door Ann discreetly kissed him goodbye. "We have to be careful because of Amanda."

'I know. I'll call you." He strode in his usual athletic lope to his truck, and then as he was about to open the truck door, turned back for a moment as though checking she was really there. He seemed to be waiting for some sign but what?

In the kitchen, Sam was pacing, his dark hair in Byronic disarray, his white shirt open to reveal a surprisingly muscular neck and chest. Was something wrong?

After Amanda left the table, Sam halted by Ann's chair. "You treated that man abominably. Ending a day like this with polite cant about the weather!"

"Amanda was here, we couldn't really talk."

"Nonsense, madam. You had a full afternoon of pleasure."

"Of comforting. That's all I wanted. He just happened to be an excellent lover too."

"Is that all?" Sam glared at her.

"Yes. I didn't spoil things by telling him Richard and I have separated."

"You used him."

After such a wonderful afternoon, she didn't need this. "I don't want advice. I don't need a built-in conscience."

"You view me as only that?" His smile was rueful "Me, Sam Johnson, 'a name at which the world grew pale, to point a moral, or adorn a tale?'"

She rushed past the moralist and turned on the television in the dining room. She would do the dishes later, or tomorrow. Sam had no right to scorn her, as though she was a ravenous housewife in one of those ancient jokes about milkmen. David had taken the initiative. His appetite had been equal to hers and he possessed unexpected reserves of endurance and strength. His body was magnificent, honed by physical exertion into an instrument of pleasure. He understood women, and he took his time. He was an excellent lover.

Sam came into the dining room. She turned on a sitcom, the kind of program he loathed. Sam sat through an hour of it, grim-faced. She left him and went upstairs to bed.

He knocked on her bedroom door. The noise was insistent and unendurable.

She opened the door and said he could enter but had to be quiet. Sam sat in a chair at the foot of her bed, his head in his hands, as though overcome. His massive shoulders were hunched, straining the fabric of his coat. From time to time he glanced at her with disgust.

She settled down with a book club novel and tried to lose herself in it.

That afternoon, she and David had slept in this same bed. And afterwards they had showered together, soaping one another. His arm muscles were sinewy but he washed her gently, as if she was an object of respect. Yes, as Sam said, it had been a full afternoon of pleasure. But something was missing. David knew it. He had turned, as he was about to drive away, and looked at her.

She couldn't concentrate on reading, not with Sam scowling. She put down her book. "Don't carry on so, Sam. It's not as though you have any experience of these things."

She turned out the light. And again she saw David waiting for her by his truck, waiting for her to make amends.

*****

David expected her phone call. At midnight, it came. Her voice seemed distant. She explained she had let things get out of control today. In a moment of weakness, she had used him. He tried to take the rejection lightly. Ever since dinner, he had been steeling himself for it. "I'll leave it up to you," he said. "Call me anytime, even if you just want to talk. You have my phone number." He gave her his home address too. "I know you have obligations, ones not easy to break."

Silence.

"Yes," she said, "I'm sorry. I think you…" For a moment she seemed to waver, as though wondering whether to confide. In a stronger voice, she said, "Thank you for being so kind."

"Kind?" He'd done her no favour. Just spoiled something promising and beautiful. He had taken her at her word, trusted she was ready, but he shouldn't have. In bed, she had urged him onward, her body had responded to every touch. Then, later, over dinner, her soul had withdrawn.

"I'd like to come over," he said, "and take you to bed, but that wouldn't be kind, and it wouldn't help."

"No. You're right, it wouldn't." She was crying.

How he hated tears. Too often they were a means of avoiding the truth. And what exactly was the truth? She had said her world was tangled, that she hardly knew right from wrong, yet she'd been a delight in bed, warm, passionate, eager. Had it had been just a blind momentary impulse, as she said, not her choice?

His throat went dry at the thought. For months, he had wanted to know more about this woman, sensed that she was the one for whom he had been searching, sensed that in some mysterious way they completed one another.… Damn it, he still believed that. Instinct couldn't be that wrong. Yet she had other obligations—to her husband and to her child.

"I don't know what's happening between you and Richard. You haven't told me and I'm worried that you haven't. I understand that you need to come to grips with your situation there and sort out your thoughts. Marriage is something I don't know much about. I've never slept with a married woman before, and I sure don't want to break up a family."

"Don't worry about that," she said. Too quickly.

So the main tie was Amanda. Ann was a good mother from what he'd seen. She and Richard had the child in common.

David said he wouldn't bother her. He said he would finish the landscaping while she was at the library.

She sounded relieved. So that was that.

Except for the feeling that it wasn't. David hung up, and went outside into the dark. It was after midnight. There was frost on the ground, and in his heart.

* * * *

Ann wiped her eyes, set the phone down, lay back on the bed and looked at Sam. Ending the budding affair was the moral thing to do. Sam was right. She had used David. Her behaviour had been shocking. How could she throw herself into a new relationship when Richard might tire of his girlfriend, and when Ann herself still needed him? David was clever about people. The fact that she hadn't told him Richard was gone showed where her loyalties lay.

Yet she was crying. Why? Whether the tears were for Richard or for David or for herself, she couldn't say.

"I know it was wrong, Sam, I'm shocked that I gave way to my desires like that, but I can't help regretting. It's been so long since I've been with a man, and I've never been loved like that." Never again to know that kind of comfortable, gentle strength. She reached for a tissue.

Sam handed it to her. "Madam, I know what it is to mourn. I loved my wife even after she took to the bottle and we lived apart. When she died, I was distraught. And later," he frowned, "there was Hester. She..." His eyes became sombre. "She was a..." He grew agitated and unable to control the shaking that plagued him. "She was a married woman."

Ann patted the bed and he sat next to her. "Tell me about her." Hearing someone else's woes might make hers feel lighter.

"I liked her husband well enough, though once when I was talking about something at dinner, he interrupted and said, 'That will be enough for one lecture.' As for Hester...." Again he became agitated.

"Such passion, after all this time!" Ann said.

"Excuse me. Even now, I can hardly say her name. She and I were friends for twenty years."

"And then she died?"

"Worse than that, far, far worse." He fell into a dismal silence.

What could have happened to the friendship?

"How did you meet Hester?"

Sam's face grew dark with suppressed emotion. "After my wife's death, I seemed broken off from mankind; a kind of solitary wanderer in the wilds of life, without any certain direction, or fixed point of view; a gloomy gazer on a world to which I have little relation."

He described exactly how she felt—adrift, unable to get her bearings, an outsider. Sam was a moral arbiter, but he was also a human being. "Because you'd lost your wife. How long did you remain in that state, Sam?"

"For years."

"Years!"

"Until I was rescued by Hester."

"So you had an affair."

"Affair! Never! There is no excuse for infidelity."

She cringed. "None? No matter what the woman's marriage was like?"

He rounded on her, his face contorted with rage. "The woman's a whore, and there's an end on't."

His moral standards were rigid. No decent woman would consider adultery. And no decent man either. Marriage was sacred. And she had done the right thing in phoning David tonight. She sighed and settled back against the pillow. She needed sleep, oblivion.

Hours passed.

Too much had happened. Too much to think about. David had held her in the kitchen, and then had let go, allowing her to choose. And she had thoughtlessly seduced him, and had chosen wrong. But she would always remember that afternoon.

She turned on the light. Three o'clock in the morning. Sam stood at the foot of the bed, obviously unable to sleep too. Because of her? Or because of virtuous Hester? Ann sat up in bed. "Hester must have been an extraordinary woman," she said.

He closed his eyes as though in pain. "I was so enraptured by her, I didn't realise how unhappy she was, married to a man who didn't love her, grieving the loss of her children, some of whom died young. I paid for my lack of sympathy."

"I'm sorry." Suddenly he seemed very human. "You told me once that you were here as my guide, because you were married, and because you travelled. You knew Hester twenty years, and lived according to your standards. What ended your friendship? Did she commit adultery? Did you?"

His face, full of suffering, faded into the wallpaper.

In panic, Ann said, "Only tell me if you want to."

A convulsion racked his body and his eyes rolled in anguish. How could he suffer so now, centuries later? Her guide's lack of tranquillity was appalling.

"She betrayed me." Sam became agitated. He twisted and twirled. The fit subsided. "Her husband died. When I heard she was to marry that damned Italian, I entreated her to see me one more time. I wrote that I found it inconceivable that she could be so...*ignominiously* married. I upset her by my views." Sam stumbled toward the bedpost and braced himself against collapse.

Betrayed after a long relationship. Poor Sam. A fellow traveller.

He lifted his head. "Eventually I wrote to give her my blessings, but from then on between us...was silence." He hid his face in his hands. His powerful shoulders heaved. In a thin voice he said, "I drove her wholly from my mind. She never wrote. I never spoke of her."

He'd been trapped in pain for centuries. Ann would have liked to hold him, comfort him if it were possible.

He sighed. "Learn from my experience."

Learn what? To hold her tongue? Or to guard her heart? "It's hard to lose a loved one to death, I know. Hester lost her babies, and I lost Edward. But it's also hard when living people turn away from you."

Sam nodded, unable to speak.

Sam and she had a lot in common. And it was strange--the better acquainted she became with him, the better he looked. He was younger now and handsome in an ugly way—sexy even. His eyes were too prominent but they were intelligent, and his lips too thick, but passionate, and his voice was resonant and as imposing as an actor's.

"I lost Richard years ago. Is that why you're my guide? So I can learn from your example to be more sympathetic with Richard?"

He stared. "I am here as your navigator"

"As navigator, tell me how to set my course."

"I am not your captain."

"You know the future, don't you?"

His head shook as he pondered her future, and his features grew dark and indistinct. "Look to the child."

She could barely hear the words. "Amanda? You mean I should ask her advice?"

"Watch her."

A great weariness overcame her. It was five a.m. She should ask more, maybe inquire about David's future, but all she wanted was the overstuffed comforter. She pulled it up over her eyes.

When she awoke the next morning, she remembered Sam's warning. Lately Amanda had been quieter than usual. Was she okay? Ann went to her daughter's bedroom. The bed with its pristine new bedspread was empty. Ann's heart tightened with fear as she hurried downstairs.

Amanda was in the living room in her pyjamas, copying pictures from an old Norwegian fairy tale.

Ann smiled with relief. Her daughter was perfectly safe.

*****

A week passed during which Ann alternated between guilt and regret. Sam had tried to comfort her, but she was confused. Sam condemned adultery, but his friend Hester had discarded him for an Italian musician. Sam had high standards. He probably would have married Hester. Sam must have been shattered, approaching old age, to be rejected like that. No wonder he had cut off all communication with Hester. Still it was tragic.

Had he been overly strict in his interpretation of immorality? Had he given her tainted advice about David?

No, she had acted thoughtlessly on impulse.

She burned with shame as she remembered the eager seduction. Sam was right. She had acted out of character. Only a week ago, she had learned about Richard's mistress. Out of anger and frustration, she had used David to satisfy her needs. If only she could have cancelled that afternoon, gone more slowly, patiently tried to learn more about him, and then, when the time was right, gone further. Too late now.

David was as good as his word. He planted the remaining trees while she was working. And that, at least was done. Richard would be happy to have the landscaping completed.

Sam was right about David, but wrong about Amanda. The child was normally quiet. She'd hardly spoken a word at Thanksgiving dinner. And she had been quiet as they shopped for the new bedspread and paint. But on Wednesday, she asked to have a weekend sleepover at Jen's house. Amanda might be quiet but she craved company and in time would be more outgoing.

But on Saturday, without Amanda, the house seemed empty and the day endless. Ann made lists of furniture she wanted to keep, and things that were Richard's, and points to be negotiated at the lawyer's. She would have gone for a walk but the weather was dreary.

At noon the dim November sun peeked over the horizon but stayed low in the sky. Ann could do anything she wanted. She could cook an elaborate meal like scallops, or Beef Wellington, or eat chocolate. She had no one to consider but herself. Somehow that wasn't enough. She turned on the television, and then turned it off. She should phone Richard and talk about selling the house. But he was with his precious Marina. And anyway, Ann would see him next week at his lawyer's.

In the living room, the fireplace yawned. She could build a fire, but it was a waste to build a fire just for her. It was the third week of November. She could shop for Christmas presents. She lay on the sofa and stared at the black hearth.

Sam paced in front of it. He had stopped wearing his horrible wig and let his natural hair show. It was curly and brown. Without the wig he was younger and sexier, and that was odd, considering his strict disapproval of adultery.

He bent to pick up a book from the floor—a Norwegian fairy tale, *East o' the Sun and West o' the Moon.*

"Amanda was reading that this morning," Ann said. "Before she went to Jen's."

Sam set the book on the coffee table and leaned close to read it, sighing and frowning as if it were a Latin text.

"I asked her if she wanted to take it with her on her sleepover. She huffed and said she was too old for fairy tales."

Sam looked up from the book. "She's abandoned childish things."

"I guess so. I commented that she had loved the story since preschool. She became strangely angry."

"Yet she made these drawings this morning." He took up several sheets of paper from the coffee table and examined them one by one.

"She yelled at me. She said I was like the mother in the story, the one who told her daughter the prince was a troll!"

Sam looked mystified.

"The story is quite funny really. Because a girl follows her mother's advice, a prince is whisked away to a faraway castle where an ugly princess enchants him. Eventually the girl finds the prince and outwits the ugly princess. I don't know what happens to the misguided mother."

Sam held up a drawing.

Ann laughed. "The ugly princess. Look how her nose reaches to her chin!"

Sam studied the drawing, and returned to the book.

Restless, Ann rose from the couch and went to the window. The newly planted birches shivered in a light breeze and cast weak shadows almost as far as the house. The sun was low now, almost gone. "David said I could phone. He gave me his address. I could drive to his house."

The ghost continued to read.

"That wouldn't be right, would it? Especially if I went at night. But I could go now this afternoon and make it a casual visit."

"Why ask me?" he said, as if her question was frivolous.

"You know morality, Sam. You can distinguish right from wrong."

"Not always, Madam. I was human."

"I don't believe you ever felt the way I do now. Longing, fearful, regretful. You were too wise."

He laughed, the laugh of a young man. He had lost weight and now she could see his neck was muscular as an ox's. His shoulders were broad. He could have been a farm labourer or a wrestler.

"I wasn't joking," she said. "You have a reputation as a moral arbiter."

He looked ashamed. "I endeavoured to make sure the world would never know of my exploits."

"Exploits?"

"Certain forays into the realm of experience." His voice became low, and seductive.

His sensuous mouth, bold, protruding eyes, and powerful frame were not the attributes of a prude.

She licked her lips. "What kind of forays?"

"I cannot say, and history will not tell you. In the last week of my life, I burned my Journal, along with other papers, but I can tell you this much. I married Tetty because she desired me. She was older but she overlooked all this," he gestured disparagingly at himself, "my blind eye, the result of scrofula, the scars from the pox, the shaking….the rest of my mannerisms."

"I hardly notice your flaws now." She had grown used to the lip smacking, the blowing, and the incessant motion.

"Tetty was lusty and I was young, and we were so besotted with one another that an actor friend would mimic us. Tetty overlooked my low birth too. When I told her one of my relatives had been hanged, she laughed. She said she had fifty who should have been hanged."

Tetty sounded nice. "From your use of the word 'foray' I thought you meant outside marriage."

"After Tetty died, I sought the consolation of certain women."

"Prostitutes?" Ann was astonished.

"Only after she died."

So in marriage, he had been faithful. He expected the same of Ann, and of Hester.

"Among those letters I burnt were some from Hester." His forehead knotted as though in spasm. "She always said our relationship was one only history would reveal. I made certain nothing would be known of it."

That sounded odd—what did they have to hide?

Anyway, Ann needed Sam's approval about her intentions. "Sam, I only want David as a friend. I won't seduce him, though I confess, I enjoyed doing that. I need advice. He's sensible and he knows about real estate. I want to ask him what price I could get for this house. A real estate agent would tell me but would inflate its value. I need to talk to someone impartial."

"David is impartial?" Sam said.

He didn't tell her *not* to go.

The small house obviously belonged to someone who loved plants. Stachys lined its driveway like grey fretwork, red berries brightened the pyracantha and skimmia and hollies, and white snowberries gleamed under Garry Oaks. At the side of the house, was a herb garden, fenced in against deer. The cottage's cream coloured stucco glowed in the dim afternoon light. The building was probably sixty years old, like the others on the street, a tiny immaculate cottage nestled comfortably under its canopy of mature oaks, a fairytale cottage the kind Amanda loved to draw.

David was planting a laurel hedge. His green mackinaw jacket blended into the shadows. She called out, and Humphrey barked. David showed no embarrassment or resentment, but greeted her calmly, and asked if she wanted tea. She told him she wanted advice.

He continued planting as she explained why she had to sell her house. She told him about Richard, said he had moved out, and said she didn't want to co-own a house with him so she would sell.

"Why don't you stay put?" he asked.

"Can't afford to."

"Me neither, up till now." He grinned. "I'm used to moving on."

Was he referring to houses, or women?

"I'll miss my house," she said. "It's full of memories, and I love the garden now."

He picked up another laurel, and she helped steady it and six more. He worked quickly, not a motion wasted. Did he resent her coming? Did he want to move on and forget her too?

The rented house was charming with its arched doorway and pointed gable and steep roof. "How do you get used to leaving everything?" she asked. "This garden for example."

In the early twilight, his hands and face looked blue.

"I'm a renter, not an owner. Every spare cent goes into the business. Right now, for instance, I need a truck to replace one on its last legs. If I had extra cash, I wouldn't buy a house, I'd buy a new boat."

"To replace *The African Queen*?"

"She's on her last legs too." He laughed and brushed the dirt from his hands. "I never really wanted to settle down, but then I never knew a librarian before. Librarians dislike change."

Was he talking about a future together? She held a laurel. Its leaves were smooth and glossy, a healthy plant.

He poured water around its roots. "One thing I never could do is stay indoors. That's why I dropped out of high school after I moved to Victoria. I've regretted it. I found that I needed to go on learning."

"I could teach you about libraries." She flushed. *Not so fast.* "If you're leaving, why are you planting this hedge?"

"Making gardens is a habit. I finish them, then move on, leave them as a kind of gift."

A gift. The beauty, the generosity and purity of it.

He put down his shovel and stretched. "Lately it's been therapy too." Only a slight wryness in his voice revealed his pain, the pain of a friend's death.

Light snow was falling. The winter moon peeked over the cottage's roof and cast shadows across white roses still in bloom.

She should leave, but she knew she couldn't, not now. She put her arms around him. His jacket was rough and it smelled of earth and smoke. For a moment she stood in the darkened garden, offering comfort. Then like an old friend, she took his hand and led him inside.

*****

When she told him Richard was gone, David had to pretend to focus on planting. One barrier had fallen. He felt joy, but this time he would not rush her. He would let her take the lead. And now they were in his bedroom, her hand rounded, firm and capable in his, her face serene. She was calmer now than the last time, and more confident. He could sense it in the proud way she moved toward the bed. The moonlight brought out her womanliness, and he wanted her even more now than before.

She waited and watched as he undressed, her eyes soft. She told him he was beautiful and he smiled. He said in the moon's cold light she was pale, luminous, and unearthly. Shadows threw into relief the generous flare of hips and waist and breasts. He left the curtains open, so he could see her, touch her burning skin. With a slow heat, they came together. Like torches they kindled and rekindled one another and lit up the night.

He had never met a woman so grateful, and the gratitude told him the history of her marriage.

Resting later, he gently probed into Richard's departure. He laughed at her description of the party and Richard's fury at being evicted. "I wish I'd been there," he said, kissing the hollow between her breasts.

"If you'd been there, I would have seduced you."

"It's one way to forget." He demonstrated his theory.

Afterwards she lay beside him, his arms around her so warm she felt no need of blankets. The sinews of his wrist showed just beneath the skin. She kissed the line they made and he stirred in his sleep.

He made love, she decided, in the same way he worked. He gave his whole heart and strength to it. There was no holding back. He spent freely, and afterwards laughed at his resulting weakness.

Nothing else mattered now. Selling the house, lack of money and insecurity were nothing beside this tenderness. She remembered how stingily she and Richard had measured out and bartered love, and she was ashamed.

David rested, holding her so her head was against his heart and the weight was familiar and right. He twirled a lock of her hair around his finger, and wondered at how the moonlight turned its darkness to shimmering silver. He brushed his lips against its smoothness. He wanted this woman and no other. He would take her child as his own too and raise her lovingly, but only if Ann decided to abandon Richard.

"How's Amanda?" he asked.

"Not doing well at school."

He heard fear. "Don't blame yourself. It's to be expected after such disruption."

"She has friends to talk to and me, but this morning I failed her. She became angry. I didn't understand why. I unfortunately didn't take it seriously." She told him about their quarrel.

He got the sense that Amanda was still loyal to her father and that worried Ann. "I know you're worried tonight, but I'm selfishly happy. I'm glad you're mine."

To cheer her, he told her about his own relationships with women. Some of the stories were funny, others just embarrassing. Like Margot who secretly wanted him to move to Ontario and take a real job. Like Jenny who thought he was rich because he owned his own company and disappeared when she found out he was poor.

"Is that why you never married?"

"I never met the right one. I knew I would. My parents have been friends and lovers for forty years. I refused to settle for anything less. And then I met you." He kissed her lightly on the shoulder." He laughed. "Even when you were drunk, that night at Government House, I wanted you."

"And I you," she said.

"At least there's no doubt about that aspect."

"No, not about that." She moved against him provocatively and he immediately came to life.

Later, when she asked about Gerry, David was careful. He told her an elaborate funeral had taken place in London, England. David hadn't gone. Instead he had attended a memorial service at Telegraph Cove. He told her about the misty water and silent fir trees and the group of friends who watched the ashes spread on the water there.

He told her many things, but he omitted one. He didn't tell her about the inheritance Gerry had left him, enough money to buy many houses and a boat.

He wanted this woman to love him for himself.

*****

She returned home an hour before Amanda. Sam greeted her at the door. His hair was tousled and his shirt undone. He looked Byronic, she decided. Except that Sam had lived long before Byron.

"Now I hope you aren't going to lecture, because I won't listen," she said. She set about making spaghetti sauce.

Sam hung around as she sautéed onions and stirred them to keep them from burning. He sniffed their fragrance but said nothing. He seemed to expect her to beg his pardon for committing adultery. After all, she had promised him not to seduce David.

But this time hadn't been like last. This time everything had been perfect. "Don't talk to me about virtue," she said.

Sam blushed, and for the first time, looked unsure of himself. He had lived by high moral standards. His love for Hester had been a true romance, unconsummated yet powerful even after all these centuries.

"How did you meet Hester?" she asked.

"Hester was twenty-four when I met her, her husband, eleven years older. He was tall, dignified and authoritative, a brewer by occupation. She was…attractive, like you…but shorter…a sprightly talker, used to entertaining older men. Intelligent, attentive and virtuous."

"Hmm," Ann said. "Unlike me."

She stirred tomatoes into the onions. Last summer, at the book club, she had ranted against romance. Now she was a believer. Celibacy had driven her to craziness and to chocolate.

"I'm happy," she said. "Celibacy is a pain, and being with David is pure pleasure."

*****

The euphoria persisted into Monday. The library patrons had probably never met such an effusive librarian.

"You're in a good mood," Colleen commented when Ann phoned to reserve a book. "I guess a single state has its advantages."

"It has," she replied smugly.

All morning she dispatched reference questions with gusto. She and Sam tackled the backlog of unanswered reference questions—information on the Nisga'a Treaty, a sample of schizophrenic handwriting, literary criticism on Shakespeare's *Troilus and Cressida*, current provincial statistics on motorcycle fatalities. Sam took a handful of the yellow Post-it notes and sprinted about the library, seeking answers. The library world had never known such a team, the librarian and the lexicographer. By eleven o'clock, the slips had dwindled to two. One was a reference to an obscure poem.

"That is easy," Sam said. "It's by Dryden. I know it by heart." He recited it in a dramatic whisper.

Ann was laughing when the reference phone rang.

The man's voice quavered. He introduced himself as a retired librarian visiting from Cincinnati. He'd been travelling in the Yukon and was back here in Victoria to catch a flight home. He edited a small periodical called *Children's Literature*. He wondered if he could publish her report.

Ann knew the periodical, but she was puzzled. "What report?"

"The one you gave at the conference, "Pictures from the Past."

"I don't understand," she stammered. "How do you know about that?"

"I was there. I heard your speech and it was very good. Would you allow me to publish it?"

"Of course, I'd be delighted." Ann swivelled in her chair and caught Sam's eye. He winked. "I'll let you have the slides too," she added.

"Could we discuss it over lunch today, or tomorrow?"

They arranged to meet in an hour for lunch. On the wheel of fortune, hers was rising. First the weekend with David, and now this!

"So much for the vanity of human wishes!" she said in triumph to Sam. "My wishes have all been fulfilled. I can't wait to tell the librarians about this. The November staff meeting is this afternoon. Librarians from every branch in Victoria will be there."

She couldn't wait to tell Amanda the news too, and David.

Then the phone rang again.

Ann cancelled lunch with the editor, and then phoned the main library and asked Colleen to find her a substitute librarian for the afternoon.

"What's wrong?" Colleen asked.

"Amanda's in trouble. I have to pick her up at school."

CHAPTER 16: THE WHITE BEAR

Amanda sat in the principal's office, head bowed, hands folded in her lap, face devoid of expression. Ann knelt beside her. "Amanda, what's wrong? Are you ill?"

No answer.

"Speak to me." She clasped her daughter's face.

Again no response. No tears, no anger, nothing.

The principal tapped Ann on the shoulder. "Dorothy Grieves would like to have a word with you in private. Don't worry. Amanda is safe here. I'll call you if there is any change."

Mrs Grieves was the counsellor, a blonde woman who was kind and overworked. Ann had met her before.

Drawings by children decorated the counsellor's homey office. Ann sat on a soft upholstered chair, and noticed the box of tissues conveniently close by.

How had this happened?

Amanda seemed okay at the beginning of the weekend—except for that quarrel, of course, but that could have been the hormones of puberty kicking in.

"Ann," the counsellor said, "I don't want to alarm you, but Amanda hasn't been herself lately. Last week, her teacher spoke to me about her concerns. I understand she also tried to contact you?"

"She did?" The last time the teacher had spoken to her was about Amanda's schoolwork, at Thanksgiving, more than a month ago. Richard's lack of interest had infuriated Ann. "I know my daughter's been having trouble with schoolwork…"

The counsellor consulted her notes. "She's been taking hours to do simple sums that she used to do in minutes. She's been talking slowly, in a monotone. Warning signs."

The words hung on the air. Ann knew now what she should have known and acted on weeks before. "What do you suspect?"

The counsellor's expression revealed nothing. "I'm not a psychiatrist, or a doctor. First, we should rule out physical causes. You should take her to emergency in case it's something like a viral infection or encephalitis or meningitis."

"Meningitis?" A dizzying white fog descended.

Dorothy Grieves consulted her notes. "Most likely it's emotional. According to her teacher, Amanda refused to help decorate a Christmas tree or make garlands for the classroom. She also refused to be in the Christmas concert."

The white fog lifted. It showed a scared girl watching her three-year-old brother in a hospital bed. "That's it. Christmas… her brother died then."

The counsellor shook her head. "Last Christmas, there were no reports of Amanda acting like this. She sang in the choir."

Last Christmas, Richard was there.

"Ann, was Amanda always a quiet child? As a toddler, for example."

As a toddler, Amanda had sat on Olive's knee, chatting to her about animals. She wanted to be a veterinarian but she couldn't pronounce the word. "As a toddler, she was happy, outgoing."

"At preschool, Amanda often sat alone reading. She learned to read long before other kids. She loved books, but made friends easily and loved her preschool teacher. We went to the teacher's wedding. Amanda had a talent for drawing. She drew pictures of the teacher in her wedding dress with every detail, even her glass earrings."

"Any change lately in her sleeping or eating habits?"

"No."

"Was she always plump?"

"No, but..." With a sinking heart Ann pinpointed the change. "I never thought of this before. She became fond of food, overly fond of food, four or five years ago, after her brother died."

"After he died. What's happened recently in her life? Are there any troubles at home?"

"No," Ann said automatically.

The woman's eyes bored into hers.

She had to be honest, for Amanda's sake. "Yes," Ann admitted. "A month ago, her father and I separated."

The counsellor's eyes flickered. "A month ago? There's nothing in her file about this. Did you tell her teacher?"

"I should have. I meant to, but I was busy."

The woman's silence condemned Ann.

Not guilty. Separating from Richard had been a simple decision, hadn't it? Ann had told Amanda everything, she hadn't neglected her had she? And it wasn't as if his leaving had meant a big change in the girl's life because he had never been there anyway.

"She's always been quiet," Ann was desperate to acquit herself. "A trait she inherited from her dad." Richard could be passive and quiet too—but not lacking emotion. He could anger, and he could love another woman.

"I'm not blaming anyone," Dorothy Grieves said, "just trying to help you find the possible cause. When did your marriage problems start?

"Seven years ago." Ann had been over that ground so often with the marriage counsellor, she knew the answer.

"How old was Amanda?"

"In pre-school, so she was four maybe. I was pregnant. I couldn't ski or play tennis."

A pattern was emerging, an unfortunate one, of eating and also of neglect. But Ann had been a good mother, hadn't she?

"Her teacher sent a note home on Friday," the counsellor said. "She's been trying to call you."

On Friday? On Saturday, Amanda left for Jen's in a huff. She'd taken her homework with her. The note must still be in her schoolbag.

"I never received the note. Amanda stayed at a friend's on the weekend." The way it sounded, no wonder the woman was giving her the third degree.

I should have checked the bag on Friday evening and asked about school. I should have seen the warning signs. Sam had told me to watch Amanda.

"That's a shame," the counselor said. "On Friday, Amanda's teacher requested an assessment because Amanda wasn't making sense. Amanda said she wanted to go Christmas shopping and buy a golden apple. Mentioned a spell and three old ladies. Said she had to be brave and take all magic as it came. The teacher recognized the allusions to a fairy tale."

"Yes. It's a Norwegian fairytale. One of Amanda's favourites."

"This one. *East o' the Sun and West o' the Moon.*" The counselor handed Ann a copy of the book. "I read it just now. You should show it to a psychiatrist."

"Thanks," Ann rejected it. "We've got a copy at home. I'll take that."

How had the sleepover gone? Usually Ann would have phoned and thanked the mother. She'd call Tara tonight.

"Amanda has deteriorated very rapidly. Don't wait for an appointment. It could take weeks to get a psychiatric assessment. I suggest you take her to emergency."

"Of course." Ann fumbled in her bag for her car keys.

Snow was falling as they left the emergency room. Ann drove carefully while Amanda slept, sedated, in the back seat.

Depression was a common reaction to loss, the E.R. doctor said. He had questioned Ann closely, asking if Amanda had mentioned death or dying lately, if she'd written or drawn pictures on that subject. Ann was puzzled until she remembered that depression is often associated with suicide.

She gripped the steering wheel. Such tendencies would be obvious, surely? She was Amanda's mother but she had encouraged the obsession with fairy tales. She had been amused by the pictures of the ugly princess. Sam had taken them seriously. "Watch the child," he said. And Ann had checked the empty bed, seen the sheet neatly tucked in under the new comforter, and pondered the possibility Amanda had run away.

The emergency doctor asked about the fairy tale. He asked Ann to outline the story. She tried to remember the gist of it. She looked to Sam who'd read it recently, but he sat silently beside Amanda, his arm around her shoulder. "There was a picture of a white bear. Amanda copied it." Slowly the details came back and she recounted the tale.

The doctor listened and stared out the window. In the parking lot, light snow dusted the cars. The doctor said nothing till she finished. "A frightening yet comforting story. The psychiatrist will want to read it. Amanda's always liked it, you say?"

"Yes, since she could read."

"The heroine is brave. If Amanda identifies with her it's a good sign. The enchanted prince could be her father."

Enchanted…distant…in a faraway castle east o' the Sun and west o' the Moon. "It could be," Ann said, "or it could be her dead brother. That would apply too."

"The ugly princess?"

Ann smiled. Richard's new woman? The usurper?

"And the place east o' the sun and west o' the moon?"

"I have no idea." Ann's eyes filled. "The kingdom of death? Or this place where she is now? Out of touch with everything."

The doctor put a reassuring hand on her shoulder. "Or the place where problems are solved."

"I should have realized something was wrong, last Saturday. She screamed at me as she left for the weekend. I should never have let her go on that sleepover. I knew something was wrong. I've suspected it for months."

"Don't blame yourself," he said. "This depression manifested itself very suddenly. In my whole career I've seen only a couple of cases like Amanda's. The decline in a matter of months, the changes in scholastic abilities, the sudden loss of movement, dissociation. But it is clinical depression, no doubt about it. The flat affect, the expressionless mask, is unmistakable."

"What will happen now? Does she have to stay in hospital?"

"No. I'm releasing her into your care. Take her home and watch her. I've arranged an appointment with a child psychiatrist and a follow-up treatment program.

"How long will she take to recover from this?" Ann asked.

"I have no idea. A clinical depression may take weeks, maybe months, or longer. But the worst is over now."

Snow was sticking to the pavement and slowing traffic. *The worst was over*. She would tell Richard that. He would meet them at home. Maybe he would feel guilty. His desertion had resulted in this.

What was in the drawings that Sam had examined so carefully? One depicted three hags giving the girl a golden apple. Another showed the girl flying on the back of the North Wind to the mysterious place where the prince was imprisoned.

Why was the prince gone? Because the girl's mother had spoiled the illusion.

In a test of wits, the girl had succeeded in getting the ugly princess's laundry clean—the peculiar test showed the folk origins of the story. Did Amanda hope to free her father from the enchantress?

But the fairy tale was not a recent favourite. Applying it to Richard's new woman was wrong. Amanda had loved the story in preschool.

Why? Because the place east o' the sun and west o' the moon was a magic land where anything was possible? That's what the doctor said.

Ann tried to remember Amanda as a preschooler. She remembered her lying on her grandmother's Persian rug, crayoning in a colouring book about children at a farm. "What colour should I do the skin," she lisped. Orange, her grandmother suggested and the two had smiled together.

In the dim residential streets, Christmas lights blinked with false cheer. A car honked and beside her, Sam stirred in his sleep.

The colouring book was important. Why?

The colour orange? Ann would have said pink for skin but orange was truer, and Amanda, from then on, used orange even for the skin of fairy princesses.

The subject of the picture? The children in the colouring book had been feeding geese.

That was it, animals! At three, Amanda adored animals, especially their pet dog, a collie. At four, Amanda had drawn calico cats and collies in strange pastel colours. That's why she liked the Norwegian tale. Not for the heroine, but for the white bear, the white bear outlined in white stars, the magical bear that appeared to the Norwegian girl, the magical bear who was the prince in disguise.

When she arrived home, she settled Amanda in bed, and then went to the basement where she had saved Amanda's drawings. She dragged the oldest box out and searched through it. When had Amanda begun to collect magazine photos of royal weddings? When had she begun drawing princesses with earrings dangling to their shoulders, exotic girls wearing long dresses, swinging, sliding, and eating? After the preschool teacher's fairy tale wedding? No. Here was a picture of a stallion and another of a swan, both drawn in kindergarten.

Here was one of a fairy tale castle, labelled Grade Three. The teacher had exhibited it at the spring craft fair. Ann remembered thinking Amanda was growing up and becoming more feminine. Four months earlier, at Christmas, Amanda had lost her brother.

That was the turning point. *After that, she'd become a solitary wanderer in a land of magic, seeking a cure for something for which there was no cure.*

Richard sat upright on the couch, listening.

Ann talked about depression. She made it clear that the cause was unknown. She explained about the change in drawings. "It's a reaction to loss, the doctor said. She's been living in a fantasy world. Devouring books, supplied by me." She swallowed, unable to go on. The doctor had said it wasn't Ann's fault. She mustn't let Richard blame her.

Richard looked at her. "I can't believe my leaving had that great an effect." His pleasure only partly concealed.

"Not just *your* leaving," she said with disgust. "First Edward, then you. It was too much for her. And lately I haven't made time for her either." She wouldn't tell him about David, not yet.

"You're looking well." He gazed at her with something like desire. "Very well."

"I've lost weight, that's all." How could he think of such superficial things now? "Amanda's upstairs, do you want to see her?"

They went up together. Amanda lay tucked into bed like an enchanted princess, her long dark hair fanned out upon her pillow. Beside her Sam sat, keeping watch.

"Hello Amanda," Richard said briskly. "How are you doing?"

The dark eyes never flickered.

"I hear you're not well."

Again no response.

As if rebuked, he reddened and stepped backward, bumping into the bedpost. He avoided people with flu. He hated germs. He was never sick himself. He stood awkwardly by the foot of the bed, touching the bedpost, clinging to it as though deriving comfort from its solidity. He stared at it then at Amanda and, almost unconsciously, ran his hand over the smooth carved oak, around and around the spindles and knobs. He'd always loved fine woodwork.

What was he thinking? He and Amanda had never been close. His daughter had been too fat for sports like tennis. He'd ridiculed her weight. Did he regret that now? Ann willed him to look at her but he looked instead at the bed, and then at the piles of books on the floor. Did he notice the new paint and new bedding?

"I'd better leave," he said almost to himself.

Amanda stirred. Her face was flushed, beautiful. He touched her forehead, and then bent to kiss it. "I won't disturb your sleep," he whispered. "I'll come back tomorrow morning."

They went downstairs, leaving Sam with Amanda.

By the front door, Richard paused and turned to Ann. "If she becomes aware, tell her I came. Tell her I love her."

His face was white and his lips thin with worry. For the first time, Ann felt pity. "I will," she said reassuringly. "And I'll call you if there's any change. The doctor said to let her rest. He gave her a sedative, and I'm to give her more if she needs it."

He zipped up his black leather jacket. "I'm sure you can handle this. You're very capable, you know. You always were."

He hadn't praised her in recent memory, except for her cooking abilities. Maybe he missed her omelettes. "Capable? How"?

"Your career and all," he said. "You had a bright future. I was sorry you gave it up when you became pregnant with Edward."

This was new. Ann smiled. "You never told me that."

He brushed a hand over his eyes. "I tried. Remember the dolphin ornament?"

"Yes." The male leading the female through a beautiful abalone sea. The ornament spinning on the formica table, and falling.

"I caught it," he said. "Because I wanted to save our relationship."

She had wondered if he caught it out of love or anger. What did it matter now? "That was before Marina," she said.

He flinched. "I don't expect you to understand. Marina was so vibrant."

"Unlike me."

"Yes, then. Edward had died, we were neither of us over that."

"And you're happy now?"

"Yes," he said with too much force. "Actually....no: Marina's still adjusting to Victoria. She misses her parents in Vernon, but I don't want to talk about her now." He took a deep breath. "I didn't realise—" he slapped the door. "Till tonight...I didn't realise how hard my leaving would be on Amanda. I'm a selfish bastard, aren't I?"

"Yes."

He said it with humility now, with no trace of vanity. He had seen Amanda. He had faced the truth. He was human after all. His eyes glistened, but he didn't turn away to hide his emotion. He wiped his eyes with a handkerchief, and then blew his nose. "These last few years have been hell."

She longed to comfort him. He was a parent. So was she. But she forced herself to remember the Richard of the secret stock purchases, and the hidden mistress.

Before he drove away, he retrieved some of his possessions from the garage. She waited until he was gone, and then, uncertain and squeamish, she went to phone David.

The snow had turned to sleet, which rattled like sand against the window. Ann shivered on the couch. Sam huddled beside her. A log crackled as David closed the fire screen and came to sit beside her. She was numb, not from cold, but from what she had just seen. They had gone up to check on Amanda. The girl was awake. Ann spoke gently and told her about Richard's visit. She told her he loved her. There was no reaction.

"This may go on for days, or months," Ann said to David. "I'll stay home from work tomorrow but I have to work, I need money. Olive will babysit and Richard will too, if necessary."

Richard was selfish but he had volunteered. And she had almost hugged him. His short greying hair and fit physique still attracted her more than she cared to admit. Some of the military starch had dissolved because of the softening influence of his mistress or because of shock. When he saw Amanda, he sagged noticeably. He looked like a prize fighter down on his knees, waiting for another blow. He loved his daughter, there was no doubt about it.

David warmed her hands between his. "You need to rest. Should I leave?" His eyes were blue and worried.

"No. Stay. It's nice to have someone here."

Someone. She was using David. She should have let Richard stay. As a father, and as her husband, he had a right.

David stared at the slush building on the windowsill. "You said Amanda was worried about Christmas."

"Yes, Christmas without Richard. She refused to have anything to do with Christmas at school. But I'll try to make the holiday as normal as possible. I'll go to Olive's for dinner. He'll be there." She tried to sound confident. Christmas was only four weeks away. Would Amanda be herself again?

David gazed calmly at the fire, and something of his calmness transferred itself to her.

"Where will you spend Christmas?" she asked.

His eyes assessed her. "That depends. With my parents maybe at Telegraph Cove. Or maybe here, with Gerry's father and Gerry's sisters."

He had family obligations. Everyone did. Her own parents in Vancouver were only a ferryboat ride away. She and Amanda could go there, but it would be noisy. Her brothers would be there with their wives and kids. There would be all the bustle of opening presents and cooking turkey. "I hate Christmas," she said.

"The shopping and the waste?"

"Yes," she said, though she hadn't meant that. She tried to laugh. "I used to be a shopper. One year, I bought a scarf for the postman and whiskey for the milkman. My friend, Colleen commented, 'What are you giving Richard for Christmas, an empty bank account?' Good old Colleen!"

David frowned. "That doesn't sound like you."

"I was like that before…before Edward died. His death made shopping seem ridiculous."

"You've never told me what happened."

"There was a Christmas concert at the school. He…" She began to shake. The nightmare, the never-ending nightmare of it.

Instantly, David pulled her to him. His lips brushed her hair. "Sorry, I shouldn't have asked, especially tonight."

She closed her eyes. She had to remain alert and think of Amanda. Not give way to memories.

"Would you like company at Christmas?" he asked softly.

Joy surged. "But what about your parents and Gerry's?"

"They'll understand." He placed her hand against his heart.

She could not speak so she kissed him. "A friend in need is a friend indeed," she said breathlessly.

"More than a friend, I hope."

His eyes were warm with mirth and suppressed passion and she wished she knew what she wanted. "I can't think about that now." She smiled to take the sting from the words.

David noted how, for the first time that evening, Ann really looked at him. It was good to see her smile at last, but he had no idea what she was thinking. Was he just a friend? Had Richard returned to her heart?

"I'd better check again on Amanda," she said.

He went upstairs with her. The girl was sleeping and that was a relief.

On their way downstairs, they passed Ann's bedroom, its door invitingly open. David considered taking her in there, but reconsidered. She was far too fragile now.

At the bottom of the stairs, Ann said, "This has been a rough day. Would you like a drink?"

"Let me." He went to the living room shelf where she kept the wine decanter.

She blushed. "Actually, you drink. I'll have tea. I need something to eat too. I'm starving."

In the kitchen, he scrambled eggs. He had to get her thinking about something positive. "I have some seed catalogues at home. Would Amanda like to look at them? She seemed to enjoy being outdoors in the garden."

"Fresh air might do her good."

He looked at the sleet outside and laughed. "Not this fresh. But we could look at catalogues together and order seeds."

"Yes, you could teach her about planting and propagating."

"And you too?" he asked with a grin to make her realise that soon life would return to normal. He flipped the omelette onto a plate "Let's eat in front of the fire." He set cups and spoons on a tray.

"I'll get a pitcher for the milk," Ann said. She reached for one on the top shelf of a cupboard. Her bottom was deliciously rounded. It was difficult to restrain himself, but he reached for the pitcher instead. Beside it was a pile of chocolate bars.

"What's that there?" He pointed.

She blushed. "Halloween candy. Have some."

He never ate sweets, but she seemed to want him to sample them so he took a couple and offered her one.

"No thanks," she said.

"You want to lead me astray?"

"Yes," she said, her eyes flirtatious.

He could have kissed her, but again, he didn't. "These things are lethal," he said. He looked at the wrapper. "Do you know how much fat's in one chocolate bar? Fifteen grams. Half your daily allowance."

Ann was horrified. She examined the tiny print, and then looked at Sam who was warming his hands on the teapot. He nodded.

She pulled a chair up to the cupboard, stood on it and scooped the candy into a plastic bowl. "I used to love these," she explained. She no longer needed them and neither did Amanda. "Amanda did too. Another one of my good influences." Amanda might have inherited her craving for sweets, but Ann could teach her not to give in to it. She could tell David about her battles with food but what did they matter? He said he had desired her even in the summer when she was heavier.

Sam winked at her like a co-conspirator. In the last month, he too had lost weight, if ghosts could be said to lose weight. He was muscular now and fit…yet she liked him as he was before, too. His previous appearance just took some getting used to.

David seemed determined to keep his distance. In the living room, he set the plates of eggs and toast on the coffee table, and sat in a chair opposite her. Just as well. All she wanted now was tea. She gulped it, as greedy as a child. The warmth flowed through her. She began to understand Sam's obsession with the comforting brew.

"Amanda will be fine." David refilled her cup. "Children come through wars where adults don't."

Ann nodded. She had to believe that. "As a Christmas present, I've thought of paying for art lessons to give her something to look forward to."

"Kids need hobbies." He spoke calmly as if nothing unusual had happened that day. "When I was fifteen, we moved to Victoria for the school year. I missed having a boat, being on the water, and having space to think. I seriously considered running away to Telegraph Cove. Then dad asked me to help him in the garden."

Careers often started as hobbies. Hers as a librarian stemmed from her love of books as a kid. "Maybe Amanda will find a career in art."

"Realistic art, I hope."

"Right. No fantasy, fairy tales or fairy games allowed."

"No?" A look of mischief came into his eyes. "I thought you liked fantasy."

He was incorrigible. "I did," she said, teasing, "until I met the man of my dreams." She stretched, feeling at ease for the first time that day. "I didn't realise, how much I needed a friend, someone to listen, someone like you, or…"

Sam sat near the fire with his feet up on the brass fender. Should she tell David about the ghost? No. He might not understand. Maybe later.

"I'm sticking to facts too, nowadays." She gestured at the books on the coffee table.

"Pretty heavy reading material. Books on forestry and on the history of lumbering."

"I only allow myself one book of fiction a month, the book club's choice. I overindulged after Richard left." She told him about her misguided speech on illustrators. She laughed. "I went crazy, and tried to prove they had their fair share of sorrow."

David chuckled. "People like hearing about disasters. The editor of that periodical was impressed."

She gasped. "The editor! I forgot he's leaving tomorrow for Cincinnati. I'll phone him first thing in the morning."

"Good. Seize the brass ring." He sat back and his eyes were serious. "You and Amanda are very alike, except for one thing. You can laugh at yourself, and she can't. Why is that?"

"I guess she's too upset."

"Art lessons will distract her, but may not help her. She's been carrying the weight of all your problems and she's staggering and trying to escape into fantasy."

"Right," Ann said with a sigh. "I feel guilty about it."

"I didn't say that to make you feel guilty, just to suggest a cure. I think Amanda needs something only you can give."

"What's that?"

"I'm no psychiatrist, but I bet she thinks the marriage troubles are her fault. You should talk to her. Tell her they're not. Maybe then, she'll want to come back."

CHAPTER 17: RECOVERY

At Government House, David's crew was taking out branches weakened by recent storms. An old plane tree by the entrance to the gardens had lost limbs. A cherry tree had died. So had a conifer. It was a shame but losses were to be expected every winter. The two copper beeches had survived though and so had the magnificent sequoia by the gates. David held the guy ropes and fed the chipper. Its noise made conversation impossible, but allowed him to think.

A week ago he had sat in front of the fire and talked to Ann as calmly as a doctor, knowing she was devastated by Amanda's illness. He had been careful to keep calm as she talked about Amanda, but he sensed her shock and fear, and a new wariness. The books on the coffee table told why. They were Richard's obviously, and Ann had been reading them. Obviously, she was not ready to let him go.

On Wednesday, when Amanda became aware of her surroundings, Ann had followed his advice, telling her daughter that the separation had nothing to do with her, and assuring her that both her parents loved her. Though groggy from medication, the girl smiled. On Thursday, Amanda spoke at last, in monosyllables and short sentences. She could recall only fragments of the weekend of the sleepover, the psychiatrist said. He thought she could start a day program in a week or so.

Amanda was starting the day program tomorrow. Ann would return to work halftime. A week had passed since her daughter became ill. David was delighted about that and about the news that Ann's speech would be published in the spring. He had phoned Ann every night, but he hadn't visited Ann. The temptation to make love was too strong, and this was a time for contemplation. He sensed that since Desolation Sound, Ann had been almost as lost as her daughter. Sometimes she had a strange faraway look in her eyes, as though she was aware of an unseen presence. Both she and Amanda needed to return to reality.

The chipper stopped its whining. The crew was taking a break. David drove the truck, loaded with prunings, down behind Government House to the stables. The truck's transmission was acting up, the reverse gear popping out. He'd had the truck since he began the landscaping firm, ten years ago, so it had served him well. After Christmas, he'd go to Vancouver and buy a new one. He dumped the prunings on the compost heap by the stables. The pruned conifer branches were still green. A hundred years ago, a gardener had planted that conifer with an eye to the future. A storm had ended that legacy, but David would replant in the spring for generations to come. As for his own immediate future, he was unsure.

On the phone, Ann mentioned her husband saw Amanda every day. She said nothing about these daily visits, or what they meant to her. And they could mean a lot. In a sombre mood, David drank coffee from his thermos. Then he walked up the driveway to the apple orchard where some of his crew were working.

A horn honked. The Lieutenant Governor's car appeared, its official flag flying. David grinned as the car stopped. Michael DeMille could never resist a chance to talk about gardens. Gerry had often laughed about His Honour's obsession.

The Lieutenant Governor got out of his car, and stood beside David. He watched the crew working and checked the apple trees for damage. He talked about the recent storms and then inquired if David would spend Christmas with him, or with his parents.

"Neither," David said. "I was going to phone you. A friend needs me. I'm sorry because I know this holiday will be difficult for you."

The older man smiled. "We'll manage. My wife and I will have our grandkids for company. Nothing like children to make you realise the meaning of Christmas."

"Right." David thought of Amanda. "I'll come out on the weekend to see the Munstead Wood project. How's the Spring Garden doing?"

"Daffodil spears are already popping up. You've missed the Aster Garden unfortunately. Before the storms the flowers were wonderful—every shade of purple and blue and white. Gerry would have liked them."

"I'm sure he would have."

The older man was silent. "There are still a few blooms left. I've taken your advice, and let the asters go to seed for the birds. You'll see plenty of other changes. I've had the tennis court taken out and am building a sandstone wall as a backbone for a new south border."

Another border? The Lieutenant Governor had royal ambitions. "I'll see you there," David said. "Maybe I'll bring some friends."

*****

Richard had changed, Ann thought. Every afternoon, he arrived punctually at four. He had always been punctual, but now, for the first time he was really talking to his daughter. He asked about her friends, about her teacher, and about her taste in food and clothing. He told her about forestry, and his work for the Commission.

He discussed current events—anything to ground her in reality. He talked about Christmas. Christmas was a month away and he planned to visit in the morning, and bring her a gift.

"What can I give you, Dad?" Amanda asked.

He hugged her. "You are all I want." He was overcome by emotion but hid it. He didn't want to upset her.

On the sixth day, Amanda came downstairs for dinner, nourishing but simple food. Afterwards she returned to bed. The next evening, Ann asked Richard to have soup and bread with them.

After Amanda went back to bed, he cleared the table. He discussed the day program, and hoped Amanda would be up to it. He volunteered to drive her home after it.

Ann said, "Till now, I never realised you even liked Amanda, or me."

Richard stacked the dirty plates. "I was afraid, especially of you."

"Afraid?" *Richard who'd charged into battle and sent bodies flying*?

"You were so damned clinging, so stubborn."

Clinging? Stubborn? How could he think that? "Richard, I *loved* you."

"I know. I think I even knew it then, but after Edward died, I'd had enough. I wanted to be free, so I was cruel." He said it dispassionately as though the means justified the end.

Did he have no shame? *Free...from responsibility? From love*? She was about to protest, but noticed his eyes filled with tears.

He wiped them away self-consciously. "It wasn't your fault," he said gruffly. "I want you to remember that."

"Whose fault then? Yours? Edward's? Amanda's?"

"No one's." He'd always wanted freedom, he said. Her second pregnancy was an encumbrance. He hadn't wanted another child.

Ann remembered his coldness during her pregnancy. Frustration had brought out the worst in her, and led to an embarrassing situation at Amanda's preschool, too embarrassing to reveal.

"But you loved Edward, didn't you?" she asked.

"Of course. He was everything to me. I had so many plans for him…I realized I had been stupid, and I realized I had hurt you so I arranged the trip to Mexico."

"In Mexico, you saved that glass ornament of the dolphins."

"Yes. But when Edward died, there was nothing left to save."

"So you started an affair. Why didn't you ask me for a divorce? Why did you disparage me so?"

"I wanted you to make that decision yourself."

She had never considered divorce. His plan hadn't worked. "Coward! I was in the dark. You led me on and you lied. You made demands. You let me flounder trying to fix an impossible relationship. You should have told me it was hopeless."

He cringed. "Yes, I was selfish and wanted nothing to do with you or Amanda. Anyway, now I've realized I love my daughter."

At last he was being honest. He loved Amanda and he loved Marina. Minutes later, he hinted that the new relationship wasn't entirely satisfactory.

Ann went to the fridge to get his favourite pecan pie, the one she'd made especially for him. She was fuming. That trip to Desolation Sound had been a last ditch effort to save her family, but Richard hadn't wanted to be with her, he'd already decided that. So he pretended they couldn't afford the trip. He'd only gone along to impress the Deputy Minister.

Sam was standing by the fridge, eyeing the pie. She had thought he was upstairs with Amanda. Had he heard Richard's confession?

"Sam, Richard once said he hoped I would learn to value *his* gifts. What about *my* gifts, Sam, what about my love? Did he value that? *No.* He called me clingy. He wanted a divorce but he allowed me to hope. I thought if I pleased him by arranging the trip to Desolation Sound, and by obeying orders—losing weight, exercising, hosting his social, and baking his bloody pies—I could regain his love, but the game was lost. He had the advantage: he knew what he wanted, and he left it to me to find out.

"Richard will never be pleased by me or by anyone else. A couple of months after moving in with Marina, he's already complaining."

"It is not easy to imagine a more unhappy condition than that of dependence on a peevish man," Sam said.

"Poor Marina," she said as she cut the pie into wedges.

Sam took two slices. "The irascibility of this class of tyrants is generally exerted upon petty provocations."

"But I allowed it to happen, and anyway, we women can be tyrants too."

"In their own way. When female minds are embittered by age or solitude their malignity is generally exerted in a rigorous and spiteful superintendence of domestic trifles. Such a woman lives for no other purpose but to preserve the neatness of a house and gardens."

"Garden, anyway." Ann smiled as she recognized herself. "Richard and I made a lovely couple, didn't we? What could we have done to prevent such pettiness?"

Sam popped a huge chunk of pie into his mouth.

How could a ghost do that? Did he have other appetites too? Better not inquire.

Sam licked his fingers. "The proper remedy against pettiness is to consider the dignity of human nature and the folly of suffering perturbation and uneasiness from causes unworthy of our notice."

"Yes, we should overlook pettiness. On the boat, you said I should endeavour to be pleased. That was marvellous advice. I've tried to follow it with David."

"And with Richard?"

The question was ridiculous. She wished Sam hadn't asked it. Sam was always promoting fidelity and marriage.

Sam's face darkened, and he vanished. Obviously he thought she hadn't tried hard enough.

She returned to Richard, plate in hand.

"You look as though you've seen a ghost," Richard said. "Did you hear a single word I said?"

"Sorry."

"I was telling you Marina misses her home in Vernon."

"Oh?"

He devoured the pie and discussed Marina's problems.

Why did she want to serve him still? Being a wife was like a flu bug she couldn't shake. Richard was delighted to see her weakness. As he was about to leave, he asked if he could stay the night.

"No," she said and handed him his umbrella.

She had herself to think of now. And David.

*****

Michael DeMille strode briskly down a grass path through birches underplanted with rhodos. In the spring, drifts of daffodils would run beneath the trees, he said.

"It will be lovely," Ann said, holding David's hand. His hand was warm and firm, his bulky beige quilted vest and loose-fitting trousers could not disguise his strong lean body. Desirable, but his spirit was equally admirable, and she needed spiritual strength now. What was she to make of Richard's odd request, his crass search for freedom, and the awful fact that she still wanted to please him.

Amanda ran ahead with David's dog, throwing a stick for him until they came to the end of the path. Beyond a forked Scots pine, was the woods. On the way back to the house, Michael pointed out the sites of future gardens. Some, like the Summer Garden and the June borders would be showy for a particular season. Others, like the main perennial border would bloom year round thanks to the shelter of the massive sandstone wall now under construction. There would be a primula garden too. And maybe he would build a new house similar to Jekyll's.

David teased him about that. "A little bit of Olde England."

"Maybe."

Ann began to grasp the size of the man's ambition. She could see why David insisted on creating one garden at a time. She could understand why he had to hurry to order plants for the Spring Garden. The ordering process was slow. Ordering was done through a Coquitlam dealer. Shipments from England took at least two months to go through quarantine inspection.

Michael stopped at the entrance to another garden. "This is my favourite garden, Ann, the Aster Garden. I'll let David show you it. He planted it last fall. Meanwhile, Amanda, would you like to see some horses?"

"Oh yes!"

He led her away with Humphrey to the stables. "Lunch is in half an hour," he called back to David.

"There's not much blooming after the storm last week," David said as they entered the aster garden.

He seemed embarrassed. "It's lovely," Ann assured him. "All these misty shades of purple, violet and white." A violet aster's petals were still soft and alive. "I'm glad you didn't cut the asters back."

"I left them to provide seeds for the birds. And mulched them against arctic winds."

"I love their pale colours. They're like ghost flowers. Except for that monster!" She pointed to a white flower that dwarfed David.

He laughed. "The Great White Hungarian Daisy."

"It's a dream garden. I've seen watercolours of the original garden but this is the real thing. Michael said you only planted it a year ago?"

"Yes."

"It looks well established. What's your secret?"

"Good soil, a well-drained site, a sheltered location and plenty of cash. Not everyone could afford to experiment on this scale."

"I sense," Ann said, "that for Michael it's an obsession, not an experiment. He knows the names and varieties of every plant. You do too. I was interested when you said modern varieties of some annuals like African marigolds are shorter and stouter than flowers Jekyll would have known."

"It's impossible to duplicate all her plants."

A wooden bench was in full sun. "Let's sit there," she said. "Tourists would love these gardens, local people too."

"Probably." David grimaced.

"Your heart isn't in the project?"

"I love the garden the way it is now, peaceful and quiet but I prefer simpler landscaping. Maintaining an Edwardian garden requires a lot of fiddling, like pegging down roses to promote bloom, filling in gaps with gypsophila or clematis or nasturtiums. Gertrude Jekyll had the patience for it. I don't. And I have no interest in creating a tourist attraction, and devising publicity, marketing plans, and so on. Unfortunately, everything Michael touches turns to gold."

She laughed at his lugubrious tone.

A robin hopped onto the Hungarian daisy.

"I will resign after Christmas," he added. "Michael has more gardens in mind but I'll find someone qualified to take over. Michael can afford to hire the best."

The asters were delicate and almost transparent. Sam would have loved these ghost flowers, but he was with Amanda.

"I'm glad you suggested coming here," she said. "It's been good for Amanda."

"And for Michael," David said. "He needs to talk to people who knew his son."

The bench was solid oak and beautifully finished. Richard would have appreciated the craftsmanship. It was a copy of one designed by Jekyll's architect friend, Edwin Lutyens.

A cloud hid the sun, and she shivered. She zipped up her jacket. "Michael will need you now, with Christmas coming."

"I will still see him." David took her hand and kissed it. "And he has other friends, including my parents who will visit from time to time."

David would keep his promise. He was reliable. He valued friendship. He valued love.

David's eyes were blue and calm. "Tell me about Edward," he said.

She shuddered. She couldn't talk to Richard about Edward. She could talk to Sam. He understood. Would David? David hadn't had children. But he had known what to do with Amanda.

The flowers vanished, the sky darkened and Edward looked up as she bundled him into a red snowsuit, a three-year-old ready to go out on a wintry night.

"There was a school concert," she began, "a big deal. Amanda had been rehearsing for months." She laughed. "I invited Richard's mum to dinner, along with my librarian friend, Colleen. Colleen refused. She said she'd had her share of concerts, and they were a great opportunity to exchange germs. I thought she was ridiculous."

Ann took a deep breath. "I planned to eat early and to tour Christmas lights on the way to the school. Just as I was taking the roast from the oven, Amanda announced she had to be at the school in fifteen minutes. Plus she needed two towels for a friend's costume. I was furious. I have a temper, you know."

"I've noticed." David squeezed her hand.

"Richard ate roast beef with his mum and Edward while, I drove Amanda to a fast food outlet, and then to school. All the way there, I lectured her about being responsible, about being prepared and on and on."

Amanda's eyes, filled with alarm, the fear would translate into guilt and then into depression.

"Finally, she interrupted me. She said she'd put a note from the teacher on my desk at home. I found it there later. It requested that parents bring two towels to be used as costumes. I felt awful about that. David, the evening was supposed to be a family dinner, a pre-Christmas celebration. I'd arranged a centrepiece of red chrysanthemums to give to Richard's mum. I wanted everything to be perfect. I was so harsh with Amanda, so angry. I spoiled everything by my temper."

"And the concert?" he prompted.

She sighed. "I dropped Amanda off at school. I returned home, found the note, dressed Edward in his snowsuit…..

She told him about Edward's sudden illness, and the trip to the hospital the next night. "The emergency room staff took charge. I had run to keep up with the stretcher. Nurses inserted tubes for a blood transfusion. Richard and I watched the clock in the lounge. Hours passed. Waiting for a miracle. The long, long winter night."

She shuddered. "I had to decide to take him off the respirator. Richard couldn't."

It was awful. David could imagine the suddenness of the illness, the need to act and the futility of action. He took Ann's hand, wanting to offer comfort, but she stared at the asters, not at him.

As if in a trance, she continued. "Richard made the coffin. He chose the finest yellow cedar. He carved teddy bears on the lid. He polished and varnished it too. He couldn't sleep. Making it gave him something to do." She began to cry. "It was so damn small."

David could not speak. He hugged her and wished he could ease her sorrow. She and Richard had endured so much. Their pain formed an unbreakable bond. He had trespassed into their private world. "I'm sorry," he said.

As though from far away, she said, "We felt so helpless, so stupid. I collected information on meningitis. We read every article. We had to find out why this had happened to our child. We had been responsible parents. We needed to find out if we could have prevented it. The articles with statistics were maddening. They lumped together all forms of meningitis. Viral meningitis is mild. Bacterial meningitis is lethal. Books should make that distinction. Not be so damned stupid." Her nails dug into the palms of her hands.

"No," David said. He gently unfolded her hands and smoothed them. Anger wouldn't turn back time.

"Sorry," she said. "I'm still angry. Our doctor knew the difference. He said bacterial meningitis kills the very old and the very young, and that it often occurs in crowded situations like barracks or bars. When he mentioned crowds. I remembered Colleen's joke about germs. 'How about school concerts?' I asked. A week later, another child died at the school, and a vaccine program began."

David could imagine how diligently she had researched, and her urgent need to understand what could never be understood. The disease had struck without warning. Fate had killed Edward and had destroyed his parents.

Ann shivered. He put his coat around her shoulders. "I can't imagine it," he said. "To lose a child. To be unable to help." The majesty of death shrank everything, made everything inadequate, especially words.

Winter birds chattered, concerned only with their midday meal. A chickadee perched on the bench, inches from his wrist, and then took flight. "Some things are beyond human understanding," he said.

Her face was pale and stubborn. "I have to try to figure it out. I always will."

She was passionate and loving, a fighter.

He realized then that retreat was no longer an option. He would stay with her forever. He clasped her hand and felt a hard, metallic band. With a shock, he realised she still wore Richard's ring.

He quickly withdrew his hand. She noticed, and looked at him. "Thank you for listening," she said.

Talking about Edward was emancipating—a taboo had been breached. He was glad she had confided in him. He knew Richard never discussed Edward's death. But Richard was still

Ann's husband, and the father of her children, and Death held them all in His grasp.

*****

Colleen gathered up her notes as Ann approached. The branch head was sick and Colleen had subbed for her that morning. Ann joined her at the reference desk. "Olive's babysitting Amanda this afternoon. She's also been driving Amanda to the day program. I'm sorry I ever said a harsh word about Olive."

Colleen laughed. "And about Richard?"

Ann didn't want to discuss Richard. "Amanda's improving. She may return to school in January."

"And you're well?" Colleen asked. "Escaped the library flu?"

"Yes."

"Well, I'd better get back to the central library. No difficult questions to pass on."

Ann glanced at the Post-its on their spike. "Actually, Colleen, Richard has changed. He's been really good to Amanda. He took her to see Christmas lights last night. He visits her every day."

"You're weakening!" Colleen looked horrified. "After all he did. Anyone could see you two didn't belong together."

Friends criticised Richard. Some hated him. But Richard once loved her. Sam merely labelled him peevish. Sam knew Richard was afraid.

Colleen changed the subject. "This morning, Elaine brought Natasha in." Elaine was the librarian whose job Ann had been filling. "The baby is almost six months old, and Elaine is glad she took unpaid leave to be with her."

"Seems like yesterday, she was pregnant." It seemed like years.

Colleen looked at her. "There's a job coming up in Acquisitions at the central library. Interested?"

Ann frowned. Acquisitions wasn't reference work. It had little to do with her specialty, children's literature. And nothing to do with the public. Should she hold out for a reference job? No. "Thanks. I need a permanent job. I'll apply. At least at the main library, I'd see more of you."

"How's your Christmas shaping up?"

"Slowly." She still hadn't done any shopping, but people were what mattered at Christmas. Not too many for Amanda. Richard and David would visit separately. Sam too, of course

Perched on the desk, Sam nodded. "Celebrate the way I did, with a fire and a meal."

Ann grinned at Colleen. "Two weeks to go, and I haven't yet bought a tree!"

She might invite Cindy and Tom for Christmas morning, to brighten Richard's visit.

A pared down Christmas was all Amanda could handle. Simple gifts. The art lessons, plus a stocking. Tonight, Ann and David would buy stocking stuffers.

Shopping for small delights was nicer than buying imposing presents, and especially nice with David as an accomplice. In the housewares section of the department store, omelette pans were on display. One was hinged, and enamelled a subtle grey-blue colour. Trendy. The type of thing Richard would like.

"What did you decide?" David asked.

"Decide?" What had they been talking about? Oh yes, the real estate agents visit last night. "Richard left the choice up to me whether to sell or not."

"Good."

"His attitude surprised me. He's thinking of resigning from the Commission too! Marina complained about all the travelling." As Ann herself had complained, long ago. "And people on the Commission have been giving him a hard time about Marina. Some of them liked me and have said nice things, including the Minister."

David laughed.

Ann stared at the omelette pan.

Last night, Richard arrived and asked if Amanda was sleeping. She was, so he went to his car and returned with an oak bookcase, his Christmas gift for Amanda. The bookcase was exactly the right height to fit under her bedroom window. Its shelves would accommodate tall books, even art books. Scrolls decorated the front of each shelf and at the top a border of oak leaves surrounded an oval.

"It's lovely," Ann said, in wonder. "Richard…you didn't make this did you?"

"Yes."

Before she knew what she was doing, her arms circled his neck and she was kissing him. His lips were warm, responsive. "Sorry," she stepped backward in a hurry, "I was just surprised, and it's so beautiful." But the kiss had felt so right, so familiar.

He was staring at her. Quickly she bent to examine the bookcase. He explained he'd taken the tools from the garage on the night Amanda became ill, and had worked on the gift in his apartment. Ann could imagine him carving the leaves, applying the varnish. This was the man she had loved once upon a time.

What had Sam said about marriage? That it was full of pain. Separation had its fair share of pain too but reunion could be delightful. The doorbell rang. If the real estate agents hadn't arrived then, what might have happened?

This was wrong, to think this way.

Richard would love this omelette pan, but someone else would have to give it to him. She put it back on the shelf.

David had seen the dreamy look before, and knew it had nothing to do with omelette pans.

"Richard's changed," she said, softly.

His blood froze at the way she said Richard's name. Two weeks had passed since they'd made love, two long weeks during which he ached to be with her. David wasn't a jealous man, but he was jealous of Richard's right, as Amanda's father, to visit Ann anytime. Richard had other rights too.

David should trust her, he knew, but after recent events, anyone would be confused. "Be honest," he said. "Have you been sleeping with him?"

"No." She whirled to face him. "How could you think that?"

He hated himself for asking, but she was blushing. "I'm sorry, but you seem different. Do you still want me to come for Christmas?" He kept his tone casual, conversational.

Her expression became opaque. "Of course."

But she seemed half-awake, dreaming of Richard, of reviving her marriage? David would not kill her dream. He would not influence her. "Considering the circumstances," he said slowly, "I think we should keep Christmas very low key."

She glanced again at the cooking display. Then she said resolutely, "And limit spending too."

"Okay. What would you like as a gift?"

She blushed again. Her eyes widened. "You," she said as if it were self-evident.

They finished shopping and hurried to his house.

In bed, it was as if they had never been apart. She was a passionate woman and she proved it, and David loved her, but afterwards, he reflected on the way she had spoken Richard's name in awe at the change in him.

Was romanticising her husband a necessity before leaving him, or before returning to him? Did Richard represent the illusion of a normal life? Was she idealising their marriage the way widows sometimes sanctify memories of miserable husbands? Amanda's illness had awakened memories of Edward's illness. It had also awakened the couple's parenting instincts and drawn them closer together.

The danger signs were there.

Did Richard represent financial security? David thought of telling her about his inheritance, and dismissed the thought as unworthy. Ann had a career, and she never talked about money. And from the sound of it, Richard had a salary from the Natural Resources Commission. Anyway money couldn't guarantee security.

David thought of Edward and shuddered. Money couldn't save the child. It also couldn't guarantee love.

She would have to choose him for himself.

He would accept the outcome even if her need for a real companion proved to be just a brief interlude, a pause, before she returned to fantasy.

CHAPTER 18: CHRISTMAS RITUALS

"I wish I'd been there," Amanda said, putting down her knife and fork. "What did they wear?"

David was glad to see the girl excited about Ann's library program. Her animation was a symptom of her recovery.

A group of preschoolers had come that morning for a Christmas program. Wearing their finest clothes, they had listened to two felt board stories, made Christmas cards and then cut loose with a rowdy imitation of Santa's reindeers landing on a roof.

What felt board stories? Amanda wanted to know. The one about the ant and the Christmas tree? What kind of presents did you put under the ant's tree? What snack did you give them? Did their parents stay with them? What kind of stickers did they put on their Christmas cards?

"Under the ant's Christmas tree we put Felt trucks and drums and dolls, and of course, the best present of all…books."

"The official library message," David said, grinning. Amanda was reliving each moment of the program and so was Ann. What a change from the withdrawn girl of three weeks ago! And what an astounding transformation from the frustrated woman at Desolation Sound! He hoped he could take some of the credit for the changes.

"Did you sing songs?"

"'Rudolph the Red Nosed Reindeer.' One boy wanted to know what 'histry' meant. It was a difficult concept to explain."

"Right up there with 'time,'" David said.

"Did all the kids take part?" Amanda asked.

"Most did. One girl sat on her mum's lap the whole time. Now eat up, Amanda."

Amanda began to eat her pasta. She had to be prompted, David noticed. She was still overly emotional.

Ann nodded meaningfully at him so she had noticed too. She described the kids decorating Christmas cards shaped like stockings.

"What kind of decorations?" Amanda wanted to know?"

"Cotton balls for fur, and stickers."

Amanda put down her fork. "What kind of stickers?"

"Bugs, paws, bones, dolphins, you name it. Christmas is such a lovely grab-bag season. The kids were so quiet all I could hear was winter snuffles. Afterwards we had a break for juice and carrot sticks. And cookies. 'Can we take two?' a boy in a red sweater asked. 'Only one,' I said. They had to learn to limit their pleasures, savor them. As I have."

She gave David a shy smile, and his heart turned over.

"After that, we acted out *The Night Before Christmas.* We dashed around the room, miming the landing on a roof, the unloading of sacks, and the journey down the chimney. They loved pretending to be stuck in it and so did I."

This new Ann was a woman who liked to play, both in bed and out of it.

She smiled at her daughter. "One girl asked why Rudolph wasn't in the *Night before Christmas."*

"What did you say, Mom?"

"I said the poem was from a time before Rudolph was born."

David laughed. "Part of his 'histry'. And which deer were his parents? That could be interesting."

After three weeks in the day program, Amanda was expressing emotion again. She was also learning to focus on people and things outside herself. If she continued to make progress, she could return to school part-time after Christmas.

"A perfect morning," David said.

"It reminded me of Amanda's preschool. One boy even whistled, he was so happy. I'm going to miss those kids. My contract ends tomorrow so I won't see them again."

"You loved being with them. That's what counts. They'll remember that."

Ann smiled. "I wanted to make the party special."

"You succeeded." He would have given anything to have seen her this morning with the children.

Amanda looked up from eating salad. "Wouldn't it be fun to have a younger brother or a sister?" She blushed. "I mean, just to play," she said hurriedly.

Ann looked uncertain. Then she hugged her daughter. "I saved something from the program for you." She reached into the cupboard and took out three tiny cookies, three perfect Christmas bells, outlined in red and green and sparkling with sugar. Delicate and fragile as new-found hope.

* * * * *

From the kitchen, an unmusical duet assaulted Ann's ears.

"*We three kings of Orient are*
One in a taxi one in a car
One on a scooter blowing his hooter
Following yonder star."

Amanda and David sang mangled carols while they did the dishes.

Ann listened with Sam at the dining-room table. They were drinking tea by candlelight, Sam's idea. He rubbed his stomach in appreciation of the dinner. He'd been anxious about it, inquiring earlier if it would include a joint of beef and a suet duff with a good sprinkling of raisins. He listed the other Christmas necessities: homemade wine, a good fire and maybe even some oranges and nuts. No turkey. He had never heard of turkey.

Ann had never heard of suet duff. It must be a pudding. The necessities had been luxuries centuries ago but were commonplace now. "Times have changed, Sam. Not just the food, the meaning too. In your day, Christmas was a super version of Sunday. Nowadays, many people don't attend church, and some churches have stopped having Christmas services. We still have Christmas trees and Christmas music but we've forgotten their meaning. We're like ignorant villagers who unknowingly continue pagan traditions."

"While shepherds washed their socks by night all seated by the tub,
A bar of Sunlight soap came down and they began to scrub."

"Pagan indeed," Sam said, listening. He leaned back in his chair while Ann refilled his cup. "I love the acquaintance of young people. Because in the first place, I don't like to think myself growing old."

Ann smiled. "Not something ghosts should worry about."

He ignored the comment. "In the next place, young acquaintances must last longest, if they do last."

"It's true," Ann whispered. David was younger than Richard and he could last longer.

Sam's eyes twinkled as if he read her mind. "And young men have more virtue than old men, they have more generous sentiments in every respect."

Ann blushed and cleared her throat. "You yourself seem younger now, more fun loving."

He laughed a young man's laugh. "Always was ready for fun. At three in the morning, some friends thundered on my door. Thinking they were thieves, I took up my poker, but when I saw whom it was I said I'd have a frisk with them. We went to Covent Garden, helped the stall owners unload their wagons, then went to a tavern. I didn't miss sleep at all. In fact, when we quaffed punch, I drank a toast to Sleep." He raised his teacup and quoted,

"Short, o short then be thy reign,

And give us to the world again!"

His voice rang out, youthful and musical. In his new necktie and well-cut vest, Sam seemed about her age. He'd donned the finery that evening when he saw her crimson dress.

"You are looking very handsome too," he commented.

As usual, he had read her thoughts.

"I bought this dress for the Natural Resources Commission social. It wasn't expensive."

He nodded. "It is foolish to spend extravagantly. Whatever you have, spend less. For the premiere of my play, *Irene*, I discarded my usual plain attire and disobeyed my own advice. I was splendid in a scarlet waistcoat and gold laced hat and I astounded my friends."

Sam in a scarlet waistcoat! "I can't imagine that!"

He grinned. "Such foolishness. The play was not a success."

She liked him in a light-hearted mood. Better than when he was moralizing. By mutual consent, they avoided the subject of adultery.

She carried the empty teapot to the kitchen and Sam followed, as usual whirling and twirling at the doorway. Ann hardly noticed it now.

Amanda was talking to David about the new paint set he'd given her. She would paint a picture of his dog. Humphrey himself was sleeping in the corner, having feasted on leftovers.

Ann dried the turkey platter and put it away in the pantry for next year.

Christmas had been merry after all. That afternoon, David had stuffed the bird so full of dressing Ann warned it might explode but it turned out splendidly. Amanda had eaten two servings and had even tried turnip, since David had prepared it. She clearly adored him. Christmas morning was a different story. Richard had visited. His gift, the new bookcase, was a hit but he seemed nervous while Amanda unwrapped it, distracted, unable to appreciate her pleasure in his gift. Ann asked if he was ill.

"No," he said. "I just don't care about much anymore."

He and Marina would eat Christmas dinner with Olive. Ann tactfully refrained from asking about their holiday plans and didn't mention her own. Amanda let slip that they would visit Vancouver with a friend. Richard would no doubt weasel the details out of Amanda later. His mood was so strange Ann was glad she had invited Cindy and Tom for coffee.

David hung up a tea towel, and Ann said, "The day improved vastly once you were here."

He grinned. "Because I did dishes?"

She swatted him with a towel.

"Dinner was excellent," he said. "I never get tired of turkey."

"Me neither," Ann said. "It doesn't have to be home cooked either. When I was single, I ate Christmas dinner with a friend in a café. The other customers were all elderly couples who couldn't cook big meals anymore. You might have thought they'd be sad, but they weren't. It was wonderful. I loved hearing them talk, their soft voices, the quiet pleasure they took in the meal."

"For them it wasn't just a dinner," David said. "It was a remembrance of Christmases past."

Amanda nodded. "Like Scrooge, reliving them."

"What was your favourite past Christmas, Amanda?" he asked.

The girl considered. "When I got a bike, that was one." She counted on her fingers. "Two, when I broke my present for Mom and she didn't mind. And three, when I sewed a pair of felt slippers for Edward." She looked at Ann. "I wonder if Edward is watching, if he knows about us, about Dad…"

Sam put his hand on Amanda's shoulder.

"I'm sure he does," Ann said.

How easily the girl spoke about her brother now. David had helped bring about that change. Ann remembered a reference question last summer, a library patron wanted books about death for her child. Ann had felt inadequate and desperate. For five years, she had avoided talking about Edward. Because of guilt.

She had taken him to that school concert. She had exposed him to germs there. He had trusted her and she had betrayed him.

Now she knew she was wrong to feel guilt and anger. Death was not the end of life. Sam had taught her that.

Richard had run away from death. He was afraid. His bookcase stood lonely and neglected in the corner of the kitchen. What kind of Christmas had he had?

After Amanda went to bed, David sat and drank brandy with Ann. The warmth of the fire and of Ann beside him contributed to a mellow optimism. Perhaps fate would smile on him. The flames changed from green to purple—probably from salts in the wood--then shot up orange and brown.

"In that dress, you remind me," he said. "of an oriental poppy, red with inner folds of rich black." He parted her hair and kissed the back of her neck.

"Thanks," she said and hugged him.

He put his feet up on the coffee table. "At Telegraph Cove, we always had a fire and a traditional Scottish dinner. I loved that, but usually, I snuck outside with Gerry for a Christmas hike in the woods, or on the beach."

He toasted his friend's memory with the brandy, and mentioned a TV show aired the previous night, an interview Gerry had done a year ago, a Christmas interview with a member of the Royal family, an interview so charming that audiences all over the world begged to see it again.

Ann squeezed David's hand. "How wonderful. I wish I'd seen it." She'd spend the previous evening playing a board game with Amanda.

David stretched. "This day qualifies as one of my favourite Christmases. Peace, a fire, and conversation, that's all I need.

Along with a few well-chosen books, of course." He referred to the gifts she'd given him, books on gardening philosophies and design.

"I'm glad we didn't go overboard on gifts," she joked. "I can't imagine you buying scarves for the postman."

He gave a mock shudder. "No, I only go overboard on eating." He patted his stomach. "I always will, even when I'm as old as those folks in the café."

"Maybe you won't eat turkey in a café. Maybe some old lady will cook it for you."

"Not just *some* old lady." He kissed her, his lips warm with brandy.

Desire leaped. Her arms and legs turned to butter.

He stared at her, his eyes mirthful. "And if we were too feeble to cook, our kids would feed us."

Kids? Maybe it was the brandy talking.

He stared at the flames. "That's what Christmas is about. Love overcoming human frailty."

That was so true, she hugged him. "Before we become too feeble," she said briskly, "let's dance." She rose and put on a CD.

He had given her CDs because he knew she loved to dance and because it was something they could do together. He said he had a second gift for her, but she wouldn't receive it until after Christmas. She wondered if it was a ring, and in a way, feared it might be.

The music began with the "Music of the Night'" from the *Phantom of the Opera*. They moved together. Eyes closed, she leaned against him and let the music take her. It was a miracle being with him, dancing with him. They had never danced before, but it came naturally, the closeness. As the music continued, she became warm from the fire, and from something more urgent.

She remembered the book from the book club, the one she'd despised, *The Bridges of Madison County*, and how the lovers had danced together. The man had the sensation of falling into the woman and the woman into him. They had kissed too, *"a long-time soft kissing, a river of it."* She had mocked those words. They seemed fitting now. How angry, how unhappy, she had been.

She kissed David's lips, and the muscles in his throat. Beneath her hands, his pulse quickened, his heartbeat too. "Do you know what we should do?" she whispered, her hands moving to his waist.

"No." His eyes twinkled.

"Yes. Our own private Christmas tradition."

*****

Through the window of the ferry's lounge, Ann watched Amanda back into the wind, her hair streaming into her face. David laughed and said something, and the girl laughed, too. No one else was on deck. Tourists were usually outside taking photographs of the mountains and islands but today, they were indoors, out of the wind, drinking coffee to warm up.

Three days had passed since Christmas and Ann was still smiling. "It was a very merry Christmas," she said to Sam, remembering the firelight tryst with David.

The ghost gave her a knowing look. Of course, he'd been there, only he had the decency to disappear during private moments. Lately he'd been disappearing a lot. She giggled. "Boxing Day was very 'merry' too."

Sam smiled. She realized what a very attractive man he was, virile, not in an eighteenth century way, but in a rougher, modern fashion.

The ship's horn sounded in Active Pass. Another ferry passed going in the opposite direction.

"You seem happy," she said to Sam. "Yet, you told me you were once very despondent…"

"I was often melancholy…"

"Before you met Hester Thrale."

"An exceeding kind couple, the Thrales. I was fifty-six. I'd just finished my edition of Shakespeare and it was a dark time. I lay on my bed for weeks, prey to gloomy forebodings. A kind of strange oblivion overspread me, so that I knew not what had become of the last year, and perceived that incidents and intelligence passed over me without leaving any impression. I was restless, pacing, unable to settle."

Restless like Richard on Christmas Day. Like Richard this morning at the lawyer's office.

"Sam, I know what that feels like. After Desolation Sound, I was full of dread and I withdrew from reality. I worried about becoming unemployed. I wrote that dismal speech. I needed someone who understood. You did."

He grimaced. "Hester and her husband visited me and they overheard me urging a friend to pray for me. I spoke with such vehemence, they said, that they grew concerned for my well-being and they invited me to stay with them in the country till I was recovered. Thanks to them I had a good library, a good table and good company, and my life was prolonged."

Hester had rescued him from suicide. She had been a true friend, but she was married and Sam hated adultery. After many years, the lively woman had abandoned him for a younger man and Sam had tried to forget her.

But he had loved her, apparently, and she had broken his heart.

On deck, Amanda's hair took on shapes worthy of an experimental beauty salon. David pointed out her reflection in the window and she laughed. The two of them attempted to braid the windblown hair.

"I hope Amanda recovers as quickly as you did," Ann said to Sam. "This mini-holiday will be good for her. A change."

In Vancouver, they would do some sightseeing, stay one night in a hotel, and buy a new truck tomorrow. Back in Victoria, Amanda would spend a few days with her grandmother while Ann prepared the house for sale. How would Richard spend the holidays?

David and Amanda were speaking to her, asking if she'd like coffee. They were rubbing their hands to warm them after their stroll on deck. She accompanied them to the cafeteria.

On Christmas morning, on Sam's suggestion, she served rum toddies to Cindy and Tom and made cocoa for Amanda. They reminisced about Desolation Sound. Tom teased Ann for screaming at the leech as though it was a rattlesnake, and teased Richard for becoming so obsessed with fishing he almost missed dinner. Cindy made fun of them all for the botched docking at Egmont. Ann laughed and recalled the barbecue falling overboard.

Richard was silent, and Ann worried that he was angry, but he suddenly he entered the conversation. He described the curious locals at the Egmont restaurant and his description was hilarious. Finally, he could see humour in the mishap.

Tom mentioned the new forestry regulations about annual allowable timber cuts. "Don't talk shop," Richard interrupted. 'It's Christmas'.

Ann almost choked on her coffee.

Richard asked about Tom's new boat, a trawler, but as Tom described it, Richard focussed on Amanda, painting a picture of the Christmas tree with her new watercolours. He gulped down his rum toddy and left, giving Ann a peck on the cheek, his eyes suspiciously bright.

David watched Ann sample the clam chowder in the ferry's café. She had been excited about this trip but now she seemed nostalgic. The mountains, she said, reminded her of those at Desolation Sound. Captain Vancouver had felt hemmed in by them but Samuel Johnson, her favourite writer, thought narrow mountainous landscapes concentrated the mind. She talked about fishing at Desolation Sound. Everything she said was disconnected. Everything centred on the past. She didn't mention

Richard, his visit on Christmas morning or their visit to the lawyer. When she reminisced, was she remembering him?

"Are you okay?" he asked.

"Yes," she said, but clearly she wasn't.

Driving into Vancouver, Ann gazed at the wide, straight streets, so different from Victoria's.

"Want to sightsee now, or after dinner?" David asked.

"I don't care," she said. At nine o'clock that morning she and Richard had stood on the steps of the lawyer's office clinging to one another desperately after signing the separation agreement. There was a finality to that which was seven years in the making.

"There's a public garden near our hotel," David said. "It's small. We could tour it."

In winter? "Okay." Ann tried to sound enthusiastic. "Nice to stretch our legs after the ferry."

"It's a Chinese garden," David said.

"If I stay here much longer," Ann said, "I'll freeze."

David wanted to wait for a tour of the Chinese garden, but the waiting room was frigid. Winter sun streamed through wooden fretwork but failed to warm the barren space. In the courtyard outside were several stringy trees, a phoney mountain and a stagnant pond. An open corridor zigzagged around the pond probably connecting with more unheated rooms.

"Forget the tour," she said. "Let's go." Without waiting for the others, she jogged into the white corridor. It widened a few times into rooms, all empty. Its windows looked inward to the courtyard and outward to a park. Nothing of interest.

"Mom, stop!" Amanda called from the door to the waiting room. "Come back."

Ann joined her.

"Let's cross the bridge to the mountain," Amanda suggested.

At the bridge, a rope barred the way and a sign prohibited crossing.

"Why would they close the bridge?" Ann glared at the green water. "You'd think someone would do something about this pond scum."

David said nothing.

A young woman was climbing the steps on the far side of the mountain. "Look at her!" Ann said indignantly. "Some people think rules apply to everyone but themselves." The woman wore a shabby quilted vest and looked like a hippie.

Sam shook his head.

Ann was disgusted. "Can you believe it? She's actually sitting in the gazebo! I'm going to tell the people in charge."

"Don't," David restrained her. "It's none of our business."

The cold room became crowded. Among the newcomers was the woman in the quilted vest. Beside her was Sam. The woman was Caucasian, but she wore layered and lumpy Chinese clothing. A cultural impostor.

"I am your guide," the imposter said in a musical voice. She welcomed everyone with a graceful gesture, and offered jasmine tea.

The scent of jasmine transformed the room and the guide. The woman was actually rather beautiful, in a calm, Zen sort of way. She had probably been meditating up on the mountain. Ann savoured her tea and calm warmth seeped into her.

David grinned. "Your second Christmas present is about to begin."

After the tour, Ann apologised. "I was so critical. I'm sorry."

"The garden is more intricate than it appears. Like life." He smiled and the weathered lines on his face vanished.

Like the garden, David too was waiting to be discovered. A door had opened, a door to which the tour had been the key.

CHAPTER 19: THE REIGN OF FANCY

"Much better than that dingy blue paint Richard picked out?" She dashed a streak of yellow paint against the wall.

Sam agreed.

Home buyers would appreciate a happier colour, the real estate agents had suggested. By lunchtime, two walls were finished. While she made a tuna salad, she and Sam talked about the Chinese garden.

She chuckled. "Sam, what if I'd yelled at that guide while she was meditating? What if I'd reported her to the administration?" She cringed. "I should've remembered David loves rocks and water in a garden. He doesn't expect me to share his tastes, but I was in such a foul mood I was oblivious to its charms. I didn't hear the trickling water, the rustling leaves, the chirping birds and the echoing footsteps. I didn't see the sunlight making the rocks look as if they were moving, or the blue tiles in the courtyard made from stones and pottery. I didn't feel anything, not the warmth of the sun on the balustrades, or the rough granite steps compared to the smooth limestone ones."

"You were preoccupied." Sam forked up tuna salad.

"Yes. Thank God I waited for the tour. "You weren't on it, I think."

"I was contemplating the view from the ting, the pavilion on top of your phony looking mountain."

She sighed. "Craftsmen took six months to build that hill, using traditional rock, limestone from Lake Tai."

"What about the 'stagnant pond' and 'pond scum'?"

She laughed. "Cloudwater. A special clay turns the water green, the colour of tranquility. The cloudiness is supposed to intensify reflections. I also missed examples of yin and yang in the garden until the tour guide pointed them out."

Sam finished eating and licked his fingers. "Each element there had history, and had been part of other peoples' lives."

Ann loaded the dishwasher. "David said the garden copies a famous Chinese garden, the Garden of the Master of the Fishing Nets. He wanted me to see it. Sam. I was so angry I almost rejected David's gift."

In the bedroom, Sam lounged on the bed. Before she started painting, she put the dolphin ornament in a drawer of the night table for safety. Her temper had always caused trouble. *One day you'll learn to value my gifts.* Richard had said. How much of the beauty of life had she missed?

Sam had urged her to be pleased with what life had to offer. Sam seemed content, a companion who appreciated her and others. Last summer, when she asked why he was accompanying her, he said he knew what marriage entailed. He also knew life and death. He knew what she and Richard and Amanda had been through. He would understand her uneasiness.

"Sam, Richard phones me every night to talk about Amanda. They've been keeping Amanda busy. Olive's been teaching her to sew. Olive thinks she has a talent for fashion design. Richard arranged a visit from Jen's father an amateur astronomer. He brought his telescope and taught the girls about the planets. Amanda can concentrate now and read, but Richard makes sure she only reads non-fiction. No fairy tales."

She painted around the baseboard. “I was happy to hear that. But when I confessed I actually enjoy aerobics now, he didn’t laugh. He didn’t mention Marina. I wonder if he’s introduced her to Amanda. I hope not. Something is wrong. Before he signed the separation agreement, he stared at me. The agreement spelled out my name and his, the date and place of our marriage, the name and birth dates of our children, as final as the words on a tombstone. His eyes looked dead. I think he’s lost.”

Sam leaned on his elbow, listening.

“I wonder if he knows what he wants, Sam. I wonder if he will remarry.”

Sam laughed. “If he does it will be the triumph of hope over experience.”

She smiled. “Poor guy.” She used a small brush to cut in the paint around the window frame. She dipped a roller in the paint. “Yellow is a good colour for a north facing room, don’t you think? I hope David likes it.”

Sam watched from the bed. He was a sexy young man now. If he hadn’t been a ghost, and if she hadn’t had David, she might have been tempted. A similar transformation had also occurred in her. Now when she looked in a mirror, she saw a desirable woman whose flaws made her unique. A happy woman. But when she looked at Richard, she saw a man whose search for physical fitness had perfected his body but dulled his spirit. He reminded her of an aging film star.

“About that Chinese garden,” Sam said. “If you knew the culture, you could decipher the symbols—the waterfall and rocks like the landscape in China, the door handles in the shape of bats a pun on the Chinese word for bat and for good fortune, and other sublime features.”

“David didn’t expect me to know those symbols. He just wanted me to appreciate it,” she pointed out the bedroom window, “Like that rock garden out there.”

"Sam, I loved the white corridor once I realized it symbolized life. It zigzagged so the view from each window was different. The guide said it zigzagged to avoid evil spirits. I couldn't escape mine."

Sam smiled. "The corridor ended in the place where life was examined, the Scholar's Garden."

"On my jog through the garden, I didn't get that far."

The paint in the bedroom was wet so she and David made up the hide-a-bed in the den and snuggled together. That progressed to more satisfying activities. Afterwards, she lay happy and contented until she remembered something Richard had said on the phone.

"Is something wrong?" David turned on the light.

"No, why?"

"You're restless."

She had been thinking so intently, she thought she had been speaking. "David, Richard resigned from the Natural Resources Commission today."

"Really?" David frowned. "Last September, at Government House, he said being appointed to the Commission was the highlight of his life!"

She remembered Richard's rage at her foolish drinking and David's patience that night. "It was strange, David. On the phone, he sounded relieved. He said he never really wanted political success, and Marina hated the travelling involved." Ann laughed bitterly. "I hated it too. If he'd resigned earlier, we might have stayed together."

David said nothing.

She realized what she had said. "Sorry, I meant, *in theory.*" How could she be so insensitive, saying that after making love? "Sorry, David. For an educated person, I'm pretty dumb."

He gazed at her for a long time, his eyes thoughtful and dark. "You can't help being linked to him." He took her hand.

"Remember the Scholar's Garden? Maybe we should make one here in your garden."

"For me?" She laughed.

"And for me." He grinned. "But mine will have willows in it."

She laughed. In the Scholar's Garden willows weren't allowed because their supple forms might remind the male scholars of women. "No willows and no women either, except me." She kissed him and wrapped her arms securely around him, feeling his strength. "Remember the three windows in the Scholar's Study and the plants in front of them--the bamboo for resiliency, the plum for ....I forget."

"Not much of a scholar." He tapped her bottom. "The bamboo for resiliency in adversity, the plum blossom for triumphal rebirth, the pine for strength and eternity."

"Great ideals, but hard to live up to. In adversity, I lose my temper, and let passion blind me."

"And what's wrong with passion?" he asked, teasing.

She kissed him. "Being a scholar in the Ming dynasty wasn't a bad career. Every household had one. They hired musicians and poets to inspire him in summer, built a special roof so he could hear the rain in winter and see the garden through a beaded curtain of water. You know, David, I'd like to go back to the Chinese Garden in a rainstorm, just to see the water curtain."

"I'm glad you liked the garden."

"It was a perfect present for an imperfect person." She reached for a glass of water and knocked it off her night table. She rose and mopped the water and rearranged the books on the table. Her hands were shaking, she noticed.

"You're worried about Richard," David said quietly.

"Yes. As you said, I feel a link to him."

"I know." David sat up in bed and took her hand. "Promise me one thing."

"Maybe." Would he tell her to avoid Richard? Surely not.

His eyes were dark with emotion. "Promise me you'll be watchful of our relationship."

"Watchful?"

"Notice if we let weeds take over. If we see weeds, we should stop, confront one another, and reconstruct the garden we want. Not establish separate gardens."

"I promise." She shook his hand sealing the bargain.

"I promise too." He kissed her. "To quote your friend, Samuel Johnson, 'Marriage has many pains'."

"And joys." She licked her lips. "And celibacy has no pleasures. None like these." She came into the circle of his arms.

The guide to the Chinese garden said moon gates often stood at the entrances to gardens. Their circle suggested heaven and perfection.

Ann closed her eyes and heard for the first time the trickling water, the rustling leaves, the chirping birds, the echo of her own footsteps in the corridor.

* * * * *

"It looks nice, doesn't it Sam?" Ann finished making the bed. The old blue and white duvet looked fresh against the yellow walls.

"New paint for a New Year." Sam looked out the window at the winter moon.

"Right. But tonight, we'll sleep on *The African Queen*. It will be cold on the water but fun to see the fireworks up close in the harbour. Like having a front row seat. You'll love them."

Sam glanced at the clock on the bedside table. "There are certain things I must do."

"Then we'll see you tomorrow, for lunch on board. Amanda will be there." She fluffed up the pillows and the duvet. "I hope David loves this old duvet as much as I do."

"He is not a peevish man."

"And I am not a peevish woman, not any more. David is bringing provisions to the boat—champagne, pizza, and a good supply of blankets. I can't wait to tell him about my new job in Acquisitions. I'll miss seeing the public, especially the kids, but until another job comes along, I'll 'endeavour to be pleased'. That's my New Year's Resolution."

Sam smiled. "Methinks it should have been your old year's resolution."

"Too true." She sat beside him on the bed. "I will be tranquil." The clock showed seven thirty. She jumped up. "Better not be too tranquil or I'll be late." She was meeting David at the harbour at ten.

She showered and dressed and packed warm clothes for herself and for Amanda. She carried the overnight bags downstairs to the front hall. The grandfather clock struck eight.

Usually Richard phoned around eight to talk about Amanda, but it was New Year's Eve and Amanda would have been delivered to the boat, and he was going to a party. Before the clock finished striking, the phone rang. Ann laughed. Even a New Year's Eve party wouldn't upset Richard's routine.

He'd taken Amanda to the museum today, he reported. He spoke against a background of music. Strange he would call from a party, but he was focussed. He wished Ann a Happy New Year, and then talked about a project he was designing, retraining loggers. Ann began to wonder why he had phoned. In the middle of describing a trivial detail, he stopped.

"Sorry for babbling," he said. "I need someone to talk to, someone who knew me before..." his voice faded.

"Before?"

"Before I was on the Commission, someone who…" again his voice faded.

"Someone who knew you before you were important?" Ann joked. "Someone who'd argue with you?"

Marina, the hometown girl, was probably still too much in awe.

"No, someone who knew Edward."

She sighed. Richard had never wanted to talk about Edward. Why would he now?

A party horn blew in the background.

"Ann, I've signed up for a course in communication. It's my New Year's resolution. To learn how to interact with people."

"People?"

"Amanda, and you."

She swallowed a laugh. The resolution was so methodical, so typically Richard. "And Marina, don't forget."

Silence. No joking allowed.

"Amanda told me you're seeing someone," Richard said.

"Yes." Communication on that topic would be minimal.

Horns blared and music sounded.

"My mom misses you, Ann,"

"Olive?" Ann just about dropped the phone. "Misses me? After all our clashes?"

"She said it wasn't a proper Christmas without a game of Scrabble with you."

After years of complaining about unsuitable Christmas gifts, maybe the woman liked Ann after all. "Did you give her a Christmas present?"

"Marina picked out something, the colour was wrong. Olive said Marina should have known pink didn't suit her."

"Olive expects a lot. Like mother, like son. Well, Richard, I'd better be going. Have a Happy New Year."

"Ann…."

"Yes?"

"I miss you, too," he blurted out. "It wasn't Christmas without you."

She hardly recognised his voice; it was so hoarse, so desperate.

"I hadn't realised," he said, "how much my life revolved around you and Amanda. Now it's revolving around a black hole."

She sighed. Too late, he appreciated what a haven their marriage could have been.

"It's New Year's Eve, Ann. So let's start this year right. I'll come over."

Come over? He never left parties early. What would Marina think?

"If you're busy, Ann, I'll usher in the New Year with my mother and Amanda."

Without Marina? A vicious stab of pleasure. Had Marina missed her family too much? Had she disliked inflexible men?

A door opened to yesterday's dream of a humble and loving Richard. "I need to think about this," she said shakily. "Can I call you back in twenty minutes?"

He said he would wait by the phone. Behind him, plates rattled. He must be in somebody's kitchen. She could imagine him huddled in a corner, cupping the phone while the party went on.

Sam pointed to the grandfather clock. It said a quarter after eight.

"Richard sounds awful, Sam. Should I phone David and say I'll be late? I could invite Richard here."

"The mind dances from scene to scene," Sam stared at her, as though willing her to understand.

"What does that have to do with Richard?"

"By degrees," Sam said, "the reign of fancy is confirmed: she grows first imperious and, in time, despotic."

"What are you talking about? The reign of fancy?" It must be an archaic meaning. She guessed at it. "By fancy, do you mean imagination?"

He smiled and continued, beating out the rhythm of his words. "When fancy grows despotic, then fictions begin to operate as realities, false opinions fasten upon the mind, and life passes in dreams of rapture or of anguish."

Dreams. Sam had lectured before about imagination and reality. *We amuse ourselves with the dance of airy images,* he had said on the upper deck of the *Maybelle.*

"Sam, if I'd listened to you at Desolation Sound, I would have seen the real Amanda, and the real Richard, but I didn't want to, the dreams were so bewitching."

The hands of the grandfather clock inched towards eight thirty. She should phone Richard, or David. No, she should think.

The clock's ticking was like a cannon firing.

Sam took a battered volume from his pocket and held it out. *The Collected Works of Samuel Johnson.* She had forgotten to return it to the library.

She would not take the book from him. She knew what was about to happen. He was leaving. How could she live without his steadying influence?

She brushed the book aside but still he proffered it. She needed Sam to guide her. He had warned her about Amanda so he must know the future. "Tell me, Sam, about the future, my future."

He stared at her, frowning. "Very well," he said. "You must figure it out. It's a long story and a parable."

She sat down on the hall bench.

He took a deep breath, and like an actor declaimed. "In my sixties, I journeyed to the Hebrides with my friend, Boswell. Bozzy and I took a boat from Skye to Iona. It was October, the season of gales, dark early and no lights except the moon. I lay in my bunk below, prey as usual to queasiness. For fourteen hours, I lay there, a dog at my back for warmth, while Bozzy was on deck."

"I know how you felt," she said. She saw the tiny boat and the cramped quarters as clearly as if images were being projected from Sam's mind to hers.

"The captain fought the storm," Sam continued, "but the wind changed and we could make no headway. Donal Mclean, a passenger, said we had to seek shelter at Mull or Coll.

"I've heard of Skye and Iona," she said. "I guess Mull and Coll must be two smaller islands nearby."

"Bozzy came below to ask me which. 'Coll for my money,' I said. Donal and the four others on deck manned ropes, goose-winging the boat before the wind. They strained their eyes for the coastline eleven miles away. The billows were high. We had to speed. We had too much sail up, but if the sail was torn to ribbons, we would end up on rocks."

He paused for dramatic emphasis.

"It must have been terrible." She saw him in the cabin, as queasy as she'd been en route to Desolation Sound. She wasn't worried, though, because she knew Sam had survived to die of old age. Sam was a ham. Was the point of this parable to show they had seasickness in common?

"We made it to Coll, and Bozzy was angry at me for being so unaffected by it all. He admired Donal Mclean, said 'he was the best of Scotland, a sailor, a hunter, a fisher, a farmer. Brave, capable, at home in the elements.' 'Almost animal-like,' I said, 'he should have had a tail.'"

Sam laughed at his own joke. Then, almost as an afterthought he said, "Anyway Donal, the brave man, got us through the storm. Two years later, he died in another."

Ann blinked. "Another storm? He died?"

"Yes." Sam's eyes were dead calm.

"Life is uncertain." She felt queasy now. Had the parable been about her or about David? David had Scottish blood. He had fought the elements on land and sea. Did a cruel future await him? She shivered. No, Sam must be speaking in general about life's hazards.

Sam turned abruptly toward her, his eyes far seeing. "We set out on a tempestuous sea in quest of some port where we expect to find rest but where we are not sure of admission. We are not only in danger of sinking on the way but of being misled by meteors mistaken for stars, or being driven from our course by the changes of the wind, and of losing it by unskilful steerage."

"Sam, my own quest for happiness was uncertain. I thought I'd find it in Desolation Sound but lost my way and lost my marriage. What would have happened if I'd stayed aboard and ridden out the storm as you did? Would I still be with Richard?"

Sam smiled. "Yet it sometimes happens that cross winds blow us to a safer coast, that meteors draw us aside from whirlpools, and that negligence or error contributes to our escape from mischiefs to which a direct course would have exposed us."

A safer course. "Sam, the trip to Desolation Sound brought accidental happiness. I came to know David, and Cindy and Tom, and you. Would it have had a happier outcome if I'd followed your advice, ignored my imagination, and tried to be appreciative? Or was everything on the trip predestined?"

Sam nodded. "Our only solace is the belief that the universe is in the hands of omnipotent goodness. And no one can tell whether the good that he pursues is not evil in disguise. As you said, life is uncertain."

"You speak in riddles, Sam."

The brave Scotsman was horribly like David. David setting off in the *African Queen* in a blaze of summer sunlight. David joyously raking and planting in the middle of winter. A man who was capable both on land and at sea, a worthy companion anywhere.

Sam looked at the clock. "It's closing time." He began to hum "The Syncopated Clock", the closing theme of the library.

Once, she had been amused by the whimsical theme. Now it was horrid.

Sam marched to the stupid tune, swinging his book like a pendulum.

"Sam, please! Stop!"

The music paused, and he did too. The ticking grandfather clock took up the beat.

Her friend was shimmering now, and fading. His feet were barely visible.

"You can't go yet, Sam," she begged. "I'll miss you too much. Besides, there's so much you haven't told me. About your life, about your work, and especially about Hester."

His expression darkened.

If she made him angry, he would stay a while. "What about the 'forays into experience' you mentioned?"

He glared. "For twenty years I loved her…loved her, esteemed her, revered her and served her." He was silent a moment, and then blurted out, "A woman has such power between the ages of twenty-five and forty-five, that she may tie a man to a post and whip him if she will."

"Whip him?" Ann asked.

Sam licked his lips. "It was a strange connection. There was a dreadful and little suspected reason for it. She said the fetters and padlocks would tell posterity the truth."

"I see." She saw too that this young man's lips curved, deliciously sensual and fleshy.

"My impulses," he continued, "were sometimes out of control."

So this counsellor, this moralist, had wandered from conventional morality.

"Madmen," he said, "are all sensual in the lower stages of the distemper. They are eager for gratifications to soothe their minds and divert their attention from the misery which they suffer; but when they grow very ill, pleasure is too weak for them, and they seek for pain."

Sadism and masochism had saved them from committing adultery? What kind of virtue was that? She and David might have committed adultery, but at least they hadn't resorted to padlocks. "This took place after your wife had died, Sam. When she was alive, did you indulge in these *forays*?"

"I lusted for my Tetty as you did for Richard. When she became an invalid, though I lay with others, I was loyal to her, and Hester was loyal to her husband."

He seemed to feel no shame at this convoluted morality. She could question it, but Sam was from a different time, an age of different morals, and he was her friend. The lovers must have endured twenty years of warped and frustrated love. They must have stifled every normal instinct, poor things! And suffered, almost to the point of madness.

He looked at her. "You have to choose between David and Richard. I cannot decide for you."

"I love David, and in a way I still love Richard. Tell me the right thing to do. Teach me."

He laughed. "I was a man only." He looked like a youth in love, full of hope and tenderness.

"Sam, you are magnificently qualified to teach."

"I am limited in death to what I said in life."

"What do you think of Richard?"

"Richard is a very good hater. An unclubbable man." Sam's neck twisted in a spasm of emotion. "I'll say what I said when Lord Chesterfield at last agreed to be my patron. I said, 'Is not a patron, my lord, one who looks with unconcern on a man struggling for life in the water, and when he has reached ground encumbers him with help?'"

"Sam, it's true that Richard watched me struggle, but he was struggling like me with death. Richard needs me."

Sam walked toward her and folded his hand over hers. "Madam, I must say farewell."

"David's too good for me…"

An awful quiet descended on the hallway. Sam was becoming transparent.

"You can't go," she said in dismay. She wiped tears away. "Don't leave without giving me some final advice."

He laughed. "I never gave advice. That's why I was popular. I merely echoed and enlarged on whatever was under discussion."

"Please, just for once, break that rule. Tell me what to do."

His eyes glistened. His shaking ceased. He drew himself up to his full height. The magnificence of his spirit towered over her. "Examine your life."

The words were like blows.

"Examine your life," he repeated, "as I examined mine and my conscience and found much wanting. Still I hope I died a Christian. On my deathbed I at times loathed sin, especially my own… At last I became calm."

Would her life bear examination?

The white corridor opened before her, the twisted corridor with windows allowing limited views, vignettes of scarred rock with leeches, of library patrons waiting for information, of Richard stubbornly fishing, of David playing with Amanda on the ferry deck, of Edward looking up trustingly as she buttoned his snowsuit. Glimpses of landscapes, miniature and large, distant and nearby, future and past. Some windows opened to the world outside. Some opened inward. All were situated so that from no one point could she see the whole garden.

At her feet, the two overnight bags were waiting, hers and Amanda's. On the boat, David was waiting too. Did she really know David? Or just know passion? What was real? Had she, like Amanda, been a prisoner of imagination? Is that why Sam had come? To set her free?

The clock resumed its ticking. Sam swayed to the beat and performed a kind of minuet. Suddenly, he bowed and kissed her hand. "When pleasure can be had, it is fit to catch it. And it has been a great pleasure discoursing with you." His voice became soft. "With you," he said, "I have known the endearing elegance of female friendship. God bless you, my dear!" He moved to embrace her.

She felt a rush of cold air. His body passed through hers. His hand clasped hers and left in it the leather-bound book.

The ticking of the clock echoed in the now empty hallway.

He hadn't even waited for the final chords of the library closing theme.

She stroked the book's leather and remembered that hellishly hot day in the library when Sam appeared. If only she could have comforted him as much as he had comforted her, been sunshine to his gloom! He had guided her through a voyage he knew too well.

The book's leather cover was marred with scratches and rubbed bare in spots, but gold leaf clung to the edge of the pages, like stardust.

The phone rang. It would be Richard, annoyed that she hadn't called. She ignored the ringing.

A laugh sounded nearby, Sam's laugh. She twirled around but the hall was empty, and quiet except for the clock marking time, waiting for her decision.

She might not be as virtuous as Sam, but she was alive. She had come ashore safely. Whatever the future on this beautiful earth, there was only one person with whom she wanted to share this garden.

Richard could wait. She would phone him later from David's boat to wish him happiness.

The music resumed, the same old tune, but there was a new singer. Ann hummed along, slowing as the tempo slowed, savouring each note especially the last.

Silence reigned.

"Good bye, Sam," she said softly.

She picked up the overnight bags, walked down the hall corridor, and opened the door.

THE END

CPSIA information can be obtained at www.ICGtesting.com
Printed in the USA
LVOW08s0859020816

498360LV00004B/10/P